A PERILOUS UNDERTAKING

PERILOUS UNDERTAKING

A VERONICA SPEEDWELL
MYSTERY

Deanna Raybourn

BERKLEY
NEW YORK

BERKLEY
An imprint of Penguin Random House LLC
375 Hudson Street, New York, New York 10014

Copyright © 2017 by Deanna Raybourn
Penguin Random House supports copyright. Copyright fuels creativity, encourages diverse
voices, promotes free speech, and creates a vibrant culture. Thank you for buying an authorized
edition of this book and for complying with copyright laws by not reproducing, scanning, or
distributing any part of it in any form without permission. You are supporting writers and
allowing Penguin Random House to continue to publish books for every reader.

BERKLEY is a registered trademark and the B colophon is a trademark of
Penguin Random House LLC.

Library of Congress Cataloging-in-Publication Data
Names: Raybourn, Deanna, author.
Title: A perilous undertaking: a Veronica Speedwell mystery/Deanna Raybourn.
Description: First edition. | New York: Berkley Books, 2017.
Identifiers: LCCN 2016019601 (print) | LCCN 2016024005 (ebook) |
ISBN 9780451476159 (hardback) | ISBN 9780698198456 (ebook)
Subjects: | BISAC: FICTION/Mystery & Detective/Women Sleuths. |
FICTION/Mystery & Detective/Historical.
Classification: LCC PS3618.A983 P47 2017 (print) |
LCC PS3618.A983 (ebook) | DDC 813/.6—dc23
LC record available at https://lccn.loc.gov/2016019601

First Edition: January 2017

Printed in the United States of America
1   3   5   7   9   10   8   6   4   2

Jacket design and illustration by Leo Nickolls
Book design by Kristin del Rosario

To the readers

I would earnestly warn you against trying to find out the reason for and explanation of everything ... To try and find out the reason for everything is very dangerous and leads to nothing but disappointment and dissatisfaction, unsettling your mind and in the end making you miserable.

A PERILOUS UNDERTAKING

CHAPTER

1

London, September 1887

"For the love of all that is holy, Veronica, the object is to maim or kill, not *tickle*," Stoker informed me, clipping the words sharply as he handed me a knife. "Do it again."

I suppressed a sigh and took the knife, grasping it lightly as I had been taught. I faced the target, staring it down as if it were an approaching lion.

"You are thinking too much." Stoker folded his arms over the breadth of his chest and looked down his nose at me. "The entire purpose of this exercise is to train you to react, not to think. When your life is in danger, your body must know what to do, because there is no time for your mind to engage."

I turned to face him, not lowering the blade. "Might I remind you that I have, upon many and various occasions, been in mortal danger and I am still here."

"Anyone can get lucky," he said coldly. "And I suspect your continued survival owes itself to a combination of good fortune and sheer bloody-mindedness. You are too stubborn to die."

"You are a fine one to talk!" I retorted. "It is not as if that scar upon your face were a love bite from a kitten."

His lips tightened. I found it entertaining that such a hardened man of the world could have gained so much experience as scientist, explorer, natural historian, naval surgeon, and taxidermist and still let himself be nettled by a woman half his size. The thin, silvered scar that trailed from brow to jaw on one side of his face was not at all disfiguring. Quite the opposite, in fact. But it was a constant reminder of the failed Amazonian expedition that had destroyed his career and his marriage and nearly ended his life. It was not entirely sporting of me to mention it, but we had begun to pluck one another's nerves in recent days, and it had been his idea to train me in the combative arts as a way to exorcise our bad tempers. It almost worked, not least because I pretended to be entirely inexperienced in the matter. Men, I had often observed, were never happier than when they believed they were imparting wisdom.

Stoker had set up a target in the gardens of our friend and benefactor, Lord Rosemorran, and we had taken the afternoon off from our various duties in the Belvedere. Situated on the grounds of his lordship's Marylebone estate, Bishop's Folly, the Belvedere was a singularly extraordinary structure. It had been built as a sort of freestanding ballroom and storehouse for an eccentric Rosemorran ancestor, and it served our purposes beautifully. The Rosemorrans were tireless collectors and had stuffed their London mansion, Scottish shooting box, and Cornish country seat clear to the rafters with treasures of every description. Art, artifacts, natural history specimens, mementos—all of them had found their way into the grasping, aristocratic hands of the Rosemorrans. After four generations of acquisition, the present earl had decided the time had come to assemble a formal and permanent exhibition, and Stoker and I had been given the task of establishing the museum. The fact that we were somewhat qualified to undertake such a feat—and recently homeless as well as in need of employment—had spurred the earl to make the thing official. The first order of business ought to have been a thorough inventory of all the Rosemorrans had acquired. It would be tiresome, backbreaking, tedious work, but necessary. Before the first display cabinet was built, before the first exhibit could be sketched or the first tag penned, we must have a complete accounting of what we had to work with.

So naturally we planned a trip instead. We had spent all of July and August of that year charting an expedition to the South Pacific, poring over maps and happily debating the relative merits of each location with regard to my interest in butterflies and Stoker's rather less elevated interest in shooting things.

"I do not shoot things for my own pleasure," he had argued indignantly. "I only collect specimens for the purposes of scientific study."

"That must be some consolation to the corpses," I returned sweetly.

"You do not hold the moral high ground there, my little assassin. I have watched you kill butterflies by the hundreds with just a pinch of your fingers."

"Well, I could pin them first, but I am not an enthusiast of torture."

"You might have fooled me," he muttered. I passed off that bit of ill humor for what it was—sulking over the fact that our patron had sided with me in choosing the Fijian islands for our expedition. The location was a veritable paradise for a lepidopterist but offered little excitement for a student of Mammalia.

"Don't grumble. The Fijian islands are rich with specimens for you to study," I told Stoker with more kindness than veracity.

He fixed me with a cold look. "I have been to Fiji," he informed me. "There are bats and whales. Do you know who is interested in bats and whales? Precisely no one."

I waved a hand. "Feathers. The Fijians boast a very nice little fruit bat you might enjoy."

What he said next does not bear repeating in a polite memoir, but I replied casually that Lord Rosemorran had mentioned calling in at

Sarawak as long as we were in that part of the world. Unlike Fiji, this destination would afford Stoker everything from panthers to pangolins for study.

He brightened considerably at this, and by the time our preparations were concluded, any casual observer might have been forgiven for thinking the destination had been his idea from the first. He threw himself into the planning with enthusiasm, arranging everything to his satisfaction—arrangements I quietly reworked to *my* satisfaction. The travel documents were in order, the trunks were packed, and a fever of anticipation settled over Bishop's Folly. All that remained was to depart, and Lord Rosemorran made a protracted leave-taking of his home, his children, his sister, his staff, and his beloved pets. It was the last that was to prove our downfall.

Returning from one last walk in the gardens where he housed his snail collection, his lordship managed to trip over his giant tortoise, Patricia, a tremendous creature who shambled about the grounds so slowly she was often mistaken for dead. How Lord Rosemorran managed to trip over an animal whose nearest relation was a boulder mystified me entirely, but the cause was not the concern. It was the effect which proved devastating. His lordship sustained a compound fracture of the thigh, a painful and thoroughly disgusting injury which Stoker assured me would take many months to heal. His experience as a naval surgeon's mate had qualified him to take one look at the protruding bone and turn to me with instructions to see to the unpacking. The Rosemorran–Speedwell–Templeton-Vane expedition was officially canceled.

Whilst Stoker was extremely useful in a crisis, his medical expertise was soon usurped by that of his lordship's own physicians and we were left cooling our heels in the Belvedere, sniping at one another in our frustration. We had each of us hoped to be shipboard once more, sea breezes blowing away the stultifying air of England as tropical climes beckoned with balmy winds and star-blazoned skies. Instead we were cooped up like hapless chickens nesting on our disappointed hopes. Even the opportunity to clear out the Belvedere did not entirely restore our good humor, although I should point out that Stoker's fit of pique lasted far longer than mine. But then, in my experience, gentlemen are champion sulkers so long as one doesn't call the behavior by that name. It was in such a state of heightened irritation that he—mindful of our previous perilous encounters—took it upon himself to instruct me in the defensive arts.

"Splendid idea," I had replied enthusiastically. "What shall we shoot?"

"I am not giving you a firearm," he told me in a tone of flat refusal. "I do not like them. They are noisy, unreliable, and can be taken away and used against you."

"So can a knife," I grumbled.

He pretended not to hear as he extracted the blade he regularly carried in his boot. He erected a target—an old tailor's dummy unearthed from the Belvedere—and set about teaching me with maddening condescension how to murder it.

"It is one smooth motion, Veronica," he said for the hundredth time. "Keep your wrist straight, and think of the knife as an extension of your arm."

"That is a singularly useless piece of instruction," I informed him, affecting a casual air as the knife bounced off the dummy's groin and flopped to the grass.

Stoker retrieved it. "Try again," he ordered.

I threw again, skimming the dummy's head as Stoker explained the desirability of various targets. "The neck is nice and soft, but also narrow and unreliable. If you really want to hinder a man, throw for his thigh. A good hit to the meat of his leg will slow him down, and if you happen to nick the femoral artery, you will stop him for good. You could try for the stomach, but if he is a stout fellow, it will merely lodge in his fat and make him angry."

He proceeded to lecture me for the next hour, about what I cannot say, for as I flung the knife with varying degrees of effort and success, I had leisure to be alone with my own thoughts.

"Veronica," he said at last as the knife sailed past the dummy altogether. "What the bollocking hell was that?" He fetched the knife and handed it back, suddenly blushing furiously.

The cause of Stoker's distress was the unexpected appearance of his lordship's sister, Lady Cordelia Beauclerk. I turned and waved the knife at her.

"Forgive his language, Lady C. Stoker is in a terrible fuss. He has been sulking ever since his lordship broke his leg. How is the patient today?"

Mindful of Stoker's baleful glance, I lowered the knife with exaggerated care.

"A trifle feverish, but the doctor says he has the constitution of an ox, although you would never know it to look at him," she said with a smile. That much was true. His lordship resembled a librarian in the latter stages of anemia—pale and stooped from too many years poring over his books. But blood will tell, and Beauclerk blood was hearty stuff. Lady C. always looked the picture of health, from her English rose complexion to her slender figure. But as I assessed her, I noted an unaccustomed furrow to her brow, and her usually pink cheeks seemed lacking in color.

"You must be working yourself to death taking care of him as well as the house," I observed.

She shook her head. "Things are a bit at sixes and sevens," she admitted. "The doctor has ordered trained nurses in to tend his lordship, and I am afraid Mrs. Bascombe doesn't care for the extra work of looking after them." I was not surprised. His lordship's housekeeper put me in mind of unripe quinces—plump and sour. Lady C. went on. "And of course it's time to pack the boys up for school and the girls have a new governess to settle in."

"For the moment," Stoker murmured. The Beauclerk girls had a habit of driving away hapless governesses with well-timed hysterics or the odd spider in the bed. I rather thought it a pity that no one had told them about the efficacy of syrup of figs dribbled into the morning tea, but it was not my place to tutor them in misdemeanors.

Lady Cordelia smiled her gentle smile. "For the moment," she agreed. "But everything seems in hand this afternoon—so much so that I have decided to pay a visit to the Curiosity Club."

My ears pricked up. Known formally as the Hippolyta Club, it was an intriguing place, founded for the purposes of free discourse amongst accomplished ladies without the strictures of society limiting their conversation. That might have been the raison d'être of the club, but like most high-minded institutions, it was entirely bound by its own set of Byzantine and impenetrable rules. Lady Cordelia had been admitted on the strength of a series of papers she had written on the subject of advanced mathematics, and it was good to see that her talents— frequently wasted in arguing with Mrs. Bascombe about the grocer's bills—were once more carrying her into the circles where her intellect was most appreciated. Her own family thought of her as a sort of performer, conjuring numbers as a dancing bear waltzes to a tune. Her grave, calm eyes never belied the frustration she must have felt at being so frequently ignored or brushed aside, even by kindly and well-meaning hands, but I harbored outrage enough for both of us.

Lady Cordelia gave me a benign look. "You have put on a brave face, but I know how disappointed you must be at not embarking upon the expedition," she began.

"Not at all." I did not make a habit of lying, but it was not Lady C.'s fault the expedition had been beached, and she had never been anything other than gracious to me. I had sensed in her—if not a kindred spirit— at least a sympathetic one.

"You lie very well," she said mildly. "But you are a world explorer, Miss Speedwell. I have heard you speak too eloquently of your travels not to understand how much you love the chase."

"Well, perhaps," I temporized.

She went on. "I know you have much work to do here, but I thought you might like to visit the club, as my guest. A little change of scene to sweeten the mood," she added with a glance to Stoker.

I pursed my lips. "If you want to sweeten the mood, you would be far better placed taking *him*. But it is kind of you to offer. Yes, thank you. I would like to go."

The little furrow between her brows smoothed, although if anything she seemed even less at ease than she had before I accepted. "Excellent. If you would like to collect your things, I will meet you in the drive."

I blinked in surprise. "Now?"

"Yes. I thought we could go for tea," she said. Her gaze drifted over my working costume. "Perhaps a change of attire?" she suggested gently.

I glanced at the enormous canvas pinafore swathing me from collar to ankles. It was an unflattering garment, to be sure, and streaked with paint, blood, dust, and the remains of a profiterole Stoker had flung at me earlier. I whisked off the offending pinafore to reveal a simple gown of red foulard. It was not a fashionable creation by any standards, but I eschewed fashion, preferring to have my working clothes tailored to my specifications rather than the latest whims of the rich and idle. Narrow skirts and an unobtrusive bustle were my only concessions to modernity.

Lady Cordelia gave a vague smile. "Very charming, I'm sure." She paused and looked to my hair, her lips parted as if to say more, but she left us then, as swiftly as she had come.

I turned to Stoker, shoving a few errant locks into the heavy Psyche knot at my neck. With a smile of deliberate malice, I turned and—in a single liquid motion—flung the blade, lodging it firmly between the target's eyes. "I am off to take tea at the Curiosity Club. Mind you take good care of that dummy."

CHAPTER

2

I settled myself comfortably opposite Lady Cordelia in one of the Beauclerk town carriages, mindful of her maid, Sidonie, who watched
balefully from an upstairs window of Bishop's Folly.

"I thought Sidonie accompanied you on all your outings," I remarked.

Lady Cordelia smoothed her black silk skirts, her expression carefully neutral. "I do not require Sidonie's company today. She is inclined
to be indiscreet at times."

I raised a brow in interest. "The Curiosity Club requires discretion?"

Almost against her will, it seemed, Lady C. smiled. "Frequently."

She seemed disinclined to conversation, but I felt obliged to speak.
"I do not know if you have considered the ramifications of being seen
with me in public," I began.

"Why should there be ramifications?"

I suppressed a snort. "We both know that my life is an unconventional
one. I might look and speak like a lady, but my choices have placed me
beyond the pale of propriety. I have traveled alone. I am unmarried, I live
without a chaperone, and I work for a living. These are not the actions of a
lady," I reminded her. I did not mention my more colorful peccadilloes. I
had made a point of choosing my lovers carefully—no Englishmen need

apply—and of entertaining them only when abroad. Thus far mere whispers of my misconduct had reached England, but one never knew when one of the dear fellows would succumb to indiscretion and Reveal All.

"Society is willfully obtuse," she returned, setting her jaw. I recognized the gesture. We had known each other only a matter of months, but I had already learnt that Lady Cordelia possessed an unbendable will when she chose. No doubt her elevated rank would protect her from the worst of the gossip.

I settled myself more comfortably as the coachman maneuvered his way through the darkening streets. A late summer storm had rolled in, blanketing the city with lowering cloud as sheets of rain began to fall, and when we reached the Curiosity Club, the windows glowed in welcome. It was an unassuming edifice, a tall and elegant house tucked in a row of other such buildings. It appeared to be a private residence, but just beneath the bell was a small scarlet plaque bearing the name of the club and the legend ALIS VOLAT PROPRIIS. "'She flies with her own wings,'" I translated.

Lady Cordelia smiled. "Fitting, don't you think?"

Before she could put a hand to the door, it swung back to reveal a portress dressed in scarlet plush, her head wrapped in a shawl of gold silk.

"Lady Cordelia," said the young woman solemnly. She was of African descent, with the innately elegant posture I had observed so often upon my travels to that continent, but her speech was London born and bred.

"Good afternoon, Hetty. This is my guest, Miss Speedwell."

Hetty inclined her head. "Welcome to the Hippolyta Club, Miss Speedwell." She turned back to Lady Cordelia as a page hurried forward to take our damp cloaks. She opened a thick leather book and proffered a pen to Lady Cordelia. "Florrie will have your things dried and brushed before you leave. Lady Sundridge is awaiting you in the Smoking Room."

I gave Lady C. an inquiring glance, but she shook her head swiftly.

"Later," she murmured. So, our visit to the club had a purpose after all, I mused. Suddenly the promise of cakes and tea took on an additional spice.

The girl named Florrie whisked herself away with the brisk rustle of starched petticoats as Lady Cordelia took the pen and signed us in with a flourish. I glanced about, registering my first impression of the club. It was smaller than I had expected, intimate, and decorated with a restraint I found relaxing. The windows were draped in scarlet velvet, almost identical in hue to Hetty's crimson plush, and the carpets were quietly patterned, tasteful things from Turkey, heavy and thick enough to muffle our footsteps. The walls were closely hung with photographs and maps, charts and memorabilia, all celebrating the accomplishments of the members. The club was fitted with gas, but a quick glimpse through the arched doorway into a large parlor revealed a fireplace in which logs were merrily crackling away. I heard the muted buzz of female conversation, punctuated here and there by excited remarks or unrestrained laughter, and I tipped my head at the sound of it.

"Debate and lively discourse are encouraged at the Curiosity Club," Hetty told me with a smile. But in contrast to the warmth of Hetty's welcome, Lady Cordelia's mood seemed to have shifted. By the time she had guided me upstairs to the closed door bearing the inscription SMOK-ING ROOM, her usual calm had faltered and the furrow had etched itself again between her brows.

She tapped lightly, darting me an anxious look before the reply sounded, swift and peremptory. "Come."

Lady C. opened the door upon a smallish, handsome room furnished in the same style as the hall downstairs. Framed maps hung upon the walls, books lined the shelves, and a table beneath the windows held celestial and terrestrial globes interspersed with a selection of potted orchids. A few comfortable leather chairs, like those in gentlemen's clubs, had been installed, and one of these was occupied by a lady dressed in subdued but extremely expensive fashion. She rose slowly as we advanced, giving me a look of frank assessment.

Lady C. made the introductions. "Lady Sundridge, may I present Miss Speedwell. Veronica, this is Lady Sundridge."

For a long moment Lady Sundridge said nothing. She merely stood in a state of composed stillness, like a figure in a tableau. But while her body was immobile, her gaze was rapacious, darting from my face to my hands and back again, as if searching for something.

As my social superior, she held the advantage. It fell to her to acknowledge me, and as long as she was content to play the mute, so was I. I returned her stare coolly, noting her fine-boned face and a tall, slender frame that she carried to elegant effect. Her hands were loaded with jewels, the facets shimmering ceaselessly in the shifting firelight.

She spoke at last. "I know the hour dictates tea, but I had in mind something more bracing." She indicated a low table before the fire. There stood a bowl of hot punch, heavily infused with rum and spices, and I took the glass she offered. She watched me as I swallowed, nodding in approval. "You are not shy of spirits."

"I am not shy of most things, Lady Sundridge."

The beautiful eyes widened for an instant. "I am glad to hear it. I asked Lady Cordelia to bring you to the club so that I might have the pleasure of making your acquaintance. You are, in some circles, quite legendary."

"And what circles might those be, my lady?"

If my forthright approach surprised her, she mastered it swiftly. She gave a dismissive little shrug. "Lepidoptery, of course. I know you trade in butterflies and publish papers very quietly, but it is not difficult to pierce the veil of anonymity if one is determined."

"And why should you be determined? Are you a collector?"

She gave a low, throaty laugh. "Of many things, Miss Speedwell. But not butterflies, alas."

"But of people, I imagine."

She spread her hands. "You astonish me. You are taking my measure," she added. But over the course of our conversation I noticed her movements, graceful and studied, and her voice, smooth as honeyed whiskey, with the barest trace of a German accent. It occurred to me that she would be violently attractive to men—and that she was entirely aware of it.

"Why should I not? You are taking mine," I returned pleasantly.

We were sparring, after a fashion, as swordsmen will do—prodding one's opponent delicately to assess the vulnerabilities in the other's defenses—but I was at a loss to understand why. Unless she suffered from some sort of professional jealousy, there was no reason for us to be at odds. And yet, Lady Sundridge was, quite obviously, sizing me up. That she was doing so in front of Lady Cordelia was even more curious, and Lady C., clearly expecting this, sat quietly sipping at her punch as her ladyship and I circled one another like cats.

"You are direct," Lady Sundridge said at length. "That can be a liability."

"Only to those who require artifice."

I heard a smothered gasp and realized Lady Cordelia was choking delicately on her punch, although from my forthrightness or the strength of the rum, I could not determine.

Lady Sundridge fixed me with a stare I found difficult to characterize. Was it assessment? Disapproval? Grudging respect?

I sipped at my punch. "I must congratulate you, my lady. I am enjoying this rather more than I expected. Generally I avoid the company of ladies whenever possible."

"You find your own sex tedious?"

"Invariably. We are educated out of common sense, curiosity, and any real merit. We are made to be decorative and worthy of display, with occasional forays into procreation and good works, but nothing more."

"You are hard upon us," Lady Sundridge remarked.

"I am a scientist," I reminded her. "My hypotheses are drawn from observation."

She nodded slowly. "Yes. You are hard upon us, but you are not wrong. Women are frequently tiresome, but not in this place. Here you will find your own kind."

"I am only a guest here," I said.

"Indeed," was her sole reply.

I finished the glass of punch and placed it carefully upon the table before I spoke. "And as much as I have enjoyed this exchange, do you not think it is time that you came to the purpose of this meeting?"

Lady Sundridge's eyes narrowed. "What purpose?"

I inclined my head graciously. "I believe you have some questions for me, Your Royal Highness."

CHAPTER

3

The silence in the room was palpable. Then Lady Cordelia began to choke again, and surged from her chair. Lady Sundridge waved her back again with an imperious gesture.

"That is quite all right, Cordelia. We ought not to have taken Miss Speedwell for a fool. I was warned not to underestimate her. Now, I am certain you would like a glass of water to settle that cough, and I think it is time Miss Speedwell and I had a tête-à-tête."

Instantly, Lady C. curtsied deeply and withdrew, but not before throwing me a thoughtful glance. I sat mutely, using silence against Lady Sundridge as she had so adroitly used it against me at the start of our meeting.

"You know who I am?" Lady Sundridge began.

"I know you are a daughter of Queen Victoria. I am not entirely certain which, the family resemblance amongst you and your sisters is strong." The fact that the lady thought she could preserve her incognita was disingenuous if not absolutely naïve. They were the most photographed family in the Empire, and scarcely a day passed without one of them turning up in the newspapers. That they bore a strong likeness to one another made it all the easier to spot one in the wild.

Unexpectedly, she smiled. "Guess."

I considered, studying the graceful bones of her face, the fineness of her tailoring, the strong hands folded prayerfully in her lap.

"Louise."

"Full marks. How did you know?"

I shrugged. "The eldest is Crown Princess of Prussia and not likely to be in London at present. Princess Alice is dead some ten years past. Princess Helena is frequently in ill health while you seem perfectly robust, and Princess Beatrice is expecting a child next month. You are slim as a willow. Besides, there is the matter of your hands."

"My hands?" She spread the long, tapering fingers so that the jewels upon them caught the light once more.

"I have heard that Your Royal Highness is a sculptress. Your hands, while lovely, show the marks of the chisel."

She sat back in her chair, steepling the fingers in question under her chin. "I am impressed with you."

"You oughtn't be," I told her. "It's little more than a parlor trick for someone in my profession. Tell me, do you know why lepidopterists make a point of following birds?" I inquired.

She blinked a little at the non sequitur. "Birds?"

"Birds are the lepidopterist's natural enemy. They feed upon caterpillars before the metamorphosis that we so desperately require in order to collect our specimens. But we have learnt to play their own game better than they. Some species of birds have been observed in the act of tracking caterpillars by looking for chewed vegetation. The lepidopterist's motto is 'Follow the bird, find the caterpillar.' Subtlety and detail are all in our pursuit."

"And are you always successful in your pursuits?" There was challenge in the princess's voice.

"Only a fool would claim perfect success. But I am better than most."

"I am depending upon that," she said slowly. She sat forward. "You and I have a mutual friend in Sir Hugo Montgomerie, I am told. I trust you remember making the gentleman's acquaintance?"

I inclined my head. Sir Hugo, head of Scotland Yard's Special Branch, had featured rather prominently in a previous adventure in detection that Stoker and I had enjoyed.

"I do."

"He remembers you as well. Acutely, in fact. I believe your last interview with him established that you might be willing to lend aid to the royal family should we have need of you."

"My recollection is slightly different," I replied with some asperity. Sir Hugo had attempted, in the common parlance, to buy me off. He had offered a substantial sum of money to me in return for my silence upon a subject which could bring the royal family considerable pain and scandal should I ever choose to reveal it publicly. The fact that my word had not been good enough for him had enraged me, and naturally I rejected the money categorically. But Sir Hugo warned me that the family might seek certain proofs of my loyalty in future, and it appeared that time was nigh.

Her Royal Highness waved a hand, diamonds glittering. "Regardless of the exact terms, I have made a study of you, Miss Speedwell. I believe I understand your character very well. In fact, I would go so far as to say that we have much in common."

"Indeed? Well, they do say blood will tell."

She flinched. My allusion to the secret I carried did not please her. Her lips went thin, but she smiled. Princesses were trained to be forbearing and polite, and she had learnt her lessons well.

"Miss Speedwell, if you know that I am the Princess Louise, then you will also know that I am married to John Campbell, the Marquess of Lorne, heir to the Duke of Argyll."

"Then why the pseudonym of Lady Sundridge?"

She shrugged. "As you have discovered in your own work, anonymity has its uses. I wanted to meet you without the burden of my position coming between us, at least not at first."

I held her gaze with my own. "Your position as princess or as my aunt?" I saw no reason to beat about the bush. I had kept my promise to Sir Hugo not to reveal my complicated parentage, but the princess clearly knew who I was—the unrecognized daughter of her eldest brother, the Prince of Wales. That alone would have been an embarrassment to the royal family; the fact that I could be considered legitimate in some circles made me dangerous. How dangerous remained to be seen. Since I discovered the secret of my birth, we had remained in a state of armed neutrality, neither party acting against the other, but making no overtures either. The fact that one of them had made the first move gave me an advantage, and I intended to use it.

Louise's lips thinned again. "The situation is complicated, and it is not of my making. I hope you will remember that."

The princess clasped her hands tightly as she fell to silence, and a sudden realization struck me.

"You want my help."

She nodded slowly. One hand crept up to play with the jewel at her wrist, a slender gold bangle set with a black enamel heart, the ebony surface marked heavily with golden initials surmounted by a coronet. She noticed the direction of my gaze and held up her wrist. I saw then that the black heart was edged in white, and the initials entwined upon the surface were *L*'s.

"A gift from Her Majesty upon the death of my brother Prince Leopold. He died three years ago. He was a lovely boy, my junior by five years. Unfortunately, he was sickly, even from childhood. You never saw such suffering—that poor, frail little body! But he bore it all with such sweetness. It seemed he would never be able to live as other men, but he had found real happiness. He married a German princess, you know, and they had children. It was the greatest joy of his life to become a father. He had such high hopes that he would outlive his illness. Fate, however, can be cruel. It was a terrible thing to lose him so young—only thirty. Not so many years older than you are now, Miss Speedwell."

Oh, it was masterfully done. Without ever acknowledging my true birth, she had drawn me into the family, appealing to my pity at the loss of an uncle I would never know. I admired and resented her for it. Suddenly, I had no stomach for the games she wanted to play.

"What do you want of me, Your Royal Highness?"

As if sensing my mood, she leaned forward, clasping her hands together. "I am desperate, Miss Speedwell. And I have no one else to whom I can turn."

"What is the trouble?"

She spread her hands. "I hardly know where to begin."

I said nothing. I might have encouraged her, coaxed the story from her, at least at the beginning, but I was conscious of a curious resentment and I held my tongue, forcing her to tell the story of her own accord.

"One of my dearest friends is dead," she managed finally.

"I am sorry for your loss—" I began.

She fluttered her hands impatiently. "I am reconciled to her death. It is not on her behalf that I have come." She paused, fixing me with a steady gaze. "Are you familiar with the Ramsforth case?"

Whatever I had expected of her, it was not this. The Ramsforth case had dominated the news for some months. The facts were simple, but the salacious details had ensured that the affair was splashed across the newspapers.

"I know a little," I told her.

"Then let me fill in the gaps. Miles Ramsforth was accused of murdering his mistress, an artist by the name of Artemisia."

"Your friend?" I hazarded.

Her lips trembled, but she brought the show of emotion under control immediately. "Yes. She was a brilliant painter, and Mr. Ramsforth engaged her to create a mural at his home, Littledown, in Surrey. They were already acquainted before the commission, but during the time she spent at his home, they became lovers, and in due course, Artemisia conceived his child. She was four or five months gone when she finished the mural."

She paused a moment as if to gather her courage to finish the story. "To unveil the piece, Mr. Ramsforth hosted an entertainment at Littledown to which many people in the artistic community, including me, were invited. During the party, Artemisia was murdered. Mr. Ramsforth discovered her, and unfortunately for him, he was found in his bedchamber with her dead body in his arms, his clothes soaked in her blood. She had been dead a very little time—perhaps half an hour. He could provide no alibi, and that fact, coupled with Artemisia's pregnancy, suggested to the police that he must have taken her life."

"For what reason?" I asked, curious in spite of myself.

"Mr. Ramsforth is married," she returned coldly. "The police believe he wanted to rid himself of her and her child before his wife discovered the state of affairs. His defense was naturally hampered by his inability to explain his whereabouts during the time of the murder, and he was found guilty and sentenced to death. He will hang next week."

I pursed my lips. "An intriguing tale, to be certain, Your Royal Highness, but I fail to see what part I am to play."

"Miles Ramsforth did not murder Artemisia!" she burst out, her iron control deserting her. She twisted her fingers together, the diamonds cutting into her flesh.

"How do you know?"

"I cannot say," she replied with a mulish set to her mouth. "Lives would be ruined if I came forward."

"What is that against a man's very existence?" I asked.

"I will not be the subject of impertinent questions, Miss Speedwell," she told me. "I am the best judge of what must be done."

"And what must be done?"

"You must find the murderer."

I gaped at her, wondering for one moment which of us had gone mad. "You cannot be serious."

"I am. A man's life—an *innocent* man's life—rests in your hands."

"It most certainly does not," I returned stoutly. "If he has an alibi, let him explain himself. If he is truly innocent, then whatever horrors the truth will unleash, they cannot be worse than his death."

"You would not say that if you knew," she told me, sudden tears filling her eyes. I might have stood then and taken my leave of her, walking out of that room and her life as easily as I had come. I might have forgot what she asked of me and never thought of her again. But for those tears. Her training, her royal blood, her position—all had failed her, and in that moment she was merely a woman who suffered. She stood on the edge of some unnameable abyss, and that I could understand. I had seen the abyss myself.

"Then tell me," I urged.

"I cannot," she said, shaking her head. "Miss Speedwell, I know I have gone about this quite badly. But you must understand, I want justice for them both. Artemisia was my friend, as is Miles. She was no encumbrance to him—he loved her! But he would go to his grave rather than speak the truth and ruin more lives, and I must honor that. Can you not see the nobility in his sacrifice?"

"I see the stupidity in it," I said, but my resolve was weakening. She must have sensed it, for she leaned forward suddenly, covering my hands with her own. They were strong, those sculptress's hands, and warm, too, and as I stared down at them, I realized that for the first time within my memory, I was being touched by a woman of my own blood. I realized, too, that she understood exactly what she was doing and that she meant to play upon my isolation, my *otherness*. They would never accept me as one of them, but she would dangle the possibility in front of me, as enticing as a lure to a rising carp. And possibly as fatal.

"Miss Speedwell—Veronica," she said softly, "please do this for me. I have no right to command, so I beg instead. Sir Hugo will not listen to me. He knows the investigation was badly handled. It would be an embarrassment for the Metropolitan Police to admit they were wrong. He is satisfied that Miles should hang for this, but if he does, an injustice will happen—a terrible injustice that you have the power to mend. Could you live with yourself if you did not even try?"

I hesitated, and with the unerring instinct of a hunter, she went for the kill. "I will not insult you by speaking of money. Sir Hugo told me of your pride, and I understand it. But I do have something to offer you for your services."

"What?" I demanded.

The grip on my hands tightened. "Your father."

I pulled my hands away sharply. "I require nothing from the Prince of Wales."

"I know," she said, her voice gentle, coaxing, insidious even. "But are you not curious? Would you not like to meet him face-to-face? I can arrange it. He will do it for me. Think of it—a chance to sit and talk to him, the father you have never known. And for nothing more than asking a few questions. It is a fair bargain, I think."

I gave her a long, searching look. I would do as she asked; we both knew that. She thought she persuaded me with her talk of family feeling and my father, but that was not why I helped her. Hatred, as it happens, can be as strong an inducement as the gentler emotions.

So I gave her a smile that hid a thousand things and settled back in my chair. "Very well. Tell me more."

Princess Louise paused a moment, her relief a palpable thing between us. Now that I had indicated I would act as her puppet, she dropped much of her pretense, speaking candidly. "I have always endeavored to do my duty to my family and to my country," she began slowly. "But as you have observed, I am an artist. As such, I have insisted upon the freedom to make friends amongst like-minded people. The cage in which I have lived my life may be gilt, but it is nonetheless a cage," she said, her lips twisting into a thin, humorless smile. "And I have beat myself bloody against the bars. Over time, I have won certain concessions, my work and my friends among them. Artemisia was one of the dearest of these friends."

"It is a curious name."

Her expression was touched with nostalgia. "An affectation. Her real name was Maud Eresby. She thought it too prosaic for an artist, so she chose another. Are you familiar with the work of Artemisia Gentileschi?"

"I am not."

She shrugged. "Few people are, and more is the pity. She was a painter of the Italian Baroque school, and she counted Michelangelo among her admirers. She often chose women for the subjects of her paintings—Judith, Bathsheba, Delilah. Her paintings are unflinching and powerful. My Artemisia aspired to the same, so she took the name."

"How did you meet her?"

"I presume you know the name Sir Frederick Havelock?" There was hardly a soul in England who didn't. He was the most accomplished artist of the age, lionized for his exquisite compositions and lavish and unexpected use of color. He had founded a new school of art, one that was decidedly English and distinctly modern, with influences of Aestheticism and Neoclassicism. He was notoriously bad-tempered and reclusive, preferring the company of a handful of chosen acolytes who lived with him in the Holland Park mansion of his own design. Seldom seen in public, he had matured from the enfant terrible who once tried to drown Dante Gabriel Rossetti to an eccentric legend bent on creating his own utopia.

"He is almost as famous as your mother," I remarked rudely.

Princess Louise overlooked the comment and went on. "Artemisia was one of Sir Frederick's protégées. She lived at Havelock House and she met Miles Ramsforth at one of Sir Frederick's entertainments. The gentlemen are brothers-in-law, and Miles has always relied upon Sir Frederick to provide him with introductions to artists to whom he might offer patronage."

"How exactly are the gentlemen connected?"

"Sir Frederick was married to Augusta Troyon, who died some years ago. Miles is married to her younger sister, Ottilie. They are still quite close to Sir Frederick, even after Augusta Havelock's death."

"And it is because of his marriage to this Ottilie that the police believe Miles was driven to kill Artemisia?"

She waved an impatient hand. "And that is where they have the wrong of it! Ottilie and Miles have a very sensible arrangement. Theirs is a friendship, a partnership of sorts. They married because Miles had an estate falling down about his ears and a bloodline that stretches back eight hundred years. Ottilie brought him a biscuit-manufacturing fortune that her uncle made. They have used her money and his connections to rebuild Littledown and travel the world, collecting art and antiquities. They have had a very pleasant life together, and Ottilie Ramsforth is far too reasonable a person to care about the occasional peccadillo in her husband's private life."

"Occasional peccadillo?" I lifted my brows in inquiry. "So there have been others?"

A fleeting smile touched her lips. "Have you seen a photograph of Miles? No? Just as well, the newspapers do not do him justice. He is a very charming fellow—not precisely handsome, you understand. His features are not nearly regular enough for that. I should never dream of sculpting him," she added with a frown. "There is something elusive about his expressions, they are so changeable. But he is a good friend. He listens, you see. And so few men know how."

Her gaze slid from mine and her expression took on a faraway, slightly disgruntled look. I wondered if she were thinking of her husband. By all accounts, the Marquess of Lorne was not the most attentive of husbands.

"And Ottilie Ramsforth didn't mind," I prodded.

Princess Louise roused herself, turning her attention back to me. "Of course not. She did what all of us do—she redecorated her house or bought a new hat or took a trip to Baden. She knew better than to take it seriously, but of course you cannot explain these things to the authorities. The investigators of the Metropolitan Police suffer from a want of imagination. They assume a man like Miles Ramsforth would wish to hide Artemisia and her pregnancy from his wife, and it made a tidy story for them. They did not trouble to look further. The verdict was precisely the one they expected." She paused, and when she spoke again, it was with real bitterness. "I spoke to Sir Hugo—at least I tried. But he believes artists are all vagabonds and wastrels. He could not say as much, not to me, but his attitude was plain. He had no wish to expend his resources upon searching for the murderer of one insignificant girl when he has the whole of the Empire under his care and a viable suspect ready to hang." That was stretching the truth a bit, I reflected. Sir Hugo was merely the head of the special department within the Metropolitan Police that handled matters touching the royal family. But it required little imagination to believe he saw his own role as much larger.

"Did he suggest you bring your problem to me?" I asked.

She shook her head slowly. "Not at first. He tried to dissuade me. But I knew of your . . . efforts . . . this past summer to uncover the truth in the matter of your own identity. And I knew that Sir Hugo considered you beholden to us."

"Beholden!" I bridled.

"Obliged," she said, gentling her tone. "He told me if I insisted upon pursuing this matter, I could not retain a private inquiry agent. It was too dangerous. But he agreed that you would understand the need for discretion—perhaps better than anyone."

"Sir Hugo has a more refined sense of humor than I would have guessed," I replied. I considered all she had told me for a long moment, and the silence stretched between us, punctuated only by the snapping of the fire and the low ticking of the mantel clock. I thought of my mother, the beautiful actress who had married in secret and borne a love child, only to have her sweet prince marry another—a woman of his own class who would fill his royal nursery with pedigreed babies while his first-born grew up motherless. And I thought of the desperation my mother must have felt when she realized she had been left all alone with me, of the black despair that must have driven her final, fatal act.

"Very well," I said as I rose. "I will be in touch when I have discovered what I can."

Her expression was one of stunned surprise. "But we have not discussed terms," she protested.

"Terms? My terms are these: I will work with my associate, Stoker. You may find him in Debrett's under the heading 'the Honourable Revelstoke Templeton-Vane, third son of the sixth Viscount Templeton-Vane.' We will bring no one else into our confidence. We will do everything in our power to bring these matters to resolution."

"I do not like it," she said, "but I suppose I have little choice in the matter."

"None whatsoever," I agreed.

She lifted her head and looked coolly down her nose at me. I returned the stare, and it pleased me when she looked away first. When she spoke her voice was marginally warmer. "You must not think me ungrateful.

I realize I am asking something quite unorthodox and possibly danger-ous of you."

I shrugged. "I am no stranger to either. In fact, some would say I actively seek the dangerous and unorthodox."

The princess looked me over slowly. "I cannot make you out, Miss Speedwell."

"Do not try, Your Royal Highness," I advised.

CHAPTER

4

The princess ended our interview by scribbling instructions on how to contact her when we had learnt anything of interest. "I think it best if we do not meet more than we can possibly help," she told me.

"My thoughts exactly."

"I will dine tonight with Sir Frederick and Ottilie. I shall explain to them that I have asked you to make inquiries."

"You did not ask them prior to speaking with me?" I was a little surprised at her temerity, but I ought not to have been. She eyed me with hauteur.

"I am not accustomed to asking permission before I take action," she informed me. "A few times each month, Sir Frederick hosts entertainments at Havelock House to introduce the public to his 'pets.' The next is tomorrow evening. I suggest you begin your investigations there. He and Ottilie will be expecting you, and I have no doubt you will enjoy their full cooperation."

"You will not attend?"

She flinched but hid it well. "I think it best if I keep my distance publicly."

I went to the door, but her voice, imperious as an empress's, called.

"Miss Speedwell?"

I turned. "Yes, Your Royal Highness?"

"If you are not successful, Miles Ramsforth will hang in one week. Do not forget that."

I did not curtsy, and I think she had learned in our short acquaintance not to expect it of me. I merely inclined my head and took my leave.

I found Lady Cordelia perched on an armchair outside the room, her expression one of faint chagrin. She rose at the sight of me. "Should I apologize? That was rather an ambush."

"But an intriguing one." I grinned to show her I bore her no ill will.

We descended the stairs, and I heard the pleasant hum of conversation from the large parlor. There was the rattle of crockery punctuated with laughter. Two women were arguing fiercely over the best fixatives for photographs, but apart from that it was a decidedly cozy environment.

The portress brought our things and when we had settled ourselves into the Beauclerk carriage, I turned to Lady Cordelia. "Do you know why she wanted to speak to me?"

She shrugged. "Royalty are eccentric, and Princess Louise is more eccentric than most. She is not an easy woman to understand. I suppose she was interested in you after our conversation."

"You spoke to her about me?"

"Yesterday. She told me she had heard of my brother's plans to organize his collections and asked me about the experts we had engaged. I told her about you and about Stoker."

Little wonder Her Royal Highness had not balked at the mention of his name. Lady Cordelia would have been fulsome in her praise of him for they were friends of long standing.

Lady C. went on. "She asked many questions about you, and my replies only seemed to kindle her interest further. She pressed me to bring you along today for an introduction but was quite adamant that I not disclose to you her identity. She wanted to meet you incognita."

"Did she tell you why?"

Lady C. waved a dismissive hand. "She often moves anonymously amongst her artist friends. A pointless affectation, really. Everyone ends up discovering who she is in the end, and those who don't—well, if she isn't treated with deference, she can be quite peremptory."

"I can well imagine," I told her. Lady Cordelia lapsed into silence then, making no further inquiries, and I was grateful. I was an accomplished liar when the occasion demanded but as a rule I preferred honesty.

As we neared Bishop's Folly, Lady Cordelia roused herself. "I must bid you farewell for a few weeks, Miss Speedwell. I am leaving to take the boys to school for the Michaelmas term, and then I am off to Cornwall to establish the girls and their new governess at Rosemorran House. His lordship has decided London offers too many diversions and thinks the girls may settle better to their lessons in the country," she told me. I was not surprised at Lord Rosemorran's decision, only that he had troubled himself to think of his children in the first place. As a rule, his lordship— a vague and gentle fellow—was far more interested in his latest scholarly project than his own progeny. He left the practical management of his children to his sister, expecting that his whims would be carried out with little fuss or bother to himself. Only Lady Cordelia's life was continually upended by his demands. It would never have occurred to him that she might have interests of her own to pursue.

"When will you return?" I asked.

She gave a tired shrug. "That depends entirely upon the children. If Rose will behave herself and stop putting frogs into the soup tureen, I might manage October sometime. Otherwise, I will have to remain until it is time to collect the boys for Christmas. I do not like leaving his lordship alone during his recovery, so I am glad to say that a relation of ours is coming to stay."

"Oh?"

"Yes, our great-aunt, Lady Wellingtonia Beauclerk."

I lifted a brow. "Wellingtonia?"

"She was born on the day Waterloo was fought. Her father was an aide-de-camp to the Duke of Wellington. She is a very interesting old lady . . . rather eccentric."

"In what way?" I asked.

"I hardly like to say," she hedged. "Far better for you to make up your own mind," she added briskly. The carriage rocked to a stop and Lady Cordelia put out her hand. "Until we meet again, Miss Speedwell."

I ran Stoker to ground in the Belvedere where he was busy cataloging the contents of a bookshelf. He gave a low, ardent groan, like that of a lover on the precipice of fulfillment. "His lordship has Pliny's *Natural History*—all thirty-seven volumes," he said, caressing book nine, one of the volumes on zoology. He looked up and must have seen something in my expression, for he put the book aside at once.

"I was going to offer tea, but I think something stronger," he said. We made our way up to the little snuggery on the first floor. Once a bolt-hole of the third Earl of Rosemorran, who had built the Belvedere to escape the demands of his wife and thirteen children, it was now our private retreat. Surrounded by shelves and case furniture, it held a comfortable sofa, an armchair, a tiled Swedish stove, and a writing table as well as a campaign bed that had once belonged to the Duke of Wellington. With the little water closet concealed behind the wall, it had provided us with a safe haven during our previous adventure, and it had become our custom to withdraw to it when we wished for seclusion. The elder Beauclerks were mindful of our privacy, but Lord Rosemorran's children were an inquisitive lot, and I was forever falling over one or another of them in the Belvedere. The snuggery was the only spot free of sticky fingerprints and prying ears. Trotting obediently at Stoker's heels came his bulldog, Huxley, and the earl's Caucasian sheepdog, Betony.

She ought to have been lying at her master's feet, offering him companionship during his recuperation, but since Stoker had come to live at Bishop's Folly, she had transferred her affections to him—and to Huxley, who seemed a little bewildered by her devotion. Huxley settled with a wet snort into his usual bed, an overturned elephant's foot, while Bet arranged her mammoth proportions into a suitably enormous basket. The fact that the basket had once served as the gondola to a balloon piloted over Versailles by the Montgolfier brothers troubled her not at all.

Stoker poured out a stiff measure of whiskey and handed me a glass. I waited until he had stirred up the fire in the stove and taken his own chair before launching into my tale. He listened, his expression carefully neutral until I finished.

His first words were cordial in tone if not in content. "Have you lost your bloody mind?"

"If you mean to abuse me, let me finish my whiskey first."

He gave an exasperated sigh. "Veronica, you have obligated us to a member of the royal family—and not for some trifling favor. You have promised that we will solve a murder."

"Yes, that is rather the idea."

"We are not investigators," he pointed out, his tone decidedly more acid. "We are natural historians."

I waved a hand. "Precisely. We are trained to observe life in the closest detail, to pursue facts, to hypothesize, to conclude—all necessary skills for a detective. We didn't do so badly this past summer," I reminded him.

"We were very nearly killed for our pains," he retorted.

"Oh, don't fuss, Stoker. The most significant injury sustained in the course of that investigation was when you stabbed me, an action for which I have entirely forgiven you."

"That was an accident," he returned, clipping the words off sharply.

"Of course it was. You would never stab me deliberately—at least, not without excellent provocation."

"Such as this?" he asked.

"Don't be peevish, Stoker. It makes your lips go thin and you have such a beautiful mouth."

He hid the feature in question by taking a swift drink of his whiskey while I continued on.

"Think of it," I urged. "The two of us, out there in the vast city, sleuthing down a murderer in a hunt of our own making. You cannot say we did not enjoy our last adventure, nor can you deny that we have both of us seen enough excelsior and packing crates to last until the New Year."

"Take me through it again," he ordered, and I did, aware that he was scrutinizing the tale this time with all the fervor of his training as a scientist. He closed his eyes and thrust his hands into his hair, tumbling the long dark locks through his fingers as he listened.

When I finished, he shook his head, dropping his hands and reaching once more for his whiskey. "I do not like it."

"Well, murder is generally regarded as disagreeable," I replied.

"I mean the whole affair. It's none of my business if half of London wants to garrote the other half and serve them up on parsley."

"Feathers," I said succinctly. "You have the most keenly developed sense of justice of any man I have ever known. You would never let an innocent fellow like Miles Ramsforth swing for a crime he did not commit."

Stoker leaned forward, his bright blue eyes glittering. "But we have only the princess's word that he didn't."

"You think she is lying." An uncomfortable snake of doubt curled itself coldly around the base of my spine.

"I think it is possible. Veronica, you must look at this rationally. If she has information that can save his life, why does she not come forward?"

"I asked her," I reminded him. "She said she could not say. That lives would be ruined."

"What is that against the death of an innocent man?" he demanded.

"Rather than agree to do this for her, you ought to have called her bluff— insisted she go back to Sir Hugo and tell the truth, whatever the cost."

I said nothing. I merely stared into the depths of my whiskey glass, surprised to find it empty.

"I know why you didn't," he told me, his voice suddenly gentle. "You think that by doing this for her—for *them*—that they will acknowledge you somehow, that it will make up for all the years of neglect."

"Of all the absurd—" I burst out, but he carried on, as implacable and unstoppable as an incoming tide.

"I understand that you believe you have something to prove to them, but you don't. You are worth a *thousand* of them, Veronica. But they will never see it. If you set yourself up as their lackey because you want their approbation, it will not stop. This is a game you cannot win, so do not play it. Walk away now, before they've got under your skin," he warned.

"Like your family have yours?" I shot back. I had not meant to say it, but once the words were there, hanging in the air between us like pieces of rotten fruit, I could not take back the stink of them.

"What do you mean?" His voice was even and calm, and that is how I knew he was truly angry. A thundering, barking, pillaging Stoker was a happy Stoker. But stillness was the thing that betrayed his deepest rage.

I rose and went to the chinoiserie cabinet in the corner. It took only a moment to lay my hand upon the letter. "This. From your brother, two weeks ago. Your father is dead and you said not a word to me. You have not been absent, so I know you did not attend his funeral. Your brother alludes to other letters written by assorted members of your family. I have searched the Belvedere and found eleven. Tell me, were there more?"

I wanted him to swear at me, something vicious and suitable for a former sailor, but he merely sat, a muscle working furiously in his jaw as he listened.

"If you truly did not care for your family, you would not have kept the letters. But you did. And they all bear the same message—your family want to see you. They implore you to name a time and place. But you have ignored them all, driving them to distraction, it seems. You have no high ground here, Revelstoke," I said coldly. "Not when you are playing a game of your own."

He passed a hand over his face, and with the gesture, the coiled anger seemed to ebb a little. "God, you have a brutal tongue when you put a mind to it. Sharp as a blade and twice as lethal." He poured out a second measure of whiskey for us both and drank his off swiftly. "Very well. My father is dead and my family beg my presence which I will not grant them. You're quite right. I have withheld myself because it gives me pleasure to think of them gnashing their teeth over it. It is a satisfaction you ought to permit yourself," he advised. "Tell the Saxe-Coburg-Gothas to go hang themselves."

"After," I said, and with that single word he suddenly understood. Comprehension broke over his features like morning across a landscape, and he shook his head slowly.

"Poor child," he murmured.

"Don't you dare. I will brook no pity from you," I warned.

"You don't want to solve this puzzle of theirs so they will like you," he said, giving voice to the feelings I could not acknowledge even to myself. "You want to do it so you can throw it in their faces."

I drained my own whiskey, taking courage from the burn of it. "Something like that," I admitted finally.

He considered this a long moment, then shrugged. "As good a motive as any. Besides, if you save a man's life and tell your family to go to the devil, it might improve that temper of yours. Don't think I haven't noticed the freight of anger you have been hauling about. And I understand it, better than anyone. You have been in a foul mood ever since we discovered the truth about your parentage."

"I have not! Besides, you only knew me for a few days before we learned the truth. How do you know what I am like? This might *be* my usual temper."

His grinned, then settled to the particulars of our investigation. "We cannot neglect our obligations here," he warned.

"Naturally," I conceded. "We shall simply have to work more quickly and finish our cataloging for the day before luncheon. That will give us the rest of each day and the evening to investigate."

He shook his head. "You are mad. And I am madder still for letting you talk me into this."

I gave him a wry smile. "We will be like Arcadia Brown and her faithful sidekick, Garvin," I said, invoking our favorite literary detective. Stoker claimed not to enjoy popular fiction, but ever since I had introduced him to the lady investigator's adventures, he had devoured them while still pretending to be above such diversions.

He narrowed his gaze. "If you are expecting me to brandish a pistol and go haring off with you, crying 'Excelsior!,' you will be waiting until the crack of doom," he warned. "I am only doing this because I know there is no point in attempting to talk you out of it, and you will need someone to watch your back with a murderer on the loose."

I grinned at him and lifted my glass in salute. "It begins."

CHAPTER

5

As natural scientists, Stoker and I approached the investigation in a suitably academic manner. First, we decided to gather as much information as possible. Stoker was finishing the mount of a particularly nasty Nile crocodile, so after speeding through my usual duties in the Belvedere, I took the opportunity to dig through Lord Rosemorran's collection of periodicals, collecting every scrap of detail regarding the Ramsforth case. It was our good fortune that Lord Rosemorran was a newspaper enthusiast, subscribing to the respectable broadsheet publications as well as the most lurid tabloids, and from every corner of the kingdom—Gravesend to John o' Groats. The cheaper publications were predictably morbid with their endless carping upon the gore-stained blood in which the victim had been found, while the broadsheets took a loftier tone of condemnation of the Bohemian life-style and its related immoralities. Hampered as we were by not examining the scene when the crime was fresh, we at least had the advantage of getting the story from every possible angle.

I pored over the newspapers until my eyes ached and my fingers were black with ink, reading aloud pertinent details and taking copious notes. I discovered Louise had been quite effective at relating the irrefutable facts of the situation: Artemisia was dead, and Miles Ramsforth, after refusing categorically to speak at all upon the subject, was about to hang for her murder. Everything else seemed open to interpretation. One scandal sheet called him a child of Lucifer while the quality press seemed to think him a rakishly charming fellow who had nobly chosen to go mutely to the gallows rather than excite further scandal by breaking his silence. The fact of Artemisia's pregnancy was seized like a moldy bone by the rabid journalists of the gutter press and neatly glossed over by their more elevated brethren. The only thing they all agreed upon was that the sooner he was hanged, the better for everyone.

The most detailed descriptions were to be found in a nasty little rag called *The Daily Harbinger*. They had created a special issue with elaborate color illustrations of the murder scene, and I waved it at Stoker.

"Here is an excellent illustration of Miles Ramsforth. He looks quite respectable in the broadsheets, but the *Harbinger* makes him look utterly villainous. Still, I think he is rather handsome, or would be if it were not for that chin."

Stoker came to look over my shoulder. "Weak," he agreed. "No doubt the reason for his muttonchops." He stroked his own jaw, looking quite satisfied, as well he might. I had seldom seen a more firmly set bone on any man.

I turned the page to find a gruesome illustration of the murder scene—Miles Ramsforth's bedchamber. It might have been an elegant room under other circumstances. It was lavishly furnished in old Tudor oak, from the linenfold paneling to the four-poster bed hung with layers of deep crimson bed-curtains. I imagined when they were drawn, the bed itself would be very cozy, a warm, scarlet womb, perfect for snuggling into on cold nights. I peered closer. "Look how frightful. They've even managed to match the blood to the bed-curtains," I said with a shudder at the puddle below the scarlet hangings. The edges of the pool were irregular, and a quick examination of the article explained. "It says the murderer must have trod in the blood at some point."

"The murderer must have been dripping in the stuff," Stoker pointed out as he returned to carefully fit an eyeball into his crocodile. He launched into a technical explanation of the velocity of the blood pumping from arterial vessels versus that of venous vessels. "I was standing next to a fellow who lost half his head to a cannonball during the Alexandria bombardment," he finished helpfully. "Looked as if we'd all been bathing in gore."

"Apparently that is how the police ruled out any other possible murderers," I said, returning to the article. "They inspected everyone's clothes and shoes—guests, staff. It says that Ottilie Ramsforth, who might otherwise have been suspected, wore unblemished white without a speck of blood anywhere upon her person. Only Miles Ramsforth was drenched in the stuff."

"If he didn't do the deed himself, how does he account for that?"

I tossed the paper aside. "He said he trod in the blood when he found the body and claimed his clothes became soiled because he was so shocked upon discovering her that he lifted her up."

"A flimsy bit of flummery," Stoker countered, and I agreed.

"Apparently that is when he stopped talking to the police. He gave them an initial statement claiming his innocence, then nothing more. He would not even help his solicitors except to say that if they could not save him without his help, he did not deserve to be saved."

"A curious line to take when one's life is at stake," Stoker put in.

We had just decided to send out for packets of fish and chips and eat à deux in the Belvedere when a note arrived from the main house. I opened it with begrimed fingers, cursing soundly as I read.

"What?" Stoker demanded.

I brandished the paper at him. "Our presence is requested for a late supper. It seems Lady Wellingtonia has arrived earlier than expected and is quite eager to make my acquaintance. We are asked to come on the hour."

Stoker glanced at the case clock and muttered something unprintable. We had scarcely a quarter of an hour to make ourselves presentable, but I always kept an extra frock close at hand, and a quick scrub in the water closet and a change into black silk effected a tremendous improvement. Stoker had no time to shave the whiskers that darkened his jaw, but he washed quickly and thrust his arms into an evening coat, snatching up a bit of discarded silk to fashion into a neckcloth as we hurried to the house. The dogs, accustomed to Stoker's habit of feeding them titbits from the table, scampered along behind us, charging off only at the last minute to chase a rabbit. The dinner gong was just sounding as we reached the drawing room, slightly out of breath and looking rather too bedraggled for a smart supper party.

The room was quiet when we entered, the only sound the frantic chirps of Lady Cordelia's lovebirds from their cage in the corner. Thinking myself unobserved, I put my hand to my hair, tucking in an errant lock with a hairpin.

"Young woman, you look like a bacchante. Have you been getting up to mischief in the bushes?" An elderly woman advanced from the shadows behind the birdcage. She came forward slowly, an ebony walking stick clutched in a gnarled hand, but I had the oddest sensation that she used it more to claim her territory than to support enfeebled legs.

The question was clearly rhetorical, so I made no effort to answer it, merely standing with my hands still as she drew near, looking me up and down, running her gaze slowly from hem to head and back again.

I took the opportunity to scrutinize her in return. She was taller than most of the Beauclerks, with a back that would have put a ramrod to shame for its straightness. She carried her chin high, and if age and a tendency to embonpoint had softened her features, it had not obscured her eyes. They were black and beautiful still, but as a hawk's are beautiful—watchful and unforgiving. The nose, too, was beakish, and the chin a trifle too sharp for handsomeness. She had clearly never been a beauty, but I could easily imagine her as a belle laide, demanding attention for her vitality alone.

"You have good posture," she said finally. "That speaks to a sturdy constitution. Whoever brought you up knew what they were about."

"I was reared by my aunts," I told her, opting for the simpler, "official" version of the truth. "One of them was kind. One was not. The one who was not fixed holly leaves to my collar to make me keep my chin up."

She nodded. "I was strapped to a board for my lessons every day. My father believed letting girls study would lead to a crooked back, so a brace was the only way he would permit me to have lessons. That's how I learnt Horace," she said grimly. "You're the Speedwell child, I take it? I am Lady Wellingtonia Beauclerk. You may address me as Lady Wellie. I do not care for ceremony, as you have no doubt observed."

"You were admiring the birds," I said by way of a conversational gambit. I nodded towards the cage where the lovebirds, Crates and Hipparchia, were wittering darkly as they looked at her.

"Pretty creatures," Lady Wellingtonia said. "But they never stop that infernal noise. I was just about to open the cage to let the cat in. Or is that cruel? Ought I to drown them straight off and have done with it?"

Before I could form a reply, Stoker came forward. "Good evening, Lady Wellie," he said, bending over her hand in a courtly gesture. He brushed his lips across the back of it and she simpered a little.

She offered him a powdered cheek. "Hello, dear boy. Give us a kiss. Now the other cheek and squeeze my hand like you mean it."

Stoker did as he was bade and stood back, grinning. "It is good to see you again, Lady Wellie."

"You're a rogue," she told him, rapping his knuckles lightly with a fan. "I have not seen you in more than six months. I like your new pet," she added with a nod towards me.

Stoker snorted, and I poked him sharply in the ribs. "That will do," I said. I turned to Lady Wellingtonia.

"Stoker and I are partners in his lordship's scheme to open the Belvedere as a public museum," I told her.

She rolled her eyes heavenwards. "A disgraceful notion. Who wants the public trampling through the gardens, leaving sweet papers and empty bottles and God only knows what other rubbish behind?"

"You don't believe the public should have access to the accumulation of human knowledge? To the accomplishment of art and exploration?"

A small smile played about her mouth. "You think the common man cares about such things? No, child. The common man cares about a full belly, warm feet, and a sound roof. But I like your idealism. It's charming, as long as you promise to lose it before you turn thirty. A woman past thirty cannot afford ideals."

"A cynical view, I think," I told her.

She pulled a face. "Stoker, the child thinks me a cynic."

Stoker gave her a bland look. "The child will think worse of you when she gets to know you."

I gaped at the rudeness, but Lady Wellingtonia threw her head back and cackled. "We shall go into dinner now because if I sit down in one of those ludicrous chairs, I might never get up again," she said with a dark glance at the low armchairs. She turned to me. "In my day, chairs were not for comfort. They were to keep your bottom from touching the floor and that is all. And be glad Cordelia is not here. She is a lovely girl, but she would swoon straightaway if she heard me use the word 'bottom' in polite company. It is the greatest advantage of getting old, you know. I can say precisely what I like and everyone excuses it because I knew Moses from his bulrush days." She took Stoker by the arm. "Take me in to dinner, boy. Miss Speedwell, you will have to walk alone, I am afraid."

Stoker obediently escorted her to the small Rosemorran supper room instead of the grand dining room. The table had been laid for four, and I raised a brow as we settled ourselves. "Is his lordship coming down? Or Lady Cordelia?"

Lady Wellingtonia paused to inspect the cold salmon mayonnaise that had been laid on the sideboard before replying. "No, child. Rosemorran is feeling feverish this evening, and I've told Cook to send him up some calf's-foot jelly and a nice blancmange. Cordelia and the children have already left." She nodded towards the extra place setting. "That is for my shadow, should he ever bestir himself to appear. He is always late."

I had just begun to wonder if the old woman's wits were wandering when the door opened and a clergyman entered, clucking apologies and tugging at his dog collar as he took his chair.

He nodded to Lady Wellie as he lifted an ear trumpet into place. "I am sorry, Wellie, but his lordship's library *will* keep me so diverted, I quite lose track of the time."

Lady Wellie sighed and spoke to him, raising her voice and speaking distinctly. "Cecil, I have seen you lose track of time by comparing the length of your shoelaces. His lordship's library has nothing to do with it. You have no discipline," she chided. But there was a note of fondness in her voice. She waved her fork. "Introduce yourself to Miss Speedwell."

The clergyman turned to me. "I am the Reverend Cecil Baring-Ponsonby. *Not* a connection to the Bessborough Ponsonbys," he added firmly. I cudgeled my brain a moment before recalling that Ponsonby was the surname of the Earl of Bessborough's family, a clan noted for its eccentricity since the beginning of the century when one of their young ladies became the mistress of Lord Byron and sent him her nether hairs in the post.

"Cecil, you've been saying that since Lady Caroline Lamb was alive. No one cares," the lady told him firmly as she forked up a fresh bit of salmon. "Stoker, you remember Mr. Baring-Ponsonby. He's still alive, as you can see. Cecil," she called, raising her voice as he lifted his ear trumpet again. "This is Revelstoke Templeton-Vane. You've met before but you won't remember, so just nod to be polite. He's an Honourable, you know. Son of a viscount I never liked."

The gentlemen exchanged cordial greetings and Stoker turned to our hostess. "What brings you to Bishop's Folly this time, Lady Wellie?"

"We are supposed to be keeping Rosemorran entertained, poor lad. Although between us, it takes an uncommonly stupid man to trip over his own tortoise. Bizarre creature. So ponderous and such a curious face—the tortoise, not Rosemorran. I say, Cecil, it's only just occurred to me, you look rather like Patricia."

"What's that?" he asked, cupping his ear.

"I said you look like Patricia! His lordship's tortoise!" she shouted back. Now that she had said it, I could not stop seeing the resemblance. I half expected Mr. Baring-Ponsonby to take offense, but he merely shrugged and applied himself to his salmon mayonnaise.

Lady Wellingtonia turned to me. "I must make a point of visiting the Belvedere whilst I am here. I haven't seen this place in forty years. Still full of rubbish, I expect."

"The collection also boasts some extremely fine examples of art and natural history," I said stoutly. The collection might have been a combination of rubbish heap and treasure trove, but I would permit no one else to think poorly of it.

"What ho! Did you hear that, Cecil? I am reproached. Never mind, my dear. You mustn't pay attention to my whims. I am glad you were free to dine with me tonight. I so wanted to meet you and put a face with a name." She gave me a long, measured look. "Miss Veronica Speedwell indeed."

"You are too kind," I replied.

She laughed, a great booming sound that seemed oddly incongruous coming from so elderly a person. "I am not kind. Ask anyone."

"No, I imagine you are not. I was merely being polite," I told her.

To my astonishment, she broke into a smile—a rather hideous smile, for it revealed a number of bad teeth. She raised a glass to me. "I have decided we are going to be very great friends, Miss Speedwell."

I lifted my glass in return and drank deeply, not certain if I was more gratified or alarmed by the prospect. Whatever peculiar fencing game she had been playing at before, she dropped it then, and we spoke of many things. Mr. Baring-Ponsonby made the occasional pithy remark, and Stoker was always good for a tale, but I was most intrigued when Lady Wellie held the floor. She was a fascinating woman, and the little glimpses I had of her past—the places she had been, the people she had known—made me all the more desirous to dig deeper.

"You have led a very interesting life," I remarked after one particularly intriguing anecdote involving an Austrian archduke.

"Have I shocked you? Remember I was born in a different time, Miss Speedwell. Virginity is Queen Victoria's legacy. The rest of us are not quite so blinkered," she told me. "Take my advice and get rid of yours as fast as you can."

I briefly toyed with the notion of telling her I had discarded mine on a hillside in Switzerland during a very pleasant interlude some seven years past.

"And if you've any sense, you will hand it to him," she added with a meaningful glance down the table towards Stoker, who was shouting remarks into Mr. Baring-Ponsonby's ear trumpet.

Just at that moment, Stoker turned, his gaze curious. "What are you two talking about? You look quite flushed."

"We were discussing horseflesh," Lady Wellingtonia said. "And how difficult it can be to find a good mount."

His response was sweetly naïve. "If you need a recommendation, I know a fellow or two."

I suppressed a laugh as Lady Wellingtonia gave him a smile that was purely feral. "I imagine you do, dear boy. I imagine you do." She turned back to me as he resumed his conversation with the little clergyman.

We chatted aimlessly until the pudding was brought in, and Lady Wellie gave a frisking little shiver of delight. "Apple snowball!" she exclaimed. "My favorite."

She glanced at Mr. Baring-Ponsonby, who had apparently drifted off to sleep sometime during the cheese course. Stoker was attacking his pudding with gusto, and an expression of pure affection gentled Lady Wellie's harsh features. "I am fond of Stoker. If I had a son, I would have wanted one like that. But it is a wretched business, this birthing of children," she added darkly. "Avoid it if you can."

"I mean to," I replied.

"That's a smart girl." She gave me a nod and a wink as I spooned up a bit of apple snowball. I did not generally care for sweets, but Cook had outdone herself with the crème anglaise accompaniment. Stoker, whose sweet tooth was legendary, had scraped his bowl clean and—I noticed with amusement—exchanged it for the slumbering Mr. Baring-Ponsonby's full one.

I turned back to Lady Wellie.

"You ought to write a memoir," I told her.

She made a dismissive gesture with her hand. "Live long enough and interesting things are bound to happen. I am older than the Nile, child. Speaking of which—" She paused and gave a quick order to Lumley, the butler. His expression faltered for an instant. "Don't be tiresome, Lumley!" she said. "I am ready for my tea, and I've no interest in hauling myself and Miss Speedwell back to the drawing room and waiting for it there. We will have it here whilst the gentlemen have their port. I daresay Mr. Baring-Ponsonby will rouse himself for that."

Lumley's color had drained, but he bowed from the waist. "Of course, my lady." Lumley, like all superior servants, was a greater stickler for conformity than the family he served. To have Lady Wellingtonia chuck the tradition of ladies withdrawing after dinner must have shocked him as deeply as if we had all begun to disrobe and dance on the tabletop.

But he was dutiful, and he appeared in due course with a decanter of port for the gentlemen and a tea service that I had never seen before. I caught my breath, and Lady Wellingtonia looked at me approvingly.

"Thought you would like that. Wedgwood," she informed me. But it was no Wedgwood I had ever seen. Cast in a deep, dull crimson, the rosso antico set featured black scenes in stunning relief. And what scenes they were! Sphinxes alternated with stylized animals and great outspread wings in bands that circled each piece, the teapot crowned with a crocodile finial. "It was created to celebrate Nelson's victory over Napoleon's navy in Egypt. Rather fun, isn't it?"

"It is splendid," I told her.

We sipped at our tea and she began to reminisce about the people she had known, never boasting, simply telling stories of the foibles that had amused her. I did not know what prompted me, but I found myself wondering if she might be useful in our current investigation.

Mr. Baring-Ponsonby had wakened with the introduction of the port, and he and Stoker were applying themselves to the judicious appreciation of his lordship's best tawny.

"I wonder, Lady Wellingtonia, if you ever had occasion to meet with Sir Frederick Havelock?"

"Freddie! I haven't seen him in years," she said with a faraway look in her eye. "He painted me twice, you know. The first was a lovely portrait for the Royal Academy before he got his Irish up and was thrown out for striking the president at the opening. The fellow made a cutting remark about the composition and Frederick never could take criticism. A bit like this one here," she said, nodding at Stoker. "Tilting at windmills. That is how he got himself thrown out of the Royal Museum of Natural History last year."

I stared at Stoker. "You hit someone?"

He shrugged and sipped at his wine. "No one who didn't deserve it."

Lady Wellie gave her cackling laugh. "I am a patroness of the place, which is a short way of saying I give them money so they invite me to all the openings. Stoker was already in disgrace, but I brought him with me as my escort and no one could say boo about it. And no one would have had Stoker not taken exception to one of the displays."

"What was so objectionable?" I inquired.

Stoker's mouth thinned with recollected fury. "The director had mounted a display of apes and fossils to demonstrate Darwinian evolution."

"That sounds reasonable," I said.

"He put a live African man in a loincloth at the end of it. *In chains,*" he said, fairly spitting the words.

"And for the director's pains, he got a tooth knocked out," Lady Wellie reminded him. She turned to me. "It took four men to pull Stoker off of him and throw him out. In the meantime, I discovered the African fellow was a qualified pastry cook without a place, so I took him off to my favorite hotel and found him employment. If you ever dine at the Sudbury, my dear, make very certain to order the croquembouche à la Beauclerk for dessert. It is his speciality," she advised me.

I thought of Stoker thrashing the director and suppressed a smile. "You said Sir Frederick painted you twice," I prompted Lady Wellie. "Did you enjoy sitting for him?"

"Enjoy? Not a moment of it. He modeled himself after Caravaggio, you know. Nothing but wine breath and grasping hands. I spent more time fending him off than actually posing. But the second was a damned fine portrait," she said, her expression dreamy. "I was quite nude. He painted me masked, of course, so no one would know. But it was a splendid portrait. Hangs over the bar at the Helicon Club."

Stoker choked lavishly then, taking some moments to recover himself. "I've seen that," he finally wheezed out.

"Rather good, isn't it?" she asked, a twinkle in her eye.

"Spectacular," he said with feeling as he raised his glass to her.

She sighed. "I was past forty when Frederick painted that. The last gasp of beauty." She turned her gaze upon me. "You should have him paint you, child. You've a face like a minor Greek goddess now, but someday it will start to slide down into your décolletage and you'll find your breasts at your waist."

Mr. Baring-Ponsonby lifted his ear trumpet. "Eh, what's that?"

Lady Wellie raised her voice. "We were talking about breasts, Cecil."

"Lovely things, breasts," he said, promptly nodding off into his port with a muffled snore. She gave him a fond look.

"He's rather like a lapdog, the dear old thing. A sweet companion in my dotage. Appendage like a donkey's, you know."

Stoker choked again on his port while I groped for a response. Lady Wellie went on in a blithe tone. "I am older than Father Thames, children, and I have made my peace with it. But I have a few years left before Death asks me to dance, and I mean to enjoy them as I have the rest. Now, tell me why you are interested in Freddie Havelock."

Before I could think of a good lie, Stoker spoke. "Building upon the work of Charles Willson Peale, I have in mind a thoroughly new means of organizing the displays of the natural history specimens his lordship has in the Belvedere. I want to place them each in a setting reminiscent of their habitat in the wild. If we were to position paintings in the background of each display, very detailed and specific paintings, we could conjure an atmosphere of reality unlike anything that has been seen before."

I gaped at him. "Stoker, that is brilliant." Too late, I realized we were supposed to be partners, and as such, I ought to have known about such a scheme.

But Lady Wellie was sharp as a talon. "You are unfamiliar with this plan, Miss Speedwell?"

"It is the first I have heard of it," I told her truthfully.

"Then why were *you* so keen to make the acquaintance of Sir Frederick?" she asked, her dark gaze inquisitive. A tiny smile curved the corners of her mouth, as if she sensed my discomfiture and it amused her a little.

"I wanted to surprise Miss Speedwell with the endeavor," Stoker lied smoothly. "It was my suggestion that we make his acquaintance with an eye to viewing his art."

She gave a slow nod, reluctantly, I fancied, accepting his explanation. "Well, Freddie is unique, and he might have done justice to your project at one time, but not now."

"Why not now?" I asked.

Lady Wellie spread her hands. "Freddie is very nearly a cripple," she said flatly. "A few years ago he began to experience episodes of tremors in the limbs. He had enough strength to do the ordinary things—shave himself, write a letter—but he hadn't the ability to hold a paintbrush for more than a few hours. He made his reputation on the size of his canvases, great hulking things, larger than life, they are. You ought to see the portrait of me in the Helicon Club—bosoms the size of an infant," she said with a raucous laugh. "But with his diminished capacity for work, a canvas of that sort would have taken him years to finish. He tried miniatures, but they demanded a finesse of which he was no longer capable. He turned his hand to designing furniture instead and decorating his house. Frightful pile of a place—looks like Brighton Pavilion inside."

"Havelock House?"

"That's the one," she said with a nod. "He inherited a tidy sum from his father—you've heard of Septimus Havelock?" She looked from me to Stoker and both of us made noises of assent. "Most famous artist of his generation, Septimus was. His portrait of Queen Victoria upon her accession secured his admission to the Royal Academy at the unprecedented age of seventeen. There was not a crowned head in Europe he didn't paint, and he finished his career at the court of the tsars as the Russian emperor's pet artist. Quite a legacy for Freddie to live up to." She paused to reach for a bowl of nuts and a nutcracker, applying herself diligently to picking out nutmeats whilst we waited for her to resume her tale. "Freddie had very little interest in his inheritance when he was young—wanted to make his own way, and I say good for him. A fellow ought not to rest upon his family name," she added with a meaningful glance at Stoker. "If he has skills, he ought to use them in service of queen and country."

Stoker studied his fingernails and made no reply.

"Sir Frederick did establish himself," I reminded her.

"That he did," she agreed. "He was a very talented painter in his own right, but he has never measured up to his father's genius and it has always been rather a sensitive point," she told me with a knowing nod. "When Frederick's body began to fail him, he built that magnificent monstrosity on the edge of Holland Park—a sort of combination of house and studio and gallery. He meant to create a salon for aficionados to gather and discuss art, but he also intended to use the space as a nursery for budding artists."

"A generous scheme," I remarked.

Lady Wellie snorted. "Generous, yes. Freddie is generous, but usually only when it benefits him."

"And how does this establishment benefit him?"

"He gets to play God. He advises them on what commissions to take, what manner of art to pursue, with whom they should sleep. With his little protégés gathered about him, he is still important, still a kind of paterfamilias to the up-and-coming. Provides them with introductions to wealthy benefactors, too—the sort of men who have more money than taste and can afford to pay handsomely to be taught what to like."

My heart thrummed with excitement. I had wondered exactly how to guide Lady Wellie onto the subject of Miles Ramsforth, but she had led us to the very edge of the story herself.

I widened my eyes, adopting an innocent expression. "Isn't Sir Frederick related to that poor Mr. Ramsforth?"

Lady Wellie's dark eyes sharpened. "Miles Ramsforth? Yes, he is. Odd to call him 'poor' when he is a convicted murderer, child," she said mildly.

"Perhaps he is innocent," I offered. "He has provided no alibi."

"Which rather points to his guilt," Lady Wellie countered. "But you are an optimist, I see, Miss Speedwell. A trait I have often observed amongst lepidopterists."

"I have pointed out that very thing to her," Stoker put in.

Lady Wellie was regarding me thoughtfully. "Yes, the butterfly hunter likes the mazy chase of the beautiful, fluttering just out of reach. But it is a curious thing, to hunt the butterfly instead of the tiger," she added in a low voice. "You mete death with your own hands, do you not, Miss Speedwell? I wonder, would you stop at a butterfly?"

I put my hand to my teacup, wrapping my fingers carefully about the warm porcelain. "Death is a necessary balance to life, Lady Wellingtonia."

She gave her cackling laugh again. "You needn't tell me, Miss Speedwell. I am nearer to it than you."

Just then Mr. Baring-Ponsonby snored loudly, rousing himself again. "Eh, what's that? Yes, I *will* have that pudding now," he said, rubbing his hands together. He looked down at his empty bowl, the merest trace of crème anglaise puddling in the bottom. "I seem to have eaten it already. How disappointing."

Stoker affected an angelic expression of innocence and Lady Wellie rose. "Never mind, Cecil. You're too fat anyway." Stoker offered his arm to her, and Mr. Baring-Ponsonby escorted me. The hour was late, the case clock in the hall chiming a quarter past midnight as we emerged from the little supper room.

"I must thank you both for a most diverting evening," Lady Wellingtonia said. She presented Stoker with her cheek to kiss but merely held out her hand to me. She wore old-fashioned mitts of lace, costly little scraps that neither veiled her aged hands nor warmed her but were worn simply to demonstrate that she had money enough for fripperies.

I touched the gnarled hand lightly, careful to avoid the fingers with their swollen joints. She wore heavy rings set thickly with old, filthy diamonds.

She gave me a slow nod. "You must let me know how you make out with Freddie," she said with an odd twinkle in her eye. "He can't paint your little landscapes, but I daresay he knows someone who will."

With that, she bade us good night and we left the warmth and light of the main house for the gardens, dark and heavy with rising fog. A lantern had been left for us, and Stoker carried it, guiding us both along the path to the Belvedere, the dogs racing up to trot dutifully at our heels. Without discussion, we chose to settle in for a nightcap in our place of work rather than repair to the separate tiny dwellings where we slept.

Lord Rosemorran had generously provided us with living accommodations on his estate, permitting us to choose from a collection of small follies scattered about the grounds, each decorated in some outlandish style and fitted with many of the modern amenities. While most young Englishmen bent on the Grand Tour spent their time collecting art and social diseases, the Beauclerk men had acquired an assortment of outbuildings, shipping them home at great trouble and hideous expense. They had variously been used as playhouses, bathhouses, summerhouses, guesthouses, and in one notable case an hermitage.

But there were no hermits in evidence when Stoker and I took up residence, he in a Chinese temple in the pagoda style and I in a Gothic chapel complete with tiny gargoyles and a vaulted ceiling painted with stars. Mercifully, the rudiments of plumbing had been installed and gas laid on, so accommodation in our tiny abodes had proven quite satisfactory.

If only the rest of the estate fared so well, I thought as we made our way down to the Belvedere. The property was a vast one by London standards, although rather mean for a man who owned more than thirty thousand acres of Cornwall. But the grounds that availed the various earls plenty of scope for their acquisitive passions also required a great deal of upkeep—upkeep that was not always forthcoming. Between the little follies and the Belvedere lay the glasshouse, a cast-iron pavilion built in the style of the Crystal Palace. In fact, it was a model, built by Sir

Joseph Paxton himself when he was tinkering with the design for the eventual site of the Great Exhibition. Once a splendid repository for the various plants and birds collected by the present earl's father, it was now an eyesore, with more windows broken than whole, fragments of glass powdering the weedy grass that had grown up around it. It was hid from the main house by a maze of hornbeam, and I doubted our patron had thought of it from one year to the next. That was a pity. The design was a miracle of modern invention, for it wedded iron and glass into a lacy, delicate structure that defied gravity, soaring like a cathedral of crystal, capturing light and multiplying it. Or it had, I imagined, before weather and neglect had had their cruel way with it. Now it stood, hunched and silent, a bedraggled figure in the fog, as if embarrassed by its wrecked splendor, like a raddled courtesan seen in the unkind light of day.

"Lord Rosemorran ought to do something with that," I grumbled. "He might pull it down and put the space to better use."

"Like a tennis court?" Stoker suggested derisively. We were united in our scorn for organized athletics.

"Like a shooting gallery," I countered. "I should like someplace to practice."

"When hell freezes solid," Stoker told me. Suddenly he stopped, rearing back so suddenly that I collided against his back, a wall of solid muscle as impassable as stone. The dogs, alerted to his mood, began to dance about, sniffing intently and whimpering.

"Stoker, what the devil is the trouble?"

He had stopped just short of the Belvedere. He said nothing but raised the lantern high and jerked his head towards the door. It was closed, as we had left it, but now a piece of paper hung there, affixed by a drawing pin.

Stoker wrenched the note loose, holding the lantern aloft so we both could see. It was a single sheet of foolscap, the writing scrawled in harsh capitals that nearly pierced the page, the ink thick and blotted, as if from a badly mended nib.

KEEP OUT OF THIS OR YOU WILL
MEET THE SAME END

All at once the dogs, who had been circling and whining, charged past, flinging themselves into the depths of the garden, giving tongue like a pack of hounds hot upon a fox as a shadow detached itself from behind the glasshouse and began to run, a black cloak billowing behind like the wings of a fallen angel.

Instantly, Stoker started off after the dogs, reaching for the knife he kept in his boot. I picked up my skirts in both hands and ran after him, hurtling over hedges as we followed the sound of the dogs. Neither of us remembered the lantern, and in the darkness I tripped—over the hapless Patricia, I noticed with some irritation—and by the time I had righted myself, it was finished. Stoker had retrieved the dogs and was returning, dripping wet from the fog and fairly vibrating with rage.

"Did you find him?"

"Gone," he said bitterly, and he tugged off his sodden coat and waistcoat. "He went clean through the gap in the east wall where the masonry is crumbling. It was all I could do to keep the dogs from following."

"Useless creatures," I said, ushering them inside and fetching them each a marrowbone for their troubles. "They might at least have provided us with a clue."

Stoker stripped off his shirt to wipe his face and sodden hair, then tugged it back on. "Ah, but they did," he told me, grinning in triumph. He tossed me a piece of fabric, no bigger than an inch by two.

"What is this?" I turned over the scrap, noticing the plain wool fabric and tiny stitches.

"Whoever he was, he wore a cloak. Huxley managed to get his teeth into the hem of it and tear that bit off as the fellow dodged through the gap."

"Well, at least you earned your marrowbone," I told Huxley, throwing Bet a reproachful glance. She panted happily as she gnawed at her undeserved prize.

"Can you tell anything from the fabric?" I asked, passing it back to Stoker.

He shrugged. "Nothing of note. But at least it is a clue of sorts. I wonder what sort of malefactor has been scampering about in the fog?"

"We are agreed that this refers to the business Princess Louise has set us upon?" I asked.

Stoker rolled his eyes. "Are you in the habit of receiving threatening missives from strangers?"

"I wouldn't call it a *habit*," I hedged.

He narrowed his gaze. "Veronica."

"Well, some butterfly collectors can be quite dogged in their pursuit. There are specimens worth more than this estate, you know."

"And have you any in your possession?"

"Not at present," I replied smoothly.

He considered that a moment. "I think I may have pursued the wrong field of natural science."

"Undoubtedly. I had five pounds off of Lord Bowen for the pretty little specimen of *Euploea mulcibes* I found him last week." Stoker raised his brows. "Striped Blue Crow," I explained. "A little brush-foot indigenous to India. I put him in touch with a dealer out of Madras who happened to have a male with the most curious mutation—"

"*Veronica.*" His voice was low and tight with the sort of control which meant I had very few seconds before he lost his temper entirely. I was halfway tempted to goad him into it—few things were more arousing to me than the sight of Stoker in full froth—but I had made a vow to myself never to bed an Englishman, and although Stoker frequently tested my resolve, I had not yet abandoned it.

"No, Stoker. I know of no one who currently has reason to threaten us."

"Us?" he queried.

"It is not addressed to me," I pointed out. "And it was placed where both of us work. It might just as easily have been meant for you."

He reared back, affronted. "I haven't given anyone reason to want to kill me."

"Are you quite certain? Think carefully. I am convinced we could compile a list," I said sweetly.

He sighed. "I spent the better part of the afternoon wrestling with a recalcitrant crocodile," he informed me. "I have no interest in crossing swords with you for the rest of the night. Come on."

He whistled up the dogs and grabbed the lantern as he seized my wrist with his other hand.

"Where are we going?" I demanded.

"To bed."

CHAPTER

6

To my mingled annoyance and relief, Stoker's invitation to bed was issued in the strictest sense of the word. He locked us into my little Gothic chapel and then proceeded to spend the night sleeping next to me, his head bumping the footboard and his feet resting on the pillow beside me. It was not the first time we had slept in such a fashion, and I doubted it would be the last. A thousand questions chased and tangled in my mind, but I thrust them aside, counting backwards from one hundred in Tagalog until I drifted off to sleep.

I awakened to the pleasant sight of Stoker stretching himself and pulling on his shirt.

"No attacks by villains bent upon writing at us?" I teased.

He favored me with a glower. "Whoever left that note was bold enough to trespass onto the private property of an earl and he was quick enough to elude apprehension."

"You needn't favor your sex so highly," I pointed out. "Our miscreant might have been a woman."

He snorted. "Do you really think a woman could elude me?" I looked him over from tumbled black hair to work-roughened hands to shoulders and thighs heavy with muscle.

"I cannot imagine the woman who would want to," I said, batting my lashes furiously.

"Stop flirting and take this seriously," he ordered. "You agreed to do this ridiculous thing for a princess and within hours we are threatened. Does that not put you off the whole business?"

"No," I replied slowly. "If anything, it has made me more determined than ever. For one simple reason."

"Bloody-minded stubbornness?" he asked.

I pulled a face. "We have not lifted a finger to begin this investigation in earnest, and already we have a clue. Whoever wrote this has just given us the first solid proof that Miles Ramsforth is innocent."

A slow smile spread across his face. "True enough. And whoever it was is clearly panicked, but why?"

"Because they know who actually killed Artemisia," I supplied.

"And they don't want the truth to come out. I will grant you that, the logic is solid. But why come after us? We haven't stirred any hornets' nests yet."

I pondered a moment. "Princess Louise did. She told me she intended to speak to Ottilie Ramsforth and Sir Frederick Havelock at dinner last night. She meant to smooth the way for us, prepare them we would be asking questions on her behalf."

"And someone didn't take it well," he finished.

"But his wife? His brother-in-law? Surely they would wish him to be exonerated! You forget, Havelock House is the nexus of the entire affair. Miles Ramsforth was a patron of the place, the dead woman lived there. Presumably her friends and most intimate connections live there as well. And Ottilie Ramsforth has come there to live since her husband's arrest. Somehow, Frederick Havelock's little commune is where the answers may be found."

"And someone there wants sleeping dogs left to lie," Stoker remarked.

I smiled. "I can think of no finer beginning to an investigation than being threatened with bodily injury," I told him. "Arcadia Brown could ask for no better."

I would have liked to have begun our inquiry at the scene of the crime— the Ramsforth estate at Littledown—but permission would have to be granted from Ottilie Ramsforth, and I must confess to a singular curiosity about that lady. I spent the day unpacking a selection of crates from the third earl's expedition to the Himalayas while Stoker energetically buffed his crocodile. After waiting as late as I dared, I lured Stoker from his work with the promise of a ham roll and a cold beef pie sent down from the Folly kitchens before sending him off to neaten himself into something approaching respectability for the entertainment at Havelock House. Shortly after the hour struck eight, we were in a hired hansom, trotting briskly towards Holland Park.

Stoker was in a predictably difficult mood. He had finally made significant progress with his crocodile, and I had dragged him away from it on what might well prove a fool's errand. I knew he did not approve of my determination to see this thing through to the end, but it was a mark of his loyalty that he was at my side, grumble though he might.

"They'll be nothing but a heap of bored aristocrats and aspiring Bohemians, and I am not certain which is the most tiresome," he warned me. "Both kinds are prone to making wild pronouncements simply for the purpose of shocking other people, and neither have the moral courage of a mouse."

In spite of his ill temper, Stoker was fairly vibrating with impatience as we approached Havelock House, quivering with the pent energy of a hound before a hunt. He might cavil at my penchant for involving us in investigations, but he was every bit as enthusiastic about the pursuit as I was. Yet even he paused on the doorstep, rocking back upon his heels as he considered Havelock House.

"It is a monstrosity," he breathed. "A very grand monstrosity."

He was not wrong. In Frederick Havelock's entry in *Notable Britons* there had been a paragraph describing the building of the place, an enterprise that had taken him the better part of a decade and the entirety of his father's fortune. At first glance it seemed a fairly plain and functional dwelling of red brick and Bath stone facings dotted here and there with mullioned windows in the Tudor style. But a closer look revealed unexpected embellishments. There were balconies and crenellations, and—looming over the east façade—a tower surmounted by a pointed roof, the witch's hat of the sort so often favored by whimsical French architects. A tiny lagoon in front of the house boasted a miniature gondola, and the portico housing the front door was hung with a series of Chinese lanterns.

Stoker's expression was rapt. "Forget what I said," he murmured. "There's genius at work here. Wild dogs couldn't drag me out of this investigation."

I grinned and we approached the open door, not surprised to find the entertainment under way. There was no servant at the door, for it was obvious Frederick Havelock did not dwell upon ceremony and all were welcome. The mood inside the house was nothing to what I had expected. Although the trappings of mourning were in evidence, a sort of carnival atmosphere prevailed. Interior doors had been thrown open and people drifted from room to room, conversing in low tones punctuated by the odd bit of muffled laughter.

The house had been built around a central hall fitted with tiles from the East, and a fountain tinkled under a gilded dome that soared overhead. A series of galleries ran the circumference of the hall, leading off in various directions to separate wings, each with a different color scheme—here Pompeiian red, there Genoan green. Only the reception hall bowed its head to the East, conjuring images of a thousand and one nights beneath an Arabian sky, for the dome was painted with a celestial scene complete with silvery constellations. In the center of the fountain, a little incongruously perhaps, stood a marble statue in the Greek style of a maiden with her hands cupped around her mouth as she gazed backwards over her shoulder. A bronze plaque at her feet was inscribed simply ECHO, and I was struck by the pathos of the nymph, for she was a masterpiece of emotion.

Apparently as welcome as anyone else, we took our time wandering about the reception hall and poking into the various workshops and studios that lined the back of Havelock House, each fitted with floor-to-ceiling windows that had been flung open to the air of the gardens, drawing in the scent of late roses and the unexpected narcotic heaviness of tuberose. Enormous bouquets of lilies had been gathered into vases that stood like fragrant sentinels at each door, and in the main drawing room a buffet of cold meats had been laid. There was a ready supply of intoxicants of every variety, and Stoker poured us both a glass of surprisingly elegant red wine as we surveyed the crowd.

And quite a crowd it was. I could not decide if the event was meant to be a sort of wake or an exhibition. A juggler vied for attention against the strains of a group of musicians playing exceedingly mournful dirges, and a contortionist twisted herself into fantastical shapes in front of a veiled and silent professional mourner draped from crown to hem in deepest, impenetrable black. I was just admiring the contortionist's flexibility when I felt the hairs upon the back of my neck prickle.

A woman dressed entirely and expensively in black glided up to us. She had a face that would never have been beautiful; the irregularity of her features would not permit it. Her nose was a trifle long, her eyes set slightly too far apart in a face so pale it reminded me of new milk. But her hands were lovely, the fingers long and tapering like a violinist's. Her hair, a dark chestnut hue shot through with grey, had been plaited and pinned into a heavy coil at her neck, and her only jewels were a slim gold wedding ring and a pair of shimmering jet earrings that trembled when she turned her head. She approached, her slender mouth parted into a modest smile of welcome.

"I think—pardon me if I am mistaken, but you must be Miss Speedwell, are you not?" Her voice, I realized, was her true beauty. It was low and soft, with an attractive musicality.

"I am."

The smile hesitated, then deepened. "I am Ottilie Ramsforth. Her Royal Highness said we might expect you. And your friend," she added quickly with a tentatively welcoming glance at Stoker.

He inclined his head. "Revelstoke Templeton-Vane, Mrs. Ramsforth."

"I know. The princess discussed you at length."

I suppressed a smile. Only the assurances of a princess could have persuaded anyone he was anything other than a buccaneer. Claiming that his eye—once the site of a grievous injury—was fatigued, Stoker had put on the eye patch that was his occasional habit, but I suspected it a gesture born of mischief. Stoker was the dedicated black sheep of the Templeton-Vane family and kept himself aloof from society whenever possible. Being thrust into the very heart of it would no doubt bring out his worse instincts for waywardness. In this case, it meant flaunting his rather alarming resemblance to a prosperous pirate, complete with overlong locks and golden earrings glinting in his lobes. The fact that the numerous tattoos acquired on his travels were hidden by his clothing was no doubt a source of great irritation to him, but the knowledge that his physique was shown to excellent effect by his tailoring must have been a consolation. It seemed to unnerve Mrs. Ramsforth, for she darted him a number of hesitant looks during our conversation.

"This is a far grander entertainment than I was anticipating," I told her. "I hope we are not intruding."

"Oh no!" she said earnestly. "Sir Frederick likes to host these gatherings a few times each month. It is an opportunity for the artists to show their work informally, to meet new patrons and models. Anyone is welcome. The affair will last far into the night, growing rather more riotous with the late hours, I am afraid," she added with a touch of asperity.

"You do not care for the exhibitions?" I asked.

She shook her head, the little jet beads at her ears clicking as they danced. "It isn't that," she protested. "These events are quite necessary for the sort of work my brother-in-law does. He has been very generous in finding his protégés suitable commissions. It is only the timing and the theme one finds difficult."

I looked from the crêpe-draped looking glasses to the ornamental professional mourner and was forced to agree. It was in questionable taste with Miles Ramsforth scheduled to hang in a week. As I watched, the professional mourner edged a little closer, clearly bent upon listening to our conversation.

"Perhaps there is somewhere more private we could talk," I suggested.

An expression of relief passed over her face. "Yes, that would be best. Won't you come up to my rooms?"

We followed Mrs. Ramsforth as she led the way through the press of people. She paused partway up the stairs, gesturing towards the statue of Echo. "If you stop at any point upon the stairs, you can hear whatever is said in the hall below," she told us. "It is a peculiar feature of this place. A whim of Sir Frederick's."

I glanced down at the press of people, wondering if any of them might have been our nocturnal visitor.

"Tell me, Mrs. Ramsforth," I said casually. "Did you have a quiet supper with Princess Louise last night?"

One elegant hand rested upon the banister. "Why, no. Sir Frederick gave a supper party almost as crowded as this one." She turned and began to climb again while I exchanged meaningful glances with Stoker. If Louise's conversation had been overheard, as seemed entirely possible in the chaos of Havelock House, any one of the guests present the night before might have slipped away to deliver the threat.

Mrs. Ramsforth led us into the wing painted Genoan green and through a small door set within an ogival arch. "Another of my brother-in-law's inspirations," she said, ushering us inside and closing the door softly behind us. We were in a small sitting room, unremarkable in its size, but unlike any room I had ever seen before. It might have been Titania's bower, for the walls were painted in shifting shades of green, with the ceiling dappled blue and festooned with drifting clouds. The furnishings were crafted of gilded wood in fanciful shapes with Gothic arches a repeating motif, and every cushion had been sewn of green velvet embellished by golden thread.

"How extraordinary," I breathed.

Mrs. Ramsforth smiled. "Sir Frederick is eccentric, but a genius. And he is very generous to me." Without asking, she poured us each a thimbleful of clear liquid into tiny crystal glasses.

"Drink carefully," she warned.

Stoker took a sip and a broad smile spread across his face. *"Tsipouro,"* he pronounced.

The placid face was lit with pleasure. "You know it?"

"I served in Her Majesty's Navy for some years," he told her. "I traveled through Greece on my way home from an engagement in Egypt."

I sipped cautiously. It was the same sort of liquid fire I had come to appreciate in the aguardiente from South America that I drank, nearly tasteless and lethally potent.

"How did you come to find such a libation?" I asked her.

She had taken no glass for herself, and she folded her hands calmly in her lap, resting the marble-white flesh on the black bombazine of her gown. "My husband and I have often traveled there as a result of his interest in Hellenic art. We purchased a villa during our last visit, and I mean to go there to live when . . . when . . ." She broke off suddenly, her voice tight with emotion.

After a moment she collected herself. "Forgive me. This has been a difficult time."

"I cannot imagine," I told her truthfully. "But we would like to help."

She clasped her hands together. "That is what the princess said. Forgive me, Miss Speedwell, but I do not see how that is possible."

Her voice was still tight, and something in her manner made her seem brittle, near to breaking. I glanced at Stoker and he gave a single quick jerk of the chin to indicate I should try a different tack. Of the two of us, Stoker had far more experience talking his way around the fairer sex, so I obliged.

"It is indeed generous of Sir Frederick to invite you to reside here, as it is generous of him to let his protégés live here and well."

She brightened noticeably at the change in subject, her hands relaxing immediately.

"He is the most openhanded gentleman you would ever encounter," she said with a firmness I had not yet seen in her.

"And this is where the unfortunate young woman—Artemisia, I believe was her name—this is where she lived as well?"

"Yes."

"Tell me about her," I invited.

She was silent a moment, then shook her head slowly. "I am not certain of how to put her into words. She was not what I would call beautiful. But she was striking. Very tall—*statuesque*," she added. "She had masses of hair. It was red, which they say is unlucky, but she wore it loose, and it was so pretty. She always gave the impression of great vitality, for she took a keen interest in things." Her expression dimmed. "She was a gifted artist, Miss Speedwell, a very gifted artist. Her speciality was murals. She had just completed one at Littledown for us when she . . ." She trailed off, then seemed to gather new strength, speaking more decisively. "She had many talents. And her death was shocking."

"I imagine it was particularly so for Sir Frederick," I said with a deliberate blandness.

She took my meaning and gave me a sharp look. "You must not think there was anything untoward between them. Frederick has always had an eye for young women, but he confines himself to dallying with the models. He would never *interfere* with an artist. He believes affairs of the heart can blunt one's ambitions, drive away the muse, as he would say."

"And he never thought to drive away the muse from Artemisia? A striking-looking young woman living under his own roof?" I pressed.

She shook her head, the jet beads clacking furiously. "No, he would not. Besides, his health would not permit—that is to say," she said with a blushing glance at Stoker, "he faces limitations in his pursuits. Since Artemisia's death he has been confined to a Bath chair. I sometimes wonder . . ."

Her voice trailed off and Stoker leaned forward, his gaze awash with sympathy. "Yes?" he asked in a far gentler voice than he ever used to me. "What do you wonder, Mrs. Ramsforth?"

"Artemisia looked a little like my sister, Augusta. I know it sounds fanciful, but I sometimes wondered if Sir Frederick's fondness for her was that he saw an echo of the woman he loved."

"When did your sister die?" I asked. The question seemed to jar her a little. She had edged forward towards Stoker like a flower to the sun, but the sound of my voice caused her to withdraw a little.

"A decade ago. In childbirth," she said, her demeanor brittle once more.

"Did the child survive?"

"No. None of hers did. Neither did mine," she answered shortly. "Our family are not blessed with fecundity, Miss Speedwell."

I flicked a glance to Stoker. My intrusive questions had nettled her; I relied upon him to soothe her back down again.

He rose to the occasion like a hero. "Tell me about Lady Havelock," he coaxed. "I imagine she was very special."

"She was," Mrs. Ramsforth said, her eyes burning with sudden devotion. "She was my elder by only eleven months, and we were raised almost as twins. Our nanny dressed us alike. Our governess taught us the same lessons. Never was there a treat for Augusta that I did not share," she added, her voice drifting into nostalgia. "She was my dearest companion. To lose her—was unthinkable." She paused then, clasping her hands together almost convulsively. "Of course it was worse for Sir Frederick. She was his wife, and he did love her dearly for all their quarrels."

"They quarreled?" Stoker prompted.

A fleeting smile touched her thin lips. "Constantly. They fought about money, about his paramours. But nothing truly divided them. They were the most devoted couple you could imagine. They throve on the fighting, you see. They were passionate." She colored again at the last word, as if embarrassed to think of the other ways in which they might have been passionate.

"I do not know how I would have managed when she died if it had not been for my husband," she went on.

"He was a solace in your grief?" Stoker suggested gently.

"He took me out of myself," she explained. "He would not let me sit and brood. He made me travel. We spent two years in Greece, scrambling over rocks and ruins, learning the language and chasing myths. It was highly therapeutic. That is why now—" She broke off, swallowing hard. "That is why now, I am planning to return there. It is what he wants."

"Mr. Ramsforth has told you this?" I put in.

She shied like a spooked horse. "I have not seen my husband in some weeks," she admitted. "He will no longer permit me to visit him. He sent word through his solicitor that I should quit England to escape the scandal. I resisted as long as I could, but now, as the end grows near—" She broke off again, clasping a hand to her mouth. Instantly, Stoker was on his knees in front of her, offering one of his enormous scarlet handkerchiefs. She took it, pressing it to her mouth as her shoulders shook silently.

After a long moment, she made to return it, but he pressed it back into her hands, clasping them with his. "Forgive the liberty, Mrs. Ramsforth," he said finally, releasing them and resuming his seat. "I never was able to resist a lady in distress."

I narrowly managed not to roll my eyes at that piece of fiction. But Mrs. Ramsforth swallowed it whole and favored him with a smile of arresting sweetness. Stoker pressed his advantage. "Mrs. Ramsforth, we have no wish to grieve you, but we do very much want to get to the bottom of this."

"The bottom of this?" She looked from Stoker to me with an expression of such naked anguish that I caught my breath. "Have you not grasped the truth yet, Mr. Templeton-Vane? You cannot grieve me further, for I have made my peace with the worst of it."

"The worst of it?" Stoker echoed.

"You have come here because you wish to prove that my husband is innocent. But that is impossible."

I gaped at her. "Mrs. Ramsforth, do you mean to say—"

"Yes, Miss Speedwell," she cut in with more firmness than she had yet demonstrated. "He murdered Artemisia. And very soon he will hang for it."

CHAPTER

7

A palpable silence filled the room after Ottilie Ramsforth's statement. It was left to me to break it.

"But Princess Louise," I began.

"Her Royal Highness is a loyal friend, to me and to my husband," Mrs. Ramsforth said calmly. "She wishes to believe he is innocent because she cannot countenance that anyone for whom she cares would be capable of such an atrocity."

"But you think he is?" Stoker put in with lightning swiftness. Ottilie Ramsforth inclined her head.

"Mr. Templeton-Vane, I have known my husband for many years—since long before our marriage. I have known him as a boy and as a man, and I can tell you that, God forgive me, I have seen weakness in him. You cannot know how it pains me to tell the truth, but I cannot lie. I have protected him from misdeeds in the past, harmless things," she said, waving a hand as I would have interrupted. "Indiscretions that would only burden a wife. He was frequently unfaithful, and that was something I was perfectly happy to accept."

"Happy!" I exclaimed. I could not imagine any woman being content to have the man she loved warming another's bed.

Her smile was fatigued, and it was the fatigue born of years. "You have never been married, Miss Speedwell. You do not yet know what it means to love someone more than yourself. I have no pride left, no delicacy. I cannot afford it. So I will tell you the truth: I wanted his happiness above all things. Unfortunately, my disappointed hopes of motherhood meant that I was unable to accommodate him in the marriage bed," she added with a studied avoidance of Stoker's gaze. "His friendships with other women were passing infatuations. Only I mattered to him, and a woman may forgive quite a lot when she is the queen of her husband's heart. I ruled alone there."

"Even when Artemisia caught his eye?" I asked. I hated the question, but it must be posed, and to her credit, she did not flinch. She spoke calmly and with perfect conviction.

"Artemisia was a lovely girl, but she was merely the latest in a long line. Miles admired her for her talent, and he was diverted by a pretty face. He would have tired of her in the end, as he did all the others."

"But there was a child," Stoker put in quietly.

"There was," she acknowledged. "And we would have done right by her and the babe. They would have been cared for, as a gentleman's mistake ought to be."

"Then what happened?" I demanded. "Why would he have killed Artemisia?"

"I don't know," she whispered, her lips tight. "I wish I did. Was it a passing madness? Was it some silly game gone awry? A prank got out of hand? If only he would say."

"But he will not," I reminded her.

"No, he will not," she burst out, "and that is why I have to think it is possible that he is guilty." She drew in a deep, shaking breath. "He always confessed his peccadilloes to me. We used to laugh about them. He was like a naughty child seeking absolution. He never felt truly at peace until he told me whatever he had done. But he will not speak of this. He will go to his death with it on his conscience, and I cannot absolve him of that. Only God can."

"What if there is nothing to absolve?" I asked.

She took another breath and the smile trembling on her lips turned sweetly seraphic. She rose and I realized our interview with her was at an end.

"Is it possible for us to visit Littledown?" Stoker asked. "Seeing where it all happened might be beneficial."

"Of course. It may take a few days," she said in an apologetic tone. "I came away quite suddenly. The newspapermen were such a frightful nuisance, and then the gawkers began to arrive—all those strangers pressed against the gates. A few of them even made it inside the grounds and came right up against the windows. I was terribly upset."

"I can imagine," Stoker said by way of consolation.

"When I came here, I closed up the house—had it shuttered and bolted and sent the key to my husband's solicitors. They have set a watchman at the place, only an elderly local man and his dog, but it is better than leaving the estate unattended. I will have to write to the solicitors to request they return the key. They may not attach much importance to such a request, what with Miles having only a few days left—" She broke off, then gathered her composure once more. "I will do my best."

She walked us to the door and shook each of our hands in turn.

"This is all so strange, I pray you will understand. I wish you the very best of luck in your inquiries, but I cannot believe you will establish his innocence, indeed, I dare not think it possible. You see, it hurts too much to hope. I must think of him as already dead, for that is what he will be, and I fear even you cannot save him."

"We will try," I promised her.

Sudden tears sprang to her eyes. "God help you, Miss Speedwell. God help you."

. . .

"A very interesting lady, Mrs. Ramsforth," I remarked as Stoker and I wended our way slowly down the stairs. He grunted by way of agreement, and without discussion we turned our steps to the drawing room where the food had been laid out. We each filled a plate as an excuse to linger, and as we nibbled at lobster patties and cold turkey, we wandered the periphery of the room, studying the art. There was a statue of Achilles as a boy that I found quite arresting, but it was an enormous canvas stretching the length of the far wall that demanded attention, a painting of no little skill and signed with a swirl of gilt paint with the name *Artemisia*.

The subject was the death of Holofernes at the hands of Judith, and the execution of it was utterly mesmerizing. The arms of the victim were thrown out in sleep, the head fallen back so that the long, sensual column of the throat was vulnerable. In contrast, the arms of his assassin were taut with intent, her expression purposeful, from the narrowed eyes to the tip of the little pink tongue caught between her teeth as she advanced upon him. Artemisia Gentileschi had painted the same scene, but unlike her predecessor, our Artemisia had chosen the moment just *before* the act. No violent spray of blood, no arms corded with homicidal effort, no rictus of pain and fear from the victim. This was a moment in which nothing had yet happened, the last instant before crossing the Rubicon. Artemisia had captured her when she might yet turn back, when she had not made a murderess of herself. That choice rendered the painting all the more powerful and poignant. It was as if the viewer, seeing it clearly, could pry the knife from her hand and guide her out of the tent, back to safety, back to innocence. The eyes were not yet those of a killer.

I scrutinized it from edge to edge and back again, from the lavish tent folds on the right-hand side of the painting through the figures and down to the tips of Holofernes' fingers, relaxed in sleep, the curving forefinger pointing to her signature, a flourish of golden paint against the white of his bedsheet. It was a clever trick; it forced the viewer to notice the signature, but in a way that was a natural extension of the work itself. Artemisia was subtly reminding everyone who saw the painting that she was as much a part of it as Judith and Holofernes, that this moment had been conjured by her and no one else.

"Stupendous," Stoker breathed, and I realized suddenly we were not alone. Standing at my elbow was a diminutive sprite of a young woman who scarcely reached my chin. She had a firm, square jaw and the most strongly marked brows I had ever seen, combining to give her a look of almost pugnacious self-confidence.

"We do not stand on ceremony here," she informed me as she thrust out her hand. "I am Emma Talbot."

"Veronica Speedwell," I replied, shaking hands. "Do you live here, Miss Talbot?"

"I do. I am a sculptress under the tutelage of Sir Frederick."

She turned to greet Stoker, and from that moment on, I might as well have been invisible. She had eyes only for him, and I was not surprised. His piratical appearance had been carefully cultivated, both as a tribute to his time served in Her Majesty's Navy, and as a means of putting off unwelcome female attentions. The poor fellow never understood that it had precisely the opposite effect. When a gentleman of excellent breeding and perfect vowels assumes the guise of a ruffian, women are frequently reduced to a state of helpless infatuation. I had seen it numerous times, that glazed look of bewilderment in a female's eyes as her interest was kindled, almost against her will. Stoker himself never took notice unless I pointed it out, at which he invariably blushed an enchanting shade of rose that only highlighted his allure. To his credit, he never abused his talent. He might have bedded half the aristocracy with his irresistible combination of good looks and brooding bad temper, but he restricted himself with the asceticism of a monk.

I sighed at the inevitable and performed the introductions.

"Mr. Templeton-Vane," Miss Talbot said, clasping his fingers in hers, the tiny hand closing carefully around his. "How enchanting to make your acquaintance."

"The enchantment is entirely mine," came the gallant reply. I rolled my eyes heavenwards, but neither of them paid me the slightest attention. I fancied I heard a slight titter of amusement from the veiled professional mourner standing against the wall, but when I shot a glance her way, she had assumed a posture of dejected sorrow.

"What brings you into our little group this evening?" she asked. "Were you a friend of Artemisia's?"

He adopted a pained expression. "Alas, I never had the pleasure. But I understand she was an artist of considerable gifts, and we are the poorer for our loss whilst heaven must rejoice at the prospect of so glorious an angel."

"My God," I muttered. I had wondered if it might be a bit too much, and to my delight Miss Talbot snorted.

"Artemisia was as original an artist as the lowest hack sketching Christmas cards for tuppence a dozen," she replied crisply. "She had talents, but her greatest by far was persuading powerful men to make much of her."

I decided I liked Miss Talbot then, but before we could question her further, she circled Stoker, eyeing him as closely as any coper at Tattersall's looking over a stallion.

"You will do quite nicely," she pronounced finally. "I should like to see your thighs before I make a final decision, but I think you would do quite nicely *indeed*."

"My thighs? I beg your pardon," Stoker managed, goggling at her.

"Don't be obtuse, Stoker," I prodded. "Miss Talbot obviously wishes you to pose for her in what one can only assume will be a state of semi-nudity."

"Semi? My dear Miss Speedwell, I have in mind to sculpt him as

Perseus at the moment of the Gorgon's defeat. He would be entirely nude," she corrected, her expression quite serious.

"Entirely nude?" Stoker repeated dumbly.

"Except for the sandals," Miss Talbot amended. "Perseus did wear the most adorable winged talaria."

"I am familiar," he told her in a clipped tone. "I suffered a Classical education."

"I think it is a marvelous notion," I said quickly. I gave him a meaningful look over Miss Talbot's head. If ever I craved the gift of telepathy, it was in that moment. If we were to poke about Havelock House, how much better to have the added excuse of a modeling engagement from one of the artists? We had no way of knowing which of them had been informed of our true purpose in being there, but the more innocuous we seemed, the better.

Before Stoker could reply, the air was rent with a wail that would have done a banshee credit. We turned as one to see a man standing in the doorway, and I felt a rush of blood straight to my sit-upon parts. He wore a jacket of peacock blue—no doubt to draw attention to his remarkable eyes, eyes that were filled with crystalline tears. His hair was not blond but gilded, as if by the hand of a Renaissance master. The cheekbones were as sweetly molded as a seraph's, giving way to a perfect jaw and a pair of rosebud lips that simply begged to be kissed, while his ears, delicately pointed at the tips, lent him the air of a young satyr waiting impatiently for his first debauchery. Clasped loosely in his hand was a bottle—of gin, it seemed—and the greater part of it had already been drunk. As we watched, the beautiful lips parted and another wail sounded, more piteous than the last.

Stoker poked me pointedly in the ribs. "For God's sake, you're staring at him as if it were the fourth year of a famine and a loin of beef just walked in the door," he muttered.

"He is very . . . noticeable," I replied faintly.

"He is a coxcomb," Emma Talbot said sourly. "No doubt he means to indulge in a performance."

As Miss Talbot suggested, the wailing continued until he had gathered the attention of everyone in the room. There was a hushed thrill of expectation as the assembled crowd watched him. Content at last that he had drawn every eye, he moved slowly towards the table, swaying only a little as he did.

"Drunk again," Miss Talbot remarked.

"Who is he?" I inquired.

"Julian Gilchrist, portraitist and ass," she answered.

Without great deliberation, Julian Gilchrist made his way to the buffet table and proceeded to climb onto it. He walked down to the middle, stepping over cruet sets and candelabra until he stood astride the punch bowl, surveying the room. His shoes had left muddy prints upon the white damask of the tablecloth, like the dirty fingerprints of an unkempt giant. "Here we are," he began, lifting the gin bottle like a torch.

Stoker snorted. "What the devil is happening? All he wants is a nice pair of breasts and he would look like *Liberty Leading the People*." Emma Talbot gave a sharp bark of laughter, like the quick sound of a fox, but I pursed my lips.

"Hush," I said softly. "No doubt you will hurt his feelings if he hears you. He clearly thinks he is being dramatic."

"Dramatic people give me a pain in my backside," he retorted.

Without further ado, Mr. Gilchrist launched into a sort of eulogy for Artemisia. At least, that is how it began. Only a few sentences in, it became a diatribe against the girl. He berated her talent, her eye, her morals, and would no doubt have gone further had not Emma Talbot stepped forward.

"Oh, do shut up, Julian," she ordered. "God knows I was not her greatest admirer, but she was twice the artist—and man—you will ever be."

"Viper!" he thundered, pointing a finger at her. "You are a viper in the bosom of this place, and I wish to God it had been you instead of her. Perhaps it will be," he said, leaning forward and very nearly, but not quite, toppling off the table. The professional mourner against the wall gave an audible gasp of horror and started forward, but a glare from Emma Talbot halted her in her tracks.

A lesser woman might have paled under the implied threat of Julian Gilchrist's words, but Miss Talbot merely curled a scornful lip. "You are only raging at me because it is true. You will never be half the artist she was and you know it, you little pustule!"

Gilchrist would have launched himself, but he tripped over an epergne, sending water and lilies cascading over the edge of the table.

"You bloody bitch," he began, waving a finger again at Emma Talbot.

I looked meaningfully at Stoker and he gave a sigh, stripping off his coat in one fluid motion. He strode to the table, grasped the tablecloth in his fists, and jerked hard. Punch bowl and platters and candelabra went flying—as did Mr. Gilchrist. He landed with a sharp thud of his beautiful head against the table, slumping instantly to unconsciousness.

Stoker reached out and easily flipped the fellow onto his shoulder. He turned to Miss Talbot, who was staring at him in open-mouthed astonishment.

"Where shall I put him?" Stoker inquired casually.

She shook herself as if to collect her wits. "He has rooms upstairs. I will show you."

She hurried out, beckoning to Stoker to follow, and he did, Mr. Gilchrist's head lolling behind.

It was the professional mourner who broke the silence. "Now, this is turning into a jolly party," she said, casting back her thick veil to reveal a wide smile. She gave me a wink. "I'm Cherry, the maid here. Come on then, miss. It's time you met the master."

CHAPTER

8

As we crossed into the reception hall, she fanned her face with the edge of her veil, scattering little pearls of perspiration from her hairline. "It's fair smothering under this lot," she complained. "But the master asked special. Said it would give the affair a bit of grav— What's the word? Sounds like gravy."

"Gravitas?" I suggested.

"That's the one. He likes an atmosphere, the master does," she told me with a fond smile. "And when he does a thing, he does it right. Hired this from Bunter and Weedman," she added with a gesture that encompassed her ensemble. I had not heard of the establishment, but it required little imagination to understand that it was one of the enormous warehouses of doleful apparel that had sprung up in the wake of the violent mourning the queen had displayed upon the death of her husband. Prince Albert might have been dead for a quarter of a century, but the industry of death showed no sign of slowing.

The maid guided me past the statue of Echo where a gentleman in a Bath chair waited, a tiny smile tugging at his lips. She fell back a respectful distance as my host beckoned to me.

As promised, Frederick Havelock was a force of nature, even in his state of infirmity. His hands were gnarled as old oak, but his entire manner was one of great vitality only lightly subdued. His hair and beard had grown together, touches of black still threading through the silvery white locks, and under his beetling dark brows, the bright eyes missed nothing. There was power in him yet, and I realized with a start that he was looking me over with the practiced eye of an artist—and seducer.

My expression must have betrayed me, for he gave another laugh and waved one of his knotted hands. "You are in no danger from me, child. I haven't been able to defile a woman properly for years. But I can still appreciate the Master's hand at work in the sculpting of a comely face," he added gallantly. "If I were able, I would strip you naked and pose you as Galatea just sprung to life under my knowing hands."

"If you were able, I would let you."

He laughed again and waved me to a cushion perched on the edge of the fountain. After Mr. Gilchrist's theatrics, the rest of the party seemed to disperse to the smaller rooms leaving us alone in the reception hall.

"Tell me your name, child."

"Veronica Speedwell."

"You are Louise's friend," he said with a nod. "She warned us you would come poking about into this business with Miles Ramsforth. Are you that rarest of birds, a lady detective?"

"I am not. I am a lepidopterist by trade."

"What ho! An educated female. Now that is an interesting creature."

"As is the artistic male," I replied.

"I presume you know who I am?" His bright eyes twinkled a little, and I could easily see him coming of age in the glamorous, feckless court of the tsars. He must have broken dozens of hearts in his day, for even now he reminded me of nothing so much as a magnificently grizzled old lion. He might be winding down, but life was not yet finished with him.

"I do. You are my host."

He raised his hands in mock horror. "Child, never call me such! Makes me sound like a sacrament. You may call me Frederick," he said with the air of one bestowing a singular honor. I wondered if he would be as quick to treat a male guest with such intimacy, but it did not matter. Like Stoker, I was not above using whatever advantages Nature had given me.

"And you may call me Miss Speedwell," I said primly.

He burst out laughing and nodded towards his pretty Echo. "D'ye see that little nymph? I sculpted her over the course of two months in the winter of 1859. It was bitterly cold that year—nothing to do but stay inside and make mischief."

"I don't remember," I said with a glance from under my lashes. "I was not yet born."

"Oh, the cruelty!" he chided. He reached out and patted my hand. "Don't draw away, child. I only hold hands these days, but it gives me comfort." He turned them over, scrutinizing my palms carefully. "You work with these hands."

"Lepidoptery is an exacting business."

"As is art," he told me, still holding my hands in his withered ones. He nodded again towards Echo. "I knew when I sculpted her I wanted a very special setting for my pretty jewel. I could not imagine how the thing was to be done, for I had conceived of the impossible—to put my little Echo in a room that would actually echo. I carted her around for years until I happened to be in St. Paul's one day, sulking at God. And then I had it—a whispering gallery," he said, gesturing expansively towards the circular hall that surrounded us. It is how I hear many things I am not meant to hear," he confided. He raised his ruined hands for my inspection. "I cannot make art these days, so I am forced to other occupations, mostly gossip and meddling."

I shrugged. "In preliterate societies, gossip is the only means of transmitting vital news and information."

"And this lot is barely lettered," he told me. "But they are my little lambs and their shepherd loves them dearly."

"I had the pleasure of meeting your sister-in-law earlier," I told him.

He gave me an enigmatic look. "And was it a pleasure? No, do not answer that. Politeness might require you to lie."

"I liked her," I told him truthfully.

"Yes, you would. Ottilie is easy to like. I think of women as elemental, Miss Speedwell. Their company is as necessary to me as air, and I have come to know them. Some women are fire, some are earth—Ottilie is water. Calm and omnipresent."

He gestured with his ruined hands to a painting hanging just under the stairs. "I painted her once. Go and see if you think it a good likeness."

I rose and went to the little niche under the stairs. The painting there was poorly lit, and the shadows that played over it seemed to change the mood. One moment it glowed with a sort of unholy light, the next it was beset by gloom. But one thing did not change—the rapt expression of the subject. If Frederick Havelock had not told me it was Ottilie Ramsforth, I would never have known her. She was wearing a loose robe of some dark stuff, and her hair was unbound, rippling over her shoulders. Her head was thrown back, eyes wide with a vision only she could see, lips parted as if caught in a sigh. One graceful hand lay draped in her lap while the other caressed a golden spear that pierced her just below the heart. The entire effect was one of arrested pleasure, the most exquisite bliss, a transient and beautiful thing, now fixed for eternity.

I returned to my perch on the edge of the fountain.

"What did you think of it?" he demanded, watching me closely.

"It is hard to say. It reminded me of one of my butterflies—something that is beautiful for only a moment. You have pinned her up for display as I might pin one of my beauties."

He gave me a slow nod of approval. "Yes. *Yes.* That is the essence of painting, child. To capture something utterly temporary and conjure permanence. That is the gift of the artist."

I glanced again to the painting. "Perhaps, too, the gift of the artist is to see what others do not. I should never have imagined Mrs. Ramsforth could look so . . . so—"

He grinned. "Exactly. I was inspired by Bernini's sculpture of Saint Teresa, that moment of exquisite ecstasy when she is lanced by the divine spear. It was heady stuff for a young artist. I would never have connected it with Ottilie myself but for a look I saw in her one day. She was newly betrothed to Miles Ramsforth. They had known each other since childhood, you understand. The match was a good one. The Troyon property had been entailed in the male line, so neither my wife nor her sister inherited the land, but the estate marched next to Littledown, the Ramsforth seat. It was a splendid house in its day, and Miles needed Troyon money to rebuild it. He also needed someone calm and settled to rein him in. Ottilie seemed the perfect choice. Augusta and I thought she would be the frost to his fire."

"And was she?" I asked.

He pursed his lips. "Not as I had expected. During the party announcing their engagement, they slipped away for a moment, stealing a kiss in the garden or some such. Miles was called for and he left us, but as he walked away I saw her watching him. It was then I saw the resemblance to Saint Teresa—a martyr who has just glimpsed her heaven. And I knew I had to paint her."

He fell silent, no doubt reminiscing, until I ventured a question.

"This must be a difficult time for her."

He nodded. "Yes. She is bearing up well, but I expect once it is finished and she has got right away to Greece, she will have the most marvelous crack-up. I wish I could say Miles Ramsforth was worth the grief she will feel, but I shall not pay you the insult of lying. This will ruin her life, and it will be one more bit of carnage to his credit," he finished bitterly.

"You do not care for him?"

He shook his head, tossing his lion's mane. "I would rather set my beard afire than spend an hour in conversation with the fellow," he told me. "We were friendly once, but I tired of him and his ways. He is the most childlike grown man you could ever meet. His enthusiasms are exhausting, and he is optimistic to the point of stupidity, always bounding from project to project. Candide would have thought him too much. He likes to be the center of attention, forever bouncing around like a jackanapes."

I could hardly point out that a craving for the limelight was clearly a quality he shared with his brother-in-law, so I said nothing. Frederick Havelock's expression sharpened.

"Did you ever meet Artemisia?"

"I did not have the pleasure. But I saw some of her work tonight. A tragic loss."

"She was a genius," he said simply. "She did not know it yet. It doesn't do to tell them too soon what they are capable of. If they are gifted, they will wreck themselves trying to make success happen. If they aren't gifted, you stifle the spirit when they might have had one good work in them."

It was a surprisingly perspicacious speech from an old roué. I regarded him with fresh appreciation. "You must be an excellent mentor."

"Mentor! D'ye know your Greek history, child?"

"When Odysseus left for the Trojan War, he gave the care of his son Telemachus to his friend Mentor, who governed the boy wisely and well," I recited.

"And no doubt had a good sniff around Penelope's skirts as well," he finished.

"No doubt," I agreed with a smile.

He regarded me from under the heavy brows. "When one is as old as I am, it is amusing to shock people, but you do not seem perturbed by anything. I shall call you the Unflappable Miss Speedwell."

"I am shocked by murder," I said simply.

"Decency must always be shocked by the indecent," he replied. The vitality seemed to ebb a little, his color turning ashen.

"Shall I call someone, Sir Frederick?" I suggested.

He waved a hand. "Not yet. Ottilie will be along shortly to fuss over me, but there's no call to weave my shroud just yet."

"You have suffered a tremendous loss," I said.

"Yes, quite," he replied, clipping off the words sharply. "I was still walking when she was alive," he added, and I knew he meant Artemisia. "I have been wasting away for years with this blasted affliction," he told me, raising his knotted hands, "but the day after she died, I suffered a fit. The shock of it, the doctors said. I was comatose for some days, and when I recovered consciousness, I found I could no longer walk, and my hands were barely more than useless."

There was no self-pity in his voice, and I liked him for that. He tipped his head as he studied me. "I do not regret the feebleness of my hands. I have worked hard to conquer my regrets. But there are moments still when I curse God that I can no longer paint. Seeing your face is one of those moments," he said. "Such coloring is rare. I have only seen violet eyes once before, and I have never painted them. I would not have got them right, but dear God, I should have liked to have tried."

"You are very kind, Sir Frederick."

A flicker of animation kindled in his face. "You were supposed to call me Frederick," he reminded me.

I smiled. "And you must call me Veronica."

"Veronica Speedwell! Ha—someone has a sense of humor," he observed. The fact that my name was a botanical pun frequently amused those who understood it. He patted my hand. "You are a kindly creature.

I do not expect you will discover anything about this business with Artemisia, but it is good of you to indulge Louise and poke about."

"You do not think Mr. Ramsforth is innocent?"

He considered that a long moment, and when he spoke, he measured his words carefully. "I do not think you will be successful in your quest to exonerate him."

"That is not the same thing," I pointed out.

"You might be too clever for your own good," he said, giving me a penetrating look. "Whatever you do, be careful. Murder is a dangerous business, sweet Veronica. And shadows are all around."

CHAPTER

9

I rose from my seat at the edge of the fountain as Stoker approached
with Miss Talbot.

"Splendid news, Sir Frederick," she said, coming to stand by her
mentor. "This is Mr. Templeton-Vane, and he has agreed to pose for me.
He will complete my gallery of Greek heroes with his Perseus."

Sir Frederick gave Stoker a long look. "How wonderful, my dear. I
hope he will be able to accommodate you while he undertakes the rest
of his obligations here at Havelock House."

Emma Talbot's expression was mystified. "Obligations?"

"Yes, child," Sir Frederick said calmly. "He is here with Miss Speedwell to ask questions about Artemisia's death. They believe they can
exonerate Miles Ramsforth."

I had heard of the blood draining from one's face, but I had never
actually witnessed the phenomenon. All the color faded from Miss Talbot's visage, even her lips went white, and she seemed to have lost the
power of speech.

"Miss Talbot?" I asked. "Are you quite well?"

She gave a sharp, angry shake of the head. "Exonerate Miles Ramsforth? It is not possible," she breathed.

Her small hands were curled into fists at her sides, and she looked at us with the ferocity of a cornered animal.

"This is the first you have heard of it?" Stoker inquired, doubtless thinking of Princess Louise and her announcement at the previous evening's supper.

"No, I was there when the princess told us. I thought she was exaggerating," she said flatly. "It cannot be done." Her grey eyes flashed with something like contempt. "If you wish to pose for me, you are welcome at any time. Otherwise, you ought to go. You should leave this place and forget what you have been asked to do. It is impossible," she finished, turning upon her heel and leaving.

"That was rather a dramatic exit," I remarked.

Sir Frederick was smiling a secretive half smile. "I do love to rile them up. It makes them indiscreet," he said by way of explanation. He gave his hands an admiring glance. "They are not good for much these days, but they can still jerk the strings of the puppets."

He beckoned to Cherry, moving towards us in her funereal garb.

"About time," she grumbled. "Mrs. Ramsforth said I was to put you to bed," she told her master.

He waved a vague hand. "Put me to bed! That makes me sound like a lettuce."

"Lettuce or no, bed is where you're bound," she told him, giving me a wink.

"I will go, but in good time. First, I wish you to take Miss Speedwell and Mr. Templeton-Vane to Artemisia's rooms."

Her face took on a shuttered look. "Those rooms are locked."

"For which we have a key," he replied firmly. "Go, girl."

She did not like it, but she did as she was bade, retrieving a key from somewhere in the domestic offices and returning to guide us up the staircase. It wound around the dome, forming a sort of gallery in places, each tiled in a different pattern of blues and golds. She led us to the floor above Ottilie Ramsforth's rooms and down a corridor painted in Venetian red.

"Here," she said, putting the key to a lock and flinging open the door. "We haven't been inside since she was buried," she told us. Stoker and I moved slowly over the threshold, but the girl lingered in the corridor.

"Are you afraid to come in?" I asked.

She hesitated. "They do say that those that have been murdered don't rest easy," she admitted. "I reckon if she has come back, Miss Artemisia would come back here."

"Why not Littledown?" Stoker inquired. "Surely she would visit the scene of her death."

Cherry gave a shudder. "I don't know about that. I do know she was happy here."

"Was she?" The question was a rhetorical one on my part, and the girl took it for such. She lingered outside the door, darting glances at Stoker. Apparently Miss Talbot was not the only one who found him interesting. I jerked my head towards the door as I moved further into the room, and he obliged, finding a coin and slipping it into the girl's palm.

"Thank you for acting as our guide," Stoker said, flashing her a devilish grin.

"Oh, *oh*," she murmured. She looked up at him, pointing with a tentative finger to his eye patch. "I know it's not my place, sir, but I am ever so curious. What happened to your eye? Did you lose it in a swordfight?"

Stoker was sweetly patient with the girl. "I haven't lost it at all," he said, flipping up the patch to show his eye, whole and undamaged save for a thin silvering scar that ran from his brow, across the lid, and down his cheek to the strong bone of his jaw.

"Then why do you wear that?" she asked, moving forward half a step.

"Because although the eye itself has healed, it is prone to fatigue. If I am too long about the fine details my work requires, its strength is taxed. It must be rested, and the patch does that."

"Fancy that," she said in a breathy voice.

Stoker did not move towards her, but his voice was warm and intimate, coaxing even. "Now that I have answered your questions, perhaps you will be good enough to answer mine."

"Oh, anything, sir!" she replied.

"Thank you. I think you are a smart girl, Cherry, and a sharp one too. I imagine little happens in this house that gets past you."

She gave him a narrow look. "Nor does it get beyond me. Thank you for the coin, sir," she said, bobbing a hasty curtsy and taking her leave.

I threw him a repressive glance. "You are losing your touch if you can't pry a little indiscreet information out of a girl like that," I told him.

He shrugged and closed the door so we should not be disturbed. Without discussion, we took the opportunity to separate. We might both claim the general occupation of natural historian, but our fields were rather different. Whereas I focused upon the intricate empire of lepidoptery, his speciality was taxidermy, the creation of animal mounts that resurrected dead specimens to a semblance of life. Both required a keen eye for detail as well as a certain creativity of thought. Our talents complemented each other perfectly.

The first room was a workroom of sorts—Artemisia's studio, stacked with canvases in various stages of completion, books on art, paints, brushes, and odd props. Enormous north-facing windows, now shuttered, must have provided her with excellent light, and even with the flickering illumination of candles—Sir Frederick had not troubled to have the highest floor fitted with gas—it was easy to see why her paintings had garnered such acclaim. She favored grand pictures, with the figures painted larger than life, the colors astonishingly brilliant. Stoker stepped to the nearest, a study of Delilah holding the shorn locks of Samson, whilst I slipped through the half-closed door into the next room.

This must have been her living quarters, for the chamber was fitted with a table and chairs, and a single armchair drawn close to the fire.

A worn but colorful rug warmed the bare boards of the floor, and an assortment of tiny cushions, each sewn from a scrap of brilliant silk, were heaped in the chair. Across the mantel marched a collection of items, framed photographs, little china animals, and papier-mâché boxes. The walls were covered in bright rose-patterned wallpaper, and nearly every square inch had been hung with art—from sketches held lightly in place with drawing pins to paintings properly framed in gilded wood. Even the scrubbed table was covered in a cloth knitted of riotous stripes of red and green and violet. Behind a découpaged screen I found a washstand and a narrow bed made up with Irish linen.

I went to the washstand and examined the few articles there. They were laid out in good order. A tooth mug with brush and powder, a hand glass, a few pots of unguents and powders, and a green glass bottle with a chemist's label pasted on the front.

"What the devil is this?" I asked, picking it up and holding it to the light. It was nearly empty, just a few drops of some greenish milky fluid left in the bottom. The label had been wetted at some point, for it had peeled away from the bottle, leaving only the start of a name and the date. *Maud Er—*

"Maud Eresby," I finished, remembering Artemisia's real name. The date was two months before her death.

"Stoker," I called. "Come and see."

He appeared in the doorway, carrying a sketchbook. I brandished the bottle at him. "What do you know of this? The label is missing."

He uncorked and gave a deep sniff, tipping his head as he considered the odor. He turned the bottle up, coaxing a pearly drop or two onto his finger. He gave it a tentative lick, holding it on his palate a long moment before swallowing.

"Raspberry leaf," he pronounced finally. "With a few other things I can't quite identify."

"Raspberry leaf? For what purpose?"

"It strengthens the womb. It is given to women who are in danger of miscarrying so they can retain the child," he explained.

I blinked at him. "She was unmarried and expecting a child by her married lover. Most women in those circumstances would welcome a miscarriage, but she took steps to prevent one?"

He shrugged. "Perhaps she wanted a babe. Many women feel the need for a child," he pointed out, tactfully avoiding my own disinclination for the event. "Or perhaps she did not want it but could not bring herself to let it die if she had the means to prevent it." His brow furrowed suddenly. "But if she were in danger of miscarrying the child, why was she in Miles Ramsforth's bed the night she died?"

I blinked again. "Is it not possible to enjoy bed sport during one's pregnancy? You mean women have to go without for the duration? Nine months without sexual congress? That's monstrous."

Stoker's complexion was tinged with pink. "If the pregnancy is a healthy one and the child well established, it is generally believed to be safe to engage in such activities. But if there is the slightest danger to the child or mother, it would be strictly forbidden."

"And why take the chance of losing a child that way if she is dosing herself with this to keep it?" I finished.

"An excellent question."

I nodded towards the sketchbook. "What have you there?"

"A bit of explanation," he said, opening the sketchbook to a page near the back. "Recognize the fellow?"

The work lacked a signature but was clearly Artemisia's. Even in miniature, I saw the same bold lines and elegant composition as her other works. It was a sketch of an unclothed male figure, graceful and lithe, stretched out upon a little sofa, his legs spread invitingly, his head crowned with the tiny tips of a satyr's horns. The face was Julian Gilchrist's.

"The sofa is in the other room," Stoker supplied helpfully. "She must have sketched it here."

"And she must have known him very well indeed," I added, noticing the state of excitation she had captured with regard to his male appendage. I leaned closer, taking a more appreciative look. "And one might congratulate her if she did."

Stoker snatched the sketchbook away, slamming it closed. "Don't be vulgar," he ordered, as cold and imperious as a Roman emperor.

I narrowed my eyes. "For a gentleman of aristocratic birth, you sometimes demonstrate the overly precious morals of a tradesman," I told him.

"What a vile thing to say." His tone was genuinely aggrieved. He might abuse his kind lavishly and even cast his vote as a Radical, but he was still an aristocrat, blood and bone, and as such deplored the notion that he might have anything in common with the middle class and its affected morality. He was no snob; he moved between the lavish decadence of the highest orders and the lax bonhomie of the lowest with equal ease, taking no more notice of a duke than a dustman, but he had no patience for the priggishness of the merchant class.

"Oh, very well, I apologize. But you have brought us a rather interesting clue," I mused. "Apparently Artemisia was on very intimate terms with Julian Gilchrist. Mightn't that be the source of his ill humor?"

"It would certainly fit," he agreed. "Particularly if she threw him over for Miles Ramsforth."

"And that would give Gilchrist excellent motive for killing her and letting Ramsforth swing for it."

Stoker rubbed his chin thoughtfully. "He's the right height for the malefactor who left us the warning last night. Did he know we were going to investigate?"

I nodded. "Remember what Ottilie Ramsforth told us about last night's dinner party. Apparently Her Royal Highness was not at all discreet about the matter."

I glanced about the room. It was quiet, so far removed from the entertainment downstairs. There was only dust and stillness and a sense of time having stopped. In a manner of speaking, it had. Sir Frederick had locked the door upon these rooms with Artemisia's death. She would never cross the threshold again, never lie upon that counterpane to sleep, never brew a cup of tea in the pot with the chipped handle. A slow breath of cold air swept across the nape of my neck, soft as a fingertip. I resisted the impulse to shudder, but Stoker must have seen something.

"What is it?" he asked softly.

"Do you believe in ghosts?"

His expression was grim. "With the life I have led, I cannot afford to."

CHAPTER

10

On our way out of Havelock House we passed Cherry bearing a basket covered with a plain black cloth. She lifted the cloth to reveal a heap of funeral biscuits wrapped together in pairs and sealed with a wafer of black wax. Each packet bore a label with a delicately scrawled dedication to Artemisia, her dates of birth and death, and a little bit of verse. "You must each take one," she instructed. "In memory of Miss Artemisia."

We obediently accepted the packets. "Please convey our regards to Sir Frederick tomorrow," I told her.

"Yes, miss. He's tucked up in bed where he ought to be. This is all a bit of a strain on him." Her chin was set with a rigid determination.

"You are very fond of your master," I observed.

"He is good to me," she said simply. "And I don't like to see him upset."

"How fortunate for him to have such a loyal champion," I told her. She gave a start and colored sharply.

"I would never presume," she began.

I touched a fingertip to her sleeve. "He is fortunate," I repeated. The angry color in her cheeks softened to a flush of pleasure.

"Thank you, miss."

Stoker put his hand to the small of my back as he guided me out the door. "What was that all about?"

"I have a feeling Cherry could prove useful to us before this business is finished. One of us has to cultivate her, and I suspect you are too modest to exert yourself to seduce her."

He blanched. "One of these days, that tongue is going to cut someone, Veronica."

"I sincerely hope so."

T he next morning I appeared at the Belvedere bright and early. I left Stoker slumbering in my bed after another chaste and pointless night. No further threat had appeared, but we had enjoyed a late drink together—a fresh batch of aguardiente had arrived from my friend in South America—and a smoke. I had finally persuaded Stoker away from his filthy cigars, preferring the fruitier aroma of my own slender cigarillos. He ate his pack of funeral biscuits, crunching through the aniseed wafers as we considered suspects and batted around theories, but in the end there was simply not enough information to permit the drawing of any conclusions. Although we had formed impressions of the various players in our little drama, it was far too soon to theorize properly, and this lack of focus left me feeling tetchy and a little irritable.

The trouble was we had no clear direction on how to proceed. I hoped a perusal of the morning's newspapers might offer a spark of inspiration, so I took myself down to the Belvedere earlier than was my custom. The hall boy, George—a sturdy lad of some eleven or twelve years—had already carried down the copy of *The Daily Harbinger*, and I had almost finished reading the last page when Stoker appeared, soaked to the skin. The skies had opened, the rain teemed, and the gardens were awash. He toweled his hair and lit the stoves while I wiped the dogs and gave them a horse's femur to gnaw companionably upon.

"Bloody hell, this hump is the work of a ham-fisted amateur." Having finished his crocodile, Stoker's newest task was the repair of the mount of an imperfectly taxidermied camel, and he swore lavishly as he inspected it carefully. "Just look at the shape of it," he demanded. "You'll not find that in nature. It looks more like a dowager duchess than a Bactrian."

I made soothing sounds as I returned to my newspaper. Stoker finished pulling the stitches from the hide and carefully peeled it away from the stuffing. Instantly, a wave of noxious odor rolled out—a combination of mold, dust, and something far worse.

"Good God, Stoker, what is that?" I demanded, covering my nose with a handkerchief.

He reached into the decaying sawdust of the humps to retrieve a nest of small corpses. "Mice. I think."

He tossed them onto the fire and I threw in a handful of dried lavender for good measure. I had learnt through experience that Stoker's experiments were invariably odiferous. He returned to his humps, lifting out a few more indelicacies as he cleaned the thing down to the bones. It was an old-fashioned mount, with the animal's skin stretched to cover the sawdust stuffing secured over the bones. In recent years, natural historians had come to favor sculpted armatures of metal or wood in place of the skeleton, leaving the bones to be displayed separately. It was a sound practice, for it afforded study of both the skeletal structure and the hide at the same time. It was also considerably more hygienic, Stoker pointed out, but required the skills of a sculptor to re-create the animal in its new form.

The thought of sculpture brought a question to mind. "When do you mean to pose for Miss Talbot?" I inquired. I leaned forward swiftly. "*The Daily Harbinger* is running a retrospective of Artemisia's murder—a different feature every day until the hanging. It is deliciously ghoulish."

Sweating from his exertions wrestling with the camel hide, he had stripped off his shirt, so frequent an occurrence in our work that I had grown immune to the sight of his exposed and formidable musculature. Almost.

He shrugged as he coaxed the skin from the beast's rump. "I do not see the purpose of posing."

"We have discussed this, Stoker. The purpose is to spend time with the possible suspects in Artemisia's death," I reminded him as I read over the article. "Ah! A new description of the death scene. In lavish detail with a stern warning for the more delicate readers," I said, rattling the newspaper.

He came to stand next to me, his skin slick with sweat and flecked with sawdust, and read the piece aloud over my shoulder. "'Miss Maud Eresby was discovered in a state of exsanguination in the great bedchamber at Littledown. She was laid out peacefully upon the bed, but the composure of her situation only served to heighten the gruesomeness of the crime itself. Gore soaked the bedding through to the floor below, leaving behind a stain that cannot be removed.'" He quirked up a brow. "Ghoulish indeed."

I sat back, giving him a thoughtful look. "Would she have really bled so much or is that an exaggeration?"

"The post-mortem report given at the inquest suggested a single slash to the throat with a very sharp instrument," he said coolly, befitting a former surgeon's mate in Her Majesty's Navy. "Once open, the sinister exterior jugular vein did its work, causing her to lose so much blood her heart had nothing left to pump."

"And the very sharp instrument was found to be Miles Ramsforth's razor, taken from the washstand across the room," I supplied. "How much force would it take to accomplish such a deed with the single slash of a gentleman's razor?"

He shrugged. "According to what we have read and heard, Artemisia was a young woman in the prime of health and statuesque in figure. A small person could not have done this. It was a man."

"Not a woman?"

He shook his head. "Not likely. For a woman to do this, she would have to be bigger and stronger than Artemisia—which certainly lets out the ladies we have met in connection with this crime. Ottilie Ramsforth is slightly below average height and slender, while Emma Talbot is smaller yet."

Stoker returned to his repulsive camel while I continued to muse. "I have met one woman who is tall . . . and she is a sculptress with strong hands," I said slowly.

"Who is that?"

"My aunt Louise."

He paused, a cloud of sawdust haloing his head. "You cannot be serious."

"It *is* a possibility," I insisted.

"It is *not*. She is a princess."

"And royalty are immune from homicidal tendencies? Study your history, Stoker. I think you will discover that is how most of them became royal in the first place."

"That is not what I mean," he countered. "I am rather more familiar with the breed than you are. Believe me when I tell you, a royal would never soil their hands when there are minions who will gladly do the deed for them. They don't handle money, they don't knock on doors—for the love of Christ, Veronica, they scarcely even wipe their own—"

I held up a quelling hand. "I take your meaning. Very well. But I still like the idea."

"I am certain you do," he replied with a curl of his handsome lip. "You would enjoy nothing better than to show them up, and I do not blame you for it. But you give them far too much credit. They have not the wit or subtlety or strength of character to accomplish a murder."

"Perhaps." I steepled my fingers under my chin. "Whom do you like as our murderer?"

"Julian Gilchrist," he said, slanting me a wicked glance.

"You are only saying that because you concussed him. Perhaps you ought to send him a nice basket of fruit by way of apology."

"Apology! The bastard came to when I went to put him down and tried to bite me. Unsporting, I'd call that," he said, his tone a trifle hurt.

"He was heavily intoxicated," I reminded him.

Just then the George the hall boy appeared. "Hello again, miss. First post," he said as he handed over a stack of envelopes. I gave them a cursory glance as he went to observe Stoker.

"That's a silly-looking horse, sir, if I do say it," George observed.

Stoker said something unintelligible. His head was firmly lodged inside the camel's rump as he excavated piles of sawdust.

"It is not a horse, George," I said absently. "The domestic horse is *Equus ferus caballus*. The specimen into which Mr. Templeton-Vane has currently thrust his head is *Camelus bactrianus*, the Bactrian camel. It is native to the steppes of Central Asia."

The boy stared goggle-eyed at the thing until I offered him a bit of honeycomb from Stoker's dwindling supply and he scampered off, sucking happily as I riffled through the post. There were advertisements and bills and one or two professional journals of little interest to either of us. *The Quarterly Report of the Society for the Protection of Lesser Marsh Beetles* was of no consequence, and I tossed it into the basket of discarded papers we kept for starting fires. Two envelopes remained, and they were equally intriguing. The first was addressed to Stoker and bore a coat of arms topped with a coronet embellished with nine silver balls. It required little effort to deduce the letter was from Stoker's brother, the new Viscount Templeton-Vane.

I dangled it from my fingertips. "A letter, Stoker. From your eldest brother, I believe."

He said something mercifully muffled by the sawdust of the Bactrian, but I caught enough to know he did credit to the reputation of naval men for fluency in the art of the profane.

"What did you say?" I called sweetly. "It sounded like something about ducks."

He pulled his head from the camel's backside, showering sawdust to the floor. His long black locks were liberally powdered with the stuff, and I felt the urge to laugh. I smothered it as soon as I saw his expression. He was white-lipped with anger, and plucked the letter from my hand without a word. He did not open it, merely consigned it to the fire and turned back to his camel.

I opened the second letter as it was addressed to both of us. I needn't have bothered to read it. I knew what it was going to say as soon as I saw Sir Hugo Montgomerie's name.

"Stoker, do stop fondling that camel and go make yourself presentable. We have been summoned to Scotland Yard."

W e said little as we made our way to the headquarters of the Metropolitan Police and less still as we waited for Sir Hugo. I had expected the head of Special Branch to leave us cooling our heels for quite a while, but it was a matter of mere moments before his junior, the charmingly ambitious Inspector Mornaday, was sent to fetch us.

"Miss Speedwell," he said, coming forward with a broad smile. "I did not think to meet you again so soon. The last time I saw you, you were preparing to leave for the South Pacific."

I gave him a thin smile of my own. "Plans, unfortunately, have changed. I am in London for the foreseeable future."

His brows lifted in interest. "Really? If that is the case, perhaps we—"

"We have been summoned to see Sir Hugo," Stoker put in flatly.

Mornaday gave him a cool nod. "Templeton-Vane. Always a pleasure."

He rested his merry dark gaze upon me, barely suppressing a smile. "Sir Hugo is ready for you."

We followed him up a flight of stairs and through corridors that twisted and turned. In spite of his elevated status as the head of Special Branch, Sir Hugo preferred to keep an inconspicuous presence at the Yard.

"I am surprised at Sir Hugo taking the time to see us," I told Mornaday. "I expect he is quite busy."

"Quite." The syllable was clipped, but Mornaday tossed a grin over his shoulder. "But you ought to know that he would never dare leave you waiting out there amongst the rabble. He is afraid of what you might say."

I snorted. Sir Hugo made no secret of his wariness where I was concerned. It still troubled him that I had refused a generous payment from the royal family to keep the truth of my birth secret. To me it stank of bribery, and I would not have a penny from them. But to Sir Hugo, it meant trusting me to keep my promise that I would never reveal it myself.

Mornaday brought us to Sir Hugo's door and scratched lightly. "Come!" Sir Hugo barked.

Mornaday opened the door for us and closed it quietly behind us. I fancied he would stay outside until our interview was concluded, playing Cerberus at the door to bar interruptions—as much to preserve our privacy as to keep our visit as discreet as possible.

Sir Hugo was sitting behind his slender Regency writing desk, a graceful piece of furniture curiously at odds with the power of his position. He rose as we entered, fixing me with a stern eye.

"Miss Speedwell, I would be lying if I said this was an unmitigated pleasure. Templeton-Vane," he added, inclining his head to Stoker.

He gestured to the chairs opposite his desk and we seated ourselves. "I will not offer refreshment," Sir Hugo informed us, "because I do not wish to prolong this meeting."

I gave him a look of gentle reproof. "That is decidedly unfriendly on your part considering how cooperative I have been."

His brows darted upwards. "Cooperative? You have never once done a single thing that I asked. How precisely do you imagine that I would ever characterize you as cooperative?"

"I may do things in my own fashion, Sir Hugo, but our aims are not incompatible," I reminded him gently.

He sighed. "That may be true. And you have managed not to flog your story to the newspapers, so I suppose I ought to be grateful for that much. Now then, I presume you know why I wished to see you today."

"I cannot imagine," I said, widening my eyes for emphasis. "Stoker, have we engaged in any felonious activity recently? Have we robbed a bank? Kidnapped a countess?" I oughtn't to have teased Sir Hugo; he was clearly in no mood for it. His expression immediately turned thunderous.

"You are here because of the Ramsforth business. I am given to understand that Her Royal Highness saw fit to involve you."

"You gave her my name," I pointed out.

"She already knew your name," he told me, then instantly looked chagrined.

I tipped my head thoughtfully. "Did she indeed?"

He sighed again and I began to worry for his digestion. "Very well. I should not have been so indiscreet, but yes, she did. She is close to . . . *him*," he said, carefully refraining from naming my father. "Princess Louise is something of a confidante to her brother. He wanted to unburden himself after that nasty business during the Jubilee," he added with a shudder of remembrance.

"I can understand that," I said, although I most certainly did not. If my father wanted to unburden himself about that "nasty business," then I was the most logical candidate. But he had made no effort to reach out to me, and I hoped he understood I would never presume to make the first move. My pride was worth more to me than a prince's acknowledgment.

"In any event, he was most impressed with your own role in the affair, and yours," he added, gathering Stoker with a glance. "No doubt his feelings made an impression on the princess when he discussed the matter with her. When this dreadful affair transpired and Her Royal Highness became convinced of Ramsforth's innocence, she asked me about you. I was bound to tell her the truth, although I did not precisely encourage her to approach you," he finished.

"Well, she did. And I wondered if you would be kind enough to share any information you might have about Artemisia's death—anything that mightn't have made it into the newspapers."

He was too self-possessed to gape, but his nostrils flared and he made an obvious effort to hold on to his temper. "No. Everything of relevance is in the newspapers because the newspapers reported the correct verdict—murder at the hands of Miles Ramsforth. Nothing else matters. It is unpalatable and the princess does not want to believe it, but there it is."

"And you are content that you are going to hang the right man?" I asked.

"I am." The words were clipped and cold. "The Yard has investigated the matter thoroughly."

I canted my head. "Did they?"

To my astonishment, Sir Hugo softened a little. "Not as thoroughly as I would have liked, if you must know." He paused, and I gave him a brightly attentive look, encouraging him to go on. He puffed out a sigh. "This estate, Littledown, it is buried in the countryside, one of those odd little corners of the Home Counties where nothing of note ever happens. The local constable was summoned when the murder was discovered. He is an elderly fellow, *quite* elderly, in fact. He has no experience of murder, and it rather got the better of him. Somehow, he let the reporters in and they trampled all over the scene like a pack of rabid wolves. There was virtually nothing left to examine."

"That is why the newspaper illustrations were so detailed—they were not working from descriptions," I worked out. "They had actually been in the room."

"For hours," he lamented. "I have already seen to it that the constable in question has been forcibly retired, but if word got out that the poor old devil mishandled things so badly, he would lose his pension. It seems rather hard to drive a man to the workhouse simply because he found himself out of his depth," he added. He seemed uncomfortable at being found to have a compassionate side, so I let it go.

"But you must admit," I began reasonably, "if the murder could not be properly investigated, it is wrong to hang Miles Ramsforth."

He recovered his usual sternness, pointing a hectoring finger at me. "It matters not one jot Miles Ramsforth has no alibi."

"The princess seems quite persuaded," I began.

"The princess is rather accustomed to getting her own way!" he replied sharply. He clamped his mouth shut, grinding his teeth together. After a moment, he spoke, his voice calm and his manner controlled. "Miss Speedwell, I understand Her Royal Highness rather better than you. After all, it has been the task of this office to ensure her safety and that of the entire family for quite some time. Princess Louise can be highly strung, nervy even."

"You sound as if you were describing a horse," Stoker put in.

A fleeting smile touched Sir Hugo's lips. "Your father used to race horses, Templeton-Vane. I am certain you understand what anxious bloodstock is like. The princess's temperament is excitable and she has been indulged, allowed to think of herself as an artist and associate with a certain raffish element," he added, pursing his lips. "This has not always been in her best interests. She is headstrong, and at this moment, she has the bit between her teeth and is running away from all common sense. She needs time to accept what Miles Ramsforth has done and that her own judgment has been flawed."

"How so?" I demanded.

He shrugged. "She considered him a friend, and he was not worthy of her friendship. To someone like the princess, accustomed to getting her own way, having obstacles smoothed before her, it rankles even worse than it does for the rest of us when things go awry. She has come to see me on several occasions on this matter, and each time, she has seemed worse, more agitated. She wanted me to reopen the investigation—an eventuality which is entirely out of the question. But I wanted to help her," he said, and I saw a sudden kindly light kindle in his eyes. For all his bluster, he did care about the family he was sworn to protect.

"The princess asked about engaging a private inquiry agent," he went on, "which I could not permit. But when she raised your name, I had already thwarted Her Royal Highness so often, I could hardly discourage her. In the end, I told her how to find you, but I made it apparent that I had reservations, and now I will make them clear to you," he said, leaning forward and gathering us both with an imperious look. "You will not meddle in this. You will not speak to the press, and you will not pervert the course of justice. Do you both understand me?"

I rose. "As you wish, Sir Hugo."

He leapt to his feet. "Oh no, you don't! I understand you well enough to know that meek acquiescence is never a good sign."

I shrugged. "And I understand men well enough to know that it is seldom profitable to argue with one who has made up his mind."

"If you choose to pursue this, I can have you stopped," he said, lowering his head like a bull.

"You can try," I said quietly.

He turned to Stoker. "Can you not talk sense into her?"

Stoker gave him a pitying glance. "If you wanted her to leave this alone, you should have ordered her to investigate. And then offered to pay her."

We left Sir Hugo sputtering. Mornaday escorted us out Sir Hugo's private entrance, giving me a wink as he closed the door behind us.

"I don't like that fellow," Stoker said as we emerged onto the pavement. The morning rain had subsided to low, threatening cloud.

"Which one? Sir Hugo or Mornaday?"

"Take your pick." He rummaged absently in his pockets for something sweet. He turned up a twist of peppermint humbugs, tearing open the packet and crunching happily into one. The sharp, cool scent blended with the aromas of sweating horse and rotting vegetables and unwashed Londoners. Over it all hung the dank green smell of the Thames, and I felt a sudden rush of affection for this city I had adopted as my own.

"We did manage to upset him rather badly," I began. "If we had told him about someone leaving a threat for us, it might have persuaded him that they have the wrong man."

He shrugged. "His pomposity needs pricking. I rather like the notion of solving this for him and presenting him with a neatly tied up murderer."

"So do I. The only question is how to proceed from here." I cudgeled my brain as we walked, mulling over the various casebooks of Arcadia Brown and considering what our next move might be.

CHAPTER

11

W e arrived back at Bishop's Folly in good time, intending to take tea before settling back to work. But just as we reached the Belvedere, we heard a low groaning sound from just under the shrubbery.

I looked at Stoker. "It is Patricia again."

"Blast that animal," Stoker said bitterly. But he accompanied me nonetheless to where the giant tortoise was upended beneath the shrubs, moaning.

"How does she *do* this?" he demanded.

In fact, there was no simple explanation. A creature of Patricia's size ought not to have been able to maneuver herself onto her back with such astonishing regularity. The fact that once there, she was utterly incapable of righting herself without assistance did not dissuade her in the slightest. And the fact that female giant tortoises were believed to be mute did not prevent her from giving loud, relentless voice to her distress.

"We cannot leave her," I reminded him. "Even if it weren't unkind, his lordship is very fond of the old girl."

I used the word "old" advisedly. Patricia had been brought from the Galapagos archipelago by Darwin himself some fifty years previously. The eminent scholar had presented a juvenile Patricia as a gift to the present Lord Rosemorran's grandfather, and she had been slowly roaming the grounds of Bishop's Folly ever since. Flinging herself onto her back and moaning for help was a new hobby of hers, and one that invariably required many hands to put right.

Stoker stripped off his coat while I attempted to leverage the beast, but we managed only to rock her a bit. "I shall try from the other side. You keep her steady," Stoker instructed as he disappeared into the shrubbery. The fact that I could hardly be expected to brace an animal of Patricia's dimensions with my slight frame seemed to have escaped him, but I did my best. I shoved with all my might against her as Stoker did the same from the other end, causing her to groan more piteously than before.

"Oh, hush, no one is hurting you, you daft creature," I told her severely.

"I say, miss, are you talking to a turtle?" inquired a polite voice from behind me. I straightened to find a young clergyman, hat in hand, wearing an expression of polite wariness.

"No, I am not. I am, in fact, speaking to a tortoise," I corrected. "A Galapagos tortoise by the name of Patricia—a most trying creature, as you can see. She has only herself to blame for her current predicament and is resistant to our efforts to help. We require another pair of hands."

I gave him a pointed look and he hurried forward. "Of course. What can I do?"

I directed him to remove his coat and then gave instruction on where to place his grip for the best hope of shifting Patricia onto her enormous feet. The delay must have irritated Stoker, for he gave a low growl.

"What in the name of bearded Jesus is taking so long?" he demanded from the other side of the shrub.

"Assistance has arrived in the form of a clergyman," I called.

"What clergyman?"

"I don't know," I told him with an apologetic look at the young man in question. "He hasn't given his name, but I rather think the formalities can wait until Patricia is righted."

The creature issued a groan of agreement, and together the three of us gave one enormous push. Watching Patricia come onto her feet again was like seeing the earth heave up a boulder, a slow, agonizing, laborious process. When it was finished, Patricia threw us one last look of loathing and began to lumber away in search of some lettuces in the kitchen garden. I dusted off my hands and turned to the clergyman.

"Your help was both timely and appreciated, sir."

He rubbed his hands frantically upon a handkerchief before taking mine. "I am glad to have been of assistance," he said, darting a nervous glance at the rustling bushes where Stoker was still concealed. The fellow made no move to tell his name, holding himself warily as Stoker emerged from the shrubbery, his hair lavishly disarranged and littered with leaves and twigs. He took one look at the younger man and gave a sigh—of resignation or disgust, I could not decide.

"What the devil are you doing here?" Stoker challenged.

I clucked my tongue. "Stoker, this young man has just helped us quite handily with Patricia. The least we can do is be courteous."

He gave me a dangerous look. "You want courtesy? Very well. Veronica, this is Merryweather Templeton-Vane, my youngest brother. Merry, I repeat: what the devil are you doing here?"

The younger man grinned broadly, but the smile was fleeting, and when he spoke, his voice cracked slightly. "Is that any way to greet your brother?"

"I have nothing whatever to say to you," Stoker told him flatly.

To his credit, the fellow stood his ground, even if his Adam's apple bobbed a bit as he swallowed hard. "Well, I have things to say to you."

"Then say them now, and say them quickly," Stoker instructed. "My patience is at an end."

The young man looked to me, and it seemed an appeal. I stepped forward to pour oil upon the troubled waters. "Pay no mind to Stoker. He is in a frightful temper, but I am afraid that is often his mood, so there is little point in waiting for a better one. Won't you come in?"

As I had anticipated, the invitation, coupled with the action of throwing open the door of the Belvedere and offering a welcoming smile, unsettled them both. The fellow looked doubtfully at Stoker, but he must have realized that following me into the Belvedere would at least get him further than standing upon the doorstep. I showed him in, turning up the gaslights as I went. Stoker trailed behind, hands thrust in his pockets, a sullen expression on his face.

I led the way to the upstairs snug so we might sit comfortably, but I did not offer refreshment. Stoker was clearly annoyed his brother had made an appearance and I knew I should have to answer for inviting him in. No sense in compounding my sins.

I gave the visitor a cordial look. He was dressed like a parson, but untidily so. His hair was a tumbled mass of ruddy waves and his cuffs were impressively smeared with ink and a substance that looked suspiciously like yellow custard. Spectacles perched low on his nose and he peered over them with a charmingly owlish expression. The scattering of freckles across his cheeks spoke to time out of doors, and with a connoisseur's practiced eye I detected a fine breadth of muscular shoulder and thigh under his unfortunate clothes.

He was staring at me in open-mouthed scrutiny, and I waited him out, saying nothing, until he collected himself with a shake and a thoroughly enchanting blush. "I say, that was terribly rude. You must, that is—I am speaking to Miss Veronica Speedwell, am I not?"

"You are," I affirmed.

"My brother Sir Rupert Templeton-Vane has described you. In exacting detail," he added in a strangled voice.

"Yes, I had the pleasure of meeting Sir Rupert a few months ago. He was very helpful in a professional capacity."

"Was he? He never said," the youngster replied, at which I felt a marginal sense of relief. Stoker and I had consulted with Sir Rupert on a matter of tremendous import and the greatest secrecy. It was comforting to know he regarded the incident as confidential.

The younger Templeton-Vane fell to silence again, staring at me, and I turned to Stoker. "Shall we ask what he wants?"

Stoker shrugged. "You invited him in. That makes him your guest, not mine."

I tipped my head as I regarded the fellow. "Is he often prone to fugue states? He looks a little slow."

Again, our caller gave himself a little shake and blushed. "I am sorry. It is only that I have never met a bad woman before."

I could not suppress a snort of laughter, but Stoker surged forward, lifting his younger brother up by his dog collar. Merryweather's feet kicked out and he grasped Stoker's steely forearm, but to no avail. Stoker was not much his superior in inches, but his strength was prodigious. He lifted the boy as if the youngster were made of thistledown.

"Apologize, you little carbuncle," Stoker instructed in a low voice. There was a strangled sound, and Stoker gave him a shake. "I can do this all day, Merry. You, I suspect, cannot."

Another strangled sound and the fellow nodded as well as he was able. Stoker merely opened his grip, dropping him to the chair where he gasped and wheezed for some minutes before he could speak. When he did, it was with considerable effort and an obvious terror of his brother.

"I . . . ap-apologize," he managed.

"Think nothing of it," I returned cordially. "But I am curious about the source of your information."

"I'm not," Stoker put in. "No parson would dare be that sanctimonious. I can smell the stink of our eldest brother all over that particular remark."

I turned to our guest. "Oh? Does the new viscount have a low opinion of me?"

The parson straightened his dog collar, now unfortunately crushed beyond all repair. "Tiberius—Lord Templeton-Vane now—has a curious sense of humor, I am afraid." He eyed me curiously. "I must say, you are taking this all awfully well."

I shrugged. "Can his lordship reconcile the competing theories of evolution proposed by Darwin and Lamarck?"

The fellow shook his head in bewilderment. "No, I am certain he could not."

"Then he is by far the least interesting of the Templeton-Vane brothers to me. His opinion therefore matters not at all," I assured him as I tossed Stoker a quick smile. Stoker had written a paper upon that very subject that was still the finest I had read. He might have spent the better part of the past four years burying himself in drink and the taxidermic arts, but I had hopes of resurrecting his career as a promising natural historian with or without his cooperation.

Stoker did not return the smile. He was too busy staring at his younger brother with an expression that would have given Medusa pause. The boy noticed and swallowed hard. At this rate, he would break his Adam's apple altogether. I sighed.

"Stoker, do stop looming over him. You have obviously given him a fright. Now, promise you won't abuse him any more on my behalf."

He grunted by way of reply, but it was enough to console his brother, and when Stoker took a chair, straddling it like a saddle and resting his forearms upon the back, the younger man relaxed a little.

"I really do apologize," Merryweather told me. "I have made quite a bad start, and really, it is a pity. I practiced it so many times."

I felt a smile tug at my lips, but I dared not give it free rein. He was so deliciously serious in spite of his youth. "Tell me, Mr. Templeton-Vane, what is your situation?"

"I am the youngest of the sons of the sixth Viscount Templeton-Vane," he replied promptly. "I have taken holy orders and I have the living at Cherboys."

"Cherboys?" I inquired.

"The family seat in Devonshire," Stoker supplied. "The village just beyond is called Dearsley, and Merry has the living there."

"How very nice," I said. "It sounds like something out of Dickens."

Merryweather pulled a face. "Not really. I don't much care for the life of a clergyman, you see. But Father insisted. He gave me the living before he died, and now I find I am rather sunk."

"How?" I asked.

"Tiberius, in his role as the new viscount and head of the family, won't hear of me giving it up."

I did not look at Stoker, but I knew he had rolled his eyes heavenwards. "For God's sake, Merry, he hasn't chained you to the bloody church. Just walk away."

Merryweather's eyes rounded in amazement. "But I couldn't."

"Why not?" I inquired. "Is there some other obligation attaching you to this church?"

"What? No, of course not. I am merely the vicar," he replied in some confusion.

"Then you can leave," I pointed out.

"Of course I can't," he argued. "One does not simply leave a family like ours."

"Stoker did," I reminded him.

"But Stoker is—" He broke off, his eyes rolling white as he cast a quick look at his elder brother.

"Go on," Stoker instructed softly. "Say it."

He bit at his lip. "I was merely going to say that Stoker is different," he said to me. "And I am not meant to be here talking about me," he went on, gaining in confidence a little. "I am meant to be talking to you." He turned to his brother. "His lordship wishes to see you. And if you will not see him, he requests that you will at least do him the courtesy of responding to the correspondence sent by the family solicitors."

Stoker roused himself a little. "I have more interest in contracting boils upon my backside than having any conversation with Tiberius."

The vicar goggled at this but bravely carried on. "Stoker, you cannot just—"

"Yes, I can," Stoker said quietly. He gave a sigh. "Merry, you're a good lad. Bloody rude to Miss Speedwell, but you have apologized like a gentleman and if she can overlook it, I will too. Tiberius ought not to have sent you to be his errand boy. If he wants to talk to me, he can come himself. Otherwise, leave it be."

There was no anger in his words, but there was also no mistaking the steel girding them. He would not be moved, and the younger Templeton-Vane let his shoulders slump in defeat. Stoker's eyes shone with malicious mischief.

"How did Tiberius get you to do this? Did you lose a coin toss?"

Merryweather flushed again and tugged at his dog collar. "We cut cards."

"And I'll bloody well bet he stacked the deck," Stoker said amiably. "Haven't you ever heard that you mustn't gamble with another Templeton-Vane? They have the devil's own luck because Old Nick always takes care of his own. He takes care of Tiberius more than most."

The young parson smiled, then turned to me. "I really am most terribly sorry. Rupert told us that Stoker had called on him in chambers with a friend, a lady. And from his description of you, I am afraid his lordship rather decided to believe the worst."

"The worst?"

He darted a nervous glance at his elder brother but went on. "That you are Stoker's . . . well, in Biblical terms, his concubine. His lordship worried that perhaps there might be an entanglement."

I laughed but Stoker shot me a glowering look that might have quelled an army. "Miss Speedwell is no man's concubine," he told his brother severely. "In fact, she takes a decidedly modern view of relations—"

"Stoker," I cut in with a warning tone. "Don't. You will only startle him and clearly he has delicate nerves." I turned back to his brother. "You have delivered your message and now you have seen me, which I suspect was a twin purpose in coming here. Please assure his lordship that I am not enjoying the fruits of connubial bliss with Stoker, nor should he expect a claim upon his fortune because I am in an indelicate condition."

Merryweather's mouth opened and closed several times in rapid succession.

"Stoker, I think he has forgot how to make words again."

Stoker shrugged. "Here is one for him to remember: 'good-bye.'" He strode to his brother, but before he could raise a hand, the younger Templeton-Vane bolted from his chair, calling a swift farewell as he showed himself out.

Stoker followed to make certain he was gone but showed little inclination to continue discussion with me. He went immediately to his Bactrian, immersing himself in his work. It was merely a delay. We would have to discuss what had just happened with his brother—and the revelation I had just discovered from a very telling slip of Stoker's tongue. But I could wait.

CHAPTER

12

A short time after young Merryweather's departure, Lady Wellingtonia appeared at the Belvedere, bringing with her the late-afternoon post—a selection of envelopes and parcels that she had ordered the hall boy to carry. Young George nearly staggered under the weight of one of the boxes, and Stoker removed himself from his Bactrian long enough to resume his shirt and liberate the boy from his burden. The youth tugged his forelock to Lady Wellie and hurried back to the main house as Stoker unpacked the parcel.

Lady Wellie gave him a long look of appreciation, making a noise in the back of her throat very like a growl. "That *is* a splendid-looking man," she said to me sotto voce. "If only I had met him when I was sixty . . ." She let her voice trail off suggestively.

I could imagine. "It was very kind of you to walk down with the post."

She waved a hand. "Kindness has nothing to do with it. I am curious to see the old place again. I haven't been here since my coming-out ball in 'thirty-three. What a night that was!"

She looked about, clearly in a nostalgic mood. She lifted her walking stick to indicate the upper gallery. "Is there still a camp bed up in the snug? I misplaced my virtue up there. Dashing fellow he was, a Scotsman, in full clan regalia. I do like a kilt," she added fondly.

Stoker, who was busy tearing the wrappings off his parcel like a child on Christmas morn, gave a shout. "They've come!" he crowed, pointing to a glass case with all the tenderness of a father tending his newborn babe. He bent over the case, slowly lowering in the remains of a desiccated rabbit.

"Who has come?" I asked as I moved near. Lady Wellie wandered off, taking a turn with her memories as she poked and prodded the various artifacts, muttering to herself.

Stoker gave a sigh of pure pleasure. "It is my colony of *Dermestes maculatus.*" A quick look at the case revealed a swarm of dark beetles happily tending to the unfortunate rabbit.

"Dermestid beetles? Whyever are you letting them dine upon a common rabbit?"

"I am experimenting. Some specimens are more valuable for the skeleton than the hide, and boiling them down to the bones makes an awful stench. So, when Huxley caught this unfortunate fellow, I left him to dry out and ordered a colony of these industrious little dermestids. If I leave these little lads to do their work, they will strip it all, clean as a new pin."

"How deliciously revolting," I said mildly.

He reared back, his expression hurt. "It is not. It is nature, red in tooth and claw," he rebuked. "They're very tidy, you know—like provincial housewives."

He bent to watching them again as they studiously began the task of stripping the dry flesh from the bones of the rabbit, and I settled to the far less gruesome chore of sorting the post while Lady Wellie moved to the display cabinet nearest the desk.

She picked up a specimen at random and turned it over, peering intently. "What is this?"

"A coprolite. Fossilized excrement," I replied helpfully. She made a moue of distaste, replacing the coprolite as I slit open a parcel. It was smaller than Stoker's beloved dermestids, a pasteboard box just large enough to hold a long iron key.

"What is that?" Lady Wellie asked, looking over my shoulder. I removed the key from its wrapping of cotton wool, hoping to find a note.

"I cannot say," I told her. "There is no letter to accompany it. Curious design, isn't it?" The key was black and as long as a man's palm. The end of it was heavily filigreed in an intricate design.

I gave a sudden sharp intake of breath, reaching for a magnifying glass.

"What do you see?" Lady Wellie demanded. I did not answer for a long moment as I scrutinized the elaborate design. At first glance it appeared to be leaves, but the longer I looked at the vine, a pattern began to emerge. It was a series of figures, male and female—some of them *aggressively* male and female—engaged in a number of spectacularly lewd acts.

I handed Lady Wellie the key and the magnifying glass. She subjected it to a thorough examination, grunting once or twice before handing them back. "Reminds me of a fellow I knew in Milan once—a contortionist. He had the most remarkable thighs." Her eyes were dreamy.

I looked over the box and wrappings once more, but there were no clues as to the identity of the sender or the purpose of the key. I returned to the key itself, making out a set of initials engraved upon the length of it. "E.G.," I murmured. "What the devil does that mean?"

Lady Wellie blinked. "It's the Elysian Grotto, of course," she said, with all the patience once might show to a moderately stupid child.

"The Elysian Grotto? What is that?"

"Oh, this younger generation," she lamented. "Your youth really is quite wasted upon you. Have you, my gentle child, ever heard of the Hellfire Club of Sir Francis Dashwood?"

"Vaguely."

"Then I will remedy the defects in your education. Some hundred years before I was born, Sir Francis Dashwood, one of society's scape-graces with more money than taste, established a club for organized debauchery. He and his fellow clubmen used to cavort there with prosti-tutes, dabbling in the occult and other mildly fiendish practices."

I raised a brow, but she waved her hand. "It sounds much worse than it was, I am told. Lots of chanting and conjuring devils but nothing more exciting happened than a few harmless orgies and perhaps the odd social disease. There were a number of copycat clubs that sprang up, and one group were the Elysian Grottoes. Where the Hellfire members devoted themselves to dark arts, the Elysians were all about pleasure. They sought to replicate the bowers of the Hedonists, giving themselves up to luxury and gratification. They built a series of grottoes around the country so they could disport themselves in comfort."

I turned the key over in my hand. "How many were there?"

Lady Wellie shrugged. "Half a dozen? No one knows. They did not last very long. As it happens, grottoes are rather uncomfortable places to pursue pleasure—terribly damp, you know. I think the members all came down with rheumatisms. Most of the grottoes were filled in or redecorated for more mundane purposes. I doubt any survive now, ex-cept perhaps the one at Littledown."

My heart gave a lurch. "Littledown? You mean Miles Ramsforth's estate?"

She nodded. "That's the one. Curious coincidence, that we were just speaking of him and now someone has sent you this key."

"'Curious' is not the word," I replied grimly.

"We are *not* using that key to break into Littledown," Stoker said, folding his arms over his chest.

I had managed to persuade Lady Wellie that I knew nothing whatsoever about the origins of the key—not a difficult task since I was mystified as to who had sent it and why—and with a great deal of careful maneuvering, finally gotten her out the door. I bolted it behind her to afford us some privacy as I coaxed Stoker away from his dermestids and told him of my plan.

"Of course we are," I said roundly. "We must. What else would we do with the key? We want to see the place where Artemisia died, and if we wait for the Ramsforth solicitors to reply to Ottilie's request to let us in, we might be cooling our heels for days. This is our way in *now*."

"Artemisia died *inside* Littledown, in the master bedchamber," he reminded me. "This Elysian Grotto is a very different sort of place."

"I am sure that it is," I said soothingly, "but it gets us far closer to Littledown than we have yet managed. We can have a good look around while we are there, perhaps turn up a clue to the real murderer."

"And perhaps get ourselves killed for our trouble," he countered, his expression implacable. "Did it never occur to you to wonder at this key just appearing out of the blue? For God's sake, Veronica, you have a substantial intellect. Perhaps you could trouble yourself to use it occasionally. This could very well be bait to lure us out there for some nefarious purpose. We have already been threatened once, and we did not heed it. Instead we plunged into the very heart of this investigation, asking questions of those who were closest to Artemisia. Did you think that would go unnoticed? It hasn't. This is no gift from a devoted admirer, you daft woman. This is a trap." I wondered how much damage his dermestids could do if I turned them loose upon his bed.

"It cannot be a trap if we anticipate that it is one," I said coolly. "We will simply go with certain precautions."

He thrust his hands into his hair, leaving the long black locks in far greater disarray than usual. "Veronica. I will speak slowly and distinctly so that even you may understand. I am not taking you out to Littledown to investigate the Elysian Grotto."

I moved forward so that I stood toe to toe with him. His superior inches meant that I had to tip my head back to look him in the eye, but I did so, giving as good as I got. "I am going to Littledown with or without you."

"You cannot go without the key," he said, reaching for me.

I thrust the key into the depths of my décolletage. "Very well. Come and get it."

He hesitated, his fingertips just brushing the tops of my breasts. I caught my breath and held his gaze, daring him to move.

"Bloody bollocking hell," he said, dropping his hand.

The trip to Littledown was accomplished in silence. Stoker was seething with barely suppressed irritation, and I was a trifle too smug to smother my satisfaction entirely. I might have teased him about his reluctance to explore my bodice in the interests of retrieving the key, but one had to be careful in taunting wolves, I decided. One never knew when they might snap those sharp teeth a little too fiercely. I had changed into my butterfly-hunting clothes, a peculiar and eminently suitable ensemble of my own design. I donned a clean shirtwaist and a pair of slim trousers, tucking them securely into flat, sturdy boots laced neatly up the front. Over it all I buttoned a fitted jacket and a long skirt with concealed slits and a clever arrangement of buttons that permitted me to drape the garment according to my activities. I had not designed a configuration for pursuing murderers, but I suspected the one I used for stalking butterflies would prove adequate. I was careful to secure the key in my pocket without mentioning to Stoker where I had put it. He might cavil at thrusting his hands into my bodice, but I was certain he would not scruple to reach into my pocket should necessity demand.

The estate was in a curious little corner of Surrey, close to the capital, but, as Sir Hugo had explained, situated in such a state of rural solitude that it might have been in the middle of Dartmoor. Stoker, with his unerring sense of direction and love of maps, had memorized the route from the station, navigating us on foot through various byways and country lanes until I began to think we were the last two people on earth. The soft whispering clicks of the crickets were punctuated by the distinctive rusty screech of a barn owl, and somewhere in the distance a fox barked. Tendrils of fog curled about our feet as we moved, shifting, ghostly fingers that seemed to point the way to Littledown. The gates of the estate were, as we had expected, closed and locked, but this was no deterrent.

Without discussion, Stoker and I scaled the stone wall of the perimeter, each using our particular skills. His height and impressive musculature lent to a quick vault and swing up to the top, while my flexibility and slighter frame dictated a swift climb, using the cracks in the mortar and irregularities in the stone as hand- and footholds. Once atop the wall, Stoker dropped down lightly, reaching up to catch me as I launched myself. That was the true measure of his character; even at the height of his irritation he would never let me fall.

Together we crossed the broad expanse of the lawns, once manicured and now left to grow wild, the weeds choking out the pretty grass and blanketing the pond with a thick layer of scum. It was the dark of the moon, and only the pale glow of starlight illuminated our way, giving a shimmering, spectral glow to the stone façade of the house softened by the rising wisps of mist. It was an unremarkable place, built in the style of Queen Anne, but someone had loved it once. I thought of Ottilie Ramsforth, who could not bear to stay in this house, and I thought too of Miles Ramsforth, who would die if we were not successful.

I reached for Stoker's hand. "I know," he said, gripping mine in return. He gave a gusty sigh. "You were right. We have to do this."

He led the way, deducing the grotto would be at some remove from the house itself, tucked discreetly out of sight but not so far the guests would find it difficult to reach. We made a slow circle around the estate until we came to a gate. Stoker dropped my hand, casting around to make certain we were alone. There was no sign of the promised watchman; nothing broke the solemn silence of the night save a soft, sighing breeze that stirred the leaves and bent the tops of the weeds, scattering patches of fog in its wake.

Content we were alone, Stoker struck a match and held it over the lock. I retrieved the key and fitted it carefully. It turned slowly, with a moan of protest. It had been months since anyone had used the gate, I realized. But whoever had been there last had left a lantern just inside, and Stoker touched the match to the wick. A warm glow of amber light filled the small rock room.

"It is an antechamber," he said. The narrow room tightened to a passage above which an inscription had been chiseled into the rock. "*Ingredi, del voluptatis causa,*" he read aloud.

"An invitation to pleasure," I replied. "How appropriate."

He did not laugh. Instead he turned and fixed me with a stern look. "I am going first. I let you talk your way around me earlier, but not this time. If anything happens, you run, do you hear me? You run and you get yourself to safety."

"Absolutely not—" I began.

He leaned close, his face a scant inch from mine. "I am not bargaining with you, Veronica. For once, do as I ask. Promise me."

"Very well. I promise," I said, crossing my fingers behind my back.

He did not look convinced, but he went, turning sideways to maneuver through the narrow rock passage. I followed, walking straight, my shoulders just brushing the stone walls. It was a short distance, just enough to make one feel quite removed from the outside world, but the path descended sharply, drawing us deeper and deeper into the earth. The passage debouched into a larger room; I could not see past Stoker, but I could hear the sudden echo of a much more spacious chamber. He paused a moment, raising his lantern high, and we surveyed our surroundings.

It was empty, at least of villains. No miscreant lay in wait for us, no would-be killer set upon us. Instead, we found ourselves in a veritable bower of pleasure.

The chamber was a natural cave, spacious and high ceilinged, and around the sides, a series of low alcoves had been carved out of the rock into makeshift divans. The purpose was not difficult to discern, but even if it had been, the decoration would have been eloquent. Everywhere one looked there were plinths and shelves devoted to the display of art—but this was no ordinary collection.

Stoker knelt to light another lamp, and as he held it aloft I realized it was a magic lantern, the sort designed to use the light to throw shapes upon the wall, entertainment via shadow pictures, although I had never before seen one quite like this. The heat of the flame caused the pictures to spin, casting silhouettes of copulating couples around us. Upon closer inspection, I realized the images were not limited to couples. Instead they featured an array of amorous engagements, each more explicit and unlikely than the last. Stoker gaped at the images as I turned to the rest of the decorations.

"Good heavens! I have never seen so many penises in one place," I blurted, heading directly for the nearest shelf. I lifted one, a smooth, thick affair made of glass, swirled and striped like a fancy sweet. "Venetian, I should guess," I said.

"No doubt," Stoker remarked in a faint voice. His attention seemed to be captured by a significantly larger apparatus fashioned of wood and leather.

"What do you think?" I asked curiously. "The lettering on the handle seems Chinese. Oh, and this one is clearly from Zanzibar. A very interesting assemblage of phalluses," I observed. "Quite a curious collection from a sociological perspective."

"There is no sociology here," Stoker corrected, his voice still tight. "These are not phalluses—at least not the sort meant for study."

I blinked at him. "Whatever do you mean?"

He was blushing furiously. "They are . . . Oh God, I can't even say the word."

"What word?"

"Dil— No, I can't. I can tell you in Greek. These are *olisboi*. Or if you prefer, in Spanish, *consoladores*."

"Consolers? But how could they console . . . oh. Oh!" I peered at the collection in renewed interest. "So they are not for study or ceremonial use but for practical application. How very intriguing." I ran a finger down the glass specimen. "Delightfully smooth, although it is too cold to be inviting. I imagine one could warm it up in hot water first—or perhaps some heated oil just to make it nicely slippy. Stoker, are you quite well? You were blushing like a queen of the May a moment ago and now you've gone white."

"I was just pondering the peregrinations of my life and wondering how I came to be here. With you. And this," he said, nodding towards the back of the room, where stood a larger-than-life-sized statue of a doubly endowed Pan servicing a pair of eager young women simultaneously.

"He is going to get a cramp doing it that way," I observed. I trailed around the chamber, exploring the collection. In addition to the phalluses of every description and material, there was a considerable compilation of pornography and some rather fine engravings of Amazonian warriors having their way with a group of captive youths. The walls were hung with velvet draperies and tapestries that upon first glance looked like Gobelins, until one realized they were comprehensively explicit.

In the center of the room stood a curious bit of furniture, like nothing I had ever seen before. Upholstered in black taffeta, the piece had an odd arrangement of arms and legs, and Stoker tossed it no more than a casual glance before replying when I asked what it might be.

"That is a *siège d'amour.*"

"A seat of love? It is a chair designed to facilitate coitus?" I murmured. "Most ingenious and very comfortable, I should think."

I settled myself onto the *siège*, gripping the arms. "Oh, there are stirrups. How clever." I raised one booted leg, but Stoker made a strangled noise somewhere between a growl and a groan.

"Veronica. For the love of all that is holy and good, get *down*," he said, in a low, tight voice unlike any I had ever heard from him before.

I slipped off the *siège*. "Quite right. We are meant to be looking for clues." We applied ourselves to searching the chamber and made quick work of it, turning over every obscene statue and peering behind every lurid tapestry. The drapery behind the statue of Pan concealed a gate of sorts, a grillwork door like the one at the front of the grotto. I summoned Stoker to try the key, but it did not budge.

He considered the position of the door. "No doubt this leads to a passage connecting the grotto to the house."

"Another entrance? To what purpose?"

He shrugged. "To spare the blushes of the host, one imagines. I suspect all the members have a key to the gate we used while this entrance is reserved solely for the club's founder. It would provide a bit of discretion, and some security. If he hired professional entertainers of this sort," he said arching a brow towards one of the silhouettes disporting itself on the wall, "he mightn't want them to have access to the house itself. And a lock on the door is also a precaution against Ottilie Ramsforth discovering his hobby."

"Do you really think she was unaware of what he got up to down here?"

"There is no institution like marriage to make a person blind," he said dryly. He turned away then to continue searching the grotto.

At length, I made my way back to the *siège*, paying particular attention to the bottom of the thing. I knocked against it, a hollow echo the reward for my efforts. I picked up the sturdiest phallus I could find and began to whack energetically at the base.

"Veronica," Stoker said in a grim tone, "in the name of seven hells, what are you doing? I asked you to leave that thing alone."

"And miss a clue?" I replied with a grin. I planted my feet and gave one final blow with the phallus, causing a hidden drawer in the base to spring open, bowling me backwards onto my bottom. I sat up to find Stoker examining the drawer and holding the remains of a lock in his hand.

"You might have let me pick the lock," Stoker remarked, but he was good enough to help me up. "Hello," he said suddenly. "What's this?"

When the drawer had flown open, a book had dropped out, and Stoker retrieved it. It was bound in black morocco figured in silver. The front cover bore a filigree design to match the key, and beneath it were scrolled the words "Elysian Grotto." Stoker flipped open the cover to a random page. It was a list of names, each with a corresponding date and a list of activities.

"It is a ledger," I said, stretching forward to look, gripping his arm in excitement. "A list of visitors and members of the Elysian Grottoes and what sort of mischief they got up to when they were here."

Stoker gave a soundless whistle. "A very dangerous book," he observed. "If this fell into the wrong hands, marriages could be wrecked, reputations ruined. It isn't just men in here," he added, pointing to a woman's signature.

I shook my head. "The date is forty years past. I hardly think anyone would care."

He gestured to the top of the page. "That entertainment was presided over by Desmond Ramsforth, Miles' father, I would wager."

"Find more recent entries," I urged.

He fanned the pages, moving further into the book. "Five years ago," he said. "Miles presiding, and what ho! Sir Frederick Havelock was a guest."

Impatient, I reached out and took the book, flipping forward. The more recent entries were less impressive. Whereas in his father's time, the club had sported viscounts and barons and the occasional earl, under Miles' primacy, it had seldom entertained anything grander than a knight, and precious few of those. The gatherings boasted fewer people than in his father's day, and it seemed likely the place had been more a curiosity used for Miles' private seductions than any proper orgiastic activity.

"Aha!" I exclaimed. "Artemisia was here, a year ago. And shortly before that, Julian Gilchrist. Curious that she did not participate in the public rituals, it seems," I observed. "It appears she only came here privately with Miles while Gilchrist was entertained with a series of paid companions. The notation for the sums is marked next to the name of each girl hired for the night along with what she was willing to do for the money. This young woman seems to have been quite accommodating," I mused as I ran down the list of her lurid accomplishments.

But Stoker was not listening. His gaze was fixed upon the page in an expression of stupefaction.

"Stoker, you've gone white as a virgin's nightgown. What is it?"

He did not reply. He merely pointed to a name I had not noticed.

"'The Honourable Tiberius Templeton-Vane,'" I read aloud. I rocked back. "But that isn't—"

"Oh, but it is," he said with a grim smile. "The newly minted Viscount Templeton-Vane. My eldest brother."

CHAPTER

13

S toker slammed the ledger shut. "I need some air."

He strode back the way we had come and it was left to me to blow out the magic lantern and follow. I did not press him. There would be plenty of time to scrutinize the ledger at our leisure once we were back at the Belvedere. Whatever implications the viscount's name raised, Stoker would require a little time to come to grips with them.

He locked the door behind us and pocketed the key carefully, giving a quick nod as I made a gesture towards the main house. He had a hunter's instinct for silence, and my years of pursuing butterflies had taught me to move without detection. We crept towards the darkened dwelling, approaching a wide garden door that most likely led to a dining room or drawing room. The windows on either side must have provided an outlook upon a pretty vista down to the pond in happier days, but they were shuttered now, the house looking blindly upon its terrace and gardens. Stoker paused a moment outside the door, weighing our options, but I had already anticipated him.

"Give me the packet of honeycomb," I instructed.

"How do you know I am carrying honeycomb?"

"You are *always* carrying honeycomb."

"This is a peculiar time for a nibble," he protested. But he handed it over without hesitation. It was very nearly empty, and I upended it, scattering the last of the sweet, sticky crumbs over the stone flags of the terrace. I unfolded the paper twist carefully and held up the side that still bore traces of the candy.

"Lick," I ordered.

Guessing what I meant to do, he complied, putting his tongue to the sheet of paper until the entire surface was gummy. With infinite care, I moved to position the paper on the glass of the garden door.

"Over one pane," he instructed softly. "The lock would be a little higher."

I did as he bade, pressing the paper to the glass until it stuck nicely. I stepped back and nodded to Stoker who handed me the ledger. He stripped off his coat, wrapping it about his hand. One quick blow and it was done. The glass broke silently, the pieces held fast by the sticky paper. I slowly pulled it free and was about to place it on the ground when Stoker stopped me.

"An animal might step on it and be harmed. 'Tis sticky as glue and full of glass," he reminded me as he took the piece of paper with its glittering shards. He turned it over and weighted the thing with a rock, only then putting his arm through the hole we had made to work the lock. It proved more difficult than we expected, and Stoker had recourse to use one of his blades before he was able to flick it open and ease the door wide. He paused to replace his knife and slip his arms back into his coat. Those few seconds were our salvation. I am not certain what we heard first—the slavering growl of the mastiff or the sleepy shouts of the watchman roused from his slumbers. The sudden cacophony rent the night, and Stoker reared back, slamming the door as we took to our heels.

We fled, across the terrace and around the pond. The shutting of the door bought us only a few seconds, for no sooner had we gained the far side of the pond than the door was flung back on its hinges and the hound burst forth. Behind it came a volley of shots, shattering stone from the edge of the terrace wall as we darted and dodged. I looked back only once to see an elderly fellow silhouetted in the doorway, the white of his nightshirt and cap stark against the dark shadows of the house. He was content to stand there, blasting away on his shotgun and hurling abuse, but his dog was not so reticent. The creature tore after us, baying with murderous intent. The soft thud of his paws was gaining on us, each stride of his powerful legs narrowing the distance between us.

"Stoker!" I panted. "We cannot outrun him!"

"No," he returned, reaching into his pocket. "But we can slow him down."

"For God's sake, you aren't going to hurt him?" I managed between breaths. I ought to have known better. For all his facility with dead animals, he was endlessly sentimental about living ones. He drew from his pocket a small parcel tied with string and flung it behind him. It struck the dog full on the snout, bursting open and spilling its bloody contents.

"What was that?"

"Calf's liver," he said, reaching for my hand as he grinned into the darkness. I marveled at his forethought. Ottilie Ramsforth had mentioned a dog, and Stoker had taken it upon himself to come armed with a meaty little distraction.

I blessed him for it as we continued to run, but I quickly realized that a calf's liver was not diversion enough for so enormous a dog. He devoured it swiftly and set off again in pursuit, tracking us through the gathering fog. Stoker, whose long strides could have easily outpaced me, refused to leave me behind and instead matched his speed to mine. The dog gained upon us, snarling as he snapped at our heels. With a single vault, Stoker was atop the wall, putting out his hands for mine. At a dead run I planted the sole of my boot on the wall, launching myself upwards as I raised my hands to grasp his.

Too late, I realized my mistake and the ledger, unwieldy and slippery, slid from my grip, tumbling to the ground.

"No!" I cried, turning to go after it, but Stoker kept a subduing arm tight about my waist. The mastiff stood upon his hind legs, his massive jaws very nearly but not quite reaching the toes of our boots as we stood atop the wall.

"The ledger is gone," I protested. "I dropped it."

"Then it will have to stay gone," Stoker said, nodding towards the direction we had come. A lantern glowed through the mist. The watchman had come after us, guided by the sound of the dog's vicious barking.

I eyed the distance to the ground. I could just see where the ledger had come to rest. The mastiff stood between me and it, but I was determined. I turned to fling myself just as another shot rang out, this one chipping the wall at Stoker's feet.

"Bloody hell," he muttered. With one graceful motion he swung me up into his arms and jumped to the lane side of the wall, landing us in a tussock of long grass. I put my hands to his chest and pushed hard.

"Why the devil did you do that?" I demanded. "I was about to retrieve the ledger!"

"I know," he said coldly as he rolled to his side and gave a great wheeze. "My God, the next time do try not to land on my stomach. I think I am going to disgrace myself."

I opened my mouth, preparing to deliver a scathing retort, but with a great effort he pushed himself to his feet, pulling me up. "Not now, Veronica. You may abuse me at your leisure, but right now we need to get away."

From the other side of the wall I could hear the dog, his howls turned to whimpers of frustration now, and the watchman, calling all varieties of insult down upon the heads of miscreants and villains who would break the peace of an old man's slumbers. He discharged the shotgun again for good measure, and I threw up my hands, admitting defeat. We might have hid for awhile until the old fellow returned to his bed, but it was just as likely he would leave the dog running loose or that he would find the ledger.

"Come along," Stoker ordered. He walked a few steps then turned, waiting, fog swirling about his legs. I sighed and swallowed my defeat. I might deplore the loss of the ledger, but Stoker would never admonish me for it. Together we walked down the lane and into the safety of the covering darkness.

W e reached Bishop's Folly and let ourselves in through the garden gate, taking the long path through the grounds so as not to disturb anyone in the main house. By silent accord we made for the Belvedere. Stoker would want a drink, and I did not want him to imbibe alone. The lamp at the door of the Belvedere had not been lit, and as we made our way in, I tripped over something on the threshold.

"What is it?" Stoker demanded, his tone irritable.

"A parcel of some sort. Perhaps our anonymous benefactor has struck again," I remarked lightly. I would not taunt him over the fact that the sender of the key had most certainly *not* attacked us or locked us in and left us for dead, but I would definitely think it.

I picked up the small parcel and carried it inside while Stoker made directly for the snug, poking up the fire and pouring out two hefty measures of whiskey.

I eyed the glass. "If you're looking to get drunk quickly, you ought to have got the aguardiente instead of the whiskey. This is going to be a waste of good single malt."

"There is no such thing as a waste of good single malt," he told me, swallowing his in a single draft. He poured another measure for himself while I plucked the strings on the little parcel. It was wrapped in plain brown paper and addressed in a nondescript hand. There was no postmark, so it had been delivered by messenger, I realized as I pulled away the paper. Inside was a simple pasteboard box and inside that was a nest of cotton wool.

"I wonder what it could be," I said as I burrowed into the fluffy cotton wool.

"Perhaps a jewel from an anonymous admirer," Stoker said nastily.

I pulled away the last of the cotton wool and stared into the box.

"What?" Stoker demanded after a long moment. "Not a jewel?"

"Not exactly," I said, steeling myself to touch the object inside.

"What, then?" he said, his irritation clearly rising. He was in no mood for games, so I would give him none.

I reached in and pulled out the object, tossing it to him in a smooth arc. "It is an eyeball."

To his credit, Stoker caught the eye without crushing it in his surprise. He held it cradled in his palm as he bent to the light. "It is not human," he said quickly.

"Any fool could see that. It is far too large and the pupil is elongated. One of the ruminants, I should think."

"A sheep, to be precise," Stoker informed me. "Of the most common domestic variety. *Ovis aries.* The sort you would see in any butcher's shop between here and the Hebrides. But why?"

"It is another threat. The meaning should be obvious, and if it were not, here is a note," I said, pulling a scrap of paper from the parcel. In block capitals were the words

KEEP OUT OF THIS OR YOU'RE EYE IS NEXT

I peered closely at the letters. "They seem to be in the same hand as the first note. Something peculiar about the letter *E*."

Stoker curled his lip. "We need to be menaced by a better class of criminal. This one cannot spell."

"Or wants us to believe he cannot," I countered. "And clearly it is someone who does not know us well, or he would never think we could be unhinged by an eyeball. There are whole jars of the bloody things about the place," I said with a wave of the arm. Stoker did keep a frankly irrational number of body parts stashed in glass bottles and cases. I was forever opening a drawer to find a disembodied eye staring up at me.

I took up my glass and settled into the chair next to Stoker while he rolled the eyeball in his fingers. "It is fresh," he told me. "If it were not, it would be soft. This one is quite firm and bounces back a bit when you press it. Like a hothouse grape."

"So our miscreant is a shepherd or farmer?" I hazarded.

Stoker shook his head. "I think not. Any butcher would have a fresh sheep's head lying about. It would be the work of seconds to get an eye out—in fact, I rather think this *was* the work of seconds. It's not been taken out neatly as a surgeon or butcher would do it. It has been gouged quite ham-fistedly. See the jagged end of the optical nerve?" He gestured to an uneven bit of white matter hanging from the back.

"Stoker, just because an eyeball does not cause me to swoon and reach for my vinaigrette does not mean I want to examine it whilst I am trying to enjoy my drink," I told him.

"Fair enough." He dropped the eyeball back into the box, turning his attention to the note and wrappings. "No postmark, no watermarks, nothing significant in any way save the resemblance to the note last night. It could be anyone."

"Even your brother," I said, taking a deep draft of whiskey and holding it on my tongue. When I swallowed, it burned all the way to my stomach, lighting my chest with the fire of its peaty warmth.

"Even Tiberius," he agreed.

"You surprise me. I thought you would fight me tooth and claw," I told him.

He shrugged. "What would be the use? His name is in the ledger. At the very least he knows something about the Elysian Grotto. At the worst—" He did not finish the statement. The possibility that Tiberius

Templeton-Vane might be somehow implicated in the murder we were investigating was too ghastly to contemplate.

"What are the viscount's interests?" I asked casually. "Is he a patron of the arts?"

"Theater," Stoker said in a distracted voice. "He does not care much for painting and such. He prefers performance. Why?"

"No matter. It just occurred to me that the players most closely involved with this little drama are artists and their patrons. We might exclude his lordship from suspicion if he does not frequent the Havelock House set."

His only reply was a noncommittal sort of grunt, what Keats might well have called a "little noiseless noise." His business with the wrappings complete, Stoker returned to his whiskey. I waited until he was well into his third glass before broaching a necessary subject.

"It was most likely someone at Havelock House who sent us this pretty present," I said in a decidedly neutral tone with a nod towards the eyeball. Stoker said nothing and I went on. "Naturally, the best way to prove that would be to visit Havelock House again and have a good nose around. Of course, it would be best to have a *reason* for our presence."

Stoker gave a gusty sigh and drained his drink. "Fine. I will take my bloody clothes off and pose for Emma Talbot whilst you play detective."

I saluted him with my whiskey. "I have no doubt you will make a fine Perseus," I said with mock solemnity. "I cannot wait to see your pretty winged sandals."

In one fluid motion he swept up the eyeball and threw it at me.

S toker was a man of his word. He rose early to look in on his sweet little dermestid beetles and scrawled a note to Emma Talbot telling her he would present himself for the purpose of being sketched. Before we could make our way to Havelock House, we received a summons. In few words, on crested paper, in an imperious hand. Princess Louise wanted a report on our progress and we were to call upon her at Kensington Palace. She provided directions to her apartments within the palace and specified that we were to be there at eleven sharp.

Stoker was irritated beyond measure. Having made up his mind to pose for Miss Talbot, he wanted nothing more than to get on with the business. He adopted an air of noble suffering, like a French aristocrat climbing into a tumbril, but I was rather more pleased. Nothing put me more on my mettle than being challenged, and Her Royal Highness had rubbed me up the wrong way.

The palace was set behind tall and imposing gilded gates, but its charms were of the homely, redbrick variety. The inner court was quite small, and we followed the directions without difficulty, presenting ourselves at the door as instructed.

A very superior butler admitted us, but before we could be announced, the princess herself appeared. "I am glad to see you count punctuality among your virtues," was her greeting. She was pale, with violet shadows under her eyes, and her movements seemed taut, as if only the force of her will kept her in a state of composure.

Before either of us could respond, a gentleman dressed in a rather ill-fitting expensive town suit descended the stairs, giving us a half-smile as if trying to place us.

"Oh, hullo, Loosy. Friends of yours?" he asked cordially. He was a tall, fair man, with disordered hair and a rather marked air of untidiness despite the costliness of his attire. He seemed perfectly affable, but his shambling ways made him an unlikely fit for the glamorous princess. She might be an artist with all that implied, but I had noted an inclination towards perfect and expensive grooming on her part.

"Lorne," she murmured. She took her husband's arm and made the introductions.

"My dear, this is Miss Veronica Speedwell and Mr. Revelstoke Templeton-Vane, son of Viscount Templeton-Vane. Miss Speedwell, Mr. Templeton-Vane, my husband, the Marquess of Lorne."

The marquess acknowledged my nod but thrust his hand towards Stoker. "One of old Reginald T-V's boys, are you? Met him several times in the Lords when my father was speaking. Always falling asleep during the debates. Frightfully loud snore."

"Indeed," Stoker returned amiably.

"I say," Lorne went on, "you're not the vicar, are you?"

"No, my lord, that is my younger brother, Merryweather."

The marquess gave a rueful smile. "I remember your father had the devil of a time getting that boy settled. Apparently he likes a little flutter on the horses now and again—and a bit of trouble at cards. I hear the lad's something of a black sheep, but not a patch on his brother, the one who went gallivanting off to—where was it? South America or South Africa? Rotten mess that was," he added. "Which of the sons was that?"

Stoker's smile was feral. "I am afraid I am the blackest of the Templeton-Vane sheep, your lordship."

The marquess's thin, sandy brows shot upwards. "Dear me, how frightfully awkward for you." Another man might have been embarrassed for himself, but I suspected it would take more than a modest social gaffe to upset the son-in-law of the queen.

Princess Louise stepped in to smooth the situation. "Miss Speedwell and Mr. Templeton-Vane are connections of Sir Frederick Havelock's. They have come to see my studio."

"Ah, more art folk! Suppose you knew the girl who lived there, the murdered one," he said. He turned to his wife. "What was her name again? Something quite outlandish."

"Artemisia," she supplied. "No, Miss Speedwell and Mr. Templeton-Vane did not have that pleasure."

"Well, perhaps it's best you didn't know her," he said to us. "Nasty business, murder. Don't like to see you upset," he told his wife gruffly. It was as close as an aristocratic Englishman could come to expressing real emotion, but it was enough for the princess. She pressed his hand.

"Dear Lorne," she said.

The butler came forward on silent feet, handing over his lordship's gloves and hat. "You caught me just as I was going out. I shall be at the club today, and I've a dinner tonight. Will you be around, Loosy?"

"I daresay," the princess replied. He brushed a quick kiss to her cheek, shook hands once more with Stoker, and nodded graciously to me before taking his leave. The princess turned to us as soon as her husband had departed. "Come. The studio is the only really private place here."

Her Royal Highness conducted us down a corridor hung with a selection of pretty watercolors to a locked door. She produced a key from her pocket and led us through a court and a little garden to a freestanding structure that seemed almost entirely made of glass. She unlocked it and lit a gasolier against the gloom of the dark, fogbound morning. The illumination was feeble, but vast expanses of windows indicated that on bright days the room would be flooded with sunlight.

"My studio," she told us. The walls were lined with shelves to hold the various tools of the sculptor's trade, and the room, a large, open space, was populated with shrouded plinths, like so many patient ghosts.

The princess led the way to a particular plinth and reached out to twitch aside the cloth that covered it. It hesitated then fell away, pooling at the feet of a statue of a young woman. She was dressed in a timeless sort of costume, a gracefully draped robe that might have belonged to any society in antiquity. But her pose was not that of a Classical beauty in repose, waiting to be admired. This figure was barely paused in the act of motion, her skirts rippling along the muscles of her thighs, the draperies along her shoulders flung back as she lifted her head, her sightless eyes fixed upon a horizon she would never see. One slim hand held the crook of a shepherdess, and I could well imagine the marble flock waiting to be gathered just out of sight. Her lips were parted and her head cocked ever so slightly, as if she heard a soundless call and had been immured in marble just at the point of responding.

"She is marvelous," I said in perfect sincerity.

"She is Artemisia," the princess replied. "That is why I wanted you to see her. I sculpted that from life, and that is how she was, tall, vigorous, full of vitality and movement. You will hear many stories of her as you investigate. Artists are famous liars," she told us with a thin smile. "But this is the truth of her. You must not forget it."

We were still standing and admiring the statue when the door opened and Ottilie Ramsforth entered.

"Loosy, the butler said you were here—" She broke off, at the sight of Stoker and me, I thought, but she was looking past us to the statue.

She came forward, her eyes alight with emotion. "Loosy! You've finished her. She's marvelous. I could almost imagine she would speak," she said, her voice breaking.

Princess Louise put an arm around her, and they clung together a long moment. Ottilie looked up, giving us a small, sad smile as tears trembled on her lashes.

"I do apologize. I did not mean to be a watering pot," she said. "It is just that seeing her there, looking so lovely and so very alive . . . sometimes I cannot quite believe things have come to this."

She broke down then, weeping on Louise's shoulder, and it was not until Stoker stepped forward with his own enormous red handkerchief that she left off. She gave a timid little laugh.

"Again you have come to my rescue, Mr. Templeton-Vane," she told him, wiping at her eyes. "You are very kind."

As ever, when someone remarked upon his better qualities, Stoker blushed and said nothing. The princess clasped Ottilie's hands. "Better now?"

Ottilie nodded. "Yes, I think so."

"Good," the princess said in a decisive tone. "Because I did not ask you here merely to see the statue. I have asked Miss Speedwell and Mr. Templeton-Vane to deliver a report upon their progress."

"Oh!" Ottilie Ramsforth's face lit with interest. "You have discovered something."

"Not precisely," I said quickly. I had no wish to give her false hope; that would be too cruel. But I could tell her what we knew. "At first, we were inclined to the view that Her Royal Highness was engaged in a bit of wishful thinking, that she did not want Miles Ramsforth to be guilty of Artemisia's murder. We now believe she might be right to trust in his innocence."

Ottilie swayed a little and Stoker leapt to put his hand under her elbow, holding her steady.

"Thank you, Mr. Templeton-Vane," she murmured. "I cannot take this in."

"It is quite true," he told her gently. "Before we even visited Havelock House, we were sent a threatening message."

"A threat!" The princess's eyes went wide. "What sort of threat?"

"A note pinned to the door of our workplace warning us to stay away. Or else," I supplied. "And last night, after we did a bit of investigative work, we were given another."

I withdrew the small box from my pocket and handed it to the princess. "Do not show it to Mrs. Ramsforth," I told her.

She gave me an imperious stare as she opened the box. A single glance inside was all it took. She shrieked, dropping the box and letting the eyeball roll under a table.

Ottilie clutched at Stoker's arm. "What was that?" she asked in a low, trembling voice. "It looked like—"

"Never mind," he said soothingly. "It doesn't matter. Suffice it to say that it came with a promise that mutilation would ensue should we continue our efforts."

Princess Louise made no effort to retrieve the eye, so I crawled under the table in considerable annoyance. I popped it back into its nest and replaced the box in my pocket. The princess was giving me a look of frank dislike, but I did not much mind.

"You might have warned me," she said coldly.

"I thought you were a student of anatomy," I replied. "Most artists are."

She said nothing to this but turned her attention to Stoker. "Is that all?"

"No," he told her. "We have apparently acquired not just an enemy, but a guardian angel of sorts. We were sent a key which we discovered fitted a very particular lock at Littledown." He watched Ottilie closely, and she pulled away, coloring a little.

"The grotto," she whispered.

"You know about it?" I asked.

She groped behind her for a place to sit and perched upon the edge of a plinth, heedless of the white dust marking her black skirts. "Of course. It is part of the history of Littledown, after all. Miles was—*is*," she corrected fiercely, "*is* so proud of the estate. The first Ramsforth was in the Domesday Book, you know. They were always reckless and lucky, the Ramsforths, always throwing the dice and landing on a winner," she said with an indulgent smile. "They have kept that bit of land since the Conquest. At least six different houses have been built there. But the last was Littledown, and Miles loves it so. I cannot tell you what it meant to him, to us, to rebuild it. We brought it back to beauty," she said with pride. "And when Miles discovered the grotto and read up on the history of it, he thought it would be a grand joke of sorts to refurbish it."

"It looks as if it has been a bit more than refurbished," I said gently.

Ottilie colored again. "I think we can have no secrets now, if you have seen the grotto," she said with a tight laugh. "I have already told you that childbearing was not easy for me." She flicked a glance to Louise who was standing stiffly to the side. "You know, my dear, the heartbreak of that kind of failure."

Louise said nothing, but her eyes were avid. She swallowed hard and gave a sharp nod. Ottilie reached out and curled her fingers around Louise's hand. "Yes, you know. Only a woman who wants desperately to give her husband a child and cannot could understand." She gave Louise's hand a final squeeze and released it. "The doctors told Miles after my last failure that it was too dangerous to try again. We should have to keep separate bedchambers for the rest of our marriage." She paused, as if picking her way through a patch of nettles. "I wanted him to be happy. I thought if he had the entertainments at the grotto to keep him diverted, he would not mind so much. And I was right. It was a bit of flummery, nothing more. He was such a boy about his collection," she said with an indulgent smile. "He thought it all so shockingly naughty. And I saw no harm in it, not really. The women who came were willing and paid well. The men . . . I do not know what prompted them, but I can guess. They were like Miles, in search of some new diversion. And they found it in the grotto."

"There were quite a few of them over the years," I commented.

Ottilie gave me a curious look. "How do you know that?"

"Because we found a ledger," Stoker told her. "A sort of guest book your husband kept."

"Unfortunately," I put in smoothly, "we were unable to examine it properly, but the short glimpse we had indicates that Mr. Ramsforth kept careful records of his visitors and their predilections."

Ottilie paled. "Oh, sweet Miles! He couldn't have been so foolish!" She reached again for Louise's hand and gripped it convulsively. "Loosy, what has he done?"

"He has been very stupid indeed," Louise said flatly, her lips thin with distaste. "What a dangerous thing to keep lying about."

"Dangerous indeed," I replied. "It is a rather good motive for letting him hang for Artemisia's murder," I pointed out. "If someone had an entry in the ledger and did not want it revealed . . ." I let my voice trail off, but the rest was clear.

Ottilie gave me a horrified look. "You don't mean that you think Miles was blackmailing someone?"

"It is possible," I began.

"It is not!" she cried, thrusting herself onto her feet. "My husband is many things, Miss Speedwell, but he is no blackmailer. To accuse him of so sordid and grubby a thing—"

"Mrs. Ramsforth, he is currently awaiting his hanging as a murderer," I said brutally. "I hardly think entertaining the possibility that he blackmailed someone is much of a stretch."

"That is enough, Miss Speedwell," the princess said in tones of chilling hauteur. "Where is the ledger now? Surely you did not leave it lying about."

"In point of fact," Stoker said, stepping up manfully, "it has been misplaced."

"Misplaced?" Louise's tone was one of frank disbelief bordering upon rage. "Of all the careless, amateurish—"

"I think Your Royal Highness is forgetting that we *are*, in fact, amateurs," I replied. "The ledger was dropped on the grounds of Littledown."

"And you did not recover it?" she demanded, looking from me to Stoker and back again.

"There was a dog, you see," I began.

She waved an imperious hand in dismissal. "Go. Now."

I shrugged and turned with Stoker to leave. "Wait," Ottilie said, coming forward, her eyes blazing. "When Loosy told me what she asked you to do, I did not know what to think. The very idea that Miles could be free, that this nightmare would at last be ended, was almost more than I could bear. I told you it hurt too much to hope you could prove him innocent. But I am past that now. I want you to do it. I see now what it will mean if he hangs. It isn't just the loss of his life—it is the loss of his reputation. People will think he did this. They will believe the worst of him, that he was a debaucher, a blackmailer, a murderer." Her voice broke upon the last word.

"Mrs. Ramsforth," I began, but she cut in sharply.

"No, we have said quite enough to one another. You will do as Loosy asks and you will prove him innocent. And when you do, I hope you have the grace to apologize for your insinuations."

I looked at the princess, but she said nothing. She merely stood, as cold and unyielding as the statue behind her.

"Very well," I said, inclining my head. "Good day to you both."

CHAPTER

14

S toker did not speak until we were in a cab. "That went splendidly," he said in a cheerful tone.

"I am in no mood," I warned him. Mentioning the loss of the ledger had been a crucial mistake, but it was done, and there was little point in treading old ground. He said nothing more until we alighted at Havelock House where Emma Talbot was waiting impatiently.

"Come! I work best in the morning and it has nearly gone luncheon," she fretted. She propelled him up the stairs to her aerie, calling to me over her shoulder. "Make yourself comfortable, Miss Speedwell. Cherry will see to you."

I roamed about the hall, now cleared of all remnants of the entertainment. After several minutes passed with no sign of Cherry, I realized her absence provided me with the perfect excuse for snooping about. I moved quietly along the ground floor, poking into various large reception rooms. Several were empty, but one was occupied by a group of young ladies intent upon sketching a bowl of pallid fruit. Sir Frederick Havelock, dressed in an artist's smock, was maneuvering himself with the aid of two sticks, making suggestions to alter the grip of a pencil here or the curve of a line there. He caught sight of me and gave a brisk nod.

"No, Miss Bricker, I am afraid that will not do," he told one of his pupils. "You are drawing a pear, not a hippopotamus. Do try to exercise a little more effort."

He left his pupil and made his way to me with a sigh, his progress slow but steady. "Miss Speedwell, what a pleasure! Shall we?" He indicated a small settee by the door and we sat, forced by the diminutive sofa to arrange ourselves thigh to thigh.

"You surprise me, Sir Frederick," I told him. "I did not realize you were able to manage without your chair."

"From time to time. On a good day," he said. "I try to haul myself about during the classes at least and give the little fledglings their money's worth. Poor wretches," he said to me in a low voice. "Their mothers send them to learn the rudiments of ladylike accomplishments, but not a single one of them has any artistic gifts. Their fruit bowls invariably look like compost heaps."

"I am surprised an artist with your substantial gifts bothers to instruct such unpromising pupils," I said.

He gave a mournful lift to his brows. "They may be hopeless, but they pay, Miss Speedwell. Handsomely." He tipped his head, pitching his voice low. "How have you fared in your investigation?"

I shrugged. "We have answers but they have only led to more questions, I am afraid."

His expression was penetrating, and I was conscious of the tremendous vitality of the man. The smell of him was an attractive combination of male flesh and clean linen and the earthy, metallic odors of the pigments he ground for his paints.

"What sort of questions?" he asked, his breath stirring the hair at my temple.

I slanted him a glance and realized he was watching me intently. There was a guardedness in his gaze and a barely suppressed excitement as well. The edges of his nostrils flared and his expression was one of expectancy. I decided then that a direct approach was the most likely to produce results. I gave him a level look.

"The sort that one finds in a place like the Elysian Grotto," I said softly, careful not to raise my voice enough to let his pupils overhear.

His mouth curved into a slow smile. "You have been to the grotto? Then you know what an interesting collection Miles has."

"Most enlightening," I agreed. "And I was deeply interested to find evidence of your presence there."

The smile deepened. "I have not participated actively in the grotto rituals in some years, but yes, I will admit to being an enthusiast once upon a time. Nowadays, one likes to watch."

"I have spoken to Mrs. Ramsforth about the grotto. She was aware of its purpose."

"Of course she was," he said roundly.

"Did she ever join in?"

He gave a quick boom of laughter, causing his pupils to look up sharply. "Back to your canvases, my doves. There is nothing to notice here," he instructed. He turned merry eyes upon me.

"Can you imagine Ottilie joining in those sorts of games?" he asked.

"I cannot," I admitted. "But she was candid about her husband's use for the place."

He shrugged. "Miles is thistledown, my dear Veronica. Blown by the wind in any direction. If he had landed with a different sort of woman, a stronger woman, she might have brought him up to scratch."

"You blame his wife for the man's infidelities?" My voice rose on an incredulous note.

He touched my arm with one gnarled, chiding fingertip, and his tone was tinged with asperity. "You are no child, Veronica. Surely you must know that there are men in this world who will only behave as they are expected to behave, men of such malleable characters that they are no better or worse than the company they keep."

I thought of Stoker, stalwart as stone. "And some who would never be swayed by anyone or anything," I countered.

"Certainly, but Miles is not one of them. He behaved badly with Ottilie because she permitted it. A woman who demanded his fidelity would have earned it."

"It is not that simple," I said.

His mouth twitched in amusement. "Of course it is. I know my sex, child. And there are those among us who will only be as good or as bad as we are expected to be. Ottilie anticipated the worst of him—she abetted it, for God's sake, by tolerating the grotto and everything that went on there. She not only turned a blind eye to his philandering, she befriended the women he bedded!"

"Surely she did not go that far," I protested.

"I watched her do it," he replied. "Over and over again. And as a strategy it has served her well enough. Women might dally with Miles, but if they were friends with Ottilie, they would not bestir themselves to try to take him away. Yes, she is a clever wife, and above all, she is Miles' friend. She knows he loves her in a way he would never love the other women with whom he toyed. Of course, if she had been a different sort of woman, she would have thrown him out bag and baggage and he would have crawled back to her over broken glass. My own Augusta told her that, time and again."

"Did Lady Havelock do that with you?" I asked.

He gave another quick laugh. "Half a dozen times or more. God, the fights we used to have! Battles of the Titans, my dear." His expression softened at the memory of his dead wife. "Augusta never stood for playing second fiddle, and I respected her for it."

"But still you were unfaithful to her."

He shook his head. "Not in my heart. The body, ah!" He made a dismissive gesture. "The body is a willful creature of passions that must be satisfied. But the heart—the heart must only be given to one. *That* is the sacred bit."

I pondered this a moment, and the only sound in the room was the gentle swish of the charcoal as his pupils sketched their pictures.

"It sounds a little too easy," I told him finally. "Convenient excuses for the worst of excesses."

"It is the truth as I have known it, sweet Veronica. My body lusted after hundreds of women. It still does," he said, giving me a sweeping look that lingered on bosom and hips. "But those hungers, once satisfied, were fleeting. I remembered none of them. I loved none of them. Only Augusta. Even after she died, the women I held, the women I kissed and petted and made love to, they have been nothing to me, as insubstantial as ghosts. Only the specter of my Augusta is real to me."

His rationale for adultery was a piece of sophistry, but his emotions were quite genuine. I covered his knotted hand gently with my own. "I think I understand."

He shook his head. "No, you do not. Because you have never given your heart to anyone."

I smiled, a small wry smile. "How can you know that?"

"Because for all your winsome ways, sweet child, there is something untouched about you."

"Would it shock you to know that I am no virgin, Sir Frederick?"

"I wasn't speaking of your body," he replied. "Did I not just tell you? Bodies are quite insignificant. The soul is a thing apart. When you decide to share that with someone, then you will know what it is to live."

I shifted on the little sofa. "We were talking about your affairs, not mine," I reminded him gently. I made to remove my hand, but he clasped it awkwardly with his.

"Sit with me awhile longer. It has been a long time since I held a woman's hand so sweetly and smelt her perfume. I am an old man now," he added with a slow smile. "I can do you no harm."

I did as he asked, leaving my hand tucked into his and wondering just how much harm he might already have done me.

As soon as I could effect a graceful exit, I left Sir Frederick. I realized with some annoyance that I had not questioned him about Julian Gilchrist's attendance at the grotto entertainments or Artemisia's, although their visits had occurred some time later than his last. There was something about his presence, a compelling trick of the personality, that made it quite difficult to keep to whatever plan I had formed. I liked the old fellow, but more than that, I felt the strength of his magnetism, the power of the man. I could not imagine what a force of nature he must have been in his younger days, but once away from him, it was easy to curse my own shortcomings.

I had in mind to search Julian Gilchrist's room but decided to look in on Stoker first. I found him alone in Miss Talbot's rooms, passing the lady as she left. She was in a fine pet, swearing inventively at the interruption and giving me only a cursory grunt. I slipped into her studio to find Stoker draped in a velvet cloak that enveloped him from head to heels.

"Whatever are you wearing?" I demanded. "That is hardly heroic enough to depict Perseus. I'd rather think you were a very unfortunate-looking vestal virgin."

He pulled a face. "It is bloody cold in here and Miss Talbot told me I could warm up while she went to fetch a fresh lot of charcoal. What have you been about?"

I sketched my conversations with Sir Frederick as swiftly as I could, naturally omitting his observations about my own romantic inclinations.

"So, he makes no bones about being a member of the grotto," I concluded.

"He is a reprobate," Stoker said flatly.

I said nothing but gave him a look which made him blush to his toes.

"Very well. I have no claim on the pinnacle of morality upon that score," he admitted.

"There is more," I said quickly, not wishing to open that particular basket of eels.

I told him about Sir Frederick getting around with the aid of sticks rather than his Bath chair. "It seems he is a bit more robust than we originally believed," I finished. "Do you think he could have done it?"

I hardly liked to pose the question, but it deserved consideration. He shrugged. "Most things are possible, particularly in the grip of strong emotion. I could engage in a little pleasant homicide myself about now," he added with a touch of bitterness.

"What ails you, Stoker?" I demanded. "You are sullen as a debutante no one has asked to dance."

He gestured to his draperies. "This! You are off cavorting with murder suspects while I am locked up here with a woman who handles me like a fresh bit of beefsteak."

I gave him a severe look. "You are supposed to be investigating *her*," I reminded him.

"Bloody difficult when she will not let me speak," he retorted.

"Whyever not?"

He flapped an impatient hand. "Something to do with my expression. She wants heroic and noble suffering, and apparently I cannot sustain it if I am chatting casually about the weather. She will not permit me to utter a word once she has posed me."

"Bad luck," I sympathized. "But she must allow you time to stretch your muscles. Perhaps you could fake a cramp of some sort. Tell her you have a rheumatism," I suggested.

"A rheumatism? I am thirty-one," he said in an aggrieved tone. "Hardly in my dotage."

"I should say," came a voice from the doorway. I had not noticed Miss Talbot's return, and I hoped she had not overlistened to our conversation. But her manner was perfectly composed, merely a little distracted with that air I had often seen in artists—a trick of appearing to be listening to music only they could hear. She bustled forward, clutching a handful of charcoal.

"Found it. That fool Gilchrist helped himself to the last of mine and thought I wouldn't notice," she muttered. She gestured towards Stoker. "Back into place, please. That is the better part of ten minutes lost."

Stoker resumed his position upon the plinth in the center of the room and she fidgeted with him, turning his limbs this way and that as if he were a manikin. There was a sword for one hand and a gruesome wax head for the other. The last was a nod to Medusa, the vanquished Gorgon whose death at Perseus' hands was his finest accomplishment.

Miss Talbot circled Stoker, stopping occasionally to adjust the angle of his head. "The head must be right, then all else will follow," she said, more to herself than either of us. She paused and considered him, then gestured for me to come forward. "The line of the throat is quite good, don't you think?" She did not wait for me to reply. "I have been working the better part of five years on my series of Greek heroes, and I am lacking only a Perseus. You've no idea how long I have searched for that perfect marriage of towering masculine strength and noble suffering united in one form," Miss Talbot said. Poor Stoker looked entirely hunted.

"How very kind. But why exactly is Perseus suffering? He defeated Medusa, did he not? And rather quickly, if memory serves."

"But at what cost?" she returned, warming to her theme. She moved to where Stoker stood, stroking his muscles as she talked. "You must remember he was a prince of Argos, conceived in a golden shower when Zeus bestowed his attentions upon the beautiful Princess Danaë against the wishes of her father, the brutal Acrisius. Imagine the scene, the angry king, locking his own daughter and grandchild into a wooden chest and hurling them into the sea so that the ancient prophecy of his own death at the hands of his grandson could not bear fruit. How long did poor Danaë and her child suffer, tossed upon the waves, fearing death at any moment, until their safe delivery onto the shores of Serifos? Such suffering must be writ in the face, do you not see it?"

"Oh, of course," Stoker temporized.

The artist continued her raptures. "Imagine him, graceful and lithe—for he was after all the son of Zeus—tasked by another jealous king with retrieving the head of Medusa. Think of him, knowing that he will likely never see his home and his family again, pitting himself against the horrors of the Gorgon cave and the monster that waits at the heart of it. Oh, I can picture it so clearly!"

She adjusted the drape of the cloak, baring Stoker's arm, her hand clenching as she prodded the muscle beneath the tattooed skin. "Such development of the biceps," she murmured.

"It seems a pity that the piece will not be seen in its proper setting," I said casually. "At least not by the man who inspired the collection."

For a moment I thought she had not heard me, lost as she was in her art. But her fingers tightened on the cape, marking the velvet. She turned, her face very white. "Miss Speedwell, I appreciate that you want to help. But what the princess has asked of you is an act of cruelty."

"Is it cruelty to save a man from the gallows?" Stoker asked without moving his head.

Her small hands curled into fists. "It is cruelty to think you can," she countered, her voice suddenly harsh. "Miles Ramsforth is going to hang. Everyone who knew and cared about him has made their peace with it. Why can't Loosy?"

"Because she does not believe he is guilty. Surely there is room for doubt?" I suggested.

"Doubt?" Her grey eyes were bleak. "This is merely theory to you, so many pieces moving about the board on squares of black and white, an academic exercise to test your own cleverness. But there are lives at stake, real lives of no consequence to you." Her posture was brittle, as if a single touch of a finger would shatter her to pieces.

"Miss Talbot," Stoker said, stepping from the plinth. "If you know anything that can help—"

"I know nothing!" she cried. "But the law has found him guilty. Who are we to say they are wrong?"

"They have been wrong before," I told her. "Why are you so certain Miles Ramsforth is guilty?"

She pressed her lips together and made no reply.

"Miss Talbot, what do you know?" Stoker urged again.

She smoothed the front of her skirt and folded back her cuffs with maddening precision. "I know that the law has said Miles Ramsforth is going to hang. And no one in heaven or on earth can stop it."

She took up her charcoal in a steady hand. "Resume your pose, Mr. Templeton-Vane, please."

Stoker gave her a long, level look, then did as she asked. He flicked me a glance, and I answered with a single shake of the head. There was no point in prolonging the interview. The opportunity for confidences was past.

I went to the door. "I've no wish to intrude upon your process. I will leave you to it."

"Good," she said. She had turned back to her work before the door even closed behind me. I stood with my back against it, breathing quite rapidly for some minutes before I collected myself.

CHAPTER

15

I sped to Julian Gilchrist's room on silent feet. I rapped lightly but received no reply. Holding my breath, I eased open the door and slipped inside. The windows were undraped and the room enjoyed excellent light, great shafts of it illuminating dancing motes of dust. This chamber had clearly escaped a housemaid's touch, and I wondered if the cleaning of it had fallen to Cherry. There was a bed in one corner, unmade and bearing the unmistakable traces of recent congress. I could smell the salty tang of sweat and something rather more intimate in the air, and I saw where a damp patch darkened the sheet. Wrinkling my nose with distaste, I slowly made a tour of the room, passing by a collection of canvases to peer at the narrow shelf of books. There were only a few volumes and all upon the subject of art, I realized as I lifted them each and ruffled through the pages.

Just as I replaced the last book, I heard the creaking of a floorboard. I whirled, realizing with a leap of the heart that I was not alone. A solid figure stood in the doorway, silent and shadowy, and it took a moment to realize it was Mr. Gilchrist. He made no move to enter, but stood as if deciding how to proceed.

Always believing that the most effective retreat is couched as attack,

I strode forward. "Mr. Gilchrist, I believe? Yes, of course. Our paths crossed the other evening here, although I doubt you will remember it. I hope you will forgive the intrusion, but I must have got quite lost. Is this your room?" I widened my eyes innocently and held my hand out expectantly. It hung in the air between us for a long moment before he shook it, almost against his will, it seemed. His hand engulfed mine in a hot, damp clasp.

"Miss Speedwell, is it not? How very unexpected," he murmured. He held my hand a long moment, searching my face with his gaze. He seemed to make a sudden decision, for he moved past me, still holding my hand, pulling me further into the room and closing the door. "Come. I want to show you something." He gestured towards his pictures. "Look at them and tell me what you think," he urged.

From the collection of canvases, I deduced that Mr. Gilchrist was strictly a portraitist. His paintings were severely restricted to depictions of ladies from the shoulders up, all the same size and all wearing almost identical expressions of rapture. I stepped to the nearest one and examined it in the light. It was of a blond woman, not so many years past thirty, I guessed, her shoulders wrapped in a cloud of green silk that brought something lively to her brown eyes. Her skin was suffused with a delicate tint of rose, flushed from some exertion, while a damp curl trailed over one bare shoulder. It required little imagination to guess what she had been doing just before that portrait was painted, and I threw him a reproachful look.

"Really, Mr. Gilchrist," I said with a touch of asperity. "I know the lady. She is wife to the director of the Royal Museum of Natural History and a very respectable mother of four."

"Not that respectable," he said demurely.

I wagged a finger in mock severity. "Do not bother to pretend you are abashed. I do not believe you."

A slow smile spread across his features. His smile was that of one of the lesser angels, the naughty sort who might have pulled Lucifer's curls or poked Saint Peter with a pin.

"Very well. Yes. I had her just before I painted that. Twice."

I gestured to the rest of the paintings. "Have you had all of them?"

He spread his hands as if to demonstrate his innocence. "No. Only most." I shook my head severely, but his expression turned earnest. "It is hardly my fault, Miss Speedwell! I am commissioned by their husbands and fathers to paint them, to make them goddesses, immortalized upon canvas for eternity. For the society beauty, nothing could be simpler. She is certain of herself, secure in her own unassailable charms. So I simply find a flaw, a nose I claim is a shade too long or a chin too pointed. Suddenly the lady is uncertain, timorous, and since I am the one who made her so, only I can restore her confidence. I compliment her on something no one else has ever noticed. The shell-like ear, so delicate and tender. The line of her neck, arched like a swan's. And they blossom like flowers."

"And the plain ones?" I asked.

The slow, lazy smile showed itself once more. "Even simpler. They are unaccustomed to being called beautiful, and they would suspect me at once if I were so clumsy. So I coax them, slowly, ever so slowly. I tell them how relaxed I am with them, and because I am at my ease, so are they. Then I tell them that I am having trouble mixing just the right color for the eyes because I have never seen such a color before. But wait! I have seen it," he said with a flourish. "In a flash of sunlight upon a sapphire sea, or in the dappled green of a forest glen, or the rich silken fur of a sable's pelt."

I snorted. "And this works?"

"Like a clockwork machine," he assured me. "Fair or plain, a woman must be complimented upon something she believes she possesses but no one else has ever noticed. That tells her that you alone see her for who she truly is. And then she is yours."

He took a step closer, and now I caught the warm smell of bed sport clinging to his skin, the damp perfume of mingled limbs. I wondered with whom he had been frolicking recently.

But his thoughts were elsewhere. "Do you know what I would compliment about you, Miss Speedwell?" he asked in a subtle, silvery tone.

"No. Do tell me," I instructed.

He came nearer still, his lips almost brushing the curve of my ear. "Nothing."

I raised a brow. "Indeed?"

He lifted a fingertip to almost but not quite stroke the line of my jaw. "Every other man who has seen you would remark upon those eyes. Violet eyes are too rare and jewel-like to go unmentioned. What man could resist the temptation? And those lips, so lush and ripe for kissing, like a pair of cherries, plump against the tongue." His gaze lingered on each feature as he spoke. "And I should not compliment you upon your wit. You are far too clever not to know your own intelligence. You are intrepid and indefatigable, so I should not remark upon those qualities you so prize in yourself," he added, almost as an afterthought. He circled slowly around me, scrutinizing me from the tips of my boots to the crown of my hat. He came behind, to the other ear, and this time his lips did touch me, the brush of them against my lobe almost indistinguishable from the whisper of warm breath as he spoke. "No, indeed, Miss Speedwell, I should compliment you upon one thing only—your utterly incomparable curiosity." He snapped his teeth upon the last word, nearly catching my lobe as he finished with a deep, wolfish growl.

His arm crept about my waist, tightening just enough to pull me against him, his chest pressing against my back so I could feel the deep inhalation as he buried his nose in my hair. He gave a groan. "You smell of roses and spices and something more," he murmured, his lips roaming from my securely pinned locks to the nape of my neck. "Warm honey, I think. I am dizzy with the scent of it," he whispered, twisting one curl about his finger and tugging it free.

"And I am appalled that you would make overtures to me when your sheets are still wet from your exertions with another woman, but I admire the effort," I told him, neatly eluding his embrace. He dropped his arm, staring at me in astonishment as I repinned the lock he had loosened.

His gaze narrowed in annoyance, but I was having none of it. "Come now, Mr. Gilchrist, do not sulk. I am certain your tricks are often successful, but I have rather more experience of seduction than you, and I can spot a stratagem at thirty paces."

His expression was mulish. "What gave me away?"

I gave him a pitying smile. "When a man truly wants a woman, he finds it difficult to hide. And some parts of him are quite impossible to conceal," I added with a meaningful look to the flat front of his trousers.

He was still sputtering when I left him.

I closed the door of Mr. Gilchrist's room behind me and descended the stairs, putting as much distance between us as I could. I had noticed a small cupboard fitted under the stairs, perfect for the hanging of coats and storing of umbrellas—and the most opportune place to keep a cloak one had worn during the doing of a nefarious deed, I decided. It took me less than a minute to find it. Someone had hid it beneath a bright green greatcoat and an ulster. I dove for it with an exclamation of glee. I had brought the scrap Huxley had secured, and it was the work of a moment to match the piece to the ragged hem left behind. I peered closer and saw a single gilt hair inside the hood, one of Julian Gilchrist's bright golden threads, I realized with a rush of satisfaction.

I turned to the lining, noticing at once the label stitched with Cyrillic letters. I was not surprised. It was a flamboyant sort of garment for a man, not in the color, of course, but in the enveloping flow of it. It seemed just the sort of thing to appeal to a person raised, as Sir Frederick had been, at the lavish court of the tsars. I put my hand into the pocket and drew out a small enameled compact, the sort that ladies are given as souvenirs from their admirers. It was a pretty thing and the bestower had thought to have it engraved. "To Emma," I murmured aloud. "Blast. That muddies the waters." Which of them had worn it last? But at least here was proof that the villain who had left the threat upon our door was a resident at Havelock House. Folding the cloak carefully over my arm, I slipped from the cupboard and closed it behind me.

As I crossed the Hall of Echoes, I saw her—the little maid, Cherry. She bobbed a curtsy and shifted her path so that she went the far way around the fountain, keeping to the opposite side from me.

"Rather like the defensive maneuver of *Phengaris alcon*," I murmured to myself. The Alcon Blue had a series of clever tricks to avoid being captured, but I knew them all. I followed the curve of the fountain around, trailing her noiselessly down the stairs to the cellars where the domestic offices were laid out. She did not look around as she darted into a room. I slipped in after her, causing her to squeak in alarm.

"Miss! What are you doing in the larder?" she demanded. "Cook will not like it."

I glanced around, noticing the shelved array of foodstuffs, a large cheese covered in a lavish coat of blue-green mold, an open jar of pickles, a bowl of brown eggs. "I wanted to have a conversation with you—mostly because you seemed so eager to avoid it."

She colored slightly. "I don't know what you mean," she said with a mulish thrust to her lower lip.

The girl had been friendly enough upon the occasion of our first meeting, and I wondered what had put her out of temper with me. Sudden inspiration struck, and I nocked an arrow for a shot in the dark. "Cherry, were you with Mr. Gilchrist in his rooms earlier? Specifically, were you in his bed?"

She raised her chin, putting her weight forward upon the balls of her feet like a pugilist about to strike. "And if I was? A girl has a right to a little fun," she told me with some heat.

"Indeed she does. In fact, I am an advocate of that very thing, and I will go so far as to say that I am quite envious of you having attended to your physical urges so recently. Mine are proving rather clamorous at present," I added regretfully.

Her mouth went slack. "You mean—"

"Yes, child. I am a firm believer that it is good for the psyche as well as the body to engage in regular activities of that nature. But most folk are not as enlightened as we are. I make a point never to indulge when I am in England."

"Then you and Mr. G., you didn't . . ."

"We did not," I assured her.

Something in her relaxed then, and she shifted her weight back onto her heels. "I did wonder. I know you were in his room, and Mr. G. is rather, well—let us just say he will take it if it's on offer, and he isn't particular."

I smiled thinly. "It was most definitely *not* on offer. I was curious about his art."

"He's a brilliant painter, he is," she said breathlessly. "But not a patch on the master." Her eyes were lit with a sort of fervor when she spoke of Sir Frederick, and I warmed to her for it.

"You are quite devoted to Sir Frederick, are you not?"

"I would die for the master," she said stoutly.

"Yes, but would you kill for him?" I murmured.

She gave a start, narrowly avoiding a plate of sliced gammon. "What's that, miss?"

"Nothing." I waved a hand. "I need the answers to a few questions, answers that might help your master," I said, engaging in only a little duplicity.

She gave me a dubious look but nodded once, her loyalty to her master trumping her natural reserve. "Well?"

"This cloak," I said, holding up the garment in question. "I know that it has been worn by Mr. Gilchrist and by Miss Talbot, also, I believe. To whom does it belong?"

She shrugged. "I cannot say, miss."

"Cannot or will not?"

"Cannot," she repeated. "It hangs in the cupboard under the stairs. Everyone uses it."

"Everyone? Surely not. The length is entirely wrong," I pointed out, shaking the garment to its full capacity.

"Miss Talbot wears it when it's foul out, to keep her skirts covered to the hem. Mr. Gilchrist likes it when he is paying a discreet call upon a lady who ought not to be entertaining him—it is very different to his usual coat."

"The green affair in the cupboard?" I asked.

"That's the one. And Miss Artemisia used to wear it as well. It did not hang so long upon her as Miss Talbot, but she liked the look of it. Rather romantical, she used to say."

"And Sir Frederick?"

"It was his to begin with. Brought it back from Russia, he did," she said, confirming my suspicion.

"I thought as much. Is there anyone in this house who has *not* worn the cloak?"

Her eyes darted about. "I am not supposed to," she hedged.

"But you have?"

"Twice," she said, jerking her chin in a mutinous fashion. "But you won't tell, will you, miss? Only I am not supposed to wear it, but it's ever so warm and the walk to the shops can be that biting."

"Never mind," I told her. I had no intention of getting the girl into trouble. Besides, I realized with a little glow of satisfaction, she had just confirmed for me that our villain was most likely *not* the Viscount

Templeton-Vane. Whoever had left the threat pinned to our door was intimately familiar with the ways of Havelock House.

Just to be certain, I put a new question to her. "Has a gentleman by the name of Templeton-Vane ever called here? Not the fellow posing for Miss Talbot," I said swiftly. "His brother. Older than he is, with a given name of Tiberius."

She furrowed her brow. "Not that I remember, and that's a curious name. I'd be sure to recollect that."

"Yes, one would imagine so. Now, tell me, Cherry, just between us. I know that Artemisia and Miles Ramsforth were lovers. I presume you knew it as well."

"Yes, miss. I saw him come out of her room early in the morning on a few occasions."

"Did you know she was expecting a child?"

She tossed her head. "I did. Told her I knew how to take care of it, but she just laughed. Said she wanted the babe, if you can believe that. In fact," she said, her tone low and confiding, "she had a scare, bleeding with a bit of cramp after the third month. She thought she was losing it, she did. You've never seen a woman in such a state."

"But she didn't lose it," I prompted.

"No, miss. I told her about my mum. She bled through all her carrying, but raspberry leaf tonic put her to rights. She kept every one of her babies, although she might have been better off if she hadn't, and that's the truth," she added.

"How many children does your mother have, Cherry?"

"Thirteen and another coming next month," she said, pulling a face. "Most of my wages go home and I've precious little to show for it, but I can't let the littles starve."

She gave a world-weary sigh, and I reached into my pocket for a coin.

"For your help," I told her.

She looked at me through narrowed eyes. "This isn't charity, is it? I'll brook no charity, miss. We pay our own way."

"I am certain you do, but it is customary to pay for information during an investigation."

Her eyes rounded with interest. "Are you an investigator, miss? A proper one?"

"No, child. I am a highly improper one, I daresay. But I was asked to look into Artemisia's death and make quite certain that the man they convicted is actually guilty."

She shook her head, making a little clucking sound as she did so. "Poor Mr. Ramsforth. I don't like to think it. None of us do. Always ready with a laugh, and generous with a coin for an extra job. There are those who pinch every penny," she said darkly, "but not Mr. Ramsforth. It will be a sad day when he hangs, and no doubt about it."

"Do you think he is guilty?"

She blinked. "Well, he must be, miss. He's been found guilty by a proper jury. Those gentlemen would know, wouldn't they?"

I almost admired her touching faith in the judicial system. "You would think so," I managed.

She took the coin from me then, tucking it into her pocket.

"Cherry, do you like Mr. Gilchrist? As a person, I mean."

She pondered that a minute. "He's beautiful," she said finally. "Course he is mean with a penny, and that's no lie, but he's so pretty to look at. And his hair is ever so soft." She paused, and I sensed something more.

I probed, gently. "What else, Cherry? What do you like about him?"

"It isn't that I like him," she corrected. "I feel sorry for him."

"Sorry for him? But Mr. Gilchrist is blessed with talent and angelic looks. He is well-connected and has a tremendous future. Why should you be sorry for him?"

"Oh, miss, I can't explain it!" She broke off, frustrated, then her furrowed brow cleared. "Do you know sheep, miss? Well, my father is a sheep farmer, and not a good one. But he's taught me enough, and I can tell you there is always one in every flock that's just not going to fit. The bummer lamb, he's called, and he will never be like the rest."

"And Mr. Gilchrist is a bummer lamb?" I asked.

"I think so. I know it isn't right for a person like me to feel sorry for a gentleman," she said hurriedly, "but you asked and I am an honest girl."

"Yes, you are," I told her. "I will leave you to your work now."

She scuttled from the larder, leaving me to follow. I turned to go, and just as I did, I caught sight of something out of the tail of my eye—a platter holding a large, indefinable object shrouded under a bit of muslin.

I lifted it carefully, but I already knew what I would find. Underneath the muslin was the head of a sheep, its mouth stiffened into a gruesome grin displaying all of its teeth. One eyeball was filmy with the cold, staring blindly ahead. The other eyeball was missing entirely.

W hen I collected Stoker, he was in a foul mood. Apparently, standing around largely unclothed in a drafty room for the better part of two hours was taxing to the temper, and I shoved a packet of honey drops at him as soon as we took our leave of Havelock House.

"I cannot believe I let you talk me into that," he muttered, conveniently forgetting that he had been as in favor of his posing for Miss Talbot as I was.

"Just think," I soothed, "you will be immortalized in marble for eternity."

He snorted and tossed a honey drop into his mouth. "It better have been worth it. What have you discovered?"

As we made our way back to Bishop's Folly and the Belvedere, I related all I had learned, eliciting the occasional grunt of interest or question.

"So, brother Tiberius falls on the list of suspects while Gilchrist is an excellent bet for our malefactor, at least as far as the threats are concerned," I concluded. "He regularly wears a cloak which appears to match that of our miscreant, and he had access to a sheep's head in the larder."

"So did everyone else at Havelock House," he pointed out.

I pulled a face. "Do you have a better idea? Someone you like more for our villain?"

He shook his head slowly. "Sir Frederick is unlikely but still possible. And Cherry was free with her confidences—perhaps too much so. She may have been telling you all of that simply to put you off suspecting her." I bridled, but he carried on, heedless. "I have my doubts about Emma Talbot. There is something going on there, something beneath the surface. She puts me in mind of a river in winter, solid ice on the surface, yet something moving in the darkness below."

"How very poetic," I told him. "But you've no proof."

He slanted me a triumphant glance. "Haven't I?" He crunched another honey drop. "Whilst you were busy running housemaids to ground in the larder and fending off Gilchrist's indecent proposals, I was searching Emma Talbot's rooms."

"You didn't!" I breathed. "When did you have time?"

He shrugged. "Posing is a thirsty business. I kept asking for tea or water. Whenever she went off to fetch something to drink, I cracked a few of her bits of charcoal so they would break when she went to use them and she would have to ferret out more. Every time she left I looked through something else."

"How very resourceful of you. What did you find?"

"This," he said, brandishing a sketch.

"Stoker! You never stole this from her sketchbook," I admonished, noticing the jagged edge where the piece had been torn from a bound book.

"In point of fact, I did not," he assured me. "It had already been ripped free and crumpled, if you will note the heavy creases, and by Emma Talbot, I suspect. She was very angry when she did that," he mused. "And at some point she had a change of heart and retrieved it. It was pressed between two large books."

I studied the drawing. It was not a masterpiece. It had been done in haste, with rough, sweeping lines. But the power of those lines! They formed the face of a man, and it took only a moment to realize his identity.

"Miles Ramsforth," I breathed. "She has sketched Miles Ramsforth." I leaned forward, inspecting the drawing more closely. "How very curious. I recognize him from the photographs in the newspapers, but she has captured something entirely different."

"How so?"

I shook my head. "I cannot say, except that he looks . . . noble here. There is something fine about his profile. And his jaw is much more serious. It's lost that bit of weakness I thought I detected. Almost as if she has drawn him as he *could* be, rather than how he is."

"You're coming over fanciful now," he said with a sudden hauteur. He took the drawing back and folded it up, thrusting it into his pocket. "I will replace it the next time we go to Havelock House. If Emma Talbot is involved in all of this, it is best she doesn't realize we have sleuthed out her connection to Ramsforth."

I tipped my head thoughtfully. "Stoker, how exactly did you manage to spirit that out of her studio? You were meant to be posing entirely nude."

He crunched yet another honey drop and shot me a dazzling smile. "That is for me to know and you to guess."

CHAPTER

16

We entered Bishop's Folly by the pedestrian gate on the far side of the property, winding through the extensive gardens and past the various follies and outbuildings until we came to the Belvedere. I nudged Stoker. "There is a caller on the doorstep."

He took one look at the visitor and began to swear. "Bloody bollocking hell," he started, but I put a hand to his sleeve and greeted our caller.

"Hello, Sir Rupert."

Sir Rupert, second eldest of the Templeton-Vane sons and a knighted barrister, doffed his hat to me as he ignored his younger brother. "Miss Speedwell, a distinct pleasure."

"It is nice to see you. Would you care to come inside?"

"He damned well would not," Stoker protested.

Sir Rupert suppressed a sigh with some effort. "I can see he is going to be tiresome about this. Yes, Miss Speedwell, I should very much like to come inside rather than conduct our family business out here with witnesses," he said with a glance to the rustling shrubbery.

"Oh, that's only Patricia. You mustn't mind her," I told him, explaining about his lordship's tortoise as we entered the Belvedere. Within a few moments I had unearthed a tin of biscuits and poured small glasses of whiskey.

Sir Rupert took a taste, rolling it over his tongue like a connoisseur. "I say, that is lovely. I was rather afraid you would offer me tea."

"I remember we resorted to strong drink the last time we met," I told him. "It seemed appropriate under the circumstances."

We exchanged conspiratorial glances and Stoker rolled his eyes heavenwards before draining his glass. "Rupert, why have you come?"

Sir Rupert took another sip of his whiskey as I regarded Stoker thoughtfully. "You really have the most appalling manners, Stoker. Sir Rupert, was he always like this?"

"Impetuous? Boorish? Entirely self-involved? Yes. From the cradle. And there was never any improving him, no matter how hard Father tried. And stubborn as the devil, too. I recall upon one occasion, Father refused him permission to ride in a local point-to-point on the grounds that he wasn't an experienced enough rider to take part."

"I imagine he sulked. He has a gift for it."

Sir Rupert shook his head. "Worse. He stole Father's favorite horse, Tinchebray, and rode him without a saddle, blazing past everyone else in the field."

"Father never criticized my riding again," Stoker put in mutinously.

"That horse was never the same," Sir Rupert told me. I smiled at him and he took another appreciative sip of the whiskey. "You have been far kinder than I deserve, Miss Speedwell. I heard of what transpired with young Merryweather, and I cannot offer enough apologies. The cub ought to be whipped for offering you such insult."

"And where did he get the notion that Miss Speedwell deserved it?" Stoker demanded with silky menace.

Sir Rupert flushed delicately, just a hint of rose at the tips of his ears. "That was my fault, I am afraid. On the evening of Father's funeral, we brothers gathered to toast him with the last of his Napoleon brandy. A toast to which you were invited," he said pointedly to Stoker. "In any event, there were rather more bottles than we remembered, and we got through them all. At one point, I mentioned that your absence was possibly due to a previous engagement with Miss Speedwell. I might have further remarked that should I ever be offered the choice between drinking with my brothers and spending the evening in such charming company, I should not hesitate to choose the latter," he added with a gallant nod towards me.

Stoker made a sound of rank disbelief, but Sir Rupert continued. "Naturally, this led to questions on the part of both of our brothers, and when I attempted to describe Miss Speedwell, I fear I may have been overwarm in elucidating her charms."

I beamed at him. "Never mind, Sir Rupert. I understand entirely."

"So do I, Rip," Stoker put in. "You were rat-arsed and no doubt made some highly vulgar observations which so inflamed Merry that he came round at the first opportunity to see Miss Speedwell for himself. He as much as insinuated she was my mistress," he said flatly.

Sir Rupert choked a little, sputtering out an apology.

"Not at all," I said graciously. "But Stoker's recollection is not entirely accurate. Merryweather made no insinuation. He stated quite plainly that he was delighted to meet a 'bad woman.'"

Sir Rupert tossed back the last of his whiskey in a single go, shuddering as it went down. "I am heartily sorry for it." He looked to Stoker. "He said you nearly whipped him, and I came to apologize to Miss Speedwell and give you a dressing-down, but I rather think I will thrash the little boil myself."

"Come now, Sir Rupert. Surely we can excuse him on the grounds of youthful high spirits. And if I am not prepared to hold a grudge, you cannot sustain one on my behalf."

"You are a truly gracious lady," he told me, holding out his glass for another. He drank it while we made polite conversation about the state of affairs in Samoa—the Germans were threatening to assume control of the islands and cut off our rather lucrative trade there—the poor showing of the buddleias in his garden, and the imminent reopening of the Haymarket Theatre after its refurbishment.

We talked until the clock struck the hour, at which point Sir Rupert leapt to his feet, rather less steadily than I had expected, exclaiming that he would be late for a dinner engagement. I walked him to the door while Stoker remained sprawled in his armchair, booted legs thrust out before him, a sullen expression on his face.

At the door, Sir Rupert shook my hand warmly. "Very kind of you, Miss Speedwell. I say, there was something I meant to discuss with Revelstoke, but devil take me if I can remember what it was . . ." His brow furrowed.

I hazarded a suggestion. "Did it have anything to do with your father's estate?"

"By Jove, yes!" he crowed. "You are a marvel, Miss Speedwell, it was indeed. But however did you guess?"

"That was part of Mr. Merryweather's mission as well."

"Ah. I daresay he was no more successful than I have been," he said with a rueful smile. He pitched his voice low. "You have influence with him, you know. Stoker, I mean. I would be most appreciative if you would use it."

"Influence! My dear Sir Rupert, you are quite mistaken. We are colleagues and sometimes friends and we bicker like the proverbial cat and dog."

His smile was wistful. "If you say so, although I have observed something quite . . . different. It really would help most awfully if he would respond to the solicitors. Tiberius—that is to say, the new Lord Templeton-Vane—is growing restive, and we do not care for Tiberius to be restive," he added with a shudder.

Seeing Sir Rupert so deeply in his cups, I realized it would be taking the most unfair advantage of the situation to question him about Lord Templeton-Vane's connection with the Elysian Grotto. Naturally, I wasted no time in doing so.

I gave him my most winsome look. "I am curious about the new viscount," I told him. "What sort of gentleman is he?"

"Dictatorial," he replied promptly. "Very much the eldest brother, bred to reign. He was badly spoilt as a child, and to his credit, he has grown out of much of that, but still he expects to be obeyed."

"A veritable Captain Bligh," I suggested.

"Oh, not as bad as that," he hastened to correct. "But he can play the martinet. The trouble with Tiberius is that he feels his responsibilities quite keenly, and that can make him difficult."

"And is there a Lady Templeton-Vane?"

He shook his head, staggered a moment, then righted himself. "Not at present. There was once, but the girl was no match for him. He only married her because she was the daughter of a duke, and he wanted to blue up the family blood even further. Much good it did him—the poor girl died within two years."

"And he has never remarried?"

Sir Rupert shrugged. "He hasn't the stomach for it. Mind you, he does like a pretty armful," he said, then put his hand to his mouth, tugging his mustaches. "Oughtn't to have said that. Do forgive me, Miss Speedwell."

"Not at all, Sir Rupert. We are, after all, adults. Surely we can discuss such things without embarrassment. It would be most surprising if a man of Lord Templeton-Vane's standing did not amuse himself. Tell me, are his amusements always of the conventional sort, or does he indulge in more esoteric pursuits?"

"Esoteric? You mean like philately?" he asked, furrowing his brows.

"No, Sir Rupert, I mean like orgies."

He sputtered, his eyes going so wide I could see the whites surrounding his pupils. "My dear Miss Speedwell! The very thought—Pardon me, I believe I am going to be unwell."

He was lavishly sick behind the nearest bit of shrubbery, returning with a handkerchief pressed to his mouth. "I think I had better take my leave of you, Miss Speedwell," he said with an air of apology. He wore the same expression Huxley did when he had rolled in something unspeakable in the garden.

"Are you quite all right to see yourself home, Sir Rupert?"

He raised a hand. "Quite. The fresh air will no doubt do me good," he assured me as he rallied. He donned his hat and thumped the brim with a jaunty gesture. "Fare thee well, Miss Speedwell!" he cried as he strolled away, only bumping into one or two bits of shrubbery on his way.

Naturally, when I returned to the Belvedere I did not approach Stoker directly on the subject of his father's estate. It has been my experience in dealing with the male of the species that the easiest way to get one to do as you wish is to encourage him to do precisely the opposite.

"I think you are quite right to ignore your family's imprecations," I began as I settled to a tray of dejected-looking *Sphingidae*.

Stoker had been reading the newspaper, but he lowered it just enough to peer suspiciously over the edge. "Do you indeed?"

"Certainly. You've had no cause to be answerable to them for years. Why bother now? In fact, you ought to throw any further missives straight onto the fire without reading them."

He snorted. "You are transparent as glass, Veronica."

"Whatever do you mean?"

He laid the paper aside and rose to his feet, coming to stand at my elbow. I did not look up from my moths. "I mean that you think you can twist me round like those insipid lovers of yours."

I reared back. "They were not insipid! Do give me a little credit, Stoker. I would never conduct an affair with a fellow who could lay claim to that word."

He folded his arms over the breadth of his chest. "Very well. What word would you use to describe men who can be bullied by a woman?"

I thrust back my chair, standing toe to toe with him. "I am not a bully."

"Of course you are," he said blandly. "You use the force of your personality to get your own way regardless of what other people may want."

"That is preposterous. I absolutely do not. I never have."

He began to tick off his fingers. "You involved me in investigating the murder of the baron," he said.

"You abducted me because you thought I had had him murdered!" I protested. "I think the fault of that investigation may be laid squarely at your feet."

"You were the one who would not turn loose of the thing," he reminded me. "You got your way about persuading Lord Rosemorran to mount an expedition to Fiji instead of Africa when you *knew* I preferred the Congo." He continued in this vein, counting off a dozen other instances while I stood by in affected boredom.

"Are you quite finished?" I asked icily when he paused to draw breath.

"Finished? I have merely scratched the surface."

"Indeed? Well, if I am to blame for those crimes, your hands are plenty dirty as well," I countered.

"The devil they are!"

I began a litany of my own. "You abducted me and forced me to live in a traveling show," I told him. "You decided it was time to begin remounting specimens in this collection when the catalog is nowhere near to completion, simply because you don't like 'busywork,' as you call it." I rattled through a dozen or more complaints of my own as we moved closer to each other, venting our mutual frustrations in a heated discussion of our various deficiencies. I called into question his hygiene, his morality, and his scientific methods. He baldly stated that my own moral standards would bear no scrutiny whilst my intellectual rigor wouldn't do credit to a child of nine.

In all, it was a most excellent quarrel—clearing the air and giving us both the opportunity to vent a little spleen. When the dust had settled and we were feeling more in temper with one another, Stoker gave me a thoughtful look.

"So what did Rupert tell you about Tiberius?"

I did not bother to ask how he knew I had prodded Sir Rupert about the viscount. Though our acquaintance was of relatively brief duration, we shared a sort of mental shorthand I had never enjoyed with anyone before. It was an odd trick of his that he could often anticipate my movements or motives, but as I could do the same in return, I was not overly discomfited.

"Nothing of significance. I introduced the subject of Lord Templeton-Vane possibly enjoying orgies. It did not prove fruitful."

Stoker's mouth quivered as if he were suppressing the urge to laugh. "I should think not. What did he say?"

"Not much. He was too busy sicking up his whiskey into the shrubbery."

Stoker swore. "That's the last time I waste good single malt on him."

I sighed and stretched. "It has been a very full day."

"And not entirely unproductive," he agreed.

"Anyone would say we had gone above and beyond what could be expected of us," I said.

"We have."

"So, we are going out tonight?"

"Certainly. I presume you want to go back to Littledown and see if we can gain access to the house itself? Or did you think to have another bash at searching Gilchrist's room at Havelock House? He might be out tonight."

"Neither." I paused and let him make the leap of logic for himself.

"Veronica, no," he said flatly.

"We have no choice. It is a possible lead and we must follow it."

"It is *not* a lead," he retorted. "It is you trying to meddle in my family business."

"Which would not be justified at all if it weren't for the fact that the name Tiberius Templeton-Vane appears in the ledger kept by Miles Ramsforth." I clapped him hard on the shoulder. "Chin up, Stoker. I shouldn't ask it of you if a man's life didn't hang in the balance, but it does. Besides," I added with an attempt at wide-eyed innocence, "if you don't go, I shall be forced to conclude that you are simply afraid to face your eldest brother."

The next few minutes were an exercise in profanity for Stoker. I let him rattle on as I mentally composed a list of the butterflies I had yet to capture. I had just reached *Greta oto*, the Glasswing, when he at last wound down.

"Finished?" I asked brightly. "Now, you say his lordship is a theater aficionado. It is not possible he would miss the opening night of the Haymarket. We can purchase late tickets for the stalls. We will dress ourselves properly and go and drink champagne, and we will 'happen' to cross paths with your eldest brother. He has been so eager to speak with you, he will certainly wish to engage in a little tête-á-tête, and that is when we will question him about the Elysian Grotto."

"A pointless exercise," Stoker said, grinding the words out through clenched jaws. "The ledger shows he has not been there in some months."

I gave him a long, level stare. "We did not have the opportunity to inspect the last page, so we cannot say that with absolute certainty. Besides that, Revelstoke Templeton-Vane, I refuse to believe you are willing to let a man hang because you do not wish to speak to your brother."

He grunted a little but said nothing intelligible, and I knew the battle was won.

"We must leave no stone unturned, and if this is unpleasant for you, I am sorry for it."

He rolled his eyes. "This entire investigation has been nothing but unpleasant for me. You have been swanning about with princesses while I am stripped naked and served up to Emma Talbot like a suckling pig."

"Next time I shall be sure to put an apple in your mouth and a nice rope of parsley about your neck. Now, hurry up and change. We haven't much time," I instructed.

My little pricks and prods had not goaded him to agree, that much I knew. Stoker could be immovable as the earth when he chose. It was the reminder that Miles Ramsforth might hang for a crime he did not commit. Whatever his other faults, Stoker was a just man, and the notion of some villain using Ramsforth as a pawn galled him as it did me.

I possessed exactly one gown suitable for attending the theater—a simply cut but rather striking violet satin—and after bullying Stoker into agreement, I hurried to my own little abode to perform my toilette. Mrs. Bascombe made me a loan of one of the housemaids, Minnie, for my preparations, and she arrived with an arsenal of feminine weapons. She was desperate to better herself and train for a lady's maid, and Mrs. Bascombe thought it far more suitable for her to practice upon me than the ladies of the family. For her part, Minnie was so grateful for the opportunity that she applied herself with real missionary zeal to the task. She dressed my hair simply, forgoing the usual frizzing irons and pads of supplementary curls in favor of piling my own black tresses loosely upon my head, securing them with a stunning number of discreetly hidden pins.

I had already rubbed my face and décolletage with my favorite cold cream of roses and applied a bit of French scent, but Minnie gilded the lily, powdering me lavishly to make my skin glow like a pearl. She touched my lips lightly with a rosy-pink paint of her own concoction, adding a little to the apples of each cheek and blending it all so skillfully that it looked as if it owed the entirety of its charm to nature rather than arti-fice. A little clever work with a pencil-thin stick of kohl and her ministra-tions were complete. After torturing me into a proper corset, she laced me into my violet silk evening gown, pulling the ribbons as tightly as she could to whittle my waist and thrust my bosom skyward. The effect was decidedly voluptuous, and I remembered again why I loathed fashionable undergarments. During my working hours I favored a simple underbod-ice that permitted great range of movement and spontaneity, but for eve-ning wear, there was no escaping a formal corset with all its attendant limitations. The result was to make of me a sort of helpless doll, with a slip of a waist and the rest so curvaceous it was very nearly indecent.

"These clothes are utterly irrational," I muttered.

"But they make you look ever so lovely," she breathed.

I smiled and fetched her a banknote from my reticule which she thrust into her pocket.

Minnie stared at me, aghast. "You have not put on your jewels!"

"I have no jewels," I told her.

She went white to the lips. "You cannot go in public in the evening without jewels. Everyone will think you are poor!"

"She will be unique," said Lady Wellingtonia as she entered without ceremony. "Every other woman will be freighted with diamonds. Miss Speedwell has not a single adornment, and for that reason, she will stand out amongst them."

Lady Wellingtonia moved closer, looking me over from head to toe with a long, measured glance. "Very effective, my dear. Do forgive me coming without invitation, but I heard Mrs. Bascombe telling Min-nie you were going to the theater tonight and I wanted to bring you a little something."

She reached into her pocket for a box, handing it over with a reverent gesture. "A loan," she said, stressing the word. "I carried it once at a ball at Buckingham Palace," she added. I opened the box to find a fan nestled in folded tissue. As I lifted it free, Minnie gave a rapturous little sigh, regarding the fan as an acolyte might a holy relic, and Lady Wellingtonia stood by with a small smile playing about her lips.

I opened the fan. The sticks and guards were of finely carved ebony, and rather than the expected leaf of silk pleated between, this fan was composed of a line of black goose feathers, so smooth they had been painted with a luscious scene of Pygmalion and Galatea. The artist had captured the pair just at the moment that Pygmalion kissed his ripe creation, his roving hands coaxing her to pink-hued life. I thought of Frederick Havelock's compliment and smiled to myself at the aptness of Lady Wellingtonia's loan.

"How lovely," I breathed, fluttering it a little.

"I am glad you like it, my dear. I have always fancied playing fairy godmother." She reached into another pocket. "Look what else I have conjured. Stoker said you mean to get last-minute tickets to the stalls, but a gown that fine ought not to be wasted amongst solicitors and merchants and their dreary wives. I have a box which I cannot use. His lordship is feeling well enough to come downstairs and he has promised to play German whist with me. He thinks we are going to play for money, but if I win, I mean to make him set those wretched lovebirds loose and finally give me some peace."

She fluttered the tickets at me and I took them with a smile. "That is very generous of you, my lady. Thank you."

"As I said, child, I have always liked the notion of granting wishes. Now, off to the ball with you, Cinderella. I have ordered the town carriage for your use tonight, but I am afraid we haven't any mice for footmen. You will simply have to make do with the ordinary kind."

She took her leave then, Minnie in tow, and I waited a moment, enjoying the feeling of being beautifully costumed and ready to make my entrance. At the last second, I opened a little pasteboard box and retrieved a small grey velvet mouse. Chester had been with me as long as I could remember, my companion through all of my adventures. "Perhaps Cinderella will have a mouse after all," I murmured, dropping him into my reticule.

I met with Stoker as he emerged from his little Chinese pagoda, dressed in the rigorous black-and-white evening formality required for gentlemen. His hair was glossy and neatly brushed into some semblance of order in spite of its length, and his chin was freshly barbered with no hint of the blue shadow that usually darkened it. He had put on an eye patch, not his usual affair of leather, but a slim scrap of black silk that matched his hair. His nails were trimmed and the knuckles had been scrubbed until they were as clean as the day he was born. Not a wrinkle or speck of dust marred the perfection of his attire, and it was a long minute before I realized I was staring.

"What?" he demanded, his expression wary.

"I have never seen you clean."

"You bloody well have," he contradicted. "If memory serves, you have seen me in a bath sheet."

I smiled at the memory of our time together in a traveling show. "That was different. You'd been doused with a bucket of tepid water. Now you look positively gleaming. And very expensive," I added, noting that this costume completely covered his tattoos. Only the glint of gold at his lobes and the length of his hair marked him as anything other than a perfectly turned out gentleman of the first order.

"And what about you?" he said, darting a glance from my piled hair to my slipper tips.

"What about me? I am always clean," I protested.

"Yes, but you usually aren't . . ." He trailed off, his gaze resting upon the exposed flesh of my décolletage.

"Well, I have to keep them covered or else you lose the power of speech," I said blandly.

He gave a start and dragged his gaze upwards, his mouth working furiously. "I do apologize," he said in a hoarse voice. "But the soul is lost in pleasant smotherings."

I smiled at the nod to Keats and tucked my hand into the crook of his elbow as we made our way to the drive where the carriage waited. "Stoker, do you remember our conversation upon the subject of physical congress?"

"With painful clarity," he said, not meeting my eyes.

Whilst I was perfectly forthright about such matters, Stoker possessed a charming reticence to discuss his baser urges. I had finally pried from him the admission that it had been some years since his last indulgence—dating to a period of debauchery in Brazil over which he firmly drew a veil. Since then he had been chaste as a monk, a state which I maintained was both unhealthful and unnatural. But as I restricted my dalliances to my travels outside of England, I too felt the insistent pressures of a treacherous body imploring me to find release. Stoker had recommended a course of cold-water baths, but from the tortured expression on his face, I surmised they worked as poorly for him as they did for me.

"I think you ought to find yourself a nice biddable maid to attend to your needs," I told him. He must have tripped in a rabbit hole, for he stumbled, and when he righted himself and took my arm again, his fingers were tight.

"You think I ought to tumble a housemaid?" he said tightly.

"Or a kitchen maid. Or a dairymaid. Yes, a dairymaid! They have sturdy arms, you know. Muscular, strapping girls. Just the sort to give you a proper seeing to."

He was silent a moment, and when he spoke, his voice was strangled. "My affairs are my own, Veronica. I will see to them without your interference."

The carriage drew up just as we reached the drive, as elegant as it was punctual.

"I was only trying to help," I told him.

"I do not require your help," was the curt reply. "Particularly in that."

He glanced once more at my lavish display of décolletage and edged as far from me as he could upon the velvet seat. He turned to look out the window, his mouth set in a rigid line, his hands clenched into fists on his thighs. I would have given a king's ransom to know his thoughts just then. But he betrayed no hint of them. And I did not ask.

CHAPTER

17

I n spite of Stoker's odd mood, I was determined to enjoy myself. We
arrived at the Haymarket in good time, and I alighted with his help,
whisking my skirts out of the way of a fresh pile of arisings from an
indelicate horse. There was a great crush of people and a tremendous
buzz of excitement in the air, like a broken hive of bees.

We settled ourselves into the plush box Lady Wellie had provided,
and I raised the tiny opera glasses I had carried in my reticule. "What do
you think of the refurbishments?" I asked Stoker. "Did you notice the
abundance of electric lights? I am not entirely certain I approve of them."

What followed was a lengthy discussion upon the merits of electric
versus gas lighting and the inherent dangers and advantages of both. I
cared less than nothing about the subject, but Stoker, like most people,
enjoyed having opinions and enjoyed sharing them even more. He
seemed to be much more himself by the time the house lights were
dimmed and the curtain rang up on *The Ballad-Monger*. It was a French
piece adapted for English theater, and Mr. Beerbohm Tree, acting as
both the leading player and manager of the Haymarket, was clearly
determined to make a success of the thing. He was very affecting in the

title role, sporting green tights and a silly cap and delivering "The Ballade of King Rope" in a voice that rang with emotion.

"How splendid," I said to Stoker when the curtain fell upon the first play.

He gave a vague nod. "I saw M. Coquelin play Gringoire at the Théâtre-Français, and I think he is Beerbohm Tree's superior. But the *ballade* was effective," he added, pitching his voice low as he recited.

> High in the branches, stretching wide,
> Where erst the thrushes piped between,
> The dead men dangle side by side,
> While ravens croak amid the green.
> Pardi! it is a lovely scene,
> Such fruit, such dainty chaplets cling;
> Fairer I think were never seen!
> It is the Orchard of the King.

I gave a little shudder. "It is a chilling thought, is it not? Dead men hanging like so much fruit upon the trees?"

"I have seen such things," he said, his expression suddenly and inexpressibly remote.

"Stoker?"

With a visible effort, he collected himself. "Never mind. We are meant to be looking for Tiberius."

I held my hand just over his, almost but not quite touching it. I knew that he had seen things, had done things, in Brazil that haunted him still. We did not speak of them, but Stoker, more than anyone I had ever known, walked with ghosts.

"Will you talk about it?"

"Someday," he told me. "I have never spoken of it. But someday I might, and if I do, you may be certain it will be with you."

He covered my hand, squeezing it sharply before he dropped it. He flicked a glance across the theater to one of the boxes opposite and rose suddenly. "There," he told me with a jerk of the chin. I rose and saw the box he indicated. A solitary figure sat in the shadows of the box.

"He is alone?"

"Unlike most people, Tiberius doesn't come to the theater to be seen. He also goes to the opera for the music. He hates conversation during a performance."

"Perhaps we should wait then. The second play is about to start," I demurred.

Stoker gave me a thin smile that was limned with malice. "If we are going to ruin his evening, let's ruin all of it."

He exited the box, seeming to care not in the slightest that I followed. He strode through the crowded foyer as if it were empty, expecting others to make way for him, and it was a testament to the forcefulness of his personality and the impressiveness of his appearance that they did. A slender usher stood at the door of the Templeton-Vane box, but one look from Stoker—and a sizable coin from me—persuaded him to step aside.

We slipped in just as the curtain was rising upon the second play. Lord Templeton-Vane looked around at the interruption, raising an imperious brow. He was younger in appearance than I would have anticipated—still on the right side of forty, I guessed. Like the rest of the Templeton-Vanes, this one had chestnut hair and grey eyes, although his bones bore the same graceful stamp as Stoker's, their mother's influence. But where Sir Rupert was clever, this one was commanding. He rose slowly to his feet. Stoker might have topped him by an inch or so, but their physiques were similarly muscular and their expressions equally forbidding.

"Revelstoke," he said quietly. "This is a surprise."

"If you didn't want to see me, you oughtn't to have sent Rupert and Merryweather," Stoker countered.

The brow rose again. "Sent them? I did not realize they had bestirred themselves to trouble you. They needn't have bothered. I have my own methods, as well they should know by now."

His gaze shifted to me. "And this must be Miss Speedwell."

To my surprise, he lifted my hand, brushing a suggestion of a kiss to the fingers. "It is a pleasure to make your acquaintance."

"How do you do?" I asked, inclining my head slightly.

Onstage, the second play was just beginning. Lord Templeton-Vane indicated the chairs in the box. "I would be delighted if you would join me for the remainder of the performance," he said to me, ignoring his brother. I seated myself next to him, leaving Stoker his choice of the seats behind us.

As we settled ourselves, his lordship leaned over to me, his breath ruffling the curl at my ear. "I suspect my brother is seething with impatience over this delay in his plans. I hope you are not likewise frustrated."

"On the contrary," I replied coolly. "Whether we speak now or later, it does not matter, my lord. I am a hunter by trade, you know. I have a great deal of practice in waiting patiently for my kill."

I gave him a dazzling smile, and to my surprise, he smiled back, his teeth gleaming white in the darkened theater.

The rest of the evening passed swiftly in a blur of electric lights and applause. The play—*The Red Lamp*—was not particularly good, but Mr. Beerbohm Tree and company excelled, and the viscount put himself out to be as gracious a host as possible. When the final curtain had rung down and the adulation had died away, his lordship rose, straightening his cuffs. He needn't have bothered. He was as fresh and uncreased as he must have been when he left his home.

"Miss Speedwell, Revelstoke, shall we adjourn to supper?" He might have been speaking to polite acquaintances, so dispassionate was his voice.

"I haven't come for food, Tiberius," Stoker replied. I trod lightly on his foot, urging him to silence. I knew he had little inclination for his brother's company, but the intimacy of a supper might prove conducive to confidences.

He slid his foot out from under mine, shooting me a dark look.

"We would be delighted," I told the viscount. He took my arm and guided me from the box without looking behind. He was clearly certain Stoker would follow and he did, rather like a resentful lapdog.

The lobby was still thronged with people, and amidst the press, I spied a familiar face. There was a start of recognition, and a quick turn of the head as if to elude me. I would not be put off.

"Mornaday!" I called, heedless of the disapproving stares of those around us.

He came to us, affecting a broad smile. "Miss Speedwell, this is a most unexpected pleasure."

"For me as well. And how is my favorite detective from Scotland Yard?"

He gave me a waggish look as he bent over my hand. "Your favorite? I say, Sir Hugo will be mightily put out when I tell him."

"No, he won't," I replied. He brushed his fingers over my hand, sending a delightful shudder up my arm.

"Well, perhaps not," he admitted.

"Lord Templeton-Vane, this is Inspector Mornaday of Scotland Yard, Special Branch. Mornaday, the Viscount Templeton-Vane."

They exchanged cool greetings. Ordinarily a viscount would never have been pressed into making the acquaintance of a police inspector, and the incongruity of the situation amused me.

"Templeton-Vane?" Mornaday asked. "You must be Stoker's brother. Where is your tame wolf, Miss Speedwell?"

"Behind you," Stoker put in coolly. Mornaday nearly leapt from his skin but managed to recover his sangfroid enough to greet him casually.

"Hello, old man. I didn't see you there."

"Obviously," Stoker replied with a bland smile. To their credit, they shook hands like gentlemen, both of them clearly disliking the gesture. It was a pity really, for they had much in common. As a policeman and a scientist respectively, they were bent upon serious occupations, both of them in possession of twisty minds, a thirst for justice, a keen intellect, and significant attractions for the fairer sex.

But that was where the similarities ended. Whilst Stoker was splendid in a rather saturnine way with a palpable air of danger, Mornaday was merry as a grig. He had brown eyes that snapped and danced, and I found him utterly charming. Stoker was somewhat less impressed. The pair had very nearly come to blows during our previous investigation, but Mornaday had done us a good turn more than once, and I believed it was knowledge of this debt more than anything that irritated Stoker. He did not care to be beholden to anyone for anything.

I turned to Mornaday. "Pay him no mind. What a delightful surprise to find you at the theater," I said, fanning myself gently. "One might even think it *too* coincidental."

"I am a devotee of the theater," he returned, sounding slightly ruffled.

"And you are not following Miss Speedwell and me upon Sir Hugo's orders?" Stoker demanded.

"Certainly not!"

I turned to Stoker. "You see, he is telling the truth. Look at how he waggles his eyebrows for emphasis."

"Sir Hugo?" put in the viscount. "Do you mean Sir Hugo Montgomerie?"

"The same," I acknowledged. "He is rather too interested in our activities, and from time to time he sets the good inspector to follow us about."

Lord Templeton-Vane gave a bland smile. "How tiresome for you.

If you will excuse me, I will see if I can find my carriage in the crush outside. I will wait there." He inclined his head with perfectly calibrated hauteur towards Mornaday. "Inspector."

"My lord."

I watched his beautifully tailored back as he moved through the crowd, never pushing, but somehow clearing a path just the same. "Rather like Moses and the Red Sea," I murmured. I turned back to the inspector. "I wish I had known you were following us, Mornaday. We would have done something far more scandalous than just attend the theater with his lordship."

Mornaday's handsome mouth curled. "Ah, a happy family occasion, is it? No ulterior motives in spending the evening with his lordship?"

I spread my borrowed fan wide, peeping over the tips of the feathers in a coquettish gesture. "But, Mornaday, what possible motive could there be? Sir Hugo has ordered us off the investigation. Of course, if you were to tell me a secret, I should be honor-bound to reciprocate." I leaned closer, eager to glean a little crumb of gossip. Mornaday had let slip once before that Sir Hugo's strings were very clearly pulled by a shadowy and powerful figure—a *female* shadowy and powerful figure, which intrigued me all the more.

"What sort of secret?" he demanded.

"Sir Hugo's puppet master. It is quite naughty of you not to tell me who she is," I remonstrated.

"I do not recall saying anything of the sort," Mornaday retorted, his voice sharp. "I don't know anything."

"Fustian," I pressed. "You told us it was a woman. What sort of woman?"

It was a sign of Mornaday's desperation that he turned an appealing gaze upon Stoker, but he was met with an indifferent shrug. "You know how she is when she wants to know something," was Stoker's only comment.

Mornaday pursed his lips. "Curious as the proverbial cat. Very well, yes. It is a woman, and from what I have been able to gather, she is highly connected. *Very* highly," he added.

I turned to Stoker. "He is waggling his eyebrows again."

Mornaday pinked, a delightful rosy shade that made me long to pinch his cheeks. There was a boyish charm about him, but he had also been blessed with substantial shoulders and a rather nice pair of thighs, I had had occasion to notice.

"I really cannot say anything else upon the matter," he said firmly.

"I do love it when you are stern," I said, putting a gloved hand to his arm.

"Oh, for God's sake," Stoker muttered under his breath.

"Ignore him," I instructed Mornaday. "He is in a pet because he had to have a bath."

"His first this year?" Mornaday asked with affected innocence.

Stoker folded his arms over his chest, affecting boredom. "Do you know what I dislike most about you, Mornaday?" he asked in a nonchalant tone. "Your utter predictability."

"Whilst I dislike most your complete and insufferable arrogance—" Mornaday began. I linked my arm with his, cutting him off neatly.

"Now, now, gentlemen. If you carry on like this you'll only end up in fisticuffs and I won't have anyone bleeding on my new gown. Stoker, perhaps you would be good enough to wait for me on the pavement with his lordship. I would like a moment's conversation with Mornaday."

Stoker eyed me for a long moment then turned on his heel, smartly making his way through the crowd. Against me, I felt Mornaday relax as the tension drained from his body.

"I cannot begin to explain how much I do not like that man," he told me.

"I know," I soothed, coaxing Mornaday to a discreet spot behind a potted palm. "And I can assure you he is equally eloquent on the subject of your defects. I expect he will spend the entire ride home cataloging them for me. But I promise I shan't listen," I assured him. "Now, I know you want me to be very discreet about Sir Hugo's superior, and I swear that I shall. But it would make it so much easier to remember if I didn't have so many questions crowding my mind about Artemisia's death . . ." I trailed off, widening my eyes as I looked at him from under my lashes.

"You little devil!" he said, his tone admiring. "You think to use your fiendish wiles upon me with no care for what might become of my position at Scotland Yard. You are an absolute monster," he told me, but he was smiling as he said it.

"Oh, don't be difficult. Come now, I only want a little piece of information."

He sighed gustily. "Very well. What?"

"I want to know if there was more to the post-mortem, any snippet that did not make it into evidence. It might be quite trivial, but if there was something, I should like to know."

He pursed his lips again. "It would be more than my position is worth to tell you. I don't even like to contemplate what would happen to me if Sir Hugo found out I was talking to you tonight." Mornaday's expression was so woebegone that I took pity upon him and brushed a kiss to his cheek, causing his eyes to gleam brighter than ever.

"There was something," he murmured into my ear. "I cannot say what, and neither can the surgeons. They are too afraid of Sir Hugo. But do not stop looking."

"Mornaday! You utter lamb." His hand tightened upon mine.

"Careful now. More of that and I will send an engagement notice to the *Times.*" He bent his head, but I eluded his grasp, slipping away as I blew a kiss in farewell.

Stoker was waiting outside for me next to the viscount's carriage. "I dismissed the Beauclerk driver. We can make our own way home after," he told me. I looked up with a meaningful glance, and he realized

I had learnt something of interest from Mornaday. "What did you winkle out of him?"

"There was something in the post-mortem. He would not say what, but it is enough to persuade me we must keep digging."

He gave a short nod and handed me into his brother's carriage, settling himself opposite us as I took the place next to his lordship.

"Where shall we sup?" I asked him in a conversational tone as the driver sprang the horses.

"Vane House," he replied. "It is my London residence, and we shall not be overheard there. I think this evening will require some privacy," he added with an oblique glance at his brother.

The carriage eventually emerged from the press of traffic in the East End and made its way into the stultified heart of Mayfair. We approached a tall, imposing house that stood aloof, keeping lofty watch over one of the more impressive squares. His lordship must have trained his staff well, for he did not even pause upon the step. The door swung open, warm amber light spilling from the large hall within. The butler who opened the door was of the most correct sort, iron grey of hair and humorless of countenance, but his expression of perfect indifference dissolved as soon as he caught sight of Stoker.

"Mr. Revelstoke!" he said, his voice warmed by the same genuine affection that caused him to smile broadly. "How very good to see you, sir."

"Collins, how have you been? The lumbago still giving you trouble?"

"Not since I began taking your advice," the butler told him. He glanced to me with a question in his eyes.

His lordship handed over his hat and gloves. "Miss Speedwell, this is Collins. He has kept the Templeton-Vanes in order for more years than I have been alive. Collins, Mr. Revelstoke's colleague, Miss Speedwell."

"How do you do?" I replied.

"Welcome to Vane House, miss," he said gravely. He turned back to the viscount. "Supper is ready, my lord. Shall I have it served?"

"Yes, in the small dining room. But give us half an hour first. We will be in my study." The viscount led us through the tall domed hall of white marble and down a long passage to a closed door which he threw open with a flourish.

The room was not as lavish as I had expected given the marble grandeur of the rest of the house. It was smaller and, while the word could never truly fit, there was a coziness within those book-lined walls I had found lacking in what I had thus far seen of Vane House. A sofa covered in red plush and a pair of armchairs, leather and deeply cushioned for comfortable reading, provided the seating. The desk was an enormous oak affair—Tudor, I thought—with heavy carving and an assortment of papers scattered about in casual disarray. A singularly beautiful bust of Athena held pride of place on a plinth in front of the long windows, overlooking a genial untidiness that seemed to be a failing of the Templeton-Vane brothers.

The viscount did not stand on ceremony. His lordship busied himself with the tantalus and gasogene, pouring out three glasses of whiskey and soda. As he handed me my drink, he leveled his grey gaze at me, and though his eyes never left my face, I realized he was taking in every detail of my appearance. When he spoke, his voice was deep as Stoker's, but a shade less rough.

"I must say, Miss Speedwell, you are not at all what I expected."

Remembering the colorful remarks made by their youngest brother, I fixed him with a smile of calculated sweetness. "I seem to have left my dreadful reputation in my other reticule."

It was a palpable hit. He flushed, the same deliciously rosy tint as I had observed in Stoker, and inclined his head. "I do not know what Merryweather may have said, but I can only guess. I would like to apologize for any lapse in manners on his behalf."

Stoker threw himself down into the nearest armchair with a gusty sigh. "I see you've settled into the role of head of the family," he observed.

His lordship gestured for me to take the other chair and waited until I had done so before seating himself. "It is my place," he reminded Stoker. "And it would have been a damned sight easier if you had replied to any of my communications, if Miss Speedwell will pardon the expression."

Stoker shrugged. "I am here now."

His lordship's mouth—a handsome facsimile of his brother's—curved into a smile of self-deprecation. "I do not flatter myself that you have sought me out from any regard for my needs."

"No, no," Stoker assured him. "I have come only out of regard for my own."

"Naturally." The word was clipped, but there was no real coldness there. It occurred to me that I was witness to some habitual pattern of communication between these two, and that the presence or absence of a third party would do little to alter it.

His lordship settled himself more comfortably. He took the opportunity to glance at me again, then shifted his attention to his brother. "What do you want, Revelstoke?"

"Information." Stoker too settled back into his chair, crossing one ankle over his knee. "Tell me about Miles Ramsforth."

His lordship's expression was carefully neutral. "What about him?"

"What do you know about his relationship with his wife, Ottilie?" I was surprised at Stoker's line of questioning and covered it by taking a swift sip of my drink. I had expected him to lead with the subject of the ledger, but I realized he would know exactly how best to handle his elder brother. The viscount's composure was impressive, and it might require a good deal of work to crack it.

The viscount shrugged. "Not much. We are, after all, only passing acquaintances. I can tell you it seems to have been a love match. No children. They travel a bit, like to go mucking about in Greece and other such places, although I think their latest pet cause is art." He narrowed his gaze. "Is that what this is about? The murder?"

"It is," I told him. "We believe Miles Ramsforth may be innocent of the crime for which he is about to hang."

His lips compressed a moment. "I cannot imagine why it is any business of yours."

"We were asked to investigate," I said. "And by whom is no business of *yours*," I added with a tart edge to my voice.

A flicker of a smile touched his mouth. "Touché, Miss Speedwell. But as I said, we are passing acquaintances. I am afraid there is nothing I can add to what you already know of Miles."

"Oh, I am sure you could think of something of interest if you cudgeled your memory," Stoker said helpfully. "Like the Elysian Grotto, for example."

The viscount's complexion did not alter. He did not flinch or give a start. Only the quick, fleeting drop of his eyelids betrayed the fact that Stoker's arrow had flown true. He took a thoughtful swallow of his drink. "Elysian Grotto?" he asked in a bored tone. "What is that? A sort of club for Hellenic fanatics? You know my preference has always been for Roman art."

Stoker gave him a thin, feral smile, baring his teeth. "You always were a slippery bastard," he said in a low tone. "But even you cannot talk your way around the fact that we found your name in Ramsforth's ledger."

The hand around the viscount's glass tensed. "What ledger?"

Stoker leaned forward, about to accomplish a killing thrust, but I suspected such brutal handling would thwart our plans entirely. I flicked him a quelling glance. "My lord, Miles Ramsforth kept a ledger, a sort of guest book of those who took part in his entertainments at the grotto. Your name was there."

"My name." He sat back in his chair, swirling the whiskey in the glass, watching the amber whirlpool as it caught sparks of light from the fire. "My name. Of course, I could lie and say it was written without my knowledge. After all, it isn't my signature, is it? You would have only his word for it that I was there, and he is about to hang. Who would believe him?" He took a deep draft of the whiskey, holding it on his tongue for a long moment before swallowing. "But I think the time for prevarication has passed." He fixed his gaze upon his brother's face. "Go on, then. Ask what you want. I will give you the truth. Do with it what you will."

Stoker eyed him suspiciously, as if he could not quite believe the viscount intended to honor his word. "That is too easy, Tiberius. What are you withholding?"

His lordship spread his hands, handsome, well-shaped hands so unlike Stoker's. They were strong and capable-looking, but they had never turned to manual labor, never even held the reins of a horse without the protection of gloves. A signet ring gleamed upon his smallest finger, the crest of the Templeton-Vanes worn almost smooth from generations of lords who had owned it before him. "I have given my word. Is that not good enough? Shall I make it a blood oath?" he asked.

"Do not tempt me," Stoker said in a voice that was nearly a growl.

I put myself forward again, pouring calming oil upon the stormy waters. "My lord, you visited the grotto, did you not? And engaged in the entertainments there?"

He inclined his head. "I did, Miss Speedwell. And I must say that I hope whatever other revelations come out tonight, they do not offend your sensibilities."

"I have none to offend," I told him frankly.

He smiled, a slow, sensual smile that excluded Stoker completely. "I find that deliciously intriguing. And I shall make a note to ask you about that at a more convenient time. But for now, I think my brother will combust if I do not satisfy his curiosity." He indicated Stoker with a tip of his glass. "He is fairly vibrating with it, like a hound at the start of a hunt. Go on then, little brother. Ask."

"Did you ever meet Artemisia there?"

"Once," the viscount replied promptly. "Early in her liaison with Ramsforth. He thought she might be interested in the goings-on, but as it happens, she proved uninterested. She watched for a little while and then left. I never saw her again. She was surprisingly provincial for a Bohemian," he added.

I licked my lips. "What sorts of 'goings-on'?"

The viscount's smile deepened. "Ramsforth's entertainments always had a Classical theme. He thought it added a fillip of excitement to the occasion. Everyone was expected to don a mask depicting a character out of Greek myth and act out the role they had been assigned."

"What was your part?" Stoker demanded.

The viscount looked at me. "Apollo. On this occasion, I had my way with a willing little Daphne who wore a crown of laurel leaves, and I do not recommend it. Damned prickly," he added.

"And then?" I asked.

The viscount took a deep breath and peered into the depths of his glass. "And then I engaged in some group pursuits and some rather more disciplined entertainments, the details I am not inclined to share for fear of scandalizing you."

"I told you, you need not worry on my account," I told him.

He raised his eyes to mine, tilting his head. "I was not speaking of *your* sensibilities, Miss Speedwell. I was worried for Revelstoke's."

He said the words as calmly and passionlessly as the rest of his remarks, but there was a watchfulness in him, a coiled tension as he awaited Stoker's reaction.

"A group," Stoker repeated. "You mean you engaged in an orgy."

"Such a vulgar word," the viscount complained. "Weighted with all sorts of unpleasant connotations. My tastes are not limited by convention. Some of them, in fact, are less than strictly legal, although such delicacy seems puritanical in the extreme, as I suspect Miss Speedwell might agree," he said with an appreciative glance in my direction. "But I imagine you understand why my appearance at the grotto might excite unwelcome speculation—particularly in light of my marital misfortune. There is a good deal of tittering in society about why I have never remarried. My expansive tastes are not the reason, but I see no point in deliberately stoking the fire."

I shrugged. "Your private life is your own, my lord."

His brows rose into elegant arches. "Miss Speedwell, I am delighted to find my assessment of your liberal thinking is accurate. To meet a lady of such broad-mindedness is rare indeed. Stoker, if you don't marry Miss Speedwell, I might."

He tossed off the last of his whiskey as Stoker glowered at him. "Tiberius, just because you are my elder and the head of the family does not mean I won't beat you senseless and leave Collins to sweep up the remains from the hearthrug."

His lordship waved a hand with lazy grace. "You always did think violence was a suitable response to any situation." He turned to me. "The fellow is a Philistine, my dear. You can do better."

"I have no intention of 'doing' at all, my lord," I told him in my most commanding tone. "I am a spinster by choice. And you are quite masterfully leading us off the subject at hand—your involvement with the Elysian Grotto. Now, help us untangle the relationships, if you will, so that we can go in to supper. I smell roasted duck."

His lordship gave me a slow, appraising smile. "So imperious! How I should like to see you wield a riding crop." Stoker started forward and the viscount held up a hand. "Sit, Revelstoke. I meant no offense, and I suspect Miss Speedwell took none." Stoker shot me a glance and subsided back into his chair while his brother regarded me thoughtfully. "I am veritable clay in your hands, Miss Speedwell. Do with me as you like. Now, what else do you wish to know?"

I had no doubt his provocative remarks were meant to raise a response, so I gave him nothing but a cool stare. "Julian Gilchrist. Do you know the fellow?"

He nodded. "He was a particularly randy Endymion at our little folly. He had had a liaison with Artemisia of a few months' duration, but she ended things when she fell in with Ramsforth."

"How did he take it?" Stoker asked.

The viscount shrugged. "How does any man take such a thing? He was resentful, and he buried himself in the nearest bit of muslin to forget it."

"What about Sir Frederick Havelock? Did you see him there?"

He tipped his head back, an expression of remembered pleasure curving his lips. "I did. A very memorable Zeus."

"Having his way with a pretty Leda or Danaë?" I suggested.

"Neither. His attentions were reserved for Hera," his lordship corrected. "Until her death, Augusta Havelock accompanied him. After she died, he continued to attend, but only as an observer, never a participant."

"His wife attended?" Stoker put in, his tone frankly disbelieving.

His lordship shrugged. "Some couples find such shared endeavors heighten their connubial relationships. Sir Frederick was not the first man to bring a wife to such entertainments."

"Did you?" I asked.

"Such boldness! Just when I thought I could not admire you more, Miss Speedwell," he said, favoring me with a smile. "No, I did not. My wife, as it happens, was a thoroughly conventional and distinctly unlovable woman chosen for me by my father. A woman like you would be a different story altogether." His gaze lingered on my décolletage a moment longer than propriety would allow.

Stoker recalled him sharply. "Did Havelock pursue anyone at the grotto? Have any entanglements of note?"

"No. He came once or twice a year and that was all. Just enough to amuse himself."

"Did Ottilie Ramsforth ever appear at these entertainments?"

"Heavens, no!" His lordship seemed genuinely shocked at the idea. "Have you met her? Eyes only for her lord and master. She is the very last woman I should expect to engage in such frivolities. To be perfectly frank, I was quite surprised that she proved so willing to turn a blind eye to them. But she is that rarest and most tragic of creatures, a woman selflessly in love with her own husband."

"What about Artemisia's relationship with Ramsforth?" I asked. "How would you characterize it?"

He considered this a long moment. "Loving. They seemed sincerely attached. In fact, after Artemisia expressed her distaste for the affairs, Ramsforth closed the grotto to group activities in deference to her wishes."

I pricked up my ears at this new bit of information. "Does that mean he did not go there again?"

He shrugged. "You would have to ask him. I know invitations were no longer forthcoming, and when I asked, he said it was down to her influence and that only private visits were permitted. He told me he would put the grotto at my disposal, but I found my interest in the place had waned. I was content to let the thing go. If nothing else, it had gotten devilishly expensive."

"Expensive?" Stoker inquired.

"Ramsforth charged admission, a sort of subscription fee," his brother explained. "Rumor has it he worked his way through most of the Troyon money Ottilie brought to the marriage in rebuilding Littledown. And he was always careful to hire professionals from the very best brothels in London. That sort do not come cheaply."

"You mean he wasn't bringing in the milkmaid or the footman at Littledown for a bit of sport?" I asked.

The viscount's expression was one of naked horror. "God forbid!

No, he only engaged professionals. He did not believe in corrupting those who were not already working in the intimate trades," he said firmly. "There is such a thing as honor amongst debauchees, you know. Besides, a professional will keep quiet about such things. Money buys discretion."

"One thing more, if you do not mind?"

His lordship leveled his gaze at me. "For you, my dear Miss Speedwell, I have all the time in the world."

Stoker made a noise of disgust, but we both ignored him. "We were sent a key to the Elysian Grotto," I told the viscount. "It was posted to us anonymously, we can only assume by a benefactor. Did you send it?"

He opened the drawer of his desk and drew out a key that matched ours in every particular. "I am, as you see, still in possession of mine. Ramsforth neglected to ask for it back after he stopped hosting entertainments. You are welcome to take it if it helps."

I could not imagine how it would, but I took it anyway, thanking the viscount for his generosity.

I looked to Stoker. "I think we have learned all we can from his lordship."

He nodded slowly, and the viscount rose with the air of a man liberated. He rubbed his hands together. "In that case, supper."

CHAPTER
18

Supper with his lordship was a strained affair. Stoker was clearly regretting the fact that I had accepted his brother's invitation. He said almost nothing over the meal, while the viscount and I discussed the theater and butterflies and my travels.

"I envy you," he said at one point as he refilled my glass of wine. "I have always longed to travel, but my responsibilities here never permitted."

He did not look at his brother as he spoke, but I knew Stoker felt the thrust of it. The tension in the air thickened, and for a moment, silence hung between them. I waited, hoping they would finally have the brawl they needed to thrash out whatever resentments still simmered, but neither spoke. Was that the root of it all then? An elder brother's jealousy that his younger sibling could evade responsibility? It seemed possible but unlikely. In the same vein, I knew full well that Stoker did not begrudge his brother the title or the obligations carried with it. He had no ambition to wear a coronet and sit in the House of Lords. The very notion of Stoker engaged in such conventional activities was laughable. And looking at the urbane and polished appearance of the viscount, I could hardly credit the fact that he might covet the freedom of a brother who had returned to England sporting tattoos and pierced lobes with his eye patch.

As the silence stretched on, I decided to take charge. I rose, and both of them leapt to their feet. Whatever their differences, they shared the rigid upbringing of aristocratic Englishmen and all its reflexive courtesies.

"It grows late," I told the viscount. "I think it is time we took our leave."

He shot a glance to his brother. "Certainly. But, Revelstoke, you and I still have business to discuss."

"Later," Stoker said in a flat tone that brooked no argument.

But his lordship was not cowed. "So you have said. Repeatedly. I want you to meet with the solicitors so we can finish settling Father's estate."

"Later," Stoker repeated.

"I want your oath on it," the viscount said, giving him a level look. "For all your sins, your word is still worth something."

"My word as a Templeton-Vane?" Stoker asked. His smile was thin and malicious. "Very well. You have my word I will meet with them. As a Templeton-Vane."

He turned on his heel and strode from the room. The viscount watched him leave, then turned to me.

"Yours is an unusual friendship," he observed.

"It is only a friendship, my lord," I said, choosing my words carefully. "I assure you, I am no threat to the Templeton-Vanes."

His only reply was the return of his enigmatic gaze.

"It was a pleasure to make your acquaintance, my lord," I said, rather surprised to find I told the truth.

The corners of his mouth quirked up slightly. "I am not quite the martinet you expected?"

"Not quite," I acknowledged.

He kept hold of my hand. "You have surprised me as well, Miss Speedwell. From Rupert's description—well, that does not bear remembering. Suffice it to say that I have not enjoyed an evening this much in a very long time. And—" He paused, studying my hand a moment as it lay in his, my smaller palm flat against his smooth, broad one. He put his other fingertip to the back of my hand, stroking it with such practiced precision that it sent a frisson of something dark and hot to the depths of my spine. "I hope you will feel free to call whenever you wish. If you wait for Revelstoke to bring you, it will be a frosty day in the netherworld."

"Perhaps," I said.

He smiled, a slightly predatory smile that was nonetheless charming. With infinite slowness and care, he bent and brushed his lips to the back of my hand.

"Until the next time, Miss Speedwell."

"My lord."

S toker said nothing until we were outside on the pavement. As soon as I appeared, he began to walk very quickly, his long-legged strides eating up the ground. I made no attempt to match his pace. He was clearly in a pet, and I was perfectly capable of seeing myself home.

But Stoker was far too well-bred for such a thing, and by the end of the block, he slowed to match my steps.

"I ought not to have sent the Beauclerk carriage on its way. Oxford is the next street. We can easily find a cab there."

"And just beyond is Marylebone. It is a fine night. Let us walk instead."

He gave a brisk nod, and we crossed the street, passing through the bright lights and congestion of Oxford Street into the relative quiet of neighboring Marylebone.

"I was very interested to hear that Miles Ramsforth was in need of money," I told him. "Does it suggest anything to you?"

He was in no mood to talk, but his agile and curious brain could never resist a challenge. "Of course," he said shortly. "Blackmail."

"Exactly. If Miles Ramsforth used his ledger to blackmail someone, they might very well be interested in seeing him hang for a murder he did not commit."

"And Artemisia would not have been a victim so much as a pawn," he added.

"Quite. Which puts rather a different spin on things."

"How do you reason?" he asked, slipping his hand under my elbow to guide me around a puddle.

"Killing her in the heat of the moment is a crime of passion, of desperation or anger or jealousy. But killing her in cold blood in order to make Miles pay the price for it—that requires a chilling sort of detachment."

"And there are any number of suspects whose names appear in that book," he groaned.

I cursed our bad luck in losing the ledger. "I don't imagine there is any hope of recovering it if we went back to search?" My tone was hopeful, but I knew the futility of it before I asked.

"The watchman would have had more than enough time to recover it at his leisure."

"Blast," I muttered.

"Indeed. We shall simply have to try another avenue," he said. We fell silent then, making our way through the shadows of Marylebone towards Bishop's Folly.

"Were you surprised?" I ventured. "About what your brother hinted about the entertainments? Orgies and riding crops and such? Do you think there were men with other men and women with other women?"

"Veronica. We do not need to discuss this."

His profile was set, his steps dogged. I gave him a kindly look. "Are you confused by the process? I am happy to offer a little elaboration. You see, when a man prefers the company of other men—"

"For the love of Christ, Veronica, I know about poofters! I was in the navy, for God's sake."

"Poofters? Did you have so many that you had to devise a name for them?" I inquired.

He rubbed a hand over his eyes. "It is what most people call them."

"Sounds rather pejorative," I mused.

"It is the best of a bad lot," he admitted. "Would you prefer 'Sodomites'?"

"Hardly. That smacks of Evangelicalism, and you know my feelings on forcible religion," I reminded him.

He gave a sigh of resignation. "There were such fellows in the navy," he told me. "We didn't discuss it. They don't hang men for it anymore, but it can still get you ten years' imprisonment. Some of the Continental navies are different—such things are done openly—but in Her Majesty's fleet, there was a veneer of propriety."

"Everything belowdecks and sub rosa?" I guessed.

"Exactly. People behave quite differently during a long haul at sea than they might at home."

"But there are fellows who always prefer the company of other men," I reminded him. "It seems terribly hypocritical to condemn them for a little discreet buggery when children are still starving in coal mines." I tipped my head. "Stoker, when you were in the navy, did you ever—"

"Yes. Once a day and twice on Sundays."

I stared at him in open-mouthed astonishment before he broke into laughter, so rare a sound for him, I almost did not recognize it.

"My God, your face," he managed, wiping his eyes.

I pursed my lips. "I assure you, I was far more shocked by your candor than the notion of you indulging in the erotic arts with a member of your own sex."

He sobered, but a wicked glint still lingered in his eyes. "No, Veronica, I did not. But for those who did, it was none of my affair. Still isn't, for that matter. I do not much care for your habit of prying into other people's bedrooms," he added in mock severity.

I shrugged. "That is where they keep the most interesting secrets."

He cocked his head. "Well, since we are peeking behind the boudoir door, as it were, have you ever sampled the Sapphic pleasures?"

"What a question!" I pronounced.

"It was a shot in the dark," he said, nearly choking, "but you've gone quite pink. Our artist friends would call the hue *cuisse de nymphe èmue*."

"Thigh of an aroused nymph?" I asked in a voice rather unlike my own.

"Yes," he told me, clearly relishing the moment. "It is meant to suggest the sweetly rosy blush of the flesh when a woman is in the throes of sexual excitement. Apropos in light of our discussion—and the question which I should like to note you have pointedly not answered."

He folded his arms over his chest and waited, his eyes bright with an unholy light.

I gave him a brisk nod. "Very well. There was a Sardinian shepherdess once. Very buxom, with pillowy lips and eyes like sloes. I kissed her— and that is all that I did. Purely out of scientific curiosity."

"Scientific curiosity? How so?" he demanded.

"Because I had just lain with her twin brother and wondered if they shared a similar technique." I put a pointed finger under his chin and pushed gently upwards. "Close your mouth, Stoker. You look like a carp."

He gulped hard and I removed my finger. "The notion of you in the arms of your shepherdess friend is one I shall want to revisit at some later time," he warned me. "But for now, I suppose we ought to think about the investigation." He shook his head hard as if to clear it.

"Were you really not surprised by the conversation with his lordship?"

He shrugged. "It is no business of mine. He can bugger a barnyard for all I care."

I turned to stare at him, the streetlight that illuminated half of his face throwing the other half in deepest shadow. "You do not see it, do you?"

"What?"

"His candor was his way of attempting to mend the breach between you."

Stoker snorted and turned to walk away. I put a hand to his sleeve, pulling him to a stop.

"He did not have to tell us anything," I reminded him. "He could have said we had imagined his name there. We do not have the ledger. We have no proof. He could have said he had only gone the one time or that his name had been forged. But he didn't."

"And?" The syllable was clipped and cold as if he had chiseled it from ice.

"It means he trusts us. If we choose to report him to the authorities, he could be put in prison, Stoker. You know the sorts of antics the Elysians got up to are illegal. He would be sentenced to hard labor."

"Peers don't go to prison," he said, curling his lip.

"Do not play the cynic with me. It doesn't suit you, and I can see right through it," I told him. "It was an olive branch, whether you choose to interpret it as such or not."

"Indeed? Veronica, he knows we cannot prove it. He was perfectly safe in sharing whatever sordid details of his life he cared to offer. Do you really not understand? He is one of them. He is an aristocrat. He is untouchable."

He turned to walk away again, but the anger seemed to have drained away. We passed the next few blocks in silence.

"I am curious how men who go with men decide who plays the submissive part," I said eventually.

Stoker made a strangled noise in the back of his throat. "Leave it, Veronica."

"Very well. I suppose I might ask his lordship the next time I see him. He doesn't seem bashful upon the subject."

Stoker stopped dead in his tracks. "What the devil do you mean 'the next time'?"

"The viscount has expressed a wish to share my company."

"The bloody hell he has!" Stoker exploded.

"Heavens, Stoker, what difference does it make to you?"

"This is just like him, thinking he can do as he damn well pleases because he is the lord of the manor," he said savagely. He turned away, then loomed back, using his height to full advantage. "You are not to go anywhere with him. You are not to call upon him. You are not to receive him."

I was so astonished I very nearly laughed aloud. "You cannot seriously think I would permit you to dictate terms to me," I began.

He leaned closer and I could smell the scent of his brother's expensive whiskey on his breath. His mouth hovered just over mine, his body brushing against me. I could see the pulse beating hard in his throat.

"I can dictate these terms," he said in a voice that was little more than a growl. "He has taken something of mine for the last time."

"I am *not* something of yours," I reminded him, scalding him with the scorn in my voice. "I don't care what bad blood there is between you, you do not get to tell me whom I see. You are not my husband!"

I pressed my hands flat to his chest and heaved, but he did not move. His hands came up to grasp my wrists hard, and for an instant I saw something like hurt flicker in his gaze. "No," he said slowly. "I am better than a husband. I am your friend."

With agonizing slowness, he dropped my hands and walked away.

CHAPTER

19

The next morning I sped through the task I had allotted myself—identifying a woefully mislabeled tray of Lepidoptera from the Americas—in the hope of spending the afternoon at Havelock House. A late-morning missive from Emma Talbot put paid to that.

"She is unable to sketch you today," I told Stoker, holding up the note she had sent the fourth delivery of the post. "She has a prior engagement. Hell and damnation," I muttered, fuming at the delay.

Stoker, who had been studying his industrious little dermestids, merely shrugged. "So we pursue another line of inquiry."

His tone was sullen, and altogether we had exchanged fewer than a dozen words throughout the morning. He had spent the better part of the time finishing the excavation of his Bactrian with the result that his chest and arms were liberally streaked with glue and sawdust and his hair was streaming with sweat. Manual labor usually had the effect of calming his temper, but in this case, it had merely given him an excuse to indulge in his more destructive tendencies. The Bactrian had been reduced to its filthy skin and a pile of untidy bones. Stoker finished folding the camel hide carefully. He would clean and dry it on a rack he had fashioned specifically for the task, but there was much work to be done first. Every bit of errant sawdust had to be cleaned from the bones and the joints assessed before he made the decision to mount the hide back on the skeleton or sculpt an armature as the new base. What he intended for the tongue and eyes did not bear thinking about.

"What are you going to do with the poor fellow?" I asked, nodding to the heap of sawdust and bones on the floor.

For a moment I thought he would not answer, but he never could resist the opportunity to discuss his work. "I shall reassemble the skeleton for display. Then I will sculpt a base for the hide and mount it, providing I can save the hide at all. The mice have got at it."

It was a tremendous amount of work; the average taxidermist would have simply mounted the hide over a bit of padding thrown over the creature's own skeleton. But Stoker was no average taxidermist. His idea of exhibiting the skeletons separately and remounting the hides on metal armatures of his devising was innovative and brilliant. Of course, I did not tell him so. It would not do to inflate his already quite healthy sense of accomplishment.

But a little feminine deference could not fail to sweeten his mood, I decided. I leaned forward in my chair, gently blowing the dust off of a delicate little specimen. "What do you suggest then as an alternate line of inquiry?" I asked casually.

He rubbed thoughtfully at his chin, leaving a dark line of sweat-dampened sawdust along his jaw. "We ought to pursue Mornaday's hint about Artemisia's post-mortem."

He settled himself on the edge of the desk and began to rummage for a bite to eat. I usually kept a tin of honeycomb on hand for emergencies, but it was empty and he grumbled his irritation. "I am sorry. I quite forgot to buy more, but you *will* keep eating it all," I told him with a touch of asperity. "That was supposed to be in case of emergency."

"This *is* an emergency. I had no breakfast. I came straight down to work, and half a pot of tea is not enough to sustain a man for a job like that," he told me with a jerk of the chin towards his Bactrian.

"Just a moment, and I will find you something. This wretched *Limenitis archippus* is masquerading as a *Danaus erippus*, and not very cleverly." I corrected the label, penning the accurate identification as Stoker gave a quick cry and dove beneath the morning's newspaper. He emerged waving a packet triumphantly.

"What have you got there?" I asked, pinning the *Limenitis* into place with a sigh of satisfaction.

"The last of the funeral biscuits," he said, tearing into the packet with his teeth. He took out the pair of biscuits inside and crunched one thoughtfully. "Aniseed again," he said after a moment. "Not my favorite, but not at all bad."

"And thoroughly ghoulish," I told him. "All of this rampant morbidity cannot be good." I picked up the discarded packet. Besides the expected advertisement for the undertakers, there was a short tribute to Artemisia and a picture of a willow bent dolorously over a grave. "There is even a poem—of the most sickeningly sentimental variety," I pointed out. "It is twaddle."

"No," he corrected, plucking the packet from my fingers with shining eyes. "It is a clue."

He turned the packet around so I could see where he pointed. "'Messieurs Padgett and Pettifer, Undertakers,'" I read slowly. "Of course! The police surgeons will never speak to us, nor will the investigators. Sir Hugo will have seen to that. Everyone associated with the case in an official capacity will close ranks against us. There is no one to whom we can turn—except the undertakers. However did you think of it?"

He shrugged. "Who knows more about a body than the men who prepare it for burial?"

"Revelstoke Templeton-Vane!" I cried. "God strike me down if ever again I question your intelligence. That is a stroke of brilliance."

He preened. "It is, isn't it? I think I shall bask in this for a little while. I do like being right."

"You are impossible," I told him, grinning.

"Only the improbable can appreciate the impossible," he said.

It took him only quarter of an hour to make himself presentable and secure us a cab. It had occurred to both of us that bursting into a respectable undertaking establishment with an eye to asking indiscreet questions was a quick route to getting ourselves thrown out with no progress made upon the investigation. It further occurred to us that it might prove awkward should the undertakers decide to report the matter to Sir Hugo.

"We will go in disguise," I pronounced.

Stoker gave me a half-smile. "What sort of disguise? I warn you, you will never pass for a corpse. You are far too loquacious."

"Very funny. We shall outfit ourselves as recently bereaved and in need of the services of Messrs. Padgett and Pettifer."

He made a token protest, but I had observed during the months of our acquaintance that Stoker was as enthralled by the unexpected as I was. He gave the driver the address of Bunter and Weedman, the warehouse Cherry had mentioned and which provided lavish funeral ensembles for hire to those who could not afford to purchase them outright. Since the death of Prince Albert, unrestrained mourning had been the order of the day, with crêpe draped at the doors and windows of houses touched by loss. Even the poorest wretch could manage a black armband, but those with the means vied to outdo one another in their trappings of grief, hiring ebony horses and equipages for the obsequies, paying funeral mutes and pallbearers to stand witness to their bereavement. Decent coin might be had by those who could look suitably downcast, summoning tears on cue, or those who could heft a coffin to a stout shoulder. The

Prince Consort's death had spawned an industry of loss, from flowers to jewelry, fabric to feathers, and shops across the city hired such things to those who had not the means or inclination to purchase them outright. It was a simple matter to outfit ourselves—Stoker in a suit of black with a tall hat and I in a gown and cape of stark jetty bombazine. The cape fell to my heels, but the thick veil at my bonnet dragged behind, muffling my steps and obscuring my features.

"You look like a ghost bride," Stoker told me as his gaze swept from the crown of my head to the sweeping hem.

"The nearest to a bride I intend ever to come," I retorted. He had worn his eye patch, and the effect as a whole was rather sinister.

The outfitting of my funereal garb had taken longer than Stoker's, and he had put the time to good use in reading the *Times*. He gestured towards the morning's obituaries.

"Our undertaker friends have a funeral this afternoon. They should be out for some hours yet," he told me.

I grinned. "The perfect opportunity to do a little sleuthing."

We made our way to the rooms of Messrs. Padgett and Pettifer. They operated out of a tall house in a respectable street in a fashionable quarter, the sort of establishment where everything would be done just so. A silent, sober porter opened the door, giving a lugubrious bow as he stepped back to let us in. I was conscious of the odor at once, a mingling of lilies and death and something else.

"Someone's been at the camphor," Stoker murmured.

I stifled a snort. He was quite right. Mourning clothes were often put aside with camphor sachets to be dragged out again when circumstances demanded, leaving a telltale odor behind. Enormous vases of lilies stood in the corners of the hall, and every door was closed, each marked with a discreet placard indicating the purpose of the room. One was a showroom for coffins, another a display room for fabrics for mourning clothes. I could not see the rest, but it required little imagination to deduce that they must be put to similar use.

The porter bowed low, his expression one of studied dolor. "How may I be of service?"

"I am Sir Hugo Montgomerie," Stoker lied smoothly. "This is Lady Montgomerie."

I choked a little but passed it off as a momentary fit of weeping.

"As you can see, my wife is quite distressed, but she would insist upon coming," Stoker said with suitable gravity. "We should like to consult with Mr. Padgett or Mr. Pettifer about arrangements for a bereavement we have suffered. It was quite sudden," he added with a mournful downturn of his mouth.

The porter tutted regretfully. "I am sorry, Sir Hugo, my lady, but I am afraid both Mr. Padgett and Mr. Pettifer are conducting a funeral at Highgate at present. If you would care to call back later—"

"We will wait," Stoker cut in.

The porter hesitated. "It might be some time," he said. "I do think it would be best—"

Sensing the opportunity slipping from our grasp, I let out a wail. "Desmond! Oh, Desmond! Taken from us too soon," I lamented.

Stoker's expression was thunderous. "Are you happy, man? Look what you've done. Lady Montgomerie is *distraught*."

I let my knees buckle a little, and Stoker's arm came around me for support. "My wife needs to sit down and collect herself. In private," he said sternly. The porter darted forward and opened a door.

"Of course, Sir Hugo, my lady. I am terribly sorry. Wait in here, please. I am certain Mr. Pettifer will not mind you using his private office."

He ushered us through the door and indicated a pair of forbidding chairs upholstered in black silk. "Is there anything I can get for the lady?" he asked Stoker.

"Thank you," Stoker replied with chilly hauteur. "I will attend to my wife."

The porter bobbed his head. "Certainly. There is brandy upon the sideboard should her ladyship require revivifying. Please do not hesitate to ring should I be able to be of service." He withdrew, closing the door firmly behind him.

Stoker arched a brow at me. "Desmond? Who in the seven devils is Desmond?"

"Our cat," I said promptly. "Dashed under the wheels of a milk wagon."

"Poor flat Desmond," he said, sweeping off his hat as he glanced about the room. "Where shall we begin?"

"With the desk," I replied. "There will be a record of the bodies they have prepared. You search the files and I will see if I can find a ledger."

We set swiftly to work, occasionally pausing to make suitably mournful noises in case the porter were listening. I wailed from time to time, making certain to sniffle loudly as Stoker bent to picking the locks on the drawers of the desk. He made quick work of it, using a pair of my hairpins for the task. We searched carefully, sifting through notebooks and the leaves of the books on the shelf, moving methodically from drawer to drawer, but there was nothing. The only promising item was a wide ledger of black kid with a list of funerals they had undertaken, noted by date. I turned quickly to the month of Artemisia's demise and found a single line—"'Maud Eresby, spinster, aged 26 years. Prepared for burial and body dispatched to family home in Kent. Account settled in full by Sir Frederick Havelock,'" I read aloud. "Hell and blast, not a mention of her condition or even that she was murdered."

"This is the business side of things," Stoker pointed out as he searched the last drawer, empty except for a box of licorice. "Perhaps Mr. Pettifer is engaged in the accounts and front-of-house arrangements. There may be notes about embalming and such in the mortuary."

I raised a speculative brow at him and he shook his head. "Absolutely not. It's too much of a risk just now." He opened the box of licorice and popped a piece into his mouth. Instantly, he gagged, spitting it into his handkerchief. He wiped his mouth and stuffed the handkerchief into his pocket.

"That tasted like Satan's shoe leather," he said, still gagging a little.

"Serves you right for being such a cowardy-cowardy custard," I taunted lightly. To my surprise, the goad worked.

"Fine. We will search the mortuary, but if we are taken up for trespassing, I shall leave it to you to explain it all to Sir Hugo," he warned.

"It is a bargain," I promised. We crept on silent feet from the room, pausing a moment to make certain the porter was not lurking about. Stoker took the lead, grasping my hand tightly in his as we slipped down the corridor towards the back of the establishment. A single door at the end was marked with the word MORTUARY, and Stoker made directly for it, putting his hand to the knob but not turning it. I looked from the closed door to Stoker's face. "Go on then," I said flatly.

"You will not be distressed?" he asked.

"Will you?" I asked with a touch of asperity that he should doubt my mettle.

A derisive snort was his only reply, and he fell back, gesturing for me to lead the way. "Excelsior," I muttered, invoking the motto of our favorite fictional detective. I pushed open the door to the mortuary, as resolute as any battlefield commander.

Instantly we were struck by the smell of carbolic—and something worse. Death has an odor of its own, sweet and heavy, and it hung in the air, enveloping us as soon as we entered. I reeled at the stench, but Stoker drew a deep breath of it. Death was his stock-in-trade, after all. There was nothing here that would frighten or disturb him.

We took a moment to get our bearings. The room was large, and along one wall ran a series of shelves neatly filled with jars of chemicals and various pieces of equipment, none of which I cared to examine further. There were assorted needles and bits of padding as well as pots of face paint and powder.

Stoker spoke in a low whisper. "Sometimes death does unlovely things. It is the undertaker's task to mask them."

My gaze went to the far side of the room where a series of marble tables stood in chilly splendor. The tiled floor below was fitted with drains, and I went to inspect in horrified fascination.

"What are these used for?" I demanded. Stoker explained the various steps of the embalming process and the necessity for drains to carry away the resulting effluvia.

"But where does it go?"

"Into the sewers," he said cheerfully.

"That is repulsive," I said, wrinkling up my nose.

"No worse than what is already there," he pointed out. "And if you find that thought too repellent, I suggest you keep far away from our silent friend," he said, nodding towards the shrouded figure lying on a table in the corner.

I went to it, pausing with my hand upon the sheet for only a moment before pulling it free. Under it lay the body of a young, naked man, the skin of his torso folded back as neatly as if it had been a shirtfront. I reeled away, and before Stoker could mock me, we heard footsteps. Without thinking, I grabbed him and vaulted onto the next table, dragging him on top of me. On his way down, he grasped the sheet and hauled it over us, shielding us from view. With any luck, whoever it was would simply complete their errand in the embalming room and leave quickly.

As we waited, tense and alert, it occurred to me that I might have arranged matters more efficiently by putting myself on top of Stoker. His weight was not inconsequential, and although he did his best not to crush me, the need to lie as flat as possible meant our bodies were thoroughly entangled in a position I knew neither of us could sustain for any length of time. His face was pressed against mine, cheek to cheek, and

I felt the rasp of his whiskers. He had shaved only that morning, but his beard was heavy, and by afternoon the shadow of it always returned. His hired suit smelt of lavender and cedar—no doubt it had been laid away in these to deter moth—but his skin was his own peculiar mixture of male flesh and leather and linen and honey, always honey. One of his errant locks tickled my nose, and I breathed in sharply to keep from sneezing. His hands were where they had landed, one gripping my hip and one behind my head, cradling it against him. Mine were clasped against his shirtfront through which I could feel the slow, steady beating of his heart. My own was flitting like a hummingbird's wings, but he was calm, and from the quick pulse of his stomach muscles clenched against mine, I knew he was stifling a laugh at the absurdity of our situation.

We clung together under the sheet, and I do not know what Stoker's thoughts were, but I was listening intently for the footfalls as the person moved through the room. It was not the porter—his step had been heavier. This was a smaller, more diminutive footstep, almost tentative. It kept to the far side of the room, some distance from our makeshift hideaway, and I began to relax. Perhaps he would not come near us after all.

I flexed one foot against Stoker's calf, easing a sudden cramp, and I felt him stiffen against me. He tightened his grip, causing me to gasp. In an instant, I heard a flurry of footsteps and then the sheet was whisked away. I looked over Stoker's shoulder, blinking at the slender gentleman who gazed down at us, his expression one of staring horror.

"But—but—who on earth . . ." he began.

From behind him, a portly fellow appeared. He scrutinized us, then a broad smile broke over his features. "Why, Mr. Pettifer," he said with terrible politeness, "do you not recognize our guests?" He fixed his rictus grin on us. "I am Mr. Padgett," he said genially. "Welcome to our establishment, Miss Speedwell and Mr. Templeton-Vane."

CHAPTER

20

Stoker showed no inclination to shift, so I prodded him with my finger. "Remove yourself from my person, Stoker. We are discovered."

He rolled off of me and landed lightly on his feet, pulling me with him. I straightened my trailing garments and squared my shoulders, setting a polite smile upon my lips. "Mr. Pettifer, Mr. Padgett. How delightful to make your acquaintance."

Mr. Padgett was having none of it. He fixed me with a glowering look and jerked his chin. "My private office, if you please."

I looked to Stoker who merely shrugged one broad shoulder and gestured for me to follow Mr. Padgett. With Mr. Pettifer bringing up the rear, we were not precisely guarded and could have made a dash for the door, but I translated Stoker's shrug to mean we might as well see what information we could glean while we were there.

Mr. Padgett led us to the office next door to Mr. Pettifer's. Clearly he was the senior partner, for his domain was far more spacious. It was furnished with the sort of fussiness indicative of too much money and too little taste. All of the wood was ebony and the upholstery was black or grey, but the rug was too thick, the draperies too full, and the furniture too plush. It was an exercise in suffocation, and I made a point of perching on the edge of the chair Mr. Padgett indicated.

But as I glanced around the room, I saw one redeeming feature—butterflies. They were subtly woven into the black silk of the chairs, and a cluster of tiny Common Sootywings—*Pholisora catullus*—hung under a glass dome on a sideboard. But the most arresting, and the thing that drove me to jump up with an exclamation of delight, was a single perfect exemplar of an enormous black butterfly framed behind the desk.

"Papilio deiphobus!" I cried, going to examine it more closely. It had been mounted with its body facing out so that the inky depth of its underside would be displayed, unrelieved in its velvety blackness save for the slender brushstrokes of grey feathering each wing between the ribs.

Mr. Padgett came to stand next to me. He was a portly man of some six and a half feet tall, and his expression suddenly changed to one of unexpected geniality. "You like my Giant Swallowtail, do you? He is a beauty, if I say it myself."

"I netted one years ago, in the Philippines," I told him. "I let him go for far too little. He was a trifle larger than this one."

"Larger!" He puffed his cheeks a little. "You are having me on," he said, narrowing his gaze.

"I am not. I was on a tour of the Asian Pacific with an eye to acquiring as many Swallowtails as I could find. My Giant was large enough to pay my passage home, although I realized later I ought to have asked double."

"You are an Aurelian," he said with some admiration, recognizing a kindred spirit at last.

"I am, sir, and I must commend you. The little Sootywings are so predictable as to be almost a cliché, but this fellow . . ." I turned again to the Swallowtail, admiring the slim, graceful arcs of his antennae and his tidy feet, gathered protectively against his body.

Mr. Padgett gave a start. "I say! Are you a connection to the V. Speed-well who wrote the most diverting piece for the *Sussex and Kent Butterfly Observer* last month? On the subject of Chalkwings?"

"I have the honor of having penned the piece myself," I told him.

He grasped my hand and pumped it hard. "This *is* a pleasure," he told me, beaming his approval. Stoker and Mr. Pettifer were excluded from the ensuing conversation on Lepidoptera. I hoped that by engaging him in his favorite interest, I might encourage Mr. Padgett to think kindly of us and overlook our unorthodox method of entry. After some spirited discussion on the difficulties of finding good specimens in a decidedly urban environment—the invariable complaint of every London butter-fly collector—Mr. Padgett fixed us with an inquiring eye.

"So, you must be wondering how I perceived your true identities," he said, clearly relishing the moment.

"I can only presume Sir Hugo anticipated us," I replied.

He blinked, a little put out at having his thunder stolen, I surmised. "Well, yes. He sent word that we might receive a visit from the pair of you," he told us, gathering Stoker into the conversation with a stern eye. Stoker yawned and scrutinized his fingernails. After a moment, he drew his knife from under his trouser leg and began to clean one of them. Mr. Pettifer, standing in the shadows in the corner, shied like a frightened rabbit.

"Stoker, do stop brandishing that blade. You have alarmed Mr. Pet-tifer, and that is very unkind. Do forgive him, Mr. Pettifer. He spent too many years on a navy ship. His manners have suffered."

"You don't know that," Stoker remarked in a lazy drawl. "I might have been worse before the navy got their hands on me."

I conceded the point. But his attempts to intimidate the undertak-ers were unworthy of a gentleman, and I glared at him until he replaced his knife with a sigh.

Mr. Padgett took a deep breath and blew it out, visibly relaxing, while Mr. Pettifer pulled out a handkerchief and mopped his brow. I turned to Mr. Padgett with a smile.

"I am sorry Sir Hugo thought to trouble you with so inconsequential a matter," I said in my most winsome tone. "Really, we only want the answer to a single question, and it hardly seemed worth troubling Sir Hugo. I am certain you know what a bore policemen can be."

I smiled and fluttered my lashes a little, but Mr. Padgett was having none of it. "I do indeed know, and I've no inclination to get on the wrong side of Sir Hugo Montgomerie. There is nothing Mr. Pettifer or I can tell you," he said, giving his colleague a meaningful look.

Mr. Pettifer rolled his eyes like a frightened horse, and I smiled at him.

"Miss Speedwell," Mr. Padgett said sharply, redirecting my attention. "I must be quite firm upon the point. Padgett and Pettifer are given a great deal of work through our connections with the Metropolitan Police and through Sir Hugo's good offices. I cannot jeopardize that. *We* cannot," he said with another firm glance at his partner.

"Certainly not," Mr. Pettifer said quietly, not meeting my eyes.

I rose gracefully. "I quite understand. Perhaps, though, in the interest of helping a fellow Aurelian, you might not mention this visit to Sir Hugo? We learned nothing," I hurried on, "so you would not even be withholding information from him."

Mr. Padgett, who had courteously risen to his feet when I did, gave me a slow, measured look. "I have an extensive collection at home, but my very first specimen, and my favorite—a Camberwell Beauty—is fading," he said. "He was once the prettiest shade of purple you ever saw, like spring violets. But he was badly fixed and is losing his luster, and I need him to complete my grouping of purple butterflies. If he were to be replaced . . ." He let his voice trail off suggestively.

"Why, Mr. Padgett," I said with wide-eyed eagerness, "you must permit me to find you another imago! It would be my pleasure to accommodate such a sympathetic gentleman."

"I understand the going rate is somewhere in the vicinity of three pounds," he said blandly.

I waved an airy hand. "How ridiculous to speak of money between friends. It would be a gift, of course," I insisted.

He came to shake my hand. "How very generous of you, Miss Speedwell. And one is so often inclined to repay generosity where one has first encountered it."

I gave him a thin smile. "I see we understand one another perfectly, Mr. Padgett."

Stoker and I went to leave, nodding towards Mr. Pettifer as we went. Just as we reached the door, Mr. Padgett called after us.

"Miss Speedwell? When you come to bring me my Beauty, perhaps you will be good enough to leave your watchdog at home," he said, giving Stoker a look of pure distaste.

By way of reply, Stoker snapped his jaws and slammed the door behind us.

After delivering our rented weeds to the funeral warehouse, we returned to the Folly so that I might apply myself to the capture of Mr. Padgett's quarry. The afternoon had turned unseasonably hot— summer's last flirtation before making her departure—and I had observed that in the lower part of the garden, past the crumbling glasshouse and the pond thick with duckweed and lily pads, a superb Camberwell Beauty had been cavorting amongst the shrubberies. Naturally, I said nothing to Mr. Padgett of the proximity of the Beauties. No butterfly hunter worth her salt shared her hunting grounds.

"Completing his collection of purples," I muttered to myself. "I have never heard anything so daft. Imagine, reducing *Nymphalis antiopa* to a pretty color."

Still, I reminded myself, netting the specimen would be a balm to my nerves, unsettled as they were by the constant demands of city life. I collected my net and slipped a few minuten—the headless pins of the lepidopterist—through the flat of my cuff. It was a neat trick, designed to hold my equipment in proximity. On my foreign travels, it also helped keep the wandering hands of importunate suitors at bay. I did not bother with a killing jar. A quick pinch to the thorax was all that was required to administer a swift, clean death. Stoker walked out with me, going as far as the pond.

"Stopping here?" I asked, checking the fastness of my pins.

He stripped off his coat. "Aye. Now turn away. I'll not have you looking upon my maidenly blushes."

Before I could remove myself, he had slipped out of his shirt and boots, pausing with his hands upon the buttons of his trousers. "Either leave or stay and help," he said, batting his lashes at me like a bashful doe.

"Ass," I said, turning away quickly. He was still laughing as I pushed my way through the foliage. A moment later I heard a hearty splash as he flung himself into the green water of tho pond. I went about my business, making straight for the little copse where I had seen several Beauties at play over the course of the past few months. It was hot work. It seemed as if summer, before she gave herself up entirely to the cooler charms of autumn, was determined to have one last hectic dance. I blotted my temples as I searched, looking low upon the branches of a plum tree for the flash of purple wings.

At last, success! A flutter of languid violet told me I had found my quarry. I crept near, my ring net clutched in practiced hands. There, beneath a plum leaf, I spied him. This fellow was fresh from his chrysalis, for his wings were damp and heavy, dragged down with his dewy liquors. He spread them slowly, flapping them open and closed to dry them in the warm air. He was a new creation, I reflected, exploring the possibility of his wings for the first time. But he had not yet felt their power. He did not realize what they could do, how they could bear him aloft on the wind, carrying him far and wide over moor and meadow, hedgerow and heath. The whole of England lay within the span of those slender wings, and he had no knowledge of it.

It was not my custom to capture the newly emerged, but the convenience was tempting. A quick flick of the wrist and my net was upon him. He was too startled to resist, I think, for he gave only a token flutter then fell still. I reached into the net and cupped him in my hand. His wings whispered against my palm—in protest? In acquiescence? I could not say. I opened my left hand to find him sheltered there in the curve of it. My right thumb and index finger formed a pincer as I eyed the spot, just below his head, where the coup de grâce would be administered.

Just then, he stirred, spreading his wings in one last flamboyant gesture of defiance. The sun touched them properly for the first time, sending warmth and life through veins no bigger than a spider's silk. He was magnificent, a perfect being, innocent and yet full of possibility. My fingertip touched the edge of his wing, and he trembled, fluttering his wings almost invitingly.

"Go now," I whispered. "Before I change my mind."

He hesitated, fanning those exquisite jeweled wings a moment more, then suddenly, with a great heave, he lurched from my palm, as graceless as a newborn colt. But then he was flying, climbing and dropping and lifting again until he rose above the plum tree, his little feet barely clearing the tips of the leaves.

"No more of that," I told myself firmly as I swallowed past the catch in my throat. "There is no place for sentimentality in science."

Thoroughly out of sorts, I strode back to the pond to find Stoker returning after having swum the length of it—several times, no doubt. His shoulders broke the water as he surged up, raising both arms and pulling himself forward in a powerful stroke. I sat upon the grassy verge and removed my boots and stockings, dabbling my toes in the green water. It was bracingly cool and smelt of duckweed and water hyacinths. Stoker turned over, floating upon his back, his black hair as dark and sleek as the pelt of a seal. He grinned when he saw me and reached a lazy hand for a convenient clump of duckweed which he dropped over his hips.

"Coming to peer at an innocent fellow while he baths—have you no shame, Veronica?" he asked lightly.

"I am disturbed—very disturbed indeed," I told him.

"That could hurt a fellow's feelings," he pointed out. "I am not that hideous to look upon."

"Not disturbed by you," I retorted. "And do not fish for compliments. It is beneath you. I found a Beauty."

"It's been a long time since anyone called me such, but I suppose it will do."

"The butterfly, you fool."

"Well done," he said, moving his arms languidly in the green water. The ripples he made touched my feet.

"I don't have it now. I let it go because I could not bring myself to kill it," I told him.

"And that disturbs you?" He closed his eyes, letting the sun warm his exposed flesh. The duckweed slipped a little on his flank, but I did not bother to tell him.

"I am a scientist," I reminded him. "What sort of professional lepidopterist cannot bring herself to kill a butterfly?" I asked in some disgust. "I might as well become a vegetarian and start eating nut cutlets and legumes," I said darkly.

He smiled but did not open his eyes. "You promised Mr. Padgett a specimen. What will you do?"

"Lord Rosemorran has several dozen in his collection. We haven't room for more than a few pairs of each, male and female. I will choose a perfectly lovely imago and send it to Mr. Padgett. I will reimburse his lordship the value out of my wages."

Stoker shrugged one shoulder, sending more ripples over my feet.

This time the water washed up to my shins, sending delicious chills up my legs. "It sounds as if you have solved the problem rather neatly. You've got rid of some of his lordship's excess collection and cleared a debt. Why are you so nettled?"

"What if I have lost my nerve?" I asked in a small voice.

He opened one eye. "Not bloody likely. You have all the nerve of a bad tooth."

I flapped my hand, sending a spray of pond water onto his face. "I mean it. What if I start thinking of all of them as creatures with feelings? What if I cannot bring myself to regard them as specimens?"

He raised his head. "I no longer hunt. It has not changed me as a scientist."

"What do you mean you don't hunt? Of course you hunt. His lordship expected you to collect specimens on our expedition in the South Pacific."

"And I would have found a way not to," he said reasonably. "I prefer to study animals, to preserve them."

"But you cannot study them if you do not first take specimens from the wild," I argued.

"There are always animals for whom it is a mercy to be killed," he pointed out. "The old, the sick, the ones that have begun to prey upon people. Besides, his lordship is so forgetful, I could easily tell him I'd shot something and he'd have forgot halfway home."

"That is diabolical."

"It is practical," he retorted.

I looked him over from head to toe, scrutinizing everything save the bit the duckweed still managed to conceal, albeit imperfectly. He still bore the scars from his last expedition, and I wondered if it had changed him. I nodded towards the long slender line that marked him from eyebrow to jaw. "Is that when you stopped? Is that why?"

He drew in a deep breath, plunging his head underwater. He stayed down for almost two minutes, finally emerging in a great plume of water, blowing out air as he rose like a magnificent son of Poseidon. "All right then. Yes," he admitted. "I didn't much like having to dispatch that jaguar, even if it was bent upon destroying me. It is one thing to slay an animal at a distance. One doesn't feel a part of it. This was entirely too personal for me. I haven't killed anything since. And I doubt I could, not something healthy and vital with a life yet to live."

I thought of the tremble of those damp wings against my palm and I understood him perfectly. "I need to get out of this city," I said finally. "I need adventure again."

He stared at me in open-mouthed astonishment. "Veronica, we are hunting a murderer. What more adventure do you require?"

"I cannot say," I told him peevishly. "I only know I am ossifying. One morning I shan't show up to work and you will come to find I have turned entirely to fossil."

"You are simply annoyed because you wanted to throw the solution to this murder in Louise's face and you have not done it yet. You are afraid Miles Ramsforth is going to hang, and it will not be the miscarriage of justice that bothers you, it will be the fact that you did not win."

"That is a vile thing to say," I told him as I collected my stockings and boots. "You think you are terribly clever, but you are not, you know. In fact, you have neglected your duckweed. You seem to have lost it entirely."

Stoker's streak of profanity lasted until we reached the Belvedere.

CHAPTER

21

B y the time evening fell, we had patched up the quarrel or at least agreed not to discuss it. We had thrown ourselves into our work for the rest of the afternoon, stopping only to eat fish and chips from a shop for our supper. Afterwards, we sat in the snuggery to smoke and drink in companionable silence. We had lit no lamps in the Belvedere; the only illumination came from the low fire burning in the stove and the glowing tips of our cigarillos. Stoker's face was thrown deeply into shadow, highlighting the strong planes of his profile. His left side was averted from me, so that I could not see his scars or his eye patch—only the splendor of the gifts nature had bestowed upon him. "'Ozymandias,'" I murmured.

"What's that?"

"Just thinking of a poem," I told him, remembering Shelley's immortal lines. *"Shattered visage" indeed,* I mused.

He pulled thoughtfully at his cigarillo. "There might be a way forward," he said slowly. "A line of inquiry we might pursue tonight—and a bit of adventure for your restless soul," he added with a lopsided little smile.

"Might there?" I leaned forward eagerly.

He twisted the glass in his long fingers, studying the golden sparks in the heart of the brandy. "Mr. Pettifer."

I thought of the diffident little fellow who hadn't said two words that afternoon and laughed. "Why on earth do you think he would be of use to us?"

He gave a sigh of purely animal satisfaction. "Because I know his dirtiest secret, one that his partner does not." He turned his head and fixed me with a sapphirine stare. "Do you remember the bit of licorice from his desk that I sampled?"

"And spat into your handkerchief? Yes."

"It was not licorice. It was opium."

"Opium! How do you— Never mind," I said hastily, holding up a hand. "I forget sometimes that your sins are as numerous as mine."

"And possibly more varied," he added with a twist of his lips. "It was quite obviously opium and furthermore, it was opium of a very decided preparation—the sort found in only one opium den in the city, to my knowledge."

"Stoker, you astonish me. You told me when we first met that you smoked opium one time, and yet you can identify a particular preparation found in a solitary location in the largest metropolis in the world."

He shrugged. "I have a gift for debauchery. It is why I have largely given it up. There is no real thrill in sinning when one has a talent for it."

I raised my glass. "I shall drink to that. Now, whereabouts is this den? The docks of the southlands? The East End?"

"In point of fact, no. It is located in Bloomsbury and it is run by a very nice elderly schoolmaster from Manchester."

"Manchester? Not exactly the exotic East, then," I complained. The latest adventures of Arcadia Brown, Lady Detective, had featured an opium den of the meanest sort in the stews of Southwark, a place of degradation and decay where the vilest examples of humanity consorted together in poverty and depravity. I longed to see such a place for myself, but a Bloomsbury location with a Mancunian schoolmaster did little to raise my hopes of pleasurable degeneracy. Still, it was something of an adventure, and I rose, stubbing out my cigarillo.

"Where are you going?" Stoker asked.

I gestured towards my gown of sober black silk. "I cannot go in this," I told him. "I am going to adopt a disguise."

"God help me," he returned, but I noticed he was smiling.

It was the work of half an hour to prepare. Having already decided that Stoker had exaggerated the mundanity of the opium den, I attired myself in what I hoped would be a suitably discreet costume for a house of corruption. Lord Rosemorran's collection afforded a gentleman's robe from China, and my own wardrobe provided slim trousers. I usually wore them under my expedition skirt, but they would serve just as well worn beneath the Chinese robe. A pair of Oriental slippers—only slightly too large—were stuffed with newspaper, and my hair was loosened from its pins, then brushed until it gleamed straight and black. I plaited it into a single thick hank down the center of my back and topped it with a small silk cap of indeterminate origin. A little judicious application of soot in the hollows of my cheeks and temples suggested bones that were more masculine than my own, and I smiled as I applied the coup de grâce. Stoker was not nearly so impressed.

"Where in the name of Christ did you get those bloody mustaches? Take them off."

"But they lend an air of verisimilitude," I protested. I had come across them in a dressing-up box that had been stored in the Belvedere and had been eagerly awaiting a chance to try them out.

Without another word, he reached out and twitched them from my face, dropping the long strands of wiry black horsehair into his pocket.

"Philistine," I muttered. "Those were works of art."

"They were damned silly," he retorted, "and likely to get us killed."

"Aha!" I cried. "So the opium den *is* a place of danger and mystery."

He rolled his eyes heavenwards and heaved a sigh. "Come on then."

During our first foray into mysterious adventure, Stoker and I had formed the habit of walking London after darkness settled. It was a thoroughly different place to the bustling and businesslike capital of the daylight hours. After night spread her inky skirts over the city, the denizens of the shadows came into their own and the business of moonlight was serious. The society types kept to streets well illuminated by gaslights and even electric bulbs. Their theaters and ballrooms shimmered and gleamed while they basked like moths in the reflected glow. But the rest of the city was where life was truly lived. The lovers who dared not be seen by daylight crept out to share embraces beneath the rustling leafy canopies in the parks. Prostitutes and thieves plied their trades in shadowy alleyways, while the organ-grinders spun melodies for stray coins and drunks stumbled loudly from the public houses on every street corner. Couples quarreled and children wept while duchesses swept past in velvet-tufted carriages. It was a glorious tumult, human life teeming under a microscope, and I had learnt from these nocturnal excursions to appreciate the city I now called my home.

This night we made our way peacefully enough through the streets of Marylebone to Bloomsbury. We were—to all appearances—a curiously imposing gentleman and his Chinese servant. I had not altered my face beyond the attempts to make it seem more masculine; I could only hope that the usual predilection to treat servants as furniture would hold.

The house was just off a quiet square, a street of respectable-looking dwellings in a respectable-looking quarter. A less likely establishment for genteel debauchery I could not imagine.

"Are you certain," I began as Stoker lifted the brass knocker upon the door. He held it out for my inspection, and I saw it was a heavy piece wrought into the shape of a dragon.

"Quite," he said with a grim smile. Before he could even drop the knocker, the door swung back and a distinctly incurious servant waved us towards a small parlor. The house was like any other in London, I reflected in heavy disappointment. There were no exotic touches to indicate this was a den of illicit doings; there was little besides horsehair furniture draped in antimacassars and a shelf of improving books. A plate bearing the legend A SOUVENIR OF MARGATE was particularly loathsome.

We waited only a moment or two before another door opened and a sober gentleman with lavish white whiskers appeared. My spirits lifted a little at the sight of him, for he wore carpet slippers in an outlandish design upon his feet, and a tiny smoking cap of orange silk perched upon a head that was bald as an egg.

"My dear friends!" he said coming forward with outstretched hands. "Welcome." He peered closely at Stoker. "Ordinarily I require a letter of introduction from a friend, but you I remember well, sir. You are welcome." He sketched a little bow and fluttered his hands. "As is your companion."

He leaned towards Stoker and pitched his voice a little lower. "I am loath to pass judgment on any gentleman's taste, but you will understand, sir, I am able to supply imperfect privacy for your . . . activities?" he asked with a suggestive wriggle of his magnificent brows.

If his assumptions surprised Stoker, he gave no sign of it. He merely offered the fellow a bland smile. "I seek only a pipe and an acquaintance I believe may be passing time here."

What happened next seemed like a sort of conjuring trick. Stoker put out his hand to the schoolmaster and the old fellow took it, shaking a moment. I saw the barest edge of a bank note as he slipped his hand into his pocket and realized Stoker had just paid him handsomely but with perfect discretion.

"The name of the one you seek?" the schoolmaster asked.

"Pettifer," was the prompt reply.

"Ah yes! He has just arrived. Your appearance is most timely, sir. I will conduct you myself."

He guided us to the door through which he had appeared, then led us into another sort of parlor, this one with several low tables where a collection of people had gathered to talk and drink tea and smoke short pipes. We did not tarry. The schoolmaster led us to the staircase at the far end of the room, and as we mounted, I realized the entire upper floor had been given over to the enjoyment of opium. What must have at one time been a series of spacious rooms had been knocked together to form an open area with little curtained alcoves for a semblance of privacy. Here the richly fruited scent of opium hung in the air, the smoke redolent of neglected orchards and barnyards after a heavy rain. The schoolmaster counted off the alcoves as he went, then paused before one shrouded in green silk, the fabric heavily figured with more dragons.

"Here you are," he said with a bow. He vanished then, leaving us to announce ourselves. With surprising delicacy, Stoker gave a low cough first, then slowly twitched the curtain aside. I do not know what he expected to find, but Mr. Pettifer was respectably attired, having removed only his coat, his collar still firmly pinned in place, his cuffs pristine. He was bent over a pipe, muttering to himself as he tried—and failed—to light it.

Mr. Pettifer looked up as the light from the outer room shone into his darkened alcove, then raised a hand to his eyes. "Who is there, please? I cannot see you."

Stoker stepped forward and I followed, letting the curtain fall behind us. The alcove was furnished with long low couches of green satin arranged around a table of the sort we had seen downstairs, lacquered black and set with the necessary impedimenta as well as a bowl of fruit and a tea service. A pair of muted lamps hung upon the walls, and a few pretty photographs of Chinese landscapes completed the furnishings.

While I took note of our surroundings, Stoker greeted Mr. Pettifer.

"Templeton-Vane. We met briefly at your mortuary today in the company of Mr. Padgett. This, in spite of her masculine attire, is Miss Speedwell."

The poor fellow paled so quickly I thought he would surely faint, but he rallied nicely although he still gaped for air as if he were suffocating.

"Stoker, you mustn't loom over people. It is unnerving," I told him. I gestured towards the pillows piled upon the divan. "Do you mind, Mr. Pettifer? I think it would be best if we made ourselves comfortable."

Without waiting for a reply, I took up two of the largest and placed them on the floor opposite the little table. Stoker and I settled ourselves, sitting in neat cross-legged fashion while Mr. Pettifer still stared at us. For a brief moment his eyes flicked to the curtain, but Stoker shook his head.

"I beg you not to raise an alarm. I am not much in the mood for a fight, but if you force the matter, I can promise you I will rise to the occasion," he said, and his lazily pleasant tone was more terrifying than any grim threat he might have offered.

Mr. Pettifer swallowed hard and attempted to light his pipe again, but his hands were trembling too badly. He dropped it, spilling the contents. Stoker reached out, but Mr. Pettifer withdrew his hands as swiftly as if he had been burnt.

"Steady, old man," Stoker said peaceably. "I only mean to light your pipe. I rather think you could do with a puff or two." He retrieved the necessary accoutrements and set to work. Within a moment he had a nicely glowing pipe ready for Mr. Pettifer, and he offered it with a genial smile. The smaller fellow took it, falling upon it like a starving man and sucking so hard I thought his eyes should pop.

But the effect was remarkable. A few minutes later his entire demeanor had changed; he was relaxed and affable, his nerves calmer, and he even managed to speak.

"You will not tell them? At the mortuary?" he asked, giving Stoker a close look.

Stoker shrugged. "Ought I to tell them? Do you work when you have been at your habit?"

The little man's expression of outrage was heartfelt. "Never! But I find the business difficult at times. And a pipe is the only thing that soothes me."

"The effect is no different than the bottle of laudanum a chemist might provide the average tradesman's wife," Stoker pointed out.

"Very true," said Mr. Pettifer, pulling on his pipe with obvious contentment. "Why have you come?"

Stoker took a moment to prepare a pair of pipes, presenting one to me with a flourish. Mr. Pettifer was by then in a froth of impatience again, and I realized that Stoker had used the delay to heighten the other man's fear rather than out of any real desire to ply me with intoxicants. Still, when in Rome, I told myself as I took a deep inhalation of the pungent smoke. I held it in my lungs as I counted slowly to ten in Mandarin, then exhaled it through my nostrils.

Stoker took a pull upon his own pipe and looked to me. We had plotted our strategy on the walk. Aware that something had been left from the official report, we concluded the only way to unearth the information was to tease it out of the diffident little undertaker, a task that seemed best suited for a woman. Bearing that in mind, I turned to Mr. Pettifer. "As you have no doubt surmised, we want to talk about the death of Maud Eresby, the artist who called herself Artemisia."

His hand stilled, and for an instant even the smoke itself seemed hesitant to move. Then it stirred, rising lazily overhead, and Mr. Pettifer gave a short nod, the tip of his nose pinched and white. "I see. And if I don't tell you, you will take news of my doings this night back to the mortuary, is that the game?"

"There is no game, Mr. Pettifer. Only fair dealing. We would like some information you possess. If you are kind enough to share it with us, we will go on our way."

"And if I don't?" he challenged. He gave a quick glance to Stoker's advantage in inches and shook his head. "Never mind. I don't want to know." He pulled at his pipe, held the smoke in his mouth a long moment, then exhaled a cloud of it, perfuming the little alcove with the scent of rotting sweetness. Stoker's own technique was more relaxed, a slow, rhythmic suck and release that kept the smoke swirling indolently above his head while I sent ribbons of grey smoke straight towards Mr. Pettifer, entwining him.

He began to speak. "I assisted Mr. Padgett when Miss Eresby arrived in our mortuary rooms. He sent me on an errand while he spoke with a fellow from Scotland Yard, but I overheard a little of what was said."

"What did this man from the Yard look like?" I put in. My tongue suddenly felt thick, and I was seized by the certainty, the unbowed conviction, that we would learn something tremendously important.

He closed his eyes and made a verbal sketch of the fellow down to his bright brown eyes and nonchalant manner. "Mornaday," I murmured to Stoker. He nodded but said nothing.

Mr. Pettifer opened his eyes again. "What did he and Mr. Padgett discuss?" I asked.

"That there was more to the death than had been written in the post-mortem," he replied promptly. He began to speak again but trailed off and sucked hard at his pipe. It seemed to be doing him little good. Stoker was growing progressively more relaxed and I was feeling no effects whatsoever, but Mr. Pettifer was taut as a drum. He took out a handkerchief and mopped at his brow.

"We know there was something curious about how she died," Stoker told him. Mr. Pettifer relaxed a little then, obviously pleased that we did not mean to force the details from him. For an undertaker, he was decidedly ill at ease with death.

"Will you tell us what that curious thing was?" I asked gently. Mr. Pettifer continued to smoke, nodding slowly as he did.

I glanced at Stoker who pursed his lips and exhaled great ribbons of smoke from his nose rather like a dragon. I narrowed my gaze at him for showing off, and his mouth twitched as if he were suppressing a smile. I puffed my own pipe heavily for several drafts, wondering if there was something faulty with my opium as I detected no change within myself except a certain lassitude that might well have been a result of the lateness of the hour.

Mr. Pettifer spoke, his voice dreamy. "She was drugged," he said finally.

"Drugged?" I fairly quivered with anticipation.

"Yes, some sort of opiate," he said, weaving slightly as he sat, his eyes slowly crossing. "A preparation of laudanum, most likely."

"But why?" I demanded. He flinched a little, and I forced myself to sit back, gentling my tone. "What purpose would there be in drugging her if a murderer meant to slit her throat?"

"Much easier," he said, his eyes going glassy. "Would take a strong man, *large* man to cut the throat of a fine, strapping girl like that. But if she were uncon—uncon . . ." His voice trailed off again and he pursed his lips as if in a soundless whistle.

I darted another look at Stoker. "A woman?" I mouthed. I thought instantly of Ottilie Ramsforth and the motivations that might lie beneath her cool, milky composure. But she had been dressed entirely in white— white that was unstained with Artemisia's blood. Who then? Emma Talbot? Little Cherry?

I turned to Mr. Pettifer. "Why would Scotland Yard not want this known?"

He gave me a vague stare. "Eh?"

"Scotland Yard, Mr. Pettifer," I replied tartly. "They suppressed this information. Can you explain that?"

"Things are being hushed up from on high," he said with a slow blinking of the eyes.

"Mr. Pettifer, are you meaning to wink at me?"

"I am," he said complacently.

"You do realize you are shutting both eyes at once?"

He blinked several times in rapid succession. "Am I indeed? How curious."

I turned to Stoker, who shrugged. "I fear Mr. Pettifer's usefulness may be at an end. But we do not need him. It's perfectly obvious why they have chosen not to make this information public."

"To keep Miles Ramsforth dangling at the end of a hangman's noose," I said bitterly. "They know if this were made public, it would open the verdict to doubt and they would rather see him hang than expose their own shoddy police work to scrutiny."

Stoker shook his head. "I doubt it is their police work they are looking to protect," he told me. He put his lips near to my ear. "Louise."

I pitched my voice to a whisper. "You really think so? That they would let Miles Ramsforth hang for a crime he did not commit just to stop any potential scandal from touching the queen's daughter?"

"They have done far worse for far less," he said flatly. "I do not claim it is a conspiracy hatched at Whitehall. I am simply pointing out that when an easy solution presented itself—a solution that would keep scandal at bay and prevent further questioning—they took it. That is all."

"Then why encourage the princess to come to me?" I demanded.

"Because I suspect they didn't believe you would get this far," he told me in a gentle voice.

I turned to my pipe, letting the cold rage wash over me. I smoked until the pipe was empty, filling myself with the odors of flowers and gunpowder and sweating horse, and when it was finished, I took a card from my case and tucked it into Mr. Pettifer's pocket. "If you should think of anything else," I told him firmly. He waved a flaccid hand and Stoker and I took our leave, pausing only long enough for Stoker to pay for our pipes and Mr. Pettifer's.

"It is the least we can do after frightening the poor fellow," he told me magnanimously. He turned to look at me and his brows snapped to-gether. "Veronica? Veronica, are you quite all right? You are weaving."

"I am not," I told him. "I am standing perfectly still." But while I was immobile, the walls had begun to move in a strange, undulating fashion.

"You're foxed," he said.

"I am no such thing. In fact, I have never felt better in my life," I replied, stretching out my arms to embrace the world.

"Bloody hell, this is all I need," he muttered. He stooped and, with no visible effort at all, hoisted me onto his shoulder so that my torso was draped down his back, affording me a lovely view of his posterior. "Don't squirm," he ordered. "I will have you outside and in a cab in a few min-utes. Try not to make a scene."

I felt a rush of gurgling laughter as he began to move. "Stoker, have I ever complimented your sitting-down parts? You have an exceptionally fine bottom."

"Veronica." I could not see his face, but I could tell the word had been issued through clenched teeth.

"I am entirely sincere," I told him, reaching out to grope the attribute in question.

"For the love of Christ," he said. He bent an arm back to swat at my hands. "Stop that."

"But it's so lovely and firm," I protested.

"Veronica, if you do not unhand me—" he began.

"What?" I demanded. "What will you do?" He did not reply and I reached further still, causing him to shy like a frightened pony.

"If you do that again, I will drop you into the nearest coal bin," he promised. "Now, take your hands from between my legs," he ordered as he yanked open the front door.

He stopped so suddenly my head struck his caudal end and bounced off. Instinctively, I tightened my grip, causing him to jump again and slap at my hand.

"Good evening, Mr. Templeton-Vane," said a familiar voice. "I presume that is Miss Speedwell draped over your shoulder?"

"It is," I called. "Superb detecting, Inspector Mornaday."

He bent and angled his head to peer between Stoker's legs, smiling broadly. "Well, well, this is an interesting development," he told me. "Unfortunately, for you it is rather your unlucky night. This establishment is being raided. And you both are under arrest."

CHAPTER

22

S toker swore as Mornaday carried on in the same cordial tone. "Mr. Templeton-Vane, if you would be so good as to relinquish Miss Speedwell's person. She will be transported in a separate conveyance."

Stoker bent, setting me gently on my feet and keeping a hand clamped to my shoulder for support. "Miss Speedwell is presently unwell and ought not to be left unattended."

Mornaday peered closely into my eyes. "Miss Speedwell has been shaking hands with the poppy," he corrected. "But we will take good care of her, as we shall you," he promised Stoker.

Stoker put out his arms, baring his wrists. "Come on then."

Mornaday's expression was gleeful as he clapped a set of irons onto Stoker and stepped back to let one of his subordinates take charge of him. The sound of pounding feet and startled shrieks from the rest of the house indicated Mornaday's compatriots at the Yard were making short work of rounding up the remaining inhabitants of the opium den.

I looked him over scornfully. "You are a nasty piece of work, Mornaday. If it were not for you, we wouldn't even *be* in this place."

He grinned. "I know, and I am sorry for it. But I didn't realize word of your visit to Padgett and Pettifer would reach Sir Hugo so quickly. He suspected me of indiscretion, so I had to make myself useful and give you up under compromising circumstances."

"He already knows about our visit to the undertakers?" I asked, struggling to follow his logic with my befogged wits. "But Mr. Padgett promised his silence!" I was outraged. And after all the trouble I had gone to in order to secure him a specimen, I reflected bitterly. "See if he gets a Camberwell Beauty out of me," I muttered.

Mornaday held up a hand. "It wasn't Mr. Padgett. It was his porter. Apparently he resides comfortably in Sir Hugo's pocket, a fact of which I was unaware."

"And now Sir Hugo wants to lecture us," I guessed. I held up my wrists. "Very well, clap me in irons as well. I expect you will enjoy it."

He gave me a look of abject horror. "Miss Speedwell! I shouldn't dream of such a thing."

"You locked Stoker up," I reminded him.

His smile was one of merry malice. "Yes, I did. But you are a different matter altogether. A spell in the Black Maria won't do him any harm. You will travel with me." He stepped back to gesture for me to precede him.

I shook my head slowly. "I do not think so," I told him.

His gaze narrowed. "Are you refusing a direct order of an officer of the law?"

"Certainly not. I am content to go with you, Mornaday. But I seem to have misplaced my nether limbs."

I looked down at my legs. I could see my appendages quite clearly, but there was simply no way to make them move. As I stared at them, they seemed to slide out of focus, drifting very far away, through a black tunnel. From outside the tunnel I could hear Mornaday's voice, but his words made no sense, and then I was flying, spiraling down on a drift of soft black wings that wrapped around me, cradling me until there was nothing but silence.

. . .

I came to on the sofa in Sir Hugo's office, my head as thick and muffled as if it had been stuffed with cotton wool.

"How do you feel?" Stoker asked, looking intently at my pupils. How he had won his release from Mornaday's custody, I did not know, but it did not surprise me in the slightest.

"A bit like a boiled owl. And my arm hurts," I told him, pointing to the spot.

"Sorry," Stoker said, pressing one of his enormous red handkerchiefs to my arm. "Hold that."

I did as he bade me, watching with casual interest as he put away a syringe and a small bottle. "What did you give me?"

"A mild solution of cocaine. You were unconscious rather longer than we liked, and a stimulant seemed indicated." He eased back and I saw that Sir Hugo was sitting behind his desk, Mornaday standing with his back to the door. Both were watching me closely, and I favored them with a wide smile.

"Good evening, gentlemen. I must say, this is a curious way to secure a lady's company, but at least one cannot fault you for dullness."

Sir Hugo slammed the flat of his hand onto his desk causing his pen to rattle in its holder. "Miss Speedwell, I am glad you are conscious because I would hate for you to miss what I am about to say—"

I sat up slowly with Stoker's aid. "Dizzy?" he asked.

"A little, but it is passing," I told him. "Your cocaine is quite efficacious."

"Not mine. It came courtesy of the supplies of the Metropolitan Police. Mind, I do not often make use of it," he said, "but for situations such as this, I find—"

Sir Hugo slammed his desk again. "If we might return to the matter at hand."

Stoker sighed and I gave an airy wave. "Save your breath to cool your porridge, Sir Hugo," I told him. "We know what you are going to say, and we have no interest in hearing it."

Mornaday's mouth went slack and Sir Hugo looked as if he were going to have an apoplexy. I pushed myself to my feet and moved forward, slowly and carefully, testing my balance until I reached the desk. Sir Hugo in a temper was always a diverting sight. He had clearly been a handsome man once and was still comely, with a commanding air and a stubborn jaw that offset a pair of delicately carved lips he attempted to hide beneath mustaches that quivered when he was angry. I longed to reach out and twitch the ends of them, although I knew that would be a step too far even for me.

I summoned a patient smile. "You are clearly angry, Sir Hugo, but I should point out that I might be just as out of temper with you," I told him.

He kept his voice low, but it throbbed with rage. "You promised not to investigate."

"Of course I did," I said pleasantly. "You would never have let me out of here if I hadn't. But I did not mean it, and you oughtn't to have extracted such a promise under duress."

For a long moment he held himself rigid, his color high, his eyes blazing in magnificent fury. And then the anger seemed to ebb. His shoulders relaxed, and his mouth went soft.

"You are right," he said simply, throwing up his hands. "I ought to have known better. Telling you to keep out of this was no different than waving a red cape in front of a bull, was it?"

"No, it was not." I turned to our two companions who were silent and slack-jawed. "Gentlemen, would you give me a moment alone with Sir Hugo?"

Stoker's reluctance was nearly palpable, but he jerked his chin towards Mornaday. "I will if he does. I wouldn't mind a moment alone with the inspector to discuss conditions in the Black Maria," he said with a thin edge of menace to his voice.

Mornaday's eyes rolled in fear, but he smiled broadly. "Nothing I would like better, but I am afraid I have a heap of paperwork to attend to." He scurried from the room, leaving the door open behind him.

Stoker paused, his hand on the knob. "I will be right outside," he said, and whether that was meant as a threat to Sir Hugo or reassurance to me, I could not have said.

The door closed and I turned back to face Sir Hugo, gentling my voice to deliberate effect. "Sir Hugo, I hope that you will believe it was never my intention to embarrass you or make your life difficult in any way."

He tipped his head, studying me. "I think those might be the first honest words I have ever had from you."

"We are not enemies," I persisted. "I know you do not trust me, but can you not at least give me the benefit of the doubt?"

"Very well," he said in a voice very different to any I had heard him use before. "Why are you pursuing this? It cannot be solely your irrepressible curiosity."

I studied him back, appreciating the lines of care at the corners of his eyes, the silver threads in his hair that had been bought with years of responsibility. The weight of it sat heavily upon him, and it occurred to me that Sir Hugo Montgomerie might be the most honorable man of my acquaintance, barring Stoker of course.

The least I could do was offer him the truth. "I wanted to succeed at something, to impress them."

I had no need to elaborate. He knew precisely to whom I referred. His blue eyes were suddenly soft as they rested upon me.

"You know that it will not matter," he said, not unkindly. "You could unmask a thousand murderers and it will not move them. They are impressed by nothing and no one."

"I realize that," I said, careful to keep my voice even. "It is a stupid reason, and it is unworthy of me, and that should convince you of my sincerity. If I were going to lie, I would have made myself look the better for it."

My voice went oddly flat on the last word, and I cleared my throat sharply. Sir Hugo, in a gesture of sensitivity that I would never have anticipated, looked away. After a moment, he turned back.

"Did she offer to introduce you to your father?" he asked.

"She did. Do not worry," I told him quickly. "I know it will not happen. It cannot."

"No," he agreed. "It cannot."

He closed his eyes for a long moment, then opened them with a sigh of resignation. "Very well."

I blinked in surprise. "What do you mean, 'very well'?"

"I mean, carry on. With limitations," he said, a touch of the old iron returning to his manner. "You will report anything of interest to me, and you will initiate no contact with Her Royal Highness. If she needs to know something you have discovered, I will relate it to her. I cannot trust you to tell me the truth otherwise," he added with some asperity.

"Agreed," I said swiftly. "Shall I swear to it?"

To his credit, he smiled. "I think we both know what your promises are worth."

"Oaths made under duress are pinchbeck promises. This I give you freely—I will share with you anything of importance that we discover."

I put out my hand and he shook it. When I went to take my hand away, he held it fast, pulling ever so gently so that I was leaning over his desk. He bent forward, putting his face close to mine. "Do not think I have forgot that I owe you a lecture, Miss Speedwell. You have got round me this time, but I am keeping an accounting."

And with that he released me suddenly, leaving me off-balance. Which, I reflected as I took my leave, was entirely appropriate.

. . .

The courtesy of the Metropolitan Police did not extend to providing transportation home. We passed Mornaday as we departed, and he had the grace to look a little embarrassed. I tipped my nose in the air and swept past him without another glance, but I did see Stoker offer an eloquently obscene gesture.

"Did you learn that in Her Majesty's Navy?" I asked as we made our way onto the street.

"Among other things." He took charge, bundling me into a cab and giving the driver directions to Bishop's Folly. I was glad of it. The interview with Sir Hugo had left me oddly unsettled—or perhaps it was the potent combination of cocaine and opium.

"How long was I slumbering in the arms of Morpheus?" I asked Stoker with a good deal more aplomb than I felt. I sagged a little against him, his shoulder hard underneath my cheek.

"Rather longer than any of us liked," he replied in a dry tone. "Sir Hugo wanted to send for a police surgeon, but I told him I could revive you perfectly well."

"I am rather surprised he agreed."

Stoker shrugged. "He did warn me he would arrest me again if I poisoned you, but I told him that hardly ever happens."

A smile tugged at his mouth, and I would have poked him pointedly, but it seemed like a great deal of trouble. I gave a great, jaw-cracking yawn.

The ride passed in a blur of lights swirling from without the windows, long trails of illumination stretching and whirling and bouncing past. It was like tumbling through a kaleidoscope, the patterns ever changing.

"Click, click, click," I said, snapping my fingers with each word.

"What are you talking about?" I heard Stoker's voice, but his face was hid in the darkness of the cab and my gaze was fixed upon the symphony of lights outside.

"I am inside the kaleidoscope," I told him, feeling a delicious lassitude creeping through my limbs.

"Home soon," he promised as we swung into Regent Street. I watched the tall, elegant sweep of buildings unroll past the window like a phantasmascope. I rested against Stoker until the cab arrived at the far gate of Bishop's Folly. I went to alight, but my limbs resisted my commands and my head lolled as Stoker reached for me.

My next recollection, dim as it is, was of coming to my senses for a moment as Stoker dropped me onto my bed. I felt his hands at my ankles, taking off the slippers, and then at my head, removing the little silken cap and unplaiting my hair. The euphoria of the pipe had crept back, seeping into my bones and lifting me, light as thistledown. Every pore, every cell, every nerve, felt open and aware, expectant even.

"The aftereffects of the cocaine wear off sooner than those of the opium," he told me. "I could try a little atropine, but far better for you to sleep it off. I am still feeling a trifle euphoric myself. We will both be sorted in the morning."

He turned to go, but I caught him by the sleeve, pulling him down as I surged up against him. The muscles of his shoulders were hard beneath my hands, and I thrust my fingers into his hair. He hesitated a moment, only a moment. And then his lips moved on mine, muttering poetry—snatches of Keats that had never sounded so beautiful and so dangerous. He tasted of honey and smoke and need, such terrible need that I tore the shirt from his body and would have clawed my way into his bones if I could. His arms were hard around me, his muscles shaking with the effort to hold something back. I pressed my mouth to the hollow of his throat, lapping at his pulse, and he gave a shudder, moving his lips to my ear as he wrapped my hair into his fists. His lips parted and a word passed between us, a moan of such desperate longing that my head snapped back and I stared into eyes that were vacant with pain and loss. He did not mean to say it; I knew that as soon as I looked at him. But he had, and that single word wrenched me free of the dreaming haze that had enveloped us. I seemed to move outside myself, for I could see my own body as if from a distance as I gave a great shuddering groan and slipped away, falling into unconsciousness, my hands untwisting from his hair as I drifted. I was truly dreaming then—a storm had risen at sea, pulling us apart. I could see his head, just above the waves as I was borne over the horizon and into blackness.

I woke some hours later. My little chapel folly was still in blackness, the hearth cold and Stoker asleep on a chaise longue in the corner. He had not shared my bed, I thought with a pang. My head was clear, the opium haze cleared as a fog blown away by a great wind. I turned on my side, listening to a nightjar in the garden, singing a plaintive song.

The drug had left my bones feeling as if they had been filled with lead, and much of the memory of the night's adventure had been lost. I pieced it together like an imperfect patchwork, recalling as much as I could of our excursion to the opium den and Scotland Yard. I put a finger to my lips. They felt tender, and when I rose later and studied them in the looking glass, I would find them swollen and bruised. And as I studied my reflection, I repeated the word that Stoker had moaned, the word that had burnt to ash whatever we had kindled between us.

"Caroline."

CHAPTER
23

The next morning I woke to a tiny sledgehammer working its way around my skull. I rose and washed and dressed slowly and with great care. I found Stoker in the Belvedere, admiring his dermestids as they tidied up the rib bones of the rabbit. He peered at me over the case.

"You look like as though you ought to be on a slab at Padgett and Pettifer's," he remarked with maddening calm. He was not wrong. Violet shadows were smudged beneath my eyes, and I was unusually pale.

"How utterly charming of you. Do you talk that way to all the ladies?"

With a sigh, he poured a foul-looking concoction into a glass and handed it over. "Here. I have brewed you something to help with the headache."

"How do you know I have a headache?" I demanded, giving it a cautious sniff.

"Veronica, I have extensive medical training as well as significant experience in debauchery. I know perfectly well that anyone who has imbibed not only a full opium pipe but a syringe of cocaine is going to feel like seven hells. Now, drink up."

He was not wrong. It smelt vile and tasted worse, but I managed to finish it to the dregs and felt marginally better, or at least more alert. The little sledgehammer had been reduced to a mallet and the ringing in my ears had dulled to a modest buzz.

"What was it?"

"You do not want to know," he said turning to his breakfast. Instead of our customary sliced bread toasted in front of the fire, a sort of buffet had been arranged upon a sarcophagus. I was not surprised at Stoker's misuse of the thing—he had a snobbish dislike for anything later than the New Kingdom, and this particular artifact was firmly Ptolemaic. But it seemed a trifle irreverent to use it for the service of food, even if the aromas were enticing. From the kitchens in the main house had come slices of cold ham, boiled eggs, a pot of quince jam, a veal pie, and fresh muffins. They were not hot; the lengthy trip to the Belvedere saw to that. But they were springy and well griddled, and Stoker pounced upon them with a sigh of pure satisfaction. He took up a pot of honey and began to scribble designs upon them, his habit when confronted with muffins, crumpets, or toast. I had yet to see him eat a breakfast without subjecting it to a little creative embellishment beforehand.

He sketched out the design of a ship on one and had just begun drizzling a cat upon the other when Lady Wellingtonia appeared.

"Good morning, my dears!" she caroled. She beamed a hearty smile at us—too hearty for midmorning, I decided. Stoker jumped to his feet, but she waved him back to his chair. She edged past the coprolite from her last visit, giving it a stern look, and nodded in approval at the sight of the muffins.

"I see Mrs. Bascombe did as she was told. When I inquired about arrangements for your board, I was told you saw to your own breakfast and were given a cold collation at luncheon. That will no longer be the case," she said with the satisfied air of one who has sailed into battle and prevailed. "You will have each morning a selection from the breakfast sideboard and a plate of hot food at midday. If you are not invited to dine with the family, you will be brought dinner as well."

"That is very kind," Stoker said through a mouthful of honeyed muffin.

She gave him a benevolent look. "I like to play Lady Bountiful. At my age, it is one of the few pleasures I have left. One loses so many opportunities for enjoyment when the knees go," she told me as a mournful aside. Stoker choked lightly but we both ignored him.

She held up a sheaf of envelopes. "I have brought the post. I confess, I would have left it to the hall boy, but I was unforgivably curious."

I took the envelopes from her and immediately saw the one that had kindled her interest, a thick specimen with a decidedly royal cipher engraved upon the reverse.

"It is from the Princess Louise," I acknowledged. There seemed no possible way—and little point—in hiding the fact.

Her brows lifted. "Indeed! What august company you keep, Miss Speedwell."

Stoker choked again, but I darted him a quelling glance. "You ought to drink something," I said. "It would be a shame if you suffocated on a muffin." I turned back to Lady Wellingtonia. "We made Her Royal Highness's acquaintance through Sir Frederick Havelock. She is a sculptress, you know. She moves in rather Bohemian circles."

"Oh, I know," she said, her shrewd eyes thoughtful. "I have often felt sorry for her."

"Sorry? For a princess?"

Her mouth twitched in amusement. "You are far too old for fairy tales, Miss Speedwell. Surely you know the life of royalty is not at all as we believe it to be. It is a prison—a gilded one—but a prison nonetheless."

"Her Royal Highness said almost exactly that to me," I replied. Too late I realized my mistake.

The shrewd old eyes sharpened. "You must have got quite close to her for the princess to make such an admission. That is quite a thing to tell a stranger."

I shrugged. "Perhaps she was in a mood to unburden herself."

"Perhaps," Lady Wellingtonia said. "Royalty can be peculiar, and Princess Louise more peculiar than most. Did she tell you about her husband?"

"The Marquess of Lorne? We met him briefly. He seemed quite cordial."

"He's a famous imbecile," she replied stoutly. "But he will be a duke and that is all that matters. Personally, I've never met a Campbell who was entirely trustworthy, but that isn't Lorne's trouble."

"What sort of trouble does the marquess have?" I inquired.

She slanted me an enigmatic look. "There is no proof, only talk, but the talk is persistent. May I sit?" she asked, indicating a camel saddle perched upon a hurdle.

"Wouldn't you prefer an armchair?" I asked, gesturing to a decaying wingback.

"Certainly not. I rode across the Syrian desert on one of these. Brings back lovely memories. I wanted to see the ruins of Palmyra," she told me as she settled herself with astonishing agility onto the saddle. "I fancied myself another Jane Digby. Are you familiar?"

"I have heard the name," I said. "An adventuress, I believe?"

She gave me a repressive look. "A woman who knew how to live," she corrected. "Took four husbands—or was it five?—and the last was a Bedouin sheikh. We were friends after a fashion, Jane and I, but she took it amiss when I had an affair with her stepson."

I smothered a laugh, and Stoker bent swiftly to his muffins, his color flaming red. Lady Wellie went on. "That sort of thing can damage a friendship, you know. Poor Jane. She's dead now—been gone some five or six years. She was a decade older than I, but I mean to see one hundred."

"I have no doubt you will," I said. "You were talking about the Marquess of Lorne," I coaxed.

She pursed her lips thoughtfully. "Yes, well, it's a tricky situation, isn't it? Louise has always been restless, always fighting against protocol. She was badly spoilt, if you ask me. The queen thought marriage might settle her down. She offered her a pair of suitors, and Louise chose Lorne as the lesser of two evils."

"That seems rather cold-blooded," I commented.

"That is royalty. It's not so much the making of marriages as the commingling of bloodstock. But there wasn't to be any commingling, not in Louise's case," she said. "They have no children."

"Barrenness is a tragedy for a woman who wants a child," I said mildly.

Lady Wellie thumped her cane against the floor. "Louise is not barren! She has a husband who won't see to her."

"The marquess is disinclined?"

"How daintily you put it, child! We were franker about these things in my day. The man won't plow his wife."

"But why not?" I asked. "The princess is pleasant and handsome. Certainly that is more than most princesses bring to the marriage bed."

"And it would have been enough if Lorne liked women."

I blinked at her. "You mean the marquess prefers men? In his bed?"

She shrugged. "That I cannot tell you. I can only say for a fact that he prefers the company of men to his wife. Whether that extends to the bedroom, only they know. There was some talk when she chose Lorne. The Prince of Wales flew into a temper and said his sister would never marry the man, but he would give no reason why. Without a compelling cause to break the betrothal, the queen let it stand. There are those who say the prince's objections were based upon the marquess's inclinations."

"But that is just hearsay," I countered.

"Hearsay that will not die. Is there at least the spark of a fire smoldering under all that smoke?" She shrugged. "Who can say? Perhaps the trouble is that Louise is frigid or in love with another man or Lorne has halitosis or likes stamps. No one really knows what goes on within the confines of a marriage. But there is talk, dreadful gossip. They say Louise has ordered the windows of the palace bricked up to stop Lorne escaping into Kensington Gardens to tryst with soldiers. Whether it is true or not, I can tell you that Louise has been unhappy. And an unhappy wife is a dangerous creature."

She paused then, letting her words sink in. After a moment, she nodded towards the envelope. "Why don't you open it and see what she wants?"

There was no reason to defer the inevitable. I picked up the horn I used as a letter opener and slit the envelope. The page was crested and the handwriting imperious. "Come at once. Do not delay and tell no one. L."

I slipped it back into the envelope and gave Lady Wellie a winsome smile. "Just a request for a subscription to a charity she supports."

Lady Wellie smiled back, and it was the smile of an old crocodile that has seen much. "So you say, child. And who am I to doubt you?" She gave a wheeze and put her stick down to dismount the camel saddle. In an instant, Stoker was at her side, helping her to her feet.

"Thank you, dear boy," she said fondly. "You are a credit to your mother. Or the navy. I never can decide."

He walked her to the door and returned, wiping the last of the honey from his mouth. "What did the letter really say?" he demanded.

"We are summoned," I told him, handing over the letter. I tipped my head as he read it over. "Stoker, why do I have the oddest feeling that Lady Wellingtonia is enjoying a joke and somehow it is at my expense?"

He flapped a hand. "That is simply her way. She likes to play with people and you are her newest bit of catnip."

"Catnip or mouse?" I asked. Only time would tell.

. . .

We made our way to Kensington Palace, following the same directions we had been given the first time. The butler had scarcely shown us in before the princess appeared. She wasted not a minute in cordiality but hurried us to her private sitting room, giving instructions that we were not to be disturbed.

Only when the door had been securely shut and we were alone did she relax a little. She plucked a letter from her sleeve and handed it over.

"Read it," she commanded.

The paper was ordinary stuff. The writing was stilted, as if someone with education and fair penmanship were endeavoring to hide them both. The edge of the paper was heavily charred and the whole smelled of smoke.

"I have the ledger," it began without salutation. "Bring your emeralds to the grotto at midnight and await further instructions. Tell no one or steps shall be taken."

I made to hand the note back, but the princess waved me off with fingers that trembled. From rage or fear, I could not tell. I passed it to Stoker who studied it in silence. We did not exchange glances, but I knew he was thinking of our abortive trip to Littledown. Someone had indeed recovered the ledger after I dropped it and seized the opportunity to put it to use.

I longed to question the princess, but I was wary of her nerves. She was pulled taut as a bowstring, and without careful handling she might well dissolve into hysterics. I chose an oblique approach instead.

"How did the note arrive?" I asked.

"It was in the morning post, mixed in with the rest."

"The envelope?"

She pulled a face. "Burnt. I wanted to destroy it, you see, so I flung both onto the fire. But I realized how foolish that was and I fetched the letter out again. It was too late for the envelope."

"Was there anything of distinction about the envelope?"

The lines in her brow deepened as she concentrated. "The post-mark was central London, but there was no other mark except for my direction."

"And was it properly addressed?"

Her smile was sour. "Yes. All the proper titles in all the proper places."

I did not want to tackle the subject of the ledger yet, and she clearly had no wish to volunteer the information. I continued to skirt the subject.

"To what emeralds does the letter refer?"

She clasped her hands together, twisting her fingers. "I have a parure composed of my wedding gifts. There is a tiara of emeralds and dia-monds given me by my husband's parents, the Duke and Duchess of Argyll. There is a bracelet, an emerald set with brilliants, and a locket, also set with brilliants. I wore it on my wedding day—it was a present from Her Majesty. There are a few smaller pieces, but those are the sig-nificant ones."

"And this villain knows all about them," I mused.

"Everyone does," she returned snappishly. "The gifts were in every illustrated newspaper in the Empire. My wedding portrait was circu-lated widely, and the locket was quite prominent."

"I presume it is of excellent quality."

"Naturally." Her mood was thoroughly awful, for which I did not entirely blame her. Hers really was a fishbowl existence, glorious as it might be, and suddenly I understood Lady Wellie's inclination to pity her. How dreadful to have millions of strangers know the intimate details of one's life, to pick over them like so many discarded bones from a banquet table, looking for the choicest bits of meat.

As if intuiting my thoughts, she began to speak, her voice low and thick with bitterness. "You have no idea how awful it is, knowing com-plete strangers are sitting in their homes, reading all about you, judging you, sometimes hating you simply because of an accident of birth. I do not know if I shall ever feel safe again leaving my house. I shall look into every stranger's eyes thinking, 'Is it you? Is it you who hates me so?'"

"I do not think you need fear the stranger on the street, Your Royal Highness," Stoker told her gently. "This is the work of someone known to you."

She blinked, her expression quite blank. "That cannot be. I will not believe it. It must be a servant. Perhaps that girl who cleans at Havelock House," she began. "Have you even investigated her? Or have you been too busy playing at this to do the job properly? Perhaps I was wrong to trust you," she blazed. "After all, it is your fault this villain has the ledger at all. And what have you managed to discover? Precisely nothing. Days wasted, and you are no closer to saving Miles Ramsforth."

My customary sangfroid deserted me at such a galling display of injustice. I made an impolite sound, and Stoker shot me a warning glance. To his credit—and my everlasting gratitude—he seized the moment. Heedless of the prohibition against touching royalty, he put a firm hand under her elbow and guided her to an armchair. When she was seated, he knelt at her feet, the very picture of devotion.

"Your Royal Highness," he said with infinite gentleness, "I understand this is difficult, and far beyond anything you have ever encountered. But we are doing everything in our power to help you."

She gave him a brief nod. "I know, Mr. Templeton-Vane. It is simply maddening, the waiting. And now this—it's monstrous."

Her lips trembled as if she would give way to tears, and he rummaged in his pocket for one of his enormous scarlet handkerchiefs. "Keep this. Just in case," he urged.

She nodded again, biddable as a child, and he took her hand in his, as gently and respectfully as he would cradle a wounded baby bird.

"Won't you tell me everything?"

Me. I noted the change of pronoun as well as the fact that he had shifted his posture slightly to put his back to me, creating an intimate twosome with the princess. He was blatantly cutting me from the conversation, but just as I opened my mouth to remonstrate with him, I saw the effectiveness of his methods.

The princess, whose sense of grandeur ought to have rebelled at having her hand held—even by the son of a peer—touched her eyes with the handkerchief and began to speak.

"I was rather rude to Miss Speedwell," she told him.

He leaned closer to her, his attitude one of conspiratorial coaxing. "I daresay she deserved it."

She smiled in spite of herself, a tiny smile, but a smile nonetheless. "The fault lies with me."

"Miss Speedwell is a stubborn and provoking woman," he said solemnly. This time the smile was real.

"I suppose she is at that. But I was peremptory with her when I did not mean to be. I need her help, quite desperately. And yours. I am so frightened, so terribly upset..."

"You are anxious and fearful," he said. "And I daresay not sleeping as well as you ought."

She closed her eyes and gave a nod of assent. I opened my mouth, and even though he never turned his head to look at me, he must have sensed I wished to speak. He made a single flicking gesture with his forefinger, warning me to silence just before she opened her eyes.

"That is true," she told him, leaning forward and pointing to her face. "You must see the shadows beneath my eyes. I have not slept properly since this business began."

"It is the most natural thing in the world that you should be gripped by violent feelings," he assured her. "And all the more reason that you should share them. It is not good for people, particularly ladies of gentle birth, to keep such tempestuous emotions locked up within them. It leads to bad health," he told her with the faintest touch of reproof.

It was an astonishing performance. With just a few words he had not only calmed her but made her feel as if she had done *right* in behaving rudely to me. Realizing that Stoker had the situation well in hand, I sat back and watched, as good as invisible to them both.

She nodded, dabbing at her pink nose with the handkerchief. "You are quite right, of course."

"Indeed I am." His tone was soothing, the sort of voice one might use to an injured animal or a querulous child. I wondered which the princess might be. Stoker moved marginally closer, increasing their intimacy as he settled himself upon a hassock at her feet. "Now, I have said I will help you, but I want you to have a greater assurance than that. You have my word as a gentleman that I will do whatever I can to unmask the villain both for your sake and that of Miles Ramsforth."

"Oh, you are kind," she told him as I resisted the urge to roll my eyes. "I know you have seen the ledger. I nearly collapsed when you told Ottilie that you had discovered it. I was so terribly afraid that you had seen my name." She broke off, her color high as she chose her words carefully. "I ought to explain about the grotto, how I came to be there."

"I know what purpose it served," he urged gently. "I have seen the place in all its glory."

She gave a grim nod. "Good. Then I needn't describe it. You must know how dreadful it's been, knowing that there was evidence I visited the grotto, that it might be discovered and brought into evidence at his trial. And then everyone would know . . ." She broke off again, pressing the handkerchief to her mouth as if to stifle rising sickness. "I understood precisely how bleak it would look for me, how salacious the press would make it seem. The newspapers, the headlines, it was a nightmare. And it was all quite innocent! Miles was simply being Miles. He amused himself by shocking people. I think he expected me to disapprove, to be like my mother. She would have been outraged," she said with a shudder. "But it was so blameless. He merely guided me through his little collection of art, showed me the ledger with all the naughty little details," she finished earnestly.

It occurred to me then that she might well be telling the truth. If she had engaged in a little sordid lovemaking with her friend's husband, it would be a scandal of immense proportions—but so would the mere appearance of impropriety. The very fact that she had been in the grotto and viewed the collection would have catastrophic repercussions for herself and the throne. Married women did not conduct themselves in such a fashion, and married princesses with Puritanical mothers were held to a higher standard still. The newspapers would make the most of the indiscretion, hounding her and the whole of the family, I had no doubt. And it would not be long before questions were raised, as they inevitably were after every royal scandal, whether England needed a monarchy at all. It would be terrible enough to endure such conse-quences if one had actually committed flagrant adultery; how much worse if one had not? It was the conundrum of Caesar's wife, ruined for the illusion of misconduct but not the act of it. The irony was too cruel.

Stoker made soothing noises and patted her hand.

"My marriage has not always been a happy one," she went on. "We care for one another, you must believe that. But my husband and I are the subject of gossip, very painful gossip which makes the round in Soci-ety circles. And every crumb of it would have been made public if I were exposed in such a fashion."

"I understand," he consoled her. "You were simply having a harmless bit of amusement, and you are entitled to a few laughs with your friends."

"How well you put it!" she said. "You understand, but the average person on the street would read those words, those horrible vulgar words, and think the worst of me. I cannot bear to think what it would do to my mother." She went white to the lips, and I realized then how completely the queen ruled her own family. She must have had Bis-marck's iron fist to keep her own daughter in such fear of her.

The princess went on. "I was not only thinking of myself, but of Lorne," she insisted. "If the popular press decided I had taken Miles

Ramsforth as my lover, then they would dredge up all the worst of the stories about my husband, his neglect of me, his disinclination for my company. And they are not true," she said fiercely. "He loves me in his own way."

Whether that was fact or wishful thinking, I would never know. No one would ever know, I supposed. But in her peculiar fashion, Louise loved her husband, and in saving Miles Ramsforth, she was really saving him.

Stoker patted her hand again. "Of course his lordship loves you," he said with a firmness that brooked no argument. "And if he only knew what agonies you have suffered on his behalf, he would treasure you all the more." He changed his tone subtly. "Now, in order to help you, I must know what happened the night Artemisia was killed. You visited the grotto. And Miles wrote your name in the ledger?"

She clutched his hand. "Yes. As a sort of joke since I had toured his collection. You didn't see it there?" she asked swiftly.

Stoker shook his head. "We had no opportunity to examine the ledger before Miss Speedwell lost custody of it," he told her, neatly portioning responsibility for the loss to me. I deserved it, and no doubt the princess was convinced of my culpability, but it rankled a little nonetheless.

Stoker went on in his soothing voice. "Were you with Miles Ramsforth when Artemisia was murdered?"

She nodded, closing her eyes and pressing the heels of her hands hard into them. "Yes," she whispered.

"And is that why Miles has no alibi? Because he was with you?"

"Yes." Her voice rose a little.

"He refuses to tell anyone the two of you were together in order to protect you," Stoker pressed.

"Yes." The voice rose higher still, verging on hysteria.

"He would rather dance at the end of a hangman's noose than betray you? That speaks to a connection more intimate than mere friendship," I put in.

They both turned to look at me, Stoker wearing an expression of exasperation while Louise's was one of mingled astonishment and dislike. "I do not expect someone of your class to understand," she said dully. "One is brought up to honor the dictates of loyalty."

I opened my mouth, but the sudden, certain futility of it all came crashing over me, and I said nothing.

Stoker resumed his masterful handling of the interrogation. "Did Miles always keep the ledger in the grotto?" he asked.

She shook her head. "I do not know. It was out when I arrived. He made a little joke about how valuable the thing was—he said even Ottilie didn't know of its existence because it would be worth thousands in the wrong hands. You must not think he would ever have used it against his friends," she hurried on. "Miles is not like that. He could have spent his last farthing and the ledger would never have seen the light of day. It was an aide-mémoire of sorts, something to remember the naughty escapades he had got up to in his youth. There was no real harm in it."

Either the princess did not realize how recently he had got up to those escapades or she was deluding herself as to the extent of Miles' cheerful debaucheries. But I suspected she was correct in her assessment of his character. If Viscount Templeton-Vane's revelations about the dwindling Ramsforth coffers were true, Miles had sat upon a potential gold mine without ever once attempting to make use of it. It spoke to a certain loyalty in the man, I decided, and I rather liked him for it.

Stoker continued on, guiding the conversation.

"Well, now someone has found the ledger and realizes that you were there, that you would pay dearly to keep this information private. And we must discover who that someone is. It is entirely probable this villain and the murderer are one and the same."

She gave a shudder. "It is a terrible thing. One reads sensational fiction, thrills to the horrors on the page, but when it is real, when it comes into your life and threatens to destroy everything . . ."

"We will recover the ledger," Stoker promised her. "And we will find the killer."

"You oughtn't promise things we might not be able to deliver," I put in sweetly. "And I am not at all certain we are the proper people to help."

"Veronica," he said through gritted teeth. The princess was regarding me with active loathing, but I did not care. I went on, recklessly.

"Before this, we had only your word that the police had got it wrong, but this," I said, holding up the note, "is proof of blackmail. That is a hanging crime. It ought to go directly to Sir Hugo Montgomerie."

"Sir Hugo!" Princess Louise fairly spat the words as she thrust herself to her feet. "He has been utterly useless. He would not even attempt to reopen the investigation when I begged him."

"I believe Sir Hugo was trying to protect you," I corrected, irritated that she would display so little appreciation for a man whose entire career was devoted to clearing up her family's messes.

"Protect me!" Scorn dripped from the words. "From what?"

"Any hint of scandal," I suggested. "As you just pointed out, if you were intimately linked with a man whose mistress was murdered in his bed, it would be a scandal of historic proportions. I imagine Sir Hugo was only too conscious of how it would look for Your Royal Highness," I told her flatly.

She curled a lip. "I do not care for the opinions of tea merchants and tailors," she said loftily.

"Of course you do," I said, striving for patience. "You care very much indeed or you would not be so terrified of the newspapers. But your greatest fear is of your mother, is it not?"

She said nothing, but it was easy to deduce how little she liked my forthright speech.

"Ma'am," Stoker began in a far more deferential tone than the one I had employed, "if you were so worried about your name appearing in the ledger, why did you not tell us about it at the start? It would have saved time and bother to know there was more to your request than saving Miles Ramsforth from the noose."

She hesitated a long moment before answering. The only noises to be heard were the soft ticking of the various clocks as they marked the seconds. "I did not know if I could trust entirely in your discretion," she said, very nearly but not entirely apologetic. "I told you as much as I dared. My hope was that the ledger had been lost or destroyed. No one knew where he kept it, and he would never tell. It was entirely possible that it would never see the light of day, and my secret would not be exposed. Then when you told Ottilie that you found the ledger and lost it again, all I could think was that it was in your power to destroy me. That is why I sent you away so quickly. I needed time to think. I decided that if I kept very quiet, you might still find the real murderer so that Miles would not hang."

"He shall if we cannot get to the bottom of this," I reminded her with brutal finality.

She said nothing but set her chin stubbornly as Stoker returned to the subject of the blackmail. "Give us them," he said. "We will hand over the jewels in your place."

She hesitated. "No police?"

"No police," he vowed, and I wondered precisely how I would be able to reconcile that with my promise to Sir Hugo. Stoker went on. "Miss Speedwell lacks your inches, but it will be dark. If the villain is about, waiting to collect his reward, he will most likely think she is you."

I folded my hands over my chest, wondering what else Stoker had planned for me since I was apparently little more than a puppet in his theater of detection.

The princess was thoughtful. "It might be dangerous. Miss Speedwell might be harmed." She did not sound unduly dismayed at the prospect, and Stoker hastened to reassure her.

"Better Miss Speedwell than you, Your Royal Highness!"

She nodded slowly. "I suppose you are correct. After all, she is an active person, experienced in this sort of thing."

"She is," he agreed. "I once saw her single-handedly extricate herself from a boat full of miscreants bent upon abducting her."

The princess roused herself to look at me, peering at me as if I were an oddity at a fair.

"I can believe it," she said at length. "She has a decidedly masculine quality," she added vaguely.

"Quite," Stoker said. "And this sort of thing requires such a quality. A delicate and feminine lady, particularly one of exalted rank, could only ever play the most marginal of roles," he assured her.

She gave him a long look. "What about my jewels? If something should go wrong, I would hate to lose them. How could I possibly explain their disappearance?"

Her manner had changed, and I detected a note of calculation behind her question. Stoker either did not notice or pretended he had not.

"I shall be at Miss Speedwell's side the entire time. They will be safe under my protection," he vowed.

She gave him a reluctant nod. "Very well. I suppose it is the best possible plan."

Stoker pressed no further. He patted her hand again, this time with something approaching reverence. "Do not trouble yourself further, ma'am."

Louise gave a nod and drew in a deep breath. "Wait here. I will retrieve the jewels for you." She proceeded from the room, and I did not even look at Stoker. I was too infuriated to speak and turned to study a landscape of Louise's hanging on the wall. It was bleak and uninspiring—Canada or Siberia or someplace equally cold and devoid of interesting butterflies. I left him to study it while the minutes ticked by. Stoker puttered about with the mantelpiece, picking up bric-a-brac and putting it down again, plucking a postcard from a litter of cards and invitations and reading it with absolutely no shame.

When Louise returned, she seemed more composed, and I caught the faintest whiff of brandy. She had clearly paused for a stiffener, and I rather resented she hadn't thought to share. She carried a small case which she handed to Stoker. He hesitated, raising a brow in inquiry. She nodded.

The case was a simple affair of blue morocco. It might have held letters or trinkets or anything at all. But instead it contained magic. Fitted into a nest of white velvet, the emeralds shone with unearthly light that shimmered and chased over the surface of the stones, diving into their hearts and exploding outwards again in an eruption of viridian splendor. The tiara, taken from its frame, curved around the other jewels protectively, gathering a fortune within its glittering embrace.

"Stunning," I pronounced.

"Irreplaceable," she corrected, reaching out and snapping the case closed. This she bundled into a small leather bag before handing over the lot of it to Stoker. "There is no way to explain what has become of these jewels if they are lost. The cost is incalculable."

"So is a man's life," I reminded her.

"We will exercise the utmost care," Stoker put in swiftly. "Do not worry, Your Royal Highness."

She straightened, raising her chin as no doubt an endless series of governesses and deportment teachers had taught her to do. "Thank you, Mr. Templeton-Vane." She gave him her hand to shake as she afforded me a curt nod of farewell. "Miss Speedwell." With that she rang the bell and the butler came to show us out of the palace.

As soon as we were outside the royal premises, I whirled on Stoker. "That was an utterly appalling display," I began.

He gave me a cheerful smile. "It was rather, wasn't it?"

I gaped at him. "You didn't mean it?"

"Not a word, which you ought to know," he said, his tone mildly aggrieved. "I am rather disappointed that you didn't, actually. You know my feelings about royalty and the general fragility of women."

"That royalty ought to be abolished and women are every bit as capable as men?"

"More so," he corrected. He tipped his head. "I oughtn't to be proud of that performance. It was frankly revolting. But it got us what we wanted. We now know why Miles cannot provide an alibi. And we are commissioned with handing over the jewels, the best lead we have had yet on unmasking the murderer. A good half-hour's work, I would say."

"I still do not understand you. How did you know it would work? You laid on the flattery with a trowel."

He gave me a pitying look. "Royalty are no different from the nobility, and you forget, I was reared amongst them. I am one of that benighted tribe, as much as I deplore it. I know what they think—and how."

"And what does the princess think?"

"That she is the center of the universe, of course. They all do. God's in his heaven, the queen's on her throne, and all creation bends a knee to them, with apologies to Browning," he told me. "It is impossible to flatter them too much. They understand nothing of true suffering or hardship or pain, so if you make them believe you think them martyrs to such emotions, they decide you are the only one who truly understands them. In the meantime, try talking to them about the plight of a Yorkshire coal miner and see how far it gets you," he added with a gesture of disgust.

"That is the most cynical thing I have ever heard you utter," I told him.

His smile was quick. "Then by all means, stay with me. I shall surprise you yet. In fact, I think I shall astonish you with this," he added, whipping a postcard from his pocket.

"What is that?"

"A scene of Bournemouth," he told me. "I stole it from the princess's mantelpiece."

"How very edifying," I pronounced.

"Turn it over, my skeptical friend."

I did as he bade, giving a crowing sound of triumph. "Stoker, you utter genius." The postcard was an afterthought, a hastily scribbled note of just a few lines addressed to Louise by a friend on holiday. But they were enough.

"Julian Gilchrist's handwriting," I breathed.

Stoker produced the blackmail note and we held them side by side. "Not a very clever chap, is he? He managed to alter the capitals only slightly, but his *E* absolutely screams the truth."

"So Gilchrist is our blackmailer as well as the author of our threat and, I suspect, the eyeball as well. All tricks to put us off the investigation."

"How do you like him for a murderer?" he asked with a forgivable air of satisfaction.

"It is possible," I temporized.

"Possible!" His lips thinned in irritation. "Veronica, I have just presented you with evidence as prettily tied up as any Christmas parcel. What more do you want?"

I shook my head slowly. "I cannot say. But we must have more proof than this. If we go to Sir Hugo with a scribble on a postcard and a threatening note, he will laugh us out of his office. It may be that Julian Gilchrist is our murderer," I said quickly, seeing his face harden. "But what we have now is not sufficient evidence to link him to the crime. He might have had nothing to do with Artemisia's death but be perfectly willing to watch Ramsforth hang for it."

"Why, precisely?" he demanded in a clipped voice.

"Jealousy," I returned. "Gilchrist was the person who enjoyed Artemisia's attentions before Ramsforth. Perhaps he could not bear the thought of losing her, of sharing her with Ramsforth. He mightn't have acted upon that feeling, but it would account for him being thoroughly happy to see Ramsforth hang for her murder."

He stopped in the middle of the pavement and stared at me. "Do you believe that? Do you believe it is possible to be so connected to another person that the very idea of losing them could drive you to watch an innocent person die without lifting a finger to stop it?"

"If I thought that person had killed them, then yes," I said levelly. "I would knot the noose with my own hands. Tell me you wouldn't do the same."

He opened his mouth, then snapped it closed. We were silent as we walked, constrained.

"Do you think Louise will come forward if we cannot catch the murderer?" I asked at length. "Or will she let Miles hang to spare herself the scandal?"

"She will have no choice," he said, an unholy light glinting in his eyes. "If she does not come of her own free will, we will go to Sir Hugo and tell him the truth."

"Again, it will not work. Without the ledger, we cannot prove Miles Ramsforth's alibi. It will be our word against hers, and precisely no one will believe us. I do not trust her to choose his life over her reputation."

"Blast," he muttered, but his failure to pursue the argument said he knew I was right. "Then we will have to catch the murderer," he said finally. "It is the only way to ensure that Miles Ramsforth doesn't hang."

We walked in silence for a long moment. "Stoker? Louise was there when we told Ottilie Ramsforth about finding the ledger. She had no way of knowing we had not seen her name. Why did she not suspect us of orchestrating the blackmail plot against her?"

He thought a moment then shrugged. "Perhaps she believes an aristocrat would never attempt to blackmail a princess. Or perhaps she thinks a woman of semi-royal blood would never do anything so dishonorable."

I mulled over the likelihood of both as we walked. "Or perhaps she lacks the imagination ever to have considered the possibility," I said finally.

Stoker snorted. "Your prejudices are showing, Veronica. It is appallingly clear how little you think of her."

I shrugged. "She is arrogant and difficult and, my God, but she always thinks she is right."

Stoker gave me a measured look from hatpin to hem and then smiled. "I cannot imagine what you mean."

He was still smiling when I pushed him off the curb.

CHAPTER

24

Calling a temporary truce, we crossed Kensington Gardens, turning our steps towards the south.

"Of course," Stoker said in a speculative voice as we fell to discussing the case again, "it may be that Gilchrist is not working alone in this. He might have a companion, someone cleverer than he who also lives and works at Havelock House."

"You suspect Emma Talbot!"

"Why not? Now that we know a woman might have done it, she is certainly an addition to the list of possible suspects."

I snorted. "If you believe that, why not add Ottilie Ramsforth's name to the list? Or don't you suspect devoted wives?"

Too late, I realized the barb was sharper than I intended. He did not put his hand to his scar or make a sound, but I knew he was thinking of the time his wife nearly cost him his life in Brazil. Caroline. The name pierced me like a lance, but I refused to speak it aloud.

"I would apologize if I thought it would help," I said after a long moment.

He gave me a faint specter of a smile. "I am not spun of candy floss, Veronica. I can take whatever pricks you choose to administer."

"I am certain you can," I said, but it was a lie and it was bitter on my tongue. He had loved her once, and he loved her still, of that I was sure. Why else cry out her name with his lips warm upon my flesh? But it had not been a cry of undiluted pleasure, that much I knew. And there was no pain sharper than that of loving someone when you would do anything to stop it.

I cleared my throat and assumed an attitude of briskness. "In any event, Ottilie is quite out of it. Remember, she was wearing white that night, and there was no trace of blood upon her. But if we are determined to consider the women, what of Louise's suggestion of Cherry?"

"Motive?" he asked, and to my relief his voice sounded almost normal.

I shrugged. "Thwarted love affair? The relationships at Havelock House seem convoluted as those of the Olympian gods, everyone sampling the connubial delights together."

He shook his head. "I cannot see it. Miles Ramsforth might be a sybarite, but he lacks imagination. He acquires beauty, and the girl is not striking enough to tempt him."

"Is Emma Talbot?" I retorted.

He considered this, his eyes crinkling thoughtfully at the corners. "She does have a certain arresting vitality. That might be enough."

My lips pursed of their own accord. "Do we know what she was wearing the night of the murder?"

"Black," he replied promptly. "At least I assume so. During my last sitting, Cherry came in with what is apparently Emma's only evening gown and got an earful for leaving a shiny mark upon it with an iron."

"Black would certainly hide the blood," I admitted.

"Furthermore, what would Cherry have been doing at an entertainment of that sort? She is the maid at Havelock House, not one of the artists."

"She might have been engaged to help serve, and if she were, she too would have been wearing black," I added with a snap of the fingers.

"All right, I will grant you that. Let us consider the men. Frederick Havelock," he pronounced. "I like him a good deal as a murderer."

"Again with the notion of that charming old man! You must be mad."

"Charm is the most effective veneer for the sinister," he told me.

"Sinister—he is in a Bath chair," I said in scornful tones.

"*In* a Bath chair, not restricted to it," he corrected. "You have seen with your own eyes that he can get about without it."

"With the aid of walking sticks!"

"One of which might easily hide a blade. No, I very much like this theory."

"It is not a theory, it is a piece of embroidered nonsense. Sir Frederick is far too feeble to caper about murdering strapping young women."

"*Now,*" he added. "But what about before his last apoplexy? He attended that evening, not in a Bath chair, and we've been told his condition deteriorated greatly after Artemisia's murder. We have no way of knowing precisely what it was before she died. And do not dismiss the fact that she was drugged. That would not benefit only a smaller woman, but a less than athletic man," he finished with a self-satisfied air.

"Fine." I begrudged him the point, but I had to concede it. "But I cannot fancy him as the person who pinned the threat to our door. Furthermore," I said, warming to my theme, "I do not expect he will tip-tap his way down to the Elysian Grotto tonight to collect Louise's emeralds. If he is involved, he must have a co-conspirator."

"Bollocking hell," Stoker said. "Just when I was convinced of it. Still," he added cheerfully, "he might be the mastermind. And in that case, I shall propose Julian Gilchrist for his puppet in light of the handwriting on the note. You liked him as the doer of deeds rather than the plotter. Why not the artist and his mentor for co-conspirators?"

"I will grant you Gilchrist as a likelier man of action, but what possible reason could he have for doing Sir Frederick's bidding?"

Stoker shrugged. "Sir Frederick could have made him promises with regard to his career. He may know something compromising about the fellow from their mutual adventures in the grotto and be holding it over Gilchrist's head."

"He could hardly do that without implicating himself," I countered.

"The reason doesn't matter," he replied with maddening calm. "Whatever links conspirators is not as significant as the fact that they *are* linked."

"And if it is not Gilchrist acting as Sir Frederick's monkey, then perhaps it is Cherry. Or Miss Talbot," I said, forestalling the inevitable. "The only way to unravel this is to get into Havelock House again and search. If we find the ledger, we will have something tangible at last."

He reached slowly into his pocket and withdrew an envelope. "This arrived earlier."

"What is that?" I demanded as I opened it. The note was written in a firm, masculine hand, but a glance at the signature told me the author was Emma Talbot. It began without preamble. "Come pose for me today, I beg you. I am desperate to work. Bring the Speedwell if you must."

"What impertinence," I tutted. "You are willing to pose for her again? Even with the possibility that she might be a murderess?"

"Well, I don't fancy standing around nearly naked," he said laconically. "But it will get us in the door, and while I am with La Talbot you will have the chance to poke your nose about and perhaps sniff something out."

I swallowed hard. I could not immediately identify the emotion welling within me. It was something akin to gratitude, but far richer. I had expected him to put himself forward, to insist upon taking the lead in the search. Instead, he had made the sacrifice of sitting out.

"How long have you had that note?" I asked as we reached the far side of the park.

"Since the second post this morning."

"Were you going to mention it?"

"No."

I gave a mirthless laugh. "At least you may count honesty amongst your virtues. What changed your mind?"

He stopped walking and gave me a look that turned my bones to water. "Seeing how Louise treated you. If we don't finish this, you will always regret it, not just because your family have let you down, but because we will have failed to save Ramsforth. I know what that sort of weight can do to a person. It crushes the soul, grinds it into the dirt until you no longer know where the gutter stops and you begin. I don't want that for you. I won't have that for you."

It was a long speech by Stoker's standards, particularly as it touched upon something he was always so careful to keep concealed from me. As if embarrassed, he turned away and walked quickly down the street. I followed, slowly, watching his broad back as he moved. He was a curious sort of champion, I reflected. But a champion he was.

We reached Havelock House a short while later. Cherry admitted us and sent us directly to Emma Talbot's studio. The artist was sitting on a virgin block of marble, smoking feverishly. As soon as she saw us, she jerked to her feet, tossing the cigarette aside. "Thank God!" she exclaimed. "I was about to run mad." She favored Stoker with a heartfelt smile, and even her greeting to me seemed sincere.

She directed Stoker behind the screen to attire himself as Perseus while she bustled around, collecting her paper, charcoal, and props.

"You seem discomposed today," I told her. She pulled a face.

"I am desperate. I want to get this sketch finished before I depart."

"You are leaving Havelock House?"

"I am," she said with some bitterness. "Mrs. Ramsforth has invited me to travel with her to Greece. She needs someone to oversee the final arrangements of the decoration and art, and there is precious little for me here, at least not now."

"Now? What has happened?"

She hesitated a moment, then burst out. "Gilchrist! He knew I was about to secure a commission to sculpt a statue for a private gallery in Birmingham. He used me to gain an introduction to the committee that oversees the place. I thought it was simply to make his name known to them for future work, but before I knew what was happening, he had persuaded them to change their minds and commission a painting instead of a sculpture."

"A painting he will execute," I guessed.

"Precisely. The little devil snaffled the job from under my nose. I will never forgive him for it. It is not uncommon in our circles, but that does not mean I have to countenance such underhanded behavior. I have no desire to remain under the same roof as the little swine."

"What did Sir Frederick have to say upon the matter?"

Her expression softened. "I couldn't tell him."

"Miss Talbot, you astonish me! Such an act of duplicity, Sir Frederick ought to be told that one of his pets has behaved badly."

"I suppose. The trouble is, I have a terrible soft spot for the old fellow. I cannot bring myself to disillusion him. Gilchrist is his beloved protégé. It would hurt him."

She fell silent, gripped by genuine emotion, and against my will, I found myself in danger of liking her. For a potential murderess, she was rather engaging.

But then, with a chill, I realized there might well be another purpose to her story of Gilchrist's treachery. It provided a perfect justification for her leaving Havelock House after Miles Ramsforth's execution. If she had plotted his judicial death, how clever of her to use his own widow as a means of getting away. She would need a convincing story as to why she had left the country, and Gilchrist's theft of her commission was a perfect one—except that she could not afford to share it with Frederick Havelock. Faced with the tale of his favorite's underhandedness, he would undoubtedly confront Gilchrist, the one course of action that Emma could not afford if it were a lie.

It was an intriguing theory, and I filed it away to share with Stoker once we were alone.

I gestured towards the block of marble. "That is extraordinary. Do you mean to use it for your Perseus?"

She grimaced. "That was my hope. But I shall not have time. I will have to complete the statue in Greece."

"I do envy you, Miss Talbot. I have never been, although Mrs. Ramsforth speaks so highly of it, she has quite persuaded me I must rectify the omission."

Her smile was vague. "Yes, she has persuaded me as well. I cannot quite believe she means to go there without—him. It will be a tremendous loss for her," she said slowly, a fierceness coming into her dark gaze. "She will walk the grounds of that villa knowing he walked them. She will sit on the furniture he chose. She will watch the sunsets he imagined. She won't go alone, you see. His ghost will be there at every turn. I think it must be a mad sort of comfort to her."

Her tone and expression were so full of emotion, I hardly knew how to respond. There was a sharpness to her I could not understand, but it occurred to me that she was under a terrible strain, like a bowed branch just before it cracks.

"Only a woman who truly loved Mr. Ramsforth would subject herself to that sort of haunted existence," I told her in a low voice. "But how fortunate for you, being on hand to work in the place where your statues will actually be installed."

"Yes," she said, coming back to herself. "I think it will make a real difference to the composition. I will have the figure decided in advance based upon my studies of Mr. Templeton-Vane, but the landscape, the feel of the thing—I am quite looking forward to seeing how Greece inserts herself into the piece." She gave me a sudden sharp look and raised her voice. "Mr. Templeton-Vane, you have been quite gentlemanly about waiting until we finished our tête-à-tête, but I know it does not take that long to put on a loincloth. Come out, please."

Stoker emerged from behind the screen with the bit of linen draped about his hips and the talaria fluttering from his ankles. I rose instantly.

"I shall leave you to it, then," I said. "Thank you for the chat, Miss Talbot. It has been most instructive."

For all I knew I was leaving Stoker alone and almost entirely unclothed in the presence of a murderess, but I was consoled that Stoker had all the instincts for self-preservation of a Bengal tiger. I had little doubt that with his superior inches and reflexes, he could best Miss Talbot if she chose to assault him. Instead I turned my attention to Julian Gilchrist's room to search for the ledger. I moved on soundless feet, a skill I had honed hunting butterflies, and gained his room without seeing anyone. I closed the door softly behind me.

It was past noon and weak sunlight slanted in. Dust motes floated in the shafts, and for some unaccountable reason I thought of Zeus visiting Danaë in the shower of gold. Shaking off the idle fancy, I started in on Gilchrist's mattress, feeling my way slowly down the length of it. It was lumpy and stained with substances I did not care to think of. But the sheets were clean, and I wondered how recently Cherry had obliged him upon them.

The mattress yielded nothing, and another perusal of his single bookshelf gave up no secrets. Open on the floor, a small valise had been packed with some of his clothes and his collection of brushes. He was clearly planning to leave Havelock House, and I wondered if the princess's emeralds were meant to finance a new life abroad. Was he intending to use the story of the commission in Birmingham to cover his disappearance?

Anything that was broken or worn had been left behind, with only the best of what he owned tucked into the valise. I searched the room carefully, finding nothing of interest. His possessions were mostly grubby, cheap things, obviously purchased at little expense and used without care. Only his brushes and pigments were quality, but they offered no clues. I poked through his clothes, searching pockets and seams, and just when I was prepared to admit defeat, I felt it—the outline of a key. He had not concealed it carefully; it was merely buttoned into the pocket of a waistcoat of a particularly virulent shade of blue. The key itself was small and heavy, fashioned of old brass that had tarnished badly. I held it in my palm, wondering what it might fit as I stood in the center of the room, circling slowly. I had examined his bed, his books, every place he might cache the ledger. Were we wrong about his involvement?

I held the key like a divining rod, as if waiting for it to point the way. But in the end, it was my talent as a lepidopterist that came to the fore. One cannot hunt butterflies without painstaking attention to detail. I had trained myself through long and arduous years to note the most minute of variations between species, for those distinctions could well mean the difference between a dinner of roast beef and one of tinned beans. I thought of the pretty *Limenitis archippus* masquerading as a *Danaus erippus* in Lord Rosemorran's collection and wondered what in this room might conceal a keyhole.

It took me less than two minutes to find it. A bit of paneling in the corner, so cleverly joined I found it by touch and not by sight. I applied my fingertips and the molding alongside shifted, giving up its secrets. "Excelsior!" I breathed, fitting the key to the lock. It turned noiselessly, and the paneled door swung open upon silent hinges. My pulse beat swiftly in my throat, percussive testament to my excitement. What would I find there? The ledger? Drafts of the blackmail note? The cupboard was deep in shadow, and I reached in with careful hands, satisfied to see that they did not tremble in spite of the burgeoning thrill of the chase.

But I was not careful enough, and with a faint whisper, a shadowy specter rushed towards me, engulfing me in its embrace. I shrieked and fell to the floor as it landed on top of me, and a good few seconds passed before I realized my assailant was, in fact, a greatcoat of some antiquity, smelling of moth. I must have brushed it free from its peg and it had fallen out, enveloping me in its heavy folds.

I muttered a curse I had learnt from Stoker and searched the garment for any clue. When I finished, I put the thing aside and rose to examine the cupboard, finding only dust and a dessicated common clothes moth for my trouble.

"*Tineola bisselliella,*" I muttered. "You are no help to me."

I picked up the greatcoat, intending to replace it. My fingers had just closed over the fabric when I realized that in the fuss of it falling out, somehow the peg had become dislodged. No doubt the weight of the coat had pulled it free, for the thing was monstrous, heavy as a bear's pelt, I observed as I put it aside again. I felt around the bottom of the cupboard for the peg, running my fingers gently over the surface. I found it at the back of the wardrobe, just out of easy reach, and with a sigh of annoyance, I hitched up my skirt and put my knee inside the cupboard to push myself further.

My hand had just closed over the peg when I heard a sharp crack and felt the perch beneath my knee give way. I leapt backwards as the pieces of the bottom fell, revealing a hidden compartment. "No doubt where he keeps his dirty underlinen," I grumbled, but nonetheless I peered inside.

The compartment was not large, but it was big enough to hold a pasteboard box. I lifted it out in eager hands. There were no markings upon the box, and it might have been a collection of saucy letters or indecent postcards, I reminded myself. There was no reason to believe it might be a clue.

And yet. My heart hammered within my chest precisely as it had just before I had spotted my first Morpho Blue.

I lifted the lid, forcing myself to set it aside before I looked at the contents. There was no ledger, no half-written blackmail note. Only a pair of ladies' dancing slippers. They were of excellent make, the soles kidskin and the uppers sewn of stiff white satin. They had been embellished with tiny beads and bits of lace, and they were fragile, beautiful creations.

Or they would have been, if they had not been stained with blood. One was merely touched with it, a slight streak across the instep, but the sole of the other had been saturated with gore, now dried to a rusted patch. I held it in my hands and thought for a mad moment of the tale of Cinderella and of the cruel stepsisters who had mutilated their own feet for a chance at a crown. It was their bloody slippers that had given them away. Who might these slippers betray?

I turned over the soiled slipper and had my answer. Stitched neatly in blue silk thread on the inside of the shoe were initials: the initials of a murderess.

"That cunning devil," I murmured.

CHAPTER

25

I rocked back on my heels, still holding the bloodstained slippers. Was it possible that the woman who owned these shoes had committed the foul deed of slitting Artemisia's throat?

I replaced the slippers in the pasteboard box and fitted the broken boards back into place. They would not stand up to scrutiny, but they would pass muster should anyone glance inside. I retrieved the peg, hung the greatcoat, and locked the cupboard, careful to pocket the key. With any luck, Gilchrist would think it simply misplaced. A more cautious man would have kept it upon his person, I reflected in disapproval. He was a woefully poor accomplice.

Unless he was no accomplice at all? What if he had done the deed and the wearer of the slippers had merely been handmaiden to the crime? But what inducement could he have offered to secure her co-operation? Perhaps he had kept the slippers to purchase her complicity, threatening her with proof of her involvement?

Before I could indulge in a brown study that would profit no one, I shook myself from my reverie and went in search of Miss Talbot and Stoker. I found them as expected in her studio, but I stopped on the threshold, my hand still upon the doorknob. She was sketching, as I had anticipated, and he was posing, yet nothing could have prepared me for the sight of him. She had, through some unholy method I could only imagine, persuaded him to leave off his loincloth entirely. He wore only a helmet and the talaria, the wings of the sandals gently brushing his ankles. His torso and arms were liberally illustrated with the tattoos of his travels, but they obscured nothing of his beautiful musculature. His back was to me, and I could see every inch of undraped flesh, from the strong neck to the shoulders corded with effort as he raised a sword in his right hand. His left arm was bent as he lifted the head of Medusa, a foul thing covered in woolen snakes with little red silk tongues that darted out as if to touch him. She had captured him at the moment of victory, Perseus triumphant, back and legs tensed against the monumental task of slaying the Gorgon. The line of his figure, curving inwards at the small of his back, outwards over firm buttocks and muscular thighs, was as graceful and powerful as anything in creation, and I stood in silent admiration for a long moment before either of them spoke.

"For the love of Christ, if you're coming in, close the door. There's a draft," Stoker ordered.

"How did you know it was I?" I asked, closing the door and advancing into the room so I could address him from the front.

He flicked his gaze to the shield propped against one leg. "The same way I am supposed to have cut off her head," he said with the barest nod to Medusa.

The shield was highly polished, and the angle afforded him an excellent view of the door.

"Are you comparing me to a Gorgon?"

"I shall compare you to worse if you don't stop distracting my model," Miss Talbot said sharply.

"My apologies." I turned my back to Stoker, and Miss Talbot sketched furiously for a few minutes more before throwing down her charcoal in triumph. Her very manner had changed. Now that she had completed her task, there was a sleekness about her, the sort of feline satisfaction I had enjoyed upon acquiring a new lover. Her artistic thirst slaked, she was relaxed as she wiped her hands.

She looked over the sheets of drawing paper. "Thank you," she said to Stoker by way of dismissal.

He stepped away from the plinth and behind the screen to resume his clothes as she turned back to me. "You saw him," she said, nodding towards the now empty plinth. Her voice was pitched low and intimate, a conversation for just the two of us. "What did you think?"

"Majestic," was the only word that served, so it was the only one I used.

She bowed her head. "He will be the making of me," she said fiercely, with an expression of rapture upon her face. So might Moses have looked upon seeing the Promised Land.

She and I said nothing more, and in a moment Stoker appeared, dressed and presentable, at least as presentable as he could be with tousled hair and a cheekful of honey pastilles.

Miss Talbot said nothing, merely smiled as we took our leave. But I noticed that her eyes fell to the parcel in my hand, and I saw too the tightness of her jaw, the quick drop of the eyelids as she clenched her fist. And when she opened her hand, I saw that she had broken her charcoal in two.

S toker and I were quit of Havelock House before he asked about the parcel. "Soon," I said, and the minute we gained the privacy of the Belvedere, I displayed my trophy.

He gave a soundless whistle and put out a finger to touch the spoiled slippers. "Do we know whose?"

"Look inside," I instructed.

He did and sat back, pursing his lips thoughtfully. "This is not enough," he said. "No jury in England will hang her on the strength of bloodied slippers. She might have trod in the stuff quite innocently."

I snorted. "Do you really believe that?"

"What I believe is immaterial. The point is what the counsel for the defense can persuade a jury to believe. And let us not forget, juries are made of men, and no man is easily swayed to believe a woman capable of such an atrocity. They will seize any excuse to avoid convicting the female of the species, particularly if it means she will swing for it. Think of the Madeleine Smith case."

"Blast," I muttered. Smith had stuffed her former lover full of arsenic—arsenic she had been proven to have purchased—yet the jury could not bring itself to return a conviction. She had not been entirely exonerated, but she had been freed just the same.

"Besides," Stoker said, holding up his fingers as he enumerated the following points. "Gilchrist wrote the threatening note to us. He wrote the blackmail note to the princess, and he kept these slippers in a secret place, no doubt to control his puppet. He must be masterminding the whole endeavor."

"Oh, there you are again—championing him for the role of criminal mastermind! In my experience," I said with a tart edge, "the female of the species is far more dangerous. I should put my money on him as cat's-paw in this plot. She gave him the slippers to hide, and the rest was done at her bidding."

Stoker said nothing, and I was surprised he had not warmed more quickly to my theory. After all, he had more reason than most men to mistrust women; his own wife had left him for dead in the Brazilian jungles. The fact that he did not hate my sex upon principle spoke to a certain native nobility in him, I decided.

I went on. "You will have to concede that I am a better judge of the character of men than you."

He made a noise I have seldom heard outside a barnyard, a sort of braying guffaw that might have suited a donkey. "You believe you know the male character better than I? Shall I remind you that I am, in fact, myself a man?"

"I am perfectly aware of that," I replied, "and it is this overfamiliarity with the gender that blinds you. You have never had cause to make a study of men because you are one, whereas I have devoted years to the subject."

"You study men?" His jaw had gone slightly slack, as if he could not entirely believe I told the truth.

"Certainly. With all the interest and vigor that I apply to my lepidoptery," I said with considerable pride.

"For what purpose?"

"Why do we study any subject?" I demanded. "To know it better. In this case, pure curiosity might have sufficed—I find the human male to be an endlessly fascinating entity. But as it happens, my more pressing motivations are twofold. First, I require men to satisfy those physical urges to which healthy adult *Homo sapiens* are prey. Now, you might imagine that securing partners for such activities is a simple matter, but I assure you, it is thoroughly complicated. One must assess a gentleman's cleanliness, his attractiveness, his education, his manners and morals, and above all his discretion. Then, one must carefully plot one's advances. A mistimed overture is a calamity."

"I can imagine," he said in a slightly strangled voice. But he had asked, and I plunged on ruthlessly.

"And the second motivation for making a study of men is my own safety. I have circumnavigated the globe three times in the past seven years, and I have found myself in every possible situation: shipwrecked, fêted, hunted, wined, dined, and very nearly served up en brochette to a rather nasty cannibal upon whose island I was forced to take refuge during a Fijian typhoon. I have endured hurricanes, volcanoes, earthquakes, malaria, Corsican brigands, Balkan Customs officials, and evangelical Christians bent upon missionary work, and had only my wits upon which to rely. My judgment, quite simply, has saved my life. I will defer to it now. Julian Gilchrist is a weak, vain man. He is nothing more than a pawn in this disgraceful game."

"Very well," he conceded finally. "Whichever of them is the author of this atrocity, we must catch them in the act of collecting the jewels. If she fetches them, that complicity plus these slippers is enough to secure her cooperation. Although I hardly think that is the case," he said coldly. "It is perfectly obvious that Julian Gilchrist is the leading figure in this drama."

I pointed to the guinea coin attached to his watch chain. "Shall we wager?" I asked with a devilish grin. We had laid a guinea upon the results of our last investigation, and he never failed to seize the opportunity to remind me that he had had the better of me. It was beyond time that I redeemed myself.

"Very well. But since I already have the coin, what will you give me if I win?" His gaze was intent, but if he meant to convey any sort of subtext to his offer, I refused to acknowledge it.

"The satisfaction of being right will have to suffice," I told him coolly. "Now, we have a few hours to make our preparations."

"Preparations?" His gaze narrowed. "What kind of preparations?"

"It is time to load the firearms," I said, rubbing my hands together.

"Absolutely *not*," he told me in a voice that brooked no argument. "I will have my knives and that is sufficient. You know how I feel about firearms. And if memory serves, the last time you went abroad armed, you ended up losing the bloody thing in the Thames—just before I almost drowned saving your life."

"That is not *quite* how I recall the events," I said. "But if it consoles you, very well. I will not take a revolver."

But Stoker said nothing about other implements of pain, and after I had repaired to my little chapel to assume my expedition costume, I slipped an assortment of minuten through the cuffs of my sleeve. The little entomological pins were slender as threads, but I had once had occasion to spend two days aboard a raft in the Yellow Sea with a Chinese gentleman who had been most instructive on the application of them to tender places. The principles behind it conflicted with Western scientific theory, yet none could deny their efficacy when implemented with a skilled hand. Unfortunately, mine was not, and the most I had done was draw a little blood and injure a bit of manly pride. Still, they gave me a touch of courage, as did the last-minute addition of my tiny velvet mouse, Chester. I tucked him into my pocket, a little murine consolation for the adventure ahead. Mindful of Stoker's admonitions against firearms, I slipped a single knife into my boot top, knowing he could hardly cavil at that since he would no doubt be equipped with at least three of his own.

I plaited my hair and wound it snugly into a Psyche knot at my nape, pinned well out of the way in case any grappling would be required of me. Everything else about my appearance was neat and tidy and deceptively simple.

After I had changed and rejoined Stoker in the Belvedere, we took a simple meal together, fortifying our strength with plates of roast beef and tall glasses of porter. Just before we left, as Stoker patted his pockets for the jewels for the twentieth time, I penned a swift note to Sir Hugo.

"Why the devil are you doing that?" he demanded.

"I gave him my word." I sealed the note in an envelope and wrote out Sir Hugo's direction at Scotland Yard. We patted the dogs and Stoker put down the remains of the roast beef for them to finish.

We left just as dusk was falling and opened the door to find Lady Wellingtonia standing there, her hand upraised as if she were about to knock.

"Hello, children!" she said in her booming voice. "I thought to invite you to take dinner up at the house, but I see you have other plans tonight."

"A lecture," Stoker said smoothly. "At the Academy."

She narrowed her eyes and folded her hands over the top of her walking stick. "*Which* Academy?"

"The Royal one," he said, his eye twitching slightly.

She pursed her mouth as if to pursue the matter, but I held up the note. "Lady Wellingtonia, I wonder if you might oblige us with a favor. I have a note here that must be delivered. Perhaps you would be so kind as to ask the hall boy to see to it? But not until tomorrow morning," I told her firmly.

She took it from me, making no bones about her curiosity. She read the address aloud with an expression of increasing incredulity. "Sir Hugo Montgomerie? Scotland Yard? What kind of business can you possibly have with the head of Special Branch?" she demanded.

"He likes butterflies," I said with a smile. "He has a particularly fine examplar of *Teinopalpus imperialis* I am longing to acquire for Lord Rosemorran's collection of Nepalese swallowtails."

"*Teinopalpus imperialis,*" she said, suspicion dripping from every syllable.

"Commonly known as the Kaiser-i-Hind," I said helpfully. "He has a female, which is the larger of the species, and it is a quite spectacular imago, isn't that right, Stoker?"

Stoker gave a start. "Yes. Imago. Quite spectacular."

I rolled my eyes heavenwards at his vagueness, but Lady Wellingtonia seemed mollified. "Very well," she said with a gracious nod. "Although I am quite disappointed you won't be joining us this evening. Perhaps tomorrow. You can tell us all about the lecture," she said with a malicious smile. "In detail."

"We shall be delighted. But now we must hurry," I said, tucking my arm through Stoker's and dragging him away. When we were out of ear-shot, I turned on him. "What in the name of all that is holy ails you?"

"I cannot lie to old women," he said, wiping his brow. "They remind me of my grandmother, a woman who had no equal for ferreting out the truth. Whenever my brothers or I were up to some mischief, it was Grandmother who invariably managed to discover the culprit. She might've given Torquemada lessons."

"Illuminating as is this insight into your childhood, we must get on," I urged. "I want to be there and in position well ahead of the appointed hour. We have the element of surprise, and we must make the most of it."

W e made our way to Littledown in silence. I could not intuit Stok-er's thoughts, but mine turned to Princess Louise. I imagined her, sitting in solitary splendor at Kensington Palace while a fortune in jewels—as well as her reputation—rested in our hands. But there was more at stake than that, and I thought too of Miles Ramsforth. I had given him little consideration as a person during our investigation. He was a cipher to me. We had collected impressions of him, glimpses given by various people, but I could not entirely grasp the whole of the man, as if someone had painted his portrait and then cut it into pieces, scatter-ing them for us to find. It was the contradictions that interested me most. He was a devoted husband, yet a faithless philanderer. He was a patron of the arts with exquisite taste, but he hosted salacious enter-tainments at the Elysian Grotto. I wondered if we would ever be able to reconcile the Janus faces of Miles Ramsforth or if he would hang in spite of our efforts. The thought might have cowed me a little, but I refused to be daunted by the task. Whatever his sins, the man was no murderer, and he would not swing for a crime he did not commit, I vowed.

We reached Littledown in good time. It lacked an hour before the appointed rendezvous with our blackmailer. I moved with the same quickness of step that I employed in the jungles as I followed the mazy paths of my butterflies. For his part, Stoker showed no sign of heightened excitement at the coming fight. He walked with his customary loose-limbed stride, the sort of gracefully lithe gait one sees in men who have spent much time astride horses or aboard ships. His hands were relaxed and his shoulders down, his brow as untroubled as if he were out for a Sunday stroll. Only the tiniest twitch of the muscle at the corner of his mouth betrayed any emotion.

Under cover of darkness, we climbed the wall at Littledown, not wishing to alert anyone to our presence just yet. We kept to the tree line as we made our way to the grotto, alert to any noise that would indicate the watchman or his dog were abroad. We reached the grotto unimpeded; I put a hand to the gate and pulled gently. It was locked, and I shot Stoker a triumphant glance. We had beaten our adversary to the field, and the advantage was ours. I drew the key from my pocket and fitted it to the lock, opening the gate just enough for us to slip inside before shutting it quietly.

We crept forward, into the darkness, and as we reached the narrow tunnel, Stoker put a hand to my shoulder, halting my movement. He struck a match and lit one of the lanterns, gesturing that he meant to go ahead of me. I pursed my lips and plucked the lantern from his hand, holding it high as I moved into the passage. He gave a sigh of irritation but let me go, following as closely behind as the modest dimensions of the space would permit.

The trip through the tunnel was much the same as the last time—the cold, clammy feel of the rock under my fingers, the dank air in my lungs—but as we rounded the last bend, I was conscious of a change. There was a glow just ahead, and a sharp metallic scent in the air.

Stoker, whose sense of smell was better than mine, knew it for what it was. He reached to pull me back, but it was too late. I stepped into the large chamber, my own little lantern unnecessary now, for the vault of the grotto was illuminated by the magic lanterns. Their flames cast the pictures of copulating couples and groups upon the walls, and the very stones seemed alive with their wild undulations.

But I was only vaguely aware of the pictures as they whirled past. My attention was fixed upon the *siège d'amour* in the center of the chamber, the seat of love that must have so often been the focus of past baccha-nals. Once more it held a naked figure, the limbs and head thrown back in a sort of parody of pleasure. One could almost imagine the parted lips were about to speak. But Julian Gilchrist, his throat slashed from ear to ear, would never speak again.

CHAPTER

26

A scarlet river of blood flowed from the obscene gash in his throat, pooling wetly in the hollows of his hips. Golden hair tumbled about his ears, and his eyes were open wide in surprise. One arm lay outstretched like that of a crucified saint, the fingers curving in a gentle arc, the forefinger extended slightly as if pointing to the blood puddling upon the floor.

Just beyond the chair, Emma Talbot stood at the edge of the shadows, her face corpse white, her eyes fixed upon the bloody blade gripped in her hand.

"Do not come closer," she warned, raising the knife. Stoker eased around me, raising his hands to show he meant her no harm.

"Emma," he said softly, "give me the knife. You do not want to harm me, nor do you wish to harm Miss Speedwell. Give me the knife," he repeated.

He edged closer, and she flinched, raising the blade level with his heart. He stood a foot or so out of striking distance but did not falter as she brandished her weapon. He merely spoke, using the same calm tone he might employ to gentle a restless animal.

"Emma, I want you to give me the knife. This will go far better for you if you cooperate," he urged.

She shook her head, blindly, as she jerked the blade again, closing a little of the distance between them.

"Emma," he said serenely, "if you do not give me the knife, I will take it from you. Now, I can see from the way you are holding it that you have no experience of such things, so believe me when I say I could take it easily, and if I have to take it from you, it will be hard and painful. I will probably break your wrist simply because you are threatening us right now, and I do not like to be threatened. Do you understand me?"

Her eyes, the irises ringed with white, widened even further. "If you are going to kill me, do it quickly," she said, fairly spitting the words.

"What do you mean if I am going to kill you? I have no wish to kill you," he told her.

"Then what about that?" she demanded. She did not say Gilchrist's name, but merely pointed with a shaking hand to the atrocity upon the chair. "You have killed him and now you want to kill me as well."

I looked at Stoker. "Is she hysterical, do you think? Shall I slap her? I wouldn't mind."

He did not turn his head, but I could see the muscles of his jaw tense. "Veronica, do not try to be helpful, I beg you."

"I am not hysterical," Emma said, her voice trembling. "But if you have done that to him, why would you spare me since I have discovered you in the act? I am a witness to your treachery."

"You are a witness to precisely nothing," I told her. "In case it has escaped your attention, you were here first. I rather think you did this and your current state of frenzy is simply a ruse to throw us off the scent."

She stared at me. "Do you really think I could bring myself to do *that*?" she demanded. "I did not like Julian, but my God!" A great shudder ran through her body and her knees buckled a little as she dropped the knife. Stoker kicked it aside and put out an arm to steady her. She took it, albeit reluctantly, as he gave me a pointed look.

"Veronica, stop tormenting Miss Talbot. You know she is innocent." He turned to the trembling woman. "Emma, we did not do this to Gilchrist, and in spite of how things look, we know you did not either."

She gripped his arm, her knuckles white against the black of his coat. "Then I was right," she said, forcing the words through bloodless lips. "She did it."

"Yes, Miss Talbot," I told her gently. "Miles Ramsforth never murdered Artemisia. Ottilie did."

She collapsed then into great heaving sobs that rocked her from head to foot. Stoker kept an arm about her while I rolled my eyes and waited for the frenzy to finish.

"I really ought to slap her," I urged Stoker again, but he merely waved me off and held her more tightly against his chest, one hand cradling her head in its broad palm. He looked like a bear with a china doll, I thought in some annoyance, and I went to pull down one of the velvet draperies to cover Julian Gilchrist. It was the least I could do to offer the fellow some dignity, I thought.

That bit of housekeeping undertaken, I returned to hold a brief council of war with Stoker. "We can hardly finish our plan with Miss Talbot in such a state," I pointed out. "We shall have to settle her somewhere until we can apprehend Mrs. Ramsforth."

Emma Talbot's artist fingers curled around Stoker's biceps. "She cannot have got far."

"Yes, Miss Talbot, that much is obvious from the warmth of the corpse and the minimal amount of clotting to the blood," I informed her.

She paled still further, and Stoker rolled his eyes. "For the love of Christ, Veronica, she is barely keeping her composure as it is."

He looked far too comfortable in the role of rescuing hero, I decided. I tipped my head as I studied Miss Talbot. "Now that you mention it, she is quite pale. Do you think we just ought to knock her thoroughly senseless until we've concluded our business? A light tap to the jaw should do it. Just below the ear," I said, pointing.

His mouth thinned, and Miss Talbot gave another deep shudder, then pushed him away gently. "Thank you, Mr. Templeton-Vane. But Miss Speedwell is correct, I must master myself and let you finish this. She must not be permitted to get away." She straightened. It took a visible effort of will, but I liked her better for it.

"She shall not elude us," I promised her. "We will take this house down brick by brick to find her if need be."

"That will not be necessary," said a voice from the shadows. Ottilie Ramsforth stepped forward, holding a small revolver in her hand. It was leveled at the group of us, and it did not waver.

"We were just talking about you," I said with a thin smile. "How very courteous of you not to make us come looking."

She advanced a little further but was careful to keep herself a good twenty feet away, the *siège d'amour* and its shrouded occupant between us. Without looking at one another, Stoker and I immediately assessed the situation and realized she was at a distinct disadvantage. She might have a revolver, but there was only one of her and two of us. If she were a very good shot—and that was a presumption indeed—she could still hit only one before the other was upon her. Naturally I did not include Miss Talbot in my calculations. She had mastered her hysteria, but I was unwilling to test her mettle in a fight. The best we could hope for was that she would throw herself to the ground and stay out of the way.

Ottilie swung the revolver from me to Stoker and back again. "Hold there, Mr. Templeton-Vane. And you, Miss Speedwell. I am a rather good shot, and unlikely to miss entirely at this distance. Miles taught me how to shoot in Greece. There are bandits there, you know. I got quite a bit of practice." She kept the barrel of the revolver trained upon me, and I stared into its unblinking black eye. It was small, a lady's toy really, but doubtless big enough to put an unwelcome hole in one or both of us. "If you advance again, Miss Speedwell, I will not shoot you. I will shoot him. And Mr. Templeton-Vane, the same goes for you. If you do not want to see Miss Speedwell harmed, stay where you are."

Stoker held up his hands. "As you wish, Mrs. Ramsforth. But I am curious as to your plan," he said in a conversational tone. "There are three of us."

Ottilie Ramsforth drew the hammer back on the revolver and pointed it squarely at the forehead of Emma Talbot. "Are there?"

Miss Talbot opened her mouth to shriek, but no sound was forthcoming. Her eyelids fluttered, and she closed and opened her mouth a few times, giving a splendid impression of a goldfish before she fell to the ground in a dead faint.

"That was certainly fortuitous," Mrs. Ramsforth said with some satisfaction. She swung her revolver back around to Stoker.

"I suppose your plan is to kill us and make away with the emeralds," I suggested.

"In point of fact, I have no interest in the jewels," she corrected. "That was Gilchrist's idea, and a thoroughly wicked one it was," she added with a severity that surprised me. "Although when I discovered why Louise was so determined to clear Miles' name, I told him to go ahead with it."

"Yes, that must have been a nasty shock," I told her, injecting my voice with suitable sympathy. "Most vexing to have devised such a tidy murder only to have it scuppered at the last minute because your bosom friend has decided to interfere."

Her mouth narrowed. "The murder came off just fine."

"I wasn't speaking of Artemisia's death. I mean the murder of Miles Ramsforth. That is what this is all about, is it not? Your primary target was never the girl. It was your own husband."

"Do not judge me!" she ordered, the hand holding the revolver shaking just a little. "Do not presume to judge me. You do not know what it was like, turning a blind eye to his adventures all those years. But I did it because it kept him close. I knew he would never leave me because he had no reason to. I loved him. *I* understood him. Not them."

"Until the money began to run out," Stoker put in. "That is when the fear took root, isn't it? That is when the uncertainty began to grow. When the money was gone, what was there to keep him?"

"He loved me," she insisted, pointing the revolver at Stoker's head.

"But not enough," I corrected, drawing her attention back to me. The revolver's eye focused upon the spot between my brows. "Without your money to support the pair of you, what was there to bind him to you? It wasn't as though you had given him a child."

The blow struck home. The revolver hand trembled, but she brought up her other hand, steadying her grip. "There had never been a child before, not in any of his liaisons. I thought perhaps it was not entirely my fault, that he might be to blame as well. But then Artemisia told him she had conceived, and it was as if he had been granted his fondest wish. You should have seen him, the proud papa," she said, her mouth twisting as it shaped the words. "He could not conceal his delight. He meant to acknowledge it. They planned it all out together—that we would go to Greece, to *our* villa, and she would have the child. And do you know who was supposed to look after it? I was. She would live with us and give him his golden child, and I was to be nothing more than a nursemaid in my own home, reduced to whatever crumbs she saw fit to leave me."

"But it wasn't her betrayal that stung the most, was it?" Stoker prodded. "It was his willingness to give up what you had built together, to include her."

"He would have made a laughingstock of both of us," she hissed. "And he did not even care, he was so happy. *He thought I would be happy.*" Her voice rose on a sob. "That is when I realized he never knew me at all. All these years of giving up so much for him, and he did not know the slightest thing about me."

"That is when you decided he had to die," I surmised. "And how better to wreak your vengeance than to kill his mistress and child and watch him hang for their murder."

"It was an elegant solution," she said. "Killing him outright would be too quick. And Artemisia would still be there with his child, a monstrous reminder. I wanted them obliterated, all of them."

"How did Gilchrist come into the plot?" Stoker asked.

"Artemisia left him for Miles. We consoled one another, as friends," she clarified quickly. "We were never lovers, although he offered." Her lips tightened in distaste. "That is how I got him here tonight. I told him I wanted to bed him, that it would be a fitting end to our partnership. Poor fool. He was stripped and onto the chair without the slightest hesitation. I told him to close his eyes while I took off my clothes. I said I was shy," she said, her voice breaking on a mirthless laugh. "He opened them when I cut his throat. He looked so surprised. Not like Artemisia. She never even stirred when I cut her."

"Because you drugged her first. How did you manage that?" I asked.

She shrugged. "A dose of laudanum in her punch. As soon as she began to feel tired, I showed her up to Miles' room to lie down for a little while. It was a crush that night, and no one noticed us slipping up the back stairs. I took her to his bed, and I helped her to lie down, and when she was sleeping, I picked up his razor from the washstand and cut her throat with it. It was so much easier than I expected."

"You were wearing white," Stoker remarked. "How did you keep from getting blood all over yourself? It must have been a very tidy murder."

"No, it wasn't. It was messy, horribly messy. But I had prepared for that. I was wearing an evening gown, so my arms were bare. All I had to do was stand behind the bed curtains and reach my arm around to do the deed. They were thick and crimson, and when the blood splashed upon them, it did not show, at least not enough to notice. I stepped out from behind the hangings without a trace upon me. Only my slippers were soiled when I trod in the blood."

"Which you noticed at once. So you gave the slippers to Gilchrist for safekeeping," I said.

"Yes. I put them into the box they came in. Emma Talbot saw me with it that night, but it meant nothing to her at the time. When she saw you today with the same box under your arm, she suddenly realized what must have happened. I said I was coming here to pack a few things I wanted for Greece. She followed to confront me. I told her it was a simple misunderstanding and that Julian was the villain. I told her I had lured him here to expose him and that I was glad of her help. Then I sent her down here to wait, knowing she would discover him and then she would know the truth." She paused. "It is not a pretty way to die, is it? I will never forget the look of horror on his face the night of the murder, when I gave him the bloodied slippers and told him what I had done. He thought we had been building castles in Spain when we talked of it, plotting their deaths. He said he didn't realize I actually meant to do it. But by then it was too late. He was my accomplice."

"Because if he had failed to do your bidding, you would have simply told the police that he had conspired to the murder with you. He could not implicate you without implicating himself," Stoker reasoned.

"Exactly. It nearly broke him. Men are not as strong as we are, Miss Speedwell," she told me with a confiding nod. "They so often let us down when we need them most. But Gilchrist delivered the threat that I told him to write, and he attempted to seduce Miss Speedwell to see how much she discovered, although he was rather a failure at that, wasn't he?" she asked.

I shrugged. "It was not entirely his fault. I have preferred dark gentlemen to fair. I also require significantly more intelligence in a man."

"Poor Julian. But he was too greedy for his own good. I knew the ledger existed, but I had never seen it. Miles was careful about that, curiously so. I did not even trouble to look for it after he was taken by the police. It did not matter to me. I almost didn't even look at it when that poor fool of a watchman sent it along to me. You gave him quite a fright, you know," she added with a touch of reproof. "He discovered it the night he chased you off. He wrapped it up most carefully and dispatched it to me at Havelock House. He said he was afraid it might be something important of the master's, and that I ought to have it. I opened it out of nothing more than idle curiosity. Imagine my surprise when I read the last entry. I never understood why Louise was so convinced of Miles' innocence. But there it was, staring me in the face." She fairly bit off the last word, her eyes gleaming with anger. "It was the worst sort of betrayal one woman can commit against another."

"The princess says they were not lovers," I told her mildly, but her eyes flashed with anger.

"That hardly matters, does it? She came down here with Miles. She knew how much I loved him, how much our life together meant to me. But she came anyway, improper as that was, and God only knows where it might have led in time. When I told Julian about Louise's name being in the ledger, he did not say much. He merely went away and said he had thinking to do. Today he told me he had sent her a note demanding her jewels. He said she ought to be made to pay, but I knew it was not my pain he cared for. He simply saw an opportunity to make himself rich— and get away. He meant to take the jewels and leave England. He thought he could escape me, escape what he had done. But there is no escape, is there? Not for any of us."

Her speech had had the air of a clockwork automaton winding down. She was finished. She gave a deep sigh of resignation and steadied her gun hand as she leveled her weapon at me. "Well, it is time."

Several things happened in an instant. Stoker, seizing his chance, reached for the knife in his boot as he lunged forward with a growl, drawing her fire. Ottilie turned the revolver to Stoker, pulling the trigger without hesitation. The noise was deafening in the stone chamber, echoing over and over again like a cataclysm. As it beat upon my ears, I bent, slipping my knife from its sheath and flinging it with the piercing howl of a Fury. It caught Ottilie full in the breast and she dropped the revolver, bringing her hands to the hilt with a look of astonishment on her face. A slow stain of crimson began to spread around the blade buried in her chest, flowering over the pale flesh of her hands. She slipped to the ground in perfect silence.

I turned to Stoker; his eyes were wide with surprise as he slowly moved towards me. Without a word, he fell heavily to his knees, and I did not understand what ailed him until he turned his head. A crimson sheet of blood cascaded down the side of his face.

I vaulted over the recumbent figure of Miss Talbot to reach him before he finished falling. I put an arm to his chest, supporting him, feeling the wet scarlet warmth of his blood seeping through my sleeve.

He sagged against me, and I forced his head back. "Do not do this," I ordered him. "Do you hear me, you stupid man? You are not allowed to die."

He opened his eyes, those impossibly blue eyes like bits of a Giotto sky. His look was one of perfect tenderness, and his hand gripped mine with all the strength he was capable of. "Veronica," he said, in a low voice that throbbed with emotion.

"Yes, Stoker?"

The grip upon my hand tightened, and he gave a great shudder. "The bloody bitch shot me." And then his eyes rolled white and he pitched forward into unconsciousness.

CHAPTER

27

The scene was something conjured out of a nightmare. The lantern images of couples disporting themselves continued to play about the room, whirling with dizzying speed. Shadow then light passed over Stoker's face in turn, illuminating the blood in stark crimson, then blackening it to ink. The blood covered my hands in a warm, sticky flow and for an instant I felt the strong urge to succumb to hysterics.

"This will *not* do," I told myself severely. I felt a rustle of movement behind me, and without forethought, my hand reached for the blade in Stoker's boot. I whirled upon my haunches, leveling it at the surprised face of Emma Talbot.

"You have recovered yourself at an opportune moment," I told her.

"I have not recovered myself at all," she corrected coolly. "I was not in a swoon. I simply thought it was an expedient way to remove myself from the line of fire."

I gave her a long look. "I am not certain whether to slap you or congratulate you, but you can tip the scales by helping me. Find something to bind his head with."

She did not hesitate. She went directly to the pile of clothing discarded by Julian Gilchrist in his haste to copulate and retrieved his neckcloth and shirt. I used Stoker's blade to cut the shirt into strips to form a sort of padded bandage and wound the neckcloth tightly to keep it in place, securing it at the ends with the minuten from my cuffs.

"It will have to do until we can fetch help," I said more to myself than to Emma Talbot. She was not beside me, and I looked up to find her standing over Ottilie Ramsforth.

"My God," she breathed. "You spitted her right through the heart. I have never seen anything like it."

"Is she dead?" I asked, fashioning my words of flint.

"She is."

"Good." I wiped my gore-streaked hands upon my skirt. "He is too large for us to move easily and I fear he will lose too much blood if we attempt it. Take a lantern and go to the front gate. If you are athletic enough, scale it. Otherwise, open it by whatever means necessary. What time is it?"

She glanced at the little watch pinned to her bodice. "It lacks twenty minutes to midnight."

"Blast. Too long," I muttered.

"Too long for what?" she demanded.

"The cavalry. Gentlemen from the Metropolitan Police will be arriving at dawn if we do not appear, but that is far too long to wait. Is there anyone else here? The watchman, perhaps? Did she keep him?"

Emma shook her head. "No one. She said she let him go, I suspect so she could do away with Julian without witnesses. So she could do away with all of us," she added with a shudder.

I gave her a close look. "Do not make me strike you, Miss Talbot. The temptation is almost more than I can bear. Now, walk down the lane until you find a house—a neighbor will do. Rouse them and find the nearest police station to organize a rescue. Or if you spy a passing bobby upon his watch, hail him. Either way, you must send for Sir Hugo Montgomerie, the head of Special Branch."

"Special Branch!" Her eyes were wide in the fitful light. "You do have an interesting acquaintance, Miss Speedwell."

"Go," I told her. "And don't dare to come back until you bring help."

She did as I bade her, leaving me alone with two corpses and Stoker. The smell of blood hung heavy in the confined space; I could taste it upon the air. The minutes ticked past and still the couples cavorted upon the walls. Stoker breathed, slowly and more shallowly than I would have liked. After some time—how long I could not say—he roused a little.

He put out a hand, and I caught it. "I am here," I told him.

"What happened? Where are we?"

"You attempted to play the hero and got yourself shot for your pains," I told him severely. "Your stupidity knows no bounds."

"Why is my face wet? Veronica, are you weeping?"

"Don't be daft. It must be blood," I said sharply. "Ottilie Ramsforth tried to kill you. Before I sorted you out, you were bleeding like a stuck pig from a wound in your temple."

"I can feel it," he told me. "It burns like the devil. I cannot remember what happened then."

"I am not surprised. You went down like a ninepin."

"At the risk of sounding ungrateful," he drawled, "I wonder if you might explain why we are lingering here in this appalling cave instead of seeking medical attention?"

"We are waiting for Emma Talbot to return with assistance," I assured him. "But this blasted place is too remote to make it a quick proposition. We are simply going to have to stay warm and quiet until help arrives."

"Like hell we will," he said, attempting to sit up.

I pushed him back with the flat of my palms. "Stop that or you will start the hemorrhage up again, and you have already bled on me enough for one night."

"Very well," he said in a deceptively meek voice. "But I should at least like to assess the damage."

"I suppose," I conceded. "Tell me what to do."

The next few minutes were unpleasant. Under his direction, I unwound the bandage, careful not to dislodge the delicate clots that had formed. "Get your flask of aguardiente," he ordered. I retrieved it and he splashed a good bit over his hand. As I watched in horror, he took his wet fingertips and ran them over the edges of the wound. "Deeper than I would like," he murmured, his face very white. "It will be difficult to stitch. I can't"—he broke off, taking a deep breath as he palpated further—"I can't feel pieces of loose bone. Do you see any?"

I steeled myself, peering into the wound. "One small chip," I told him.

He handed me the flask. "Be quick about it."

I splashed the aguardiente on my hand, running the strong spirit over my skin until it stung. When my fingers were as sterile as I could make them under the circumstances, I reached into the gaping wound. As gently as I could, I grasped the tiny bit of chipped bone and pulled it free. I held it up to him and he slowly closed his eyes in approbation.

"Good girl," he muttered.

"What shall I do with it?" I asked, staring at the slender whiteness of the shard against the puddled blood in my hand.

"Keep it for a souvenir," he suggested. "You have to wash out the wound now. God, what I wouldn't give for a nice bit of carbolic. The aguardiente will have to do."

"It will hurt," I warned him.

He opened one eye. "I should think you would enjoy that."

"Stupid man," I retorted. I poured out the aguardiente in a slow, steady stream, trickling it from one end of the wound down, flushing it as clean as I could. It bled afresh then, but stopped almost immediately, and I wrapped his head with his own shirt turned inside out to make as clean a bandage as possible. He made no sound as I tended him, but his hands were clenched, his knuckles white to the bone, and when I finished, he gave a sigh, his mouth going slack.

"I forgot to ask—are you hurt?" he demanded suddenly, trying once more to sit up. I pushed at his shoulders with both hands.

"Lie back, idiot. You oughtn't to move. If you will give me your handkerchief, I will mop up your face as best I can."

He pointed to his pocket and I wiped at his face. The blood was too dry to come away, and the effect was ghoulish, but at least it gave me something to do. I removed my jacket and folded it to make a pillow for his head. I settled him on it and he stared for a long moment at the whirling figures. "They are giving me the collywobbles," he said in a faint voice. I rose and went to find a lamp, lighting it with a match from the box in my pocket. When it was burning well, I blew out the magic lantern, causing the couples to cease their endless copulating. I came back to Stoker, lamp in hand.

"What in the name of Satan's arsehole is that?" he demanded.

"The genitals of a very healthy young man," I told him, waving the phallus-shaped lamp.

He began to laugh then, a laugh that ended in a wheezing cough. "I refuse to die with that my last sight."

"You are not going to die," I told him severely. "I have already forbidden it."

"I will obey," he said solemnly.

But I did not like his color. He was a ghastly shade of pale, his lips almost white now, his breathing slow. I put a hand to his cheek and it was cold. I cursed the rock floor upon which he lay. The chill of it was seeping into his bones, I had no doubt, robbing him of whatever strength remained to him. I left him again to find something with which to make him a pallet. I went to the velvet curtains which screened off the passageway to the main house. With hands shaking with rage, I tore them down, bundling them into my arms to make a nest for Stoker. I deliberately did not look at the supine form of Ottilie Ramsforth.

Stoker was sleeping when I returned, rousing with some difficulty and a little confusion.

"What is happening?" he demanded.

"Nothing," I soothed. "But you must be warm." I arranged the velvet in folds, saving out one panel with which to cover him. When I was done, I coaxed him onto the pallet, heaving him as he was in no state to move himself. I spread the velvet over him, tucking it tightly to hold in his warmth, and then I lay beside him, pressing close.

He drifted to sleep again but woke a little while later, nearly frantic with thirst. I held the last of the aguardiente to his lips as he drank deeply. I questioned the wisdom of giving him intoxicants, but he was already in so weakened a condition, it could hardly hurt. Besides, I reasoned, it might blunt the edge of the pain in his head.

He closed his eyes but did not sleep again. Instead, he pushed his arms out of the velvet coverings, muttering about the heat.

"You must not take a chill," I insisted. I made to tuck him in again, but he grunted in protest, wrapping his arms about me instead.

"Stay," he mumbled. And I did. I stayed, clasped to his chest as a child might hold a beloved toy, closely and with something like reverence.

It seemed like the time for confidences. He had not fallen into unconsciousness again, but drifted, and I ventured a question as much to distract him as to satisfy my own curiosity. "Stoker," I began, "during Merryweather's visit, there was a slip of the tongue when you were talking to him. I don't even think you realized it," I said softly.

He was silent so long, I wondered if he had swum into sleep again. But at length his chest rumbled with a reply. "I did. As soon as it passed my lips."

"'You mustn't gamble with a Templeton-Vane,'" I quoted. "'They have the devil's own luck.' *They.*"

"You saw Rupert," he reminded me in a thick, slow voice. "And you saw Merry, and you have seen Tiberius. Peas in a pod, the Templeton-Vanes. They always breed true—auburn hair and grey eyes. My mother even had the same coloring. She was a distant cousin, one of the Vanes."

I looked into his eyes, blue as an equatorial sea beneath hair so black a raven would envy it. "When did you realize?"

He shrugged. "The cuckoo in the nest never sounds quite the same as the other nestlings. Always something that marks you as different. His lordship, the old viscount—the one they call my father," he said with a twist of his handsome mouth, "he did what they all do. He gave me his name and pretended not to notice. But he noticed. And through a thousand ways, he showed me he noticed."

I said nothing and he went on, talking almost as if I were not even there, purging himself of the memories. My teeth showed an alarming tendency to chatter, so I clenched my jaw tightly and listened. "He had a stormy relationship with my mother. It was an arranged marriage—aren't they all? She had money, he had the name and the title. They got along tolerably well for a while, I'm told. There was Tiberius the heir and Rupert the spare. But then something happened. He took to drink. So did she, to hear Rip tell it. And they began to quarrel. He got a child on a housemaid and Mother found out about it. Things went from bad to worse. He decided to have her portrait painted as a sort of peace offering. He commissioned a Welshman to do it." He broke off and smiled bitterly to himself. "Well, he did more than paint her. And the result was a black-haired infant in the nursery who looked exactly like the painter."

"These things are not always certain," I began.

He attempted to shrug and winced, thinking better of it. "This is. The viscount went abroad for a while. He was not within a thousand miles of his wife when the deed was done. Everyone knew what I was before I did," he added simply. "I understood I was different from the first. I did not know why until Tiberius very kindly informed me of it during a childhood quarrel. The word isn't a pretty one. When I asked Nanny what it meant, she washed my mouth out with soap and his lordship whipped me. I never told them where I heard it. Tiberius expected me to. I saw it in his face as the viscount was whipping me—oh, his lordship always made us watch when he inflicted punishments upon the others. He thought it would teach discipline. It just made us hate him more, but I was the only one honest enough to say it aloud. I got whipped for that too."

"But surely your mother—"

"My mother was a very beautiful, very weak woman who would have lost everything she loved most in the world if she had ever stood up to him." He broke off with a sudden groan. "You're shivering. It is the shock. You killed her, didn't you? You killed her for me, and now you are sick with it."

"I am not sick," I told him, holding him more tightly.

"Of course you are," he said in a slurring voice. "It takes you like that, the first time. Battle is one thing, you are prepared for it. You expect it. But this is something altogether different. How were you to know?"

"I did know," I said in a small voice.

"You can't," he insisted. "And you did it for me."

"You tried to leap on her to save me," I reminded him. "Of all the woolly-witted, ham-headed, thoroughly stupid things to do—" I broke off, unable to finish.

"But you did it instead and now you have to live with it. It changes you, that first time you take a life. And I am sorry it is because of me," he said.

I put my face to his neck, feeling the pulse there as I hid my eyes. "It is not the first time, Stoker. I have taken a life before. And I would take a thousand more if it meant I could save you. But I cannot talk about it. Not now. Talk to me so I don't have to think about it," I ordered, desperate. "Tell me about your mother, your beautiful mother with the grey eyes."

For a long moment I did not know how he would react to my

confession. Any other man would have shoved me away, would have repudiated me for carrying the mark of Cain upon my brow. But Revelstoke Templeton-Vane was not any other man. With infinite care, he raised his arm and put it about me, drawing me closer as he began to speak.

"She didn't love the painter, you know. You mustn't think I was conceived in some grand passion or deathless love affair. It was a sordid little interlude between a fellow on the make and a woman who was in need of some kindness. As it happens, the painter was a bounder whose silence upon the matter was bought and paid for."

I felt a little of the chill ebb from my body as I realized he was not going to make me speak of things I could not. Instead he was offering up his own tragedies to spare mine. It was an act of true generosity. He put his palm to my cheek, catching my tears and letting them run through his fingers. "Your family paid him hush money?"

"Every month until I left home. After that, the viscount washed his hands of me. Said he didn't much care if my paternity was exposed. I was a troublesome child who had caused him nothing but grief when I ought to have been grateful." He fairly spat the last word. "I ran away. Frequently. The first time, my mother was still alive, and she is the one who forced him to set a detective upon me."

"That was when you met Sir Hugo Montgomerie," I put in.

"Yes. I eluded them for six months, and those were the happiest days of my life. I think his lordship would have been willing enough to let me go, but Mother forced the issue. They had made up, you see. After my birth, they realized how close they had come to wrecking everything. The possibility of divorce and public scandal was too horrifying to contemplate. So they put a happy face upon things. Merryweather was the result of that, the embodiment of their determination to make a go of things." His expression was thoughtful. "I've often wondered if it makes a difference, you know, the circumstances of conception in the character of a child. He has always been a sunny little fellow, happy as a lark. And I have always been . . . other. Does that mark a child forever?"

"I am perhaps not the person to ask," I reminded him.

"Damn me," he muttered. "I forgot." I had not yet come to terms with the circumstances of my own conception. I wondered sometimes if I ever would.

"Never mind," I said. "It does not matter."

"Of course it does. It matters more than anything. It shapes us. Don't you see that?" I drew back to look at him. The pain in his eyes was unlike anything I had ever seen before. I had seen his undraped body, but this was true nakedness. I looked away, studying my fingernails instead. His blood was caked beneath them, thin scarlet moons.

"We are both of us children of the wilderness," I said lightly. "All the more reason to send their opinions to the devil. What care we for the judgments of others?"

"Very convincing. I might almost have believed you," he said, brushing his fingertips over my damp cheek to collect my tears. "But for these."

"I am not weeping about your silly brother," I told him, drying my eyes on my sleeve. "It is that wretched story of your childhood. The whippings and the coldness, being shut out of the rest of the family. At least I had Aunt Lucy. She was warm and real."

"But she wasn't yours," he said softly. "She lied to you as much as they lied to me. And now we've broken free of the lot of them. Let them keep their shame and their secrets. We shall take life on its own terms."

I gave him a watery smile. "There is an old Spanish proverb: *Take what you want. Take it,* said God. *And pay.*"

"We have paid every minute of our lives. Let someone else pay," he said with a rough edge to his voice. "Presuming we get out of here," he added.

"We will," I promised. I did not doubt Emma's resourcefulness. But it could take many hours to find the authorities at this time of night, persuade them of the urgency. And I wondered how long he could last on a cold stone floor without proper treatment.

The hardest lesson I had learnt upon my travels was patience. There are times when every muscle, every nerve, screams for movement, when every instinct urges escape. But the instinct to fly is not always a sound one. There are occasions when only stillness can save you. I wanted to do nothing more than lift Stoker's recumbent form onto my back and stagger out of that place. It was a futile thought; with the difference in our sizes, I could not have managed more than a few hundred yards before putting him down. And in the meantime, I could do incalculable damage by disturbing whatever fragile clots had formed to protect him. It was a measure of my regard for him that I smothered every inclination to action and simply put my arms about him and held him close, giving him my warmth and letting my own worst imaginings devour me.

I must have drifted off to sleep, for the next thing I knew, the sound of approaching footsteps echoed through the grotto. I can only blame the disorienting effects of deep sleep when surrounded by corpses—as well as the suddenness of my coming awake—for what happened next. My wits were clouded with slumber and not entirely recovered from Ottilie Ramsforth's homicidal attack; I was conscious only of the need to protect my injured and vulnerable partner. I grabbed the first thing that came to hand, raising my weapon just as a figure emerged from the shadows of the narrow corridor. With a fair imitation of the Maori battle scream I had been practicing for some years, I leapt forward, bringing my weapon down hard upon the head of the man who entered.

"What the bloody hell was that?" Mornaday roared, clutching his head as he fell to his knees.

Sir Hugo Montgomerie stepped into the grotto and took in the scene with a glance. "I believe," he said acidly, "Miss Speedwell has just knocked you about with a very large lobcock."

I looked to my weapon and realized then that I had snatched up one of Miles Ramsforth's prized phalluses and used it to assault a member of Special Branch. I held it out for Sir Hugo. He reared back and gestured for one of his assorted underlings to take possession of it. They surged into the room, a crowd of the plainly clothed Special Branch investigators, asking no questions but carrying out their superior's orders with alarming efficiency.

"Miss Speedwell will come with us," Sir Hugo told them.

"Miss Speedwell will do nothing of the sort," I countered. "Not until Mr. Templeton-Vane has had medical treatment."

Sir Hugo looked at Stoker's recumbent form. In spite of the chaos and noise, he had not moved, not even stirred in his sleep. "What the devil is ailing him?"

"He was shot in the head by Ottilie Ramsforth," I informed him. "And he needs proper treatment. Surely Emma Talbot informed you."

"Miss Talbot gave a somewhat garbled story to which I was not privy," he told me. Sir Hugo waved a beckoning hand to one of his subordinates, a police surgeon as it happened.

The fellow made a swift but thorough assessment of Stoker's condition. "Pulse is strong but slow. Given the look of him, I would wager he has lost a fair bit of blood, but he should be right enough with rest and time. The shot grazed the bone," he informed Sir Hugo.

I sagged in relief, and Mornaday, who ought to have held a grudge, kindly offered his arm in support.

"Aren't you angry?" I asked.

"My head hurts like the very devil," he told me. "But you look like seven hells."

I could well imagine. My hair was half undone, snarling nearly to my waist, whilst my face and hands were streaked with Stoker's blood. Soot from the guttering lamp had no doubt left black ash on my skin, and I was certain that sleeplessness had marked dark shadows under my eyes.

"Don't be ridiculous," I said, tucking my hair up and straightening my shoulders. "I am perfectly well. What has become of Emma Talbot?"

Sir Hugo spoke up. "Miss Talbot's appearance at the nearest police station occasioned a bit of alarm. The superior officer there decided her story was untenable and held her on suspicion of being an escaped lunatic. She has only just now been released."

"Then how on earth did you know to come here?" I demanded.

"I am afraid that is down to me," said Lady Wellingtonia from the doorway.

CHAPTER

28

It was some days before Stoker was recovered enough for us to assemble in Lord Rosemorran's drawing room for a proper discussion of the curious conclusion of the Ramsforth case. He suffered from the occasional headache and his hair, shaven at his temple to permit suturing—by his own hand at his insistence—was just beginning to grow in, pure white against his black locks. He wore his eye patch to help with the ache in his head, and he looked every inch the dangerous malefactor as her ladyship organized the seating arrangements. Sir Hugo appeared, as did Emma Talbot and Sir Frederick Havelock, accompanied by the maid, Cherry. She pushed his Bath chair with an officious air and wore the starched uniform of a private nurse with great pride. Whatever had caused him to elevate her status in his household, she was clearly determined to make the most of it.

But Lady Wellingtonia was more discreet than I had given her credit for being. She inclined her head when Cherry had settled Sir Frederick near the fire. "Thank you, my dear. Mrs. Bascombe will be very pleased to entertain you in her parlor," she said in a tone that brooked no contrariness. Cherry withdrew with a single backwards glance, pregnant with longing. I could not blame her. It seemed hard that she should know so much of the affair and not the conclusion. I only hoped Sir Frederick would take pity upon her and relate the story in time.

After tea had been served and a quantity of excellent sandwiches and cakes eaten, Lady Wellingtonia took the lead.

"It behooves me to begin with an explanation, which I believe is perhaps long overdue," she said.

"Too right," I said with deliberate firmness. Whatever explanations she had been about to offer the night of Stoker's shooting had been pushed aside in favor of prompt medical attention. Since then, we had been left to our own imaginings. I had not wanted to leave Stoker long enough even to go up to the main house, but instead played nursemaid, an endeavor that required minding his dermestid beetles and reading out the journals of the various zoological societies of which he was member. (A brisk argument on an article about the relative merits of the Batavian method of preserving specimens had marked a turning point in his recovery, I am happy to report.)

Lady Wellingtonia's mouth curved into a smile. "I am the reason you were brought into this affair, Miss Speedwell—and by extension, you, Stoker. Although even I could not have anticipated the dangers." Her tone was almost apologetic, but her entire manner seemed to have changed. The aging grande dame had assumed a new authority, and it was with mingled admiration and shock that I discovered Sir Hugo deferred to her.

"I have, in the course of my long life, been fortunate enough to be on intimate terms with the royal family," she said. "I do not like to make much of it, because there are those who will seek to play upon such connections, but I have always been deeply concerned with their well-being, and even, upon occasion, privy to their secrets," she said with a meaningful glance at me.

Quick heat rose in my face, and I bent over my teacup. I understood her perfectly, and I also understood the reason for her oblique explanations. Whatever the sins of my father, she would not want them exposed in front of others.

She went on smoothly. "When this terrible business happened, I was abroad. I knew little of what had occurred, but when I returned a few weeks ago, Princess Louise came at once to see me. She was distraught. She said a terrible injustice was about to occur—that a man, a very good friend of hers, was about to be hanged for a murder he did not commit."

She gave a little cough. "Now, from time to time, the little problems of the royal family have caused me to rely upon the diligence of Sir Hugo," she said with a nod to him. "But in this matter, his hands were tied. He could not subvert the course of British justice, and British justice had condemned Miles Ramsforth."

Emma Talbot gave a little shudder and took a hasty sip from her tea-cup. Lady Wellingtonia looked at her thoughtfully. "There is a rather good single malt in the decanter upon the sideboard," she instructed. "Pour a measure into everyone's tea, child. I think we could all use a stiffener."

Emma rose and moved about the room, pouring a considerable bit of amber consolation into each cup. When she had taken a sip of her own and the color had come back to her cheeks, Lady Wellie resumed her narrative.

"With Sir Hugo unable to help and Louise unable to explain exactly why she was convinced of Miles' innocence, it occurred to me that the princess might do something desperate. She might engage a private inquiry agent, someone indiscreet and unreliable. And that I could not condone. My thoughts, therefore, turned to Miss Speedwell," she said, inclining her head to me. "And naturally to Mr. Templeton-Vane, with whom I was already well acquainted. I knew him to be a resourceful and intelligent man of action, and I had heard Miss Speedwell was nothing if not damnably curious. If there was some means of overturning the con-viction, surely they could find it, I reasoned." I bridled a little at the description of myself as "damnably curious," but Stoker was grinning into his cup. Lady Wellie went on. "And so I suggested to Louise that she confide in Miss Speedwell and set her to investigating. In the meantime, I arranged to take up residence in my nephew's house so I could keep an eye upon things at close quarters and perhaps provide a little support should it be required."

"Such as supplying little titbits of information about Sir Frederick and his household," I put in.

Sir Frederick roused himself. "Yes, Lady Wellie and I are indeed old friends. I am sure she had much to say."

"Not *that* much," Lady Wellie contradicted swiftly. "Some things were not at all pertinent to this affair." She looked to me. "That last night, when you left here, you gave me a message that was to be delivered to Sir Hugo in the event you did not return by the following morning. I confess to anticipating your need for him and instructing—*suggesting*," she corrected quickly, "that he come to your aid with all expedience. But that is the extent of my involvement."

I might have believed her had it not been for that little slip. She would not admit it, I realized, not even if I confronted her directly. But I had small doubt she was the puppet master who pulled Sir Hugo's strings. Why she occupied the role of guide and protector of the royal family, I could not imagine, but her function as éminence grise was indisputable. I flicked a glance to Stoker and saw him watching her closely. Before she noticed, he dropped his gaze to his cup.

"One thing further I must confess," she said in a tired voice. "I quite thought that Louise was being an hysteric about the whole affair. I never expected there to be an actual murderer on the loose, and I certainly never expected there to be any real danger. At most, I thought dabbling in an investigation would be a way to distract her, to give her a little peace of mind and the drama she so loves."

"You know," Stoker said quietly, "there are places in Africa where, when one wants to hunt a lion, one tethers a goat to serve as bait while one lies in wait for the lion to come. I presume one doesn't tell the goat, but it does seem a trifle unfeeling, doesn't it?"

She lifted her chin, but something of the fight seemed to have gone out of her. "I deserved that hit, boy. And I will take my lashes. I made a mistake and you nearly died for it."

Stoker colored quickly. "It was nothing," he assured her. "A mere scratch."

"It is a lie," she returned with a ghost of her usual bravado. "But I appreciate it nonetheless." She took a deep breath. "That is the extent of my involvement and the enormity of my failure. I am leaving tomorrow for my shooting box in Scotland where I plan to meditate upon my shortcomings."

"No sackcloth and ashes on my account," Stoker told her. Her lips twitched as if suppressing some strong emotion, but she said nothing.

Sir Hugo stirred the whiskey into his tea. "The necessary formalities have been concluded," he told us. "The inquest into the deaths of Julian Gilchrist and Ottilie Ramsforth concluded this morning and the verdicts have been returned."

I gaped at him. "But Stoker and I were not asked to give evidence. How is it possible that you have held the inquests?"

He gave me a smooth smile. "The evidence was quite incontrovertible. Julian Gilchrist was murdered by Ottilie Ramsforth—who, in an act of contrition for her crimes, took her own life."

"Took her own life?" My voice was hollow to my ears.

"Yes," Sir Hugo replied. "There were no witnesses to the contrary."

"I was there!" I protested.

"Were you? I do not recall seeing you." He plucked a piece of lint from his trousers before flicking it away.

"Miss Talbot and Mr. Templeton-Vane were both there," I reminded him.

"Could Miss Talbot swear to what happened in that grotto?" he asked. "Could Mr. Templeton-Vane?"

"Well, no," I faltered. I turned to both of them in turn. "Miss Talbot? Stoker?"

Emma Talbot shrugged. "I was lying upon the floor. I never *saw* what happened. I only made the assumption that you killed her. I might have been wrong."

I gaped, and she smiled at me, the first real smile I had ever seen upon her face. It kindled something quite beautiful in her expression, and I realized that she was, for the first time in the short history of our acquaintance, happy.

I turned my gaze to Stoker. "I was unconscious. I remember nothing of that moment," he said truthfully. "I could not give evidence."

"Satisfied, Miss Speedwell?" asked Sir Hugo. "There is no one to give evidence that the blade in Ottilie Ramsforth's heart was delivered there by any hand but her own."

"But why—"

"It was necessary," he said quickly. "I presented in evidence a written confession discovered in her room at Havelock House detailing her crimes and acknowledging her murderous activities. She took responsibility for the deaths of Artemisia and Julian Gilchrist, as well as the intention to see her husband hang."

"A confession?" Stoker asked.

Sir Frederick spoke at last. "Perhaps the handwriting was a little different to Ottilie's," he said in a decidedly neutral tone. "But since I was the one to confirm that it was in her hand, my word was believed."

"But who—" I began.

Emma Talbot put aside her cup and smoothed her skirts. "One woman's hand looks very like another."

"You wrote her confession?" I stared at her in astonishment. From her I looked to Sir Hugo, Sir Frederick, and Lady Wellingtonia. "You conspired to do this, all of you. Why?"

It was Sir Hugo who replied. "Expediency, Miss Speedwell. When I presented a confession in evidence, everything fell into place. Ottilie Ramsforth was condemned for the murderess that she was. Miles Ramsforth has been exonerated fully and will be released this afternoon as soon as the necessary formalities are completed. The ledger has been recovered from Ottilie Ramsforth's possessions and destroyed. The princess's property has been returned to her," he said with a delicate hint at the jewels, "and her name has not been mentioned in connection with the affair."

Something unpleasant gnawed at me. "I have to know—would she have let him hang? Or would she have come forward and told the truth?"

He spread his hands. "Miles Ramsforth is an incurably optimistic fellow. He put his faith in her, always believing she would repay his loyalty. And she did, after a fashion," he reminded me. "She brought you and Templeton-Vane into the investigation. That decision, as much as I deplored it, has led to this rather convenient outcome. It is finished to everyone's satisfaction."

"Except mine," I retorted. "It is not the truth."

"There are many truths," Lady Wellingtonia said firmly. "And this is as much truth as the public requires. We, all of us in this room, have done what was necessary to bring justice to bear in this case, and she has prevailed."

I did not like it, but I could not fault her logic. Miss Talbot poured out another measure of whiskey and when it was finished, we began the lengthy task of saying our good-byes. Sir Hugo was the first to leave. "Must get on," he said, rising and straightening his waistcoat. "Goodbye, Aunt Wellie," he murmured, pressing a kiss to her wrinkled cheek.

When he left, I gave her a piercing look. "*Aunt* Wellie?"

She waved a hand. "An honorific. I am, in fact, his godmother."

"Among other things," I said, sotto voce. Lady Wellie smiled her crocodile's smile.

I sought out Sir Frederick to shake his hand before Cherry came to claim him. "The girl is a marvel," he told me. "Quick as a hare and cheerful as a lark. She is fine company. I mean to shut up the house and take her to the seaside. I think a good long rest is just what I require."

"Thank you for your help," I told him. "All of it," I added with a significant lift of the brows.

Sir Frederick smiled. "When did you guess?"

"That you sent the key to help us in our investigations? Not until I found the slippers," I confessed. "There were numerous possibilities for our anonymous benefactor, but when I found the slippers, it was proof that this foul plot was hatched under your own roof, by your own sister-in-law. And I remembered the painting you had done of her, how you captured the violence of her emotion. I wondered then if you suspected her and tried, after a fashion, to guide us."

He sighed. "Ottilie did not love Miles. She was obsessed with him. You may think these emotions are the same, but they are not, my dear child. They are opposite sides of the same coin, yet one of them will destroy you. I was fortunate. With my Augusta, I had love. We fought and laughed and spent every minute living to the fullest. But Ottilie's passions were different. I saw it from the first. She became attached to him in a way that no human being should ever be attached to another. She was consumed with him, consumed *by* him. That is why I painted her as I did. I saw it, even then."

"That is her tragedy," I observed.

"And his. Although I suspect this will change him. All of his frivolity, his dissipation, will be burnt away by this experience. He will emerge from prison an altered man."

"Altered for the better," Miss Talbot said as she joined us. The happiness I had observed in her still illuminated her face. She looked tired and a little thinner, but the radiance was unmistakable.

She turned to me with a shining countenance. "I have been able to send messages to him and receive them in kind," she said. "As soon as his liberty is restored we are leaving England."

Sir Frederick's heavy brows rose. "You? And Miles?"

Stoker stepped into our little circle as I spoke. "Miss Talbot has always been in love with him, isn't that right?"

She nodded. "Yes, and hated myself for it. He was everything I despised—devoted to dissipations and changeable as a winter sea. But I could not help myself. Even at his worst, he could be so sweetly good, like a wayward child. There was no malice in him, no real wickedness. He was inconstant as a weather vane, but so ready to believe the best of people, even when they let him down. He always expected everything would be quite all right, no matter the situation. And everyone indulged him, as if it were some great joke that he was less than he ought to have been. I was the only one ever to be angered by it. I thought I concealed my feelings. How did you know?" She slanted me a curious glance.

"Stoker found a sketch of Miles that you drew. We had seen photographs of him in the newspapers, but your sketch was something altogether different. You gave him a nobility we had not seen in him," I told her with gentle tact.

"I drew him as I wanted him to be, as I knew he *could* be. I never imagined he would feel the same, but he tells me that he always believed himself unworthy of me," she said, lifting her chin proudly. "We have vowed to put aside all such barriers. We will leave for Greece as soon as possible. He will want to be away from the newspapers and the gossiping tongues. We will find peace there."

"You will be missed," Sir Frederick told her. "And mind you do not neglect your art."

"There will be time to say good-bye," she assured him. She bade us farewell, pressing our hands in turn before going to find Cherry.

I turned to Sir Frederick. "Godspeed, Sir Frederick." Impulsively, I kissed his cheek, and he lifted my hands to his lips.

"If I were a younger man," he said, a wistful tone to his voice. I turned away sharply and left Stoker to say our farewells.

There was little more to be said. When everyone else had left that evening and Stoker had whistled up the dogs to make his way slowly to his little temple, I remained behind. I poured a fresh measure of whiskey, waiting until Lady Wellingtonia and I were alone. She came to sit by the fire, taking the chair next to me as Crates and Hipparchia fussed in the corner.

I stared into my glass, watching the sparks in the heart of the crystal as the firelight played over the surface. "So, everything is sorted," I said. "How very tidily it has all been managed. You must be very proud."

Something in my tone alerted her ladyship. She gave me a level stare. "We did what we had to do, Miss Speedwell. I regret that Stoker was harmed. But that is not what this is really about, is it, child? You are angry at being kept in the dark."

"I am angry at being used as a pawn," I retorted. "I am not your chess piece to move as you see fit, my lady. I was not engaged upon this investigation simply because you wished to amuse Her Royal Highness or make certain Miles Ramsforth didn't hang. You were testing me."

She gave me a thin smile that did not quite reach her eyes. "Why on earth should I want to do that?"

"Because when Sir Hugo offered me a pension—their money to keep my silence about who I am—I refused it. And that has made you uneasy. You did not know how far you could trust me, so you took the first opportunity to challenge me."

"I am old, my girl. I have not many years left, and I must be efficient with them. I took the opportunity to peg two little birds with one well-placed stone. Surely you do not blame me for that."

"I will not be part of your games," I told her. "I explained to Sir Hugo that I want nothing from them, and now I am telling you. They are nothing to me, and I am nothing to them. They have made that perfectly clear." The fact that Louise had accepted the return of her jewels without so much as a line of thanks had angered me beyond reason, but her neglect to follow through on her promise to introduce me to my father had shown me my true worth in her eyes.

"You want your father." There was no triumph in her voice, but she had thrown a gauntlet. "Child, you try my patience!" she said, bringing her stick down sharply upon the floor. "Who do you think insisted upon this piece of theater that Sir Hugo has played out in the inquest? Who do you think demanded that Ottilie Ramsforth's confession be written and submitted into evidence?"

Ice numbed my spine. "If I had given evidence, I might have been charged with Ottilie's death," I said, groping slowly towards understanding. "He could not take the chance that I would be exposed."

"He could not stand that his own child would suffer," she corrected. "He did this for *you*."

It was a long moment before I spoke again. "It was considerate of you to look away," I told her finally as I put aside my handkerchief.

"I do not like maudlin displays," she said, wiping her own eyes. Her voice was suddenly gentle. "You must understand their limitations. He cannot acknowledge you. He cannot even meet you. But there is not a day goes by that he does not think of you."

I rose. "I want nothing," I said, and this time I meant it.

Lady Wellie cocked her head and studied me from hem to head. "If they could see you now, they would clap a tiara on your head and give you a title. Imperious as a duchess, and that is something one cannot be taught."

"I have no doubt you intend that as a compliment," I told her. "But I find it hard to take it as one."

She rose slowly to her feet, using her stick for support. "I know you deplore my methods, Miss Speedwell, but my cause is just. So goes the family, so goes England. And so goes England, so goes the world."

"I understand that the feelings of one person cannot interfere with what is best for the country," I said haltingly.

"Then you understand *them*. Whether you like it or not, your fate is now entwined with theirs," she told me. And I did not know if that was a threat or a promise.

CHAPTER

29

The next week, Stoker and I sat out in the grounds of Bishop's Folly, enjoying the last of the sunshine of St. Martin's summer. Autumn had officially come a fortnight before, but the gardens were warm and bursting with rosehips and turning leaves, apples and quinces weighing the branches of the orchard with ripe promise. Patricia lumbered about in search of late lettuces, and Betony, to everyone's surprise, was round with a pregnancy that could only have been caused by the lowly Huxley. Quite how he managed it was a subject of much speculation in the house and even a few bawdy wagers on the part of the housemaids. Lady Wellingtonia, now settled in her shooting box in Scotland with Mr. Baring-Ponsonby, had already claimed a pup as soon as they were weaned.

Stoker and I quarreled happily over tracks that had appeared in the garden—he insisting they were those of a fox while I maintained such a creature would never be so bold as to encroach upon Huxley's territory—and the sun shone down, gilding the late-afternoon scene to a picture that would have sent Constable scurrying for his brushes.

Another letter had come from Stoker's family, a rather gentler invitation from his eldest brother, the viscount. I said nothing, but I noticed that this one had not been consigned to the wastepaper basket as quickly as the others. There was a new thoughtfulness about Stoker, and I wondered if perhaps a rapprochement was in the works. I was equally silent upon the subject of Caroline, the name he had uttered when I kissed him in my opium-stoked delirium. Whatever hold his former wife had upon him, she possessed it still, and that knowledge stood between us, unspoken, but a thing unto itself.

Caroline had left her scars and this investigation had left one as well, I reflected as I glanced to his temple. The wound would heal cleanly, but the white streak at his temple would always remind him—and me—that he had thrown himself in front of a revolver for me. Caroline might have her claim upon him, but I had one of my own, I decided. And mine was the stronger because I demanded nothing of him save friendship. His soul was his own.

"You're pensive today," he said lazily.

"I am content," I told him truthfully.

"Veronica." The word was soft as a prayer. I did not turn my head. I knew it was an invitation to talk, but it was an invitation I could not accept.

"Not yet," I told him. I knew he had questions about what I had told him the night Ottilie Ramsforth had died, questions about my past and the life I had taken. But I had no answers ready to give. I smiled and repeated what he had told me at the Haymarket. "I have not spoken of it. I may never. But when I do, it will be with you."

He gave a nod and I turned to watch a pretty Camberwell Beauty flapping a lazy path through the air, the light glowing violet on his wings as he fluttered around a privet hedge. Beyond, sounds of clattering and hammering and breaking of glass rose and fell along with the cheerful voices of workmen set to their tasks.

"What is all the palaver about? Has his lordship formed a new enthusiasm?" I asked. Lord Rosemorran had decided that a heated plunge pool would be just the thing to speed his recuperation and had installed one in his Roman folly at hideous expense. But the thing had been finished a fortnight before and no doubt our benefactor was haring off after a new diversion.

"His lordship is restoring the glasshouse," Stoker told me, his gaze suddenly intent.

"For what purpose?" Anticipation quickened in my blood.

"For the purpose of breeding butterflies."

"He means to install a vivarium?"

"We cannot mount an expedition for some months yet, and the gardens here can only offer you so much diversion for the hunting of butterflies. But a proper vivarium will give you a place to breed your own, to study them. He means to stock the place with the right sort of plants, and he wants you to compile a list of the larvae you will require to begin."

A vivarium! My mind reeled at the possibilities. The glasshouse was an enormous thing; to fill it with hundreds of fluttering jewels of every description, to watch them metamorphose from dull, lumpen larvae to spin their silken cocoons and emerge, damp-winged and laden with lustrous possibility . . . it was almost more than I could bear.

"In time," Stoker went on, "it might make a good addition to the museum. People could enjoy and appreciate the butterflies without having to pin them to the walls. They could watch them fly about and feed and rest." He paused. "Veronica, you have not said a word. Are you happy?"

Happy? It was too puny and small a notion to describe my eruption of joy. I reached out and took his hand, squeezing it so hard, I could feel his bones shift.

"Well," he said gently, "you may not have said a word, but you have spoken."

"You did this," I said at last when I could speak. "You told him to do this. For me."

His gaze held mine for only a moment, then he looked away, watching the Beauty as he dropped to feed upon a berry. "When I most had need of you, you did not leave me. Whatever this thing is that makes us different, this thing that makes quicksilver of us when the rest of the world is mud, it binds us. To break that would be to fly in the face of nature."

He tightened his grip on my hand for a moment, then let it slip away. The warmth of his skin lingered upon my palm. He reached for his watch chain to unfasten the guinea that hung there.

"I seem to recall you won the wager," he began. I put a finger to his hand, stilling it.

"Keep it. We will wager double or nothing next time," I said with a grin.

What the future held, I could not say. But we would have more adventures together, of that I was certain, and I could not wait to begin them.

Until then, I turned my face to the light and closed my eyes as the Camberwell Beauty dipped his wings and soared over the privet hedge against the setting sun.

ACKNOWLEDGMENTS

This is where all the gratitude happens. I would like to express my most heartfelt appreciation to the following:

For all of their enthusiasm and support, the fine folks at Penguin, with special recognition of Craig Burke, Loren Jaggers, Claire Zion, and Kara Welsh for their championing of Veronica. I am immensely grateful to the art department for their glorious work, as well as the dedication of the sales, marketing, editorial, and PR teams. Always and forever, particular thanks to Ellen Edwards for bringing Veronica home.

For shepherding Veronica with kindness, skill, and immense creativity, my editor, Danielle Perez. I am more grateful than I can say for you.

For almost two decades of care, hard work, and friendship, my agent, Pam Hopkins. There are not words, but I think you already know.

For generosity and expertise in their various fields: Jen Stayrook, Mary Williams, Susan Ellingson, and Lindsay Carlson.

For support, friendship, and edification: Blake Leyers, Benjamin Dreyer, Ali Trotta, Joshilyn Jackson, Ariel Lawhon, Delilah Dawson, Rhys Bowen, Alan Bradley, Susan Elia MacNeal, Lauren Willig, Nathan Dunbar, Stephanie Graves, Holly Faur, and Carin Thumm, all of whom have offered kindness when it was most needed. For providing the name "Miles Ramsforth" in a burst of creative brilliance, Jeff Abbott.

For administrative work and attention to detail: the team at Writer-space. Special thanks to the irrreplaceable Jomie Wilding for truly spectacular endeavors.

For generosity of spirit: Fernando Velasquez whose gifted compositions have been the soundtrack of my writing and whose kind messages have buoyed my creativity.

For endless cups of tea, understanding, patience, and fortitude: my family.

For everything, for always: my husband.